PHOENIX

A **BLACK CITY** NOVEL

ELIZABETH RICHARDS

G. P. PUTNAM'S SONS
AN IMPRINT OF PENGUIN GROUP (USA) INC.

G. P. PUTNAM'S SONS
An imprint of Penguin Young Readers Group.
Published by The Penguin Group.
Penguin Group (USA) Inc., 375 Hudson Street, New York, NY 10014, USA.
Penguin Group (Canada), 90 Eglinton Avenue East, Suite 700, Toronto, Ontario
M4P 2Y3, Canada (a division of Pearson Penguin Canada Inc.).
Penguin Books Ltd, 80 Strand, London WC2R 0RL, England.
Penguin Ireland, 25 St. Stephen's Green, Dublin 2, Ireland
(a division of Penguin Books Ltd).
Penguin Group (Australia), 707 Collins Street, Melbourne, Victoria 3008, Australia
(a division of Pearson Australia Group Pty Ltd).
Penguin Books India Pvt Ltd, 11 Community Centre, Panchsheel Park,
New Delhi–110 017, India.
Penguin Group (NZ), 67 Apollo Drive, Rosedale, Auckland 0632, New Zealand
(a division of Pearson New Zealand Ltd).
Penguin Books South Africa, Rosebank Office Park, 181 Jan Smuts Avenue, Parktown
North 2193, South Africa.
Penguin China, B7 Jiaming Center, 27 East Third Ring Road North,
Chaoyang District, Beijing 100020, China.
Penguin Books Ltd, Registered Offices: 80 Strand, London WC2R 0RL, England.

Published simultaneously in Canada. Printed in the United States of America.
Design by Ryan Thomann. Text set in Sabon.

Library of Congress Cataloging-in-Publication Data is available upon request.
ISBN 978-0-399-15944-2
3 5 7 9 10 8 6 4 2

For Rob.
"So begins my heart . . ."

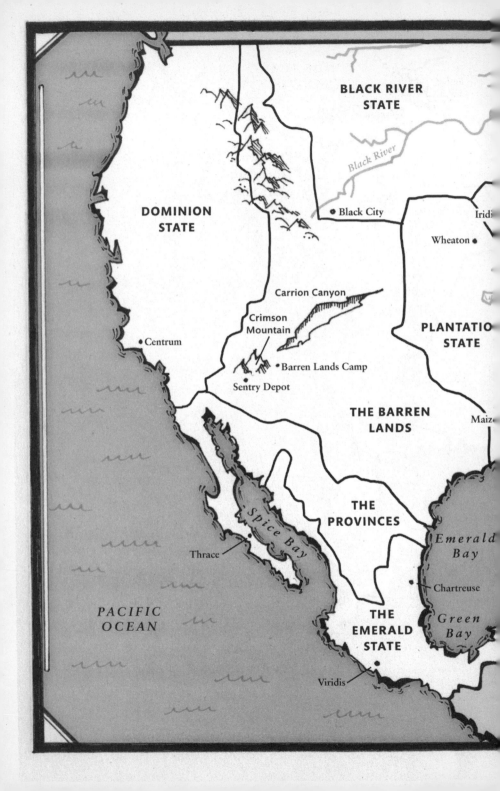

PART I

BLACK CITY BURNING

PROLOGUE

PURIAN ROSE STEPPED OUT onto the balcony of the Golden Citadel, adjusting the white cotton glove on his right hand. The sun had just started to set over the city, making the giltstone buildings shimmer gold. He was greeted by the melody of a million voices calling out to him across the metropolis, united in their evening prayer. Normally this would bring a smile to his thin lips. Centrum was his creation, his perfect vision of the world: purity, faith and power combined.

But not tonight.

How could he be happy when everything he had worked so hard for was in jeopardy? It had taken fifteen years of bloodshed, bribery and sheer determination to build his utopia, but that half-breed and his race-traitor girlfriend had threatened to unravel it all. Rose flexed his right hand, irritated that the glove wasn't fitting correctly. Everything had to be flawless; too much was at stake to allow for even the slightest imperfection.

In the city square below him, a team of workmen were preparing the stage for the televised referendum in a couple of days, when the whole country would vote for his segregation laws.

The ballot was meant to have taken place two months ago, but after everything that had happened in Black City—the riot between his Sentry guards and the Darklings, which resulted in a teenage boy being killed; Emissary Buchanan's imprisonment for poisoning its citizens with a drug known as Golden Haze; and the attempted execution of the half-blood boy they were now calling Phoenix—well, it hadn't seemed like the right time. Public opinion of his government had never been so low.

But that was a few weeks ago, and people's memories were short. He was a patient man, able to bide his time until it was the right moment to strike, even though he was itching to punish the citizens of Black City for defying him. *No fear, no power!* they had chanted. It had enraged him at first, but he had found a way to turn the situation in his favor. He was, if anything, resourceful.

His eyes caught on two black ants crawling along the golden balustrade that ran around the edge of the balcony, and a flicker of annoyance crossed his gray eyes. Despite all his power, he still couldn't prevent His Mighty's smallest creatures from invading his carefully crafted world. Just like the rebels in Black City.

The sound of footsteps made him turn. By the doorway stood his servant—a young man named Forsyth, who was dressed in long white robes with a red rose emblem on his chest. It was the uniform of the Pilgrims—the devoted followers of the Purity faith, the religion that Rose had founded. The servant bowed.

"Your Transporter is ready, Your Excellency," Forsyth said.

Rose simply nodded, dismissing the man, and turned his attention back to the ants. He watched the insects for a moment longer before crushing them under the thumb of his white-gloved hand.

He had waited long enough. The moment had come to put his plan into action. It was time he reminded Ash Fisher and Natalie Buchanan why they should fear him.

1.

ASH

A STEAM-POWERED STREETCAR rattles along the tracks beside me, spewing clouds of soot into the gray skies shrouding Black City. I take a cigarette from my packet of Sentry-regulation smokes and slip it between my lips, but don't bother to spark up. Nicotine doesn't give me the same buzz that it used to; nothing gets me as high as the heart beating inside my chest. I only carry the smokes to give me something to do with my hands when I'm nervous. My fingers find the small parcel inside my jacket pocket, and my stomach flips.

I stroll through the Rise, the poorest district in the city, and turn down Cinder Street—a narrow alleyway wedged between rows of tightly packed Cinderstone buildings. Three boys are playing in the street, blocking my path. Two of them brandish toy wooden swords, pretending to be Sentry guards. They're chasing the third boy, who is dressed in black clothes, the sleeves decorated with orange ribbons that look like flames when he runs. It takes me a moment to realize the boy is pretending to be me. My chest tightens as I watch him play, thinking about the real fire that blazed up my arms, burning the flesh off my bones . . .

The boy looks up at me with wide brown eyes.

"Phoenix!" he cries out.

The children run over to me.

"I saw you on the news the other day," Little Phoenix says. "Did you really hijack those Sentry trucks?"

"Yeah," I say, putting my unlit cigarette back in the packet.

"And steal all those medical supplies from Sentry headquarters?" he asks.

"Yup," I say.

"Wow," all the boys say in unison.

Since the uprising two months ago, the Sentry government has been finding ways to lash out at us, such as withholding medical supplies from our hospitals or stopping Synth-O-Blood shipments into the Darkling ghetto, known as the Legion. I've been working with Humans for Unity—the rebel group campaigning to unify our species—to protect the people of this city. The front door of the house behind them opens, and a pretty middle-aged woman with sandy blond hair appears, wiping her hands on an old dishcloth. I've seen her at a few of the rebel meetings, although we've never spoken. I think her name's Sally.

"Boys, get inside this minute and leave that young man alone," she says.

"Aww, *Mom*," Little Phoenix whines.

"Don't 'aww Mom' me," she says, ushering them inside.

She gives me a shy smile once they're in the house.

"I really admire what you've been doing," she says in a quiet voice. "I think you're very brave to stand up to Purian Rose. It's given so many others in this country the courage to finally do the same."

"Thanks," I say, rubbing the back of my neck.

She blushes slightly. "Well, good luck at the ballot tomorrow. I'll be voting against Rose's Law," she says. "The war's over; it's time we all forgave each other and moved on."

"I appreciate your support," I reply. "See you tomorrow."

I head toward the small house at the end of the lane and dart around the back of the one-story building. As I'd hoped, the bedroom window is open. I climb through, being careful not to make a sound as I land on the other side.

The tiny room is crammed with old furniture: a desk, two beds, two dressers and a wardrobe. Day's side of the room is immaculate, while Natalie's is strewn with magazines, shoes and laundry. Her nightstand is covered in makeup, plus a small container of heart medication that I stole from the Sentry when we raided their medical supplies. I carefully navigate the mess and lean over her bed. Only Natalie's face peeps out from behind the handmade quilt, her golden curls spilling across the pillow.

"Happy birthday, blondie," I whisper.

Sunlight catches on her blond lashes as they sleepily flutter open.

"I was just dreaming about you," she says.

"All good things, I hope?" I say, shrugging off my jacket.

She grabs my belt and pulls me onto the bed with her, making the wooden frame creak under our weight. I worry that Sumrina—Natalie and her sister Polly's guardian—might hear us, but that thought is quickly pushed aside when Natalie presses her lips against mine. Everything melts away, and it's just the two of us, our hearts beating in unison. My hand glides down her body, skimming over the soft cotton nightdress until I find the silken smoothness of her legs. My fingers brush over a small mark on her calf muscle where a Darkling bit her a few months ago. Natalie suddenly stops kissing me and bolts upright, cheeks flushed, to look toward Day's bed. She lets out a long sigh when she realizes it's empty.

"That could have been embarrassing," she says.

I chuckle. "I would've restrained myself if she'd been here."

Natalie raises a brow at me.

"Okay, maybe not."

"Well, since we're alone . . ." She playfully runs her fingers down my shirt, undoing the buttons.

"Natalie, don't," I say, holding her wrists.

A small frown crosses her lips. "I just thought, since it's my birthday—"

"You know I can't."

"The doctor said your burns were healing nicely. Couldn't we at least *try*? It's been so long since we . . ." She doesn't need to finish the sentence. It's been over two months since we were last physical with each other. "I love you, Ash. I don't care what you look like."

"Then I guess it's lucky I'm such a stud," I tease.

She attempts a smile, but the disappointment is evident in her eyes.

"I do want you," I say, gently running my thumb over her cheek.

"Really?" she whispers.

"Of course. It's pretty much all I think about, *trust* me."

"Then why can't we . . . ?"

My body tenses up. *Because I'm a freak?*

"I'm sorry, Ash. I didn't mean to push things," she says, sensing my discomfort. "I can wait, it doesn't matter. Forgive me?"

I kiss her again. This time it's urgent, hungry, showing her how much she means to me. I do want her—boy, do I want her;

that was never the issue. She sighs as my fangs gently nip on her bottom lip.

Fragg it.

I shrug off my shirt, tossing it on the floor. I lie down, pulling Natalie on top of me, my heart racing. This is the first time she's seen my scars since I was taken to the hospital after my failed execution. Her fingers inquisitively explore my skin, her touch feather-light as she skims over the patchwork of burnt flesh on my upper body. I flinch slightly; the scars are still tender.

The burns on my back, neck and hands have almost gone, and in a few more months, the ones on my shoulders and arms will look less alarming. I wish they'd heal entirely; I hate being reminded of that day. But that will never happen. So instead I'm wrenched awake every night, thrashing and screaming, convinced I'm on fire.

"What were you so worried about, silly?" Natalie finally whispers. "Did you honestly think I'd be put off by a few scars?"

"I'm not exactly the guy you fell in love with," I say.

"That's true," she says, placing a hand over my racing heart. "You're *better*. You sacrificed yourself to save me, Ash. Trust me, that earned you a few extra boyfriend points."

I grin. "Maybe I can stick to buying you flowers in the future." She laughs.

I gently cup her face with my hands, and she stops laughing, the mood shifting. My eyes drink her in, admiring the cute dimple in her cheek, the cornflower blue of her eyes, the gentle curve of her rose-pink lips.

My stomach clenches as I get this sudden, panicked feeling in my gut that I'm going to lose her. It's the same sensation I've been getting since my crucifixion. So far Purian Rose has left us alone, but how long will this last? I kiss her, forcing those dark thoughts aside.

"What would you like to do today, birthday girl?" I murmur against her lips.

"This," she replies.

"Sounds good to me."

Our plans are immediately dashed when there's a brisk knock on the door. We barely have time to pull the covers over us as Sumrina, my dad and Beetle enter the room. Beetle smirks when he sees me, the pink flesh of his scarred cheek puckering—a nasty remnant of the bombing that took down part of the Boundary Wall. Sumrina can't hide her shock at the sight of my burns, muttering "mercy" under her breath, while Dad just gives me a weary look, the lines on his forehead furrowing. His hair has turned as gray as his minister's tunic, making him look decades older than he is. The stress of losing Mom, followed by my murder trial and crucifixion, has taken its toll on him.

"I thought you might be here." He passes my shirt to me.

"Natalie and I were just talking," I say in a rush, shrugging on my top as Natalie sinks farther under the sheets.

Beetle laughs, then quickly tries to disguise it as a cough when I glower at him.

"I'm guessing this isn't a social visit?" I say to him.

"Sorry, bro. You're needed at the Legion. There's been an incident," Beetle replies, adding quickly: "No one's dead. But it's probably best if Roach fills you in on the details."

I frown. It must be pretty serious if he's leaving it up to his aunt Roach—the head of Humans for Unity—to tell me what happened.

"Am I needed too?" Natalie asks.

Beetle glances at the ground. "No, just Ash."

"Oh," she says, deflated.

I rub the back of my neck, flicking a look at Natalie.

"It's okay, Ash," she says. "You should go; it sounds important. See you tonight?"

I give her a chaste peck on the cheek, not wanting to give my dad any more reasons to have a hernia.

"Catch you later, birthday girl," I say, slinging on my jacket. "I'll give you my gift tonight."

I slip my hand into my pocket to check that the parcel is still there, and my stomach fills with nerves, both excited and anxious about this evening. I'm throwing her a surprise birthday party, which I've been planning for weeks, but that's not all. Tonight, I'm going to ask Natalie to marry me.

2.

ASH

WE PUSH OUR WAY down Bleak Street, which is heaving with bleary-eyed commuters heading to work. Some of them nod at me as we pass by. Plastered across shop windows, walls and lampposts are hundreds of Humans for Unity flyers, with slogans like NO FEAR, NO POWER! and ONE COUNTRY UNITED and VOTE NO TO ROSE'S LAW! On all of the posters is an image of me staring moodily off into the distance with smoke billowing behind me—a phoenix rising from the ashes. Roach shortened my name from Black Phoenix to Phoenix, thinking it would sound snappier in the promos.

Beetle suddenly cuts across the road and I hurry after him, weaving through the steam-powered streetcars.

"Aren't we supposed to be going to the Legion?" I say.

"Yeah, but there's something going on at the Chimney you need to check out first," he says. "It won't take long."

We cross Union Street and head toward the factory district called the Chimney, where most of the city's poorest citizens, known as Workboots, earn their living. It's a bleak place, with noisy Cinderstone refineries belching out toxic smoke into the sky, contributing to the thick black cloud that permanently lingers over the city.

The only splash of color comes from the giant digital screens on top of the buildings, which constantly stream the latest news from the government-owned channel, SBN. The monitors flicker, and an attractive blond presenter, February Fields, appears on all the screens across the city, smiling down at us with her plumped-up red lips.

"And now an announcement from your government," she says.

The footage cuts to a picture of an attractive young boy and girl, both blond and blue eyed. Written below them is the phrase ONE FAITH, ONE RACE, ONE NATION UNDER HIS MIGHTY. Rose has been running these commercials for weeks, in the run-up to the referendum tomorrow. My stomach knots just thinking about it. If we lose the vote, then my people will be trapped behind the Boundary Wall forever. *No pressure.*

The newsfeed is suddenly interrupted, and my image appears on-screen.

"And now an announcement from your liberators," a female voice says. It belongs to Juno Jones, lead reporter at Black City News and one of the highest-ranking members of Humans for Unity. We've distorted her voice so she can't be recognized.

Recently, the rebels have been running their own promo spots in retaliation to Purian Rose's commercials, by hacking into the government feed. The footage is of me walking through the Darkling ghetto—a run-down, diseased shantytown with filth and sewage in the streets. Emaciated Darkling children reach out to me, and I pass them bags of Synth-O-Blood from the Sentry trucks we hijacked last week. The shot changes and now I'm inside a crowded hospital, where medical supplies are being handed out to nurses tending to the Wraths—Darklings infected with the deadly C18-Virus. The promo ends with our slogan: NO FEAR, NO POWER!

The picture returns to the usual government feed.

"So are you all ready for Natalie's party tonight?" Beetle asks as he leads me up a steep hill overlooking one of the Cinderstone factories.

My fingers find the parcel in my jacket pocket again. "Yeah, I think so."

"I've got all the stuff at the barge. I just need to set it up. She'll love it."

"Are you sure? It has to be perfect," I say.

"Stop stressing, mate."

At the top of the hill, we meet a young, petite black woman with closely cropped hair, dressed in dull gray overalls like the other factory workers.

"Ash, this is Freya," Beetle says. "She recently joined us from the Ember Creek branch of Humans for Unity."

In the past two months we've managed to organize fifteen new factions of Humans for Unity around the country, increasing our membership to over five thousand, and it's growing every day. It's still a drop in the ocean compared with Purian Rose's forces, but it's a promising start.

"It's a pleasure to meet you, Phoenix," Freya says.

"Likewise. Black City's a long way from Ember Creek," I say.

"I wanted to be at the heart of the action."

"So what's going on?" I ask.

"I've been tracking some suspicious activity in the Cinderstone factories," Freya explains. "I first noticed it happening in Ember Creek, and when I told Roach, she said the same thing was occurring here. So she asked me to investigate."

I slide a questioning look at Beetle. "Why didn't I know about this?"

The tips of his ears turn pink. "Roach didn't want to bother you, bro. She thought you had enough on your plate with the ballot, but I thought you'd like to know."

"Thanks," I say. "So what's this 'suspicious activity'?"

Freya points toward the factory at the base of the hill. Everything seems pretty standard to me—just workers loading trucks with Cinderstone bricks, the slow-burning fuel that's used to power factories, trains and streetcars. Then I see them—three men dressed in dark red clothing emerging from the factory. Each of them is over seven feet tall, with heavy brows and reflective, silver eyes. Their heads are shaved, except for a narrow strip of long, fur-like hair down the center of their scalps.

Lupines.

The only people the Darklings hate as much as the Sentry are the Lupines, since they sided with the government during the war. The tallest of the Lupines wears a bloodred leather frock coat and has human teeth woven into his silver hair. He barks some orders at the other two Lupines, then goes back into the factory while they climb into the trucks and drive off.

"They've been taking all the shipments to the Mountain Wolf State," Freya says.

"What's there that requires so much fuel?" I say. "That shipment alone was enough to power a whole city for a year."

"I don't know yet, but I've been trying to gain access to the head office, to download the shipment logs," Freya says. "It's not easy, though. They've got armed guards securing the office, but I'm trying."

"Do your best. Keep me posted," I reply.

We leave Freya and head back into the city. Pain throbs at my temples, and I massage them with my fingertips.

"You okay, mate?" Beetle asks as we turn onto City End— the street that runs parallel to the Boundary Wall, which encloses the Darkling ghetto.

I nod. "Just stressed about tomorrow."

"It'll be fine." Beetle checks his watch. "I better head to the barge and get it prepared for tonight."

Nerves bubble in my stomach again.

"Don't worry, mate—she's going to love it," he says.

Beetle crosses over the streetcar tracks while I continue down City End, not worrying too much about running into any Trackers—the Sentry's elite military group who hunt and kill rogue Darklings—although I know they've been keeping tabs on me. If I turn around now, I'm sure I'll see one of their goons darting into an alleyway, acting like he wasn't following me. But it's no big deal; I can shake them off when I need to.

Since the unrest at my crucifixion, the Sentry government has kept a low profile in the city. Now isn't the time for the government to be seen wielding its power—"crushing the little man," as Roach puts it—since it would only add fuel to our fire. That's something Purian Rose is very concerned about. He told me as much when he paid me an unexpected visit after I was released from the hospital.

The government is still here, though; it's just they're working more covertly now. I hear rumors of people tied to the rebellion mysteriously disappearing. There's no proof the government has been involved, so we can't do anything about it. But we know. Yet we continue with our underground meetings and pirate radio shows, all in the hopes of gathering the support we need for tomorrow. I honestly have no idea how it's going to go. All I can do is hope I've persuaded enough people to vote against Rose's Law.

The sound of hooves startles me out of my thoughts. I whip around. Two black horses canter toward me, their footsteps stirring up the ash on the cobblestones. They're pulling a closed-top carriage, which bobs up and down on the uneven road. I flatten my back against the concrete wall before the vehicle runs me over. It draws to a halt, and a moment later, the door swings open and Sebastian Eden steps out.

He's dressed in a new version of the Tracker uniform: a black flat cap with a rose emblem on the front, a fitted black military coatee, tight black slacks and matching leather jackboots. With his shaved head, the overall look is more severe than the stylish red-and-black uniform from a few months ago. Pinned to his chest is a rose-shaped silver medal, indicating his high rank in the Tracker squad. His green eyes flash with contempt, an expression that I know is mirrored on my own face. Sebastian used to be Natalie's bodyguard and boyfriend, and a couple of months ago, he tried to rape her. We got into a fight about it, and it was this incident that sparked the riot that got Gregory Thompson killed and me subsequently arrested and convicted of his murder.

"Get in," he orders.

I laugh. "Yeah, like I'm going to do that."

His upper lip twitches, his eyes flicking toward the vehicle. I catch a glimpse of a shadowy figure inside, and the hairs on the back of my neck prickle.

"One of my men is standing outside Natalie's house as we speak," Sebastian says in a low voice. "So it's in your best interest to get into the carriage, nipper."

"If you lay one finger on her, I swear—"

"What?" A cruel smile plays across his lips. "She'll be dead before you can reach her."

There's no way to be certain whether Sebastian is telling the truth or not, but I can't risk it. I step inside the carriage.

My blood turns to ice when I see who is sitting opposite me. *Purian Rose.*

He studies me with cold, gray eyes. Unable to help myself, I shudder. There's something deeply disturbing about his face, which looks all stretched and waxy. The carriage lists slightly to one side as Sebastian takes the seat next to the driver. Rose taps the roof of the carriage, and the vehicle begins to move. I try to rein in my panic.

"What do you want?" I ask.

"Not even a hello?" he says, amused.

"Hello," I say. "What do you want?"

He runs his tongue over his top teeth and studies me for a long moment. I fidget in my seat, waiting for him to speak.

"I've been keeping a close eye on you, Mr. Fisher," Rose finally says. "I must confess I admire your tenacity. It's an admirable quality to keep trying so hard when there's no hope of success."

"Um, *thanks*?" I say. "But I'm guessing you didn't come all this way to tell me that. So what do you want?"

"Always to the point, aren't you?"

"It's one of my many 'admirable qualities,'" I retort.

He leans forward, and I crush my back into the purple velvet seat.

"What I *want*, Mr. Fisher, is for you to vote in favor of Rose's Law tomorrow," he says.

I laugh. "You're joking."

"No, I'm not really one for humor."

"No kidding," I mutter. "Why on earth would I do that?"

He smiles. "You might remember, the last time we met, I promised to break you down, piece by piece?"

"I vaguely recall something along those lines."

"Well, it's time I acted on that promise," he says. "If you don't vote yes tomorrow, then I'm going to take Miss Buchanan."

My heart stops.

"And let me be clear," he continues. "I won't kill her straight away. Instead, my guards will slice bits off her, *piece by piece,* until she's begging for death. Do you understand?"

I nod faintly. "Don't hurt her," I whisper.

"Now, that depends entirely on you." He gives me a cold smile. "So, what's it to be?"

His ultimatum lingers in the space between us.

Natalie or my people?

I look down at my feet.

Her life in exchange for their freedom?

"Think it over, Mr. Fisher," he says. "I have faith you'll do the right thing."

He taps the carriage roof again, and the vehicle shudders to a halt. He opens the door for me, and I step out, the cold air rushing against my skin.

"Good day," he says, then as an afterthought: "And wish Miss Buchanan a very happy birthday from me. Make sure it's not her last."

3.
ASH

PURIAN ROSE'S THREAT rings in my ears as the carriage rides away. As soon as the vehicle rounds the corner, I slump down on the curb, my whole body shaking with adrenaline.

"What I want, Mr. Fisher, is for you to vote in favor of Rose's Law tomorrow."

Can I honestly go through with this?

He'll torture Natalie. I can't let him do that.

But how can I betray my people? I know my vote alone doesn't have the power to stop these segregation laws from passing, but people *are* expecting me to lead the way. If I vote in favor of Rose's Law, what sort of message does that send? Why should the humans put their necks on the line for the Darklings when the rebellion's poster boy won't even do it? We'll lose the vote, and Purian Rose will have defeated us without even raising a gun.

I consider telling Roach what happened, but immediately scrap that idea. I'm certain she'd advise me to vote against Rose's Law, despite the risks to Natalie. The rebellion is the only thing that matters to her; she'd sacrifice her own nephew,

Beetle, if she thought it was necessary. I admire her dedication to the cause, but not her willingness to allow people to die for it.

I don't know how long I sit on the curb, but when I eventually stand up, my legs feel numb. I find a pay phone and call Natalie.

"Hello," she says on the other end of the line.

I shut my eyes, relieved to hear her voice. "Hey."

"Everything okay?" she says distractedly as Day and her younger brother, MJ, have an argument in the background.

I can't dump this on her now; it's her birthday.

"Ash?"

"Everything's fine," I say. "Look, I bumped into Sebastian a few minutes ago. There might be a Sentry guard outside your house, so keep an eye out."

"Yeah, we saw one hanging around earlier, but he's gone now."

I press my forehead against the phone booth. So Sebastian wasn't lying.

"What did he want?" Natalie asks.

"To wish us good luck for tomorrow," I say.

Natalie laughs. "Sure he did. Are you okay?"

"I'm fine. It's nothing to worry about. I'll see you later."

I hang up and head to the Legion to find out what this "incident" was that Roach needed to tell me about, my footsteps leaden, still undecided about what I'm going to do tomorrow.

Twenty minutes later, I'm staring at the empty storeroom that was once stocked to the ceiling with military-grade guns and ammunition, which Humans for Unity had stolen from the Sentry. Seems like the government decided to take them back.

"They cleared us out during the night," Roach says beside me.

She's wearing a man's gray shirt tucked into black pants, and scuffed work boots. Her dreadlocks, which have been newly dyed blue, hang down to her trim waist. Next to her is one of the Darkling ministers, Logan. She's more handsome than beautiful, with startling lilac eyes and rippling black hair. She glances at me with her usual mixture of irritation and guilt. Logan was one of the three judges, known as the Quorum of Three, who oversaw my trial two months ago and sentenced me to death. Something like that tends to strain a working relationship.

"How did the Sentry get into the ghetto undetected?" I say.

Logan and Roach share a knowing look.

"What?" I say.

"We believe it was an inside job," Logan replies.

"Fragg," I mutter.

"Suspicious timing, don't you think?" Roach says. "The public vote is tomorrow and suddenly all our weapons go missing."

I rake a hand through my hair. How in the hell are we going to run a rebellion without any weapons? I suspect Purian Rose was somehow behind the theft. He must've had a spy working for him inside the Legion this whole time. The timing is too neat to be a coincidence.

"Does Sigur know about this?"

"He is speaking with the other ministers now," Logan replies.

"There's going to be an inquest," Roach adds. "But for now, we need to watch our backs. I'm going to kill those traitorous bastards when I get my hands on them!"

We leave the empty storeroom, and Logan closes the door.

"Do we have *any* weapons?" I ask as we walk down the corridor.

"I've told the lieutenants to gather what they can," Roach

says. "But we haven't had much response so far—just some rifles and enough parts to cobble together some bombs."

"We're totally screwed, aren't we?" I say grimly.

"It doesn't look great," she admits. "Look, let's keep this on
a need-to-know basis for now. For morale, you know?"

I nod. With the ballot tomorrow, the last thing our support-
ers need to hear is that we have no means to defend ourselves
if we lose the vote and the Sentry come for us. Purian Rose's
threat flashes through my head again. What am I going to do?

The door to Sigur's office opens and Juno Jones pops her
head out. Her fiery red hair has been pulled back into a slick
ponytail, and her pale blue eyes are rimmed with Cinderstone
powder. She's wearing a pair of indecently tight black leather
pants and a white corset blouse with a ruffled collar.

"I thought I heard your voice," she says, bundling me into
the office. "I need you to shoot some promos for tomorrow."

Roach and Logan smirk at me as Juno shuts the door.

"From the top," Juno says an hour later.

We've been recording two speeches to run after tomorrow's
ballot—one a rousing victory speech if things go well, and a second speech if things don't. They both feel like losing speeches
to me, knowing that whatever I choose tomorrow, someone
important to me is going to suffer. The question is *who?*

I shift in my seat, trying to get comfortable, although I'm
unbearably hot in my battered Legion Liberation Front jacket.
The coat's been dyed black to match the rest of my uniform,
which was carefully put together by the rebel leaders to create the character of Phoenix. The LLF jacket represents the
Darkling rebellion, while the black slacks and boots are from
my old Tracker uniform. Now, instead of hunting Darklings,

I'm "hunting down freedom," according to one of our slogans anyway.

Our cameraman and technician, Stuart—a gangly man with spiky brown hair—fiddles about with the sound levels while Juno's younger sister, Amy, hurries over to me to redo my makeup. This is another thing putting me in a bad mood. They've painted a band of Cinderstone powder down the bridge of my nose and around my eyes, so I look more "phoenixy," in Juno's words. She thought it would make me easier to identify when we do the crowd shots. In fairness to Amy, she's done a good job, but I still hate it.

She blushes as she dabs more Cinderstone powder onto my face, her fingers light and warm. She's a year younger than me, and I vaguely remember seeing her around school—when we used to attend it. We haven't been in months, since joining the rebellion. But our parents tutor us whenever they can so we don't fall too far behind in our education. Amy looks like Juno, with the same auburn hair and pale, freckled skin. On her wrist is a tattoo of a burning black flower, dubbed the Cinder Rose, which has become the symbol of the rebellion. Beetle came up with the design. The color represents Black City, while the burning rose signifies our destruction of the Sentry government . . . or something. I sort of stopped listening when Beetle explained it to me.

"You're doing much better," Amy says.

"I suck," I say, adjusting my microphone. "Don't tell your sister, but I much prefer doing the promos with James and Hilary on Firebird radio. At least I don't have to wear makeup."

"Your secret's safe with me," Amy says, smiling.

Before we can carry on filming, Sigur sweeps into the room, his ice-white hair flowing around his shoulders. He's wearing loose purple robes that conceal his fragile wings. One of his eyes is milky white, where he was blinded, while the other glimmers orange.

"Excuse me, but I have some important business to discuss with Ash," he says.

Juno tries to stifle her frustration. "Okay, let's call it a day. I think I've got enough footage to cobble *something* together, although I can't guarantee it'll be any good."

"I'm certain it will be a masterpiece, as always," Sigur says. "What would we do without you, Juno?"

"I'm only in it for the fame and glory, you know," she replies.

It's hard to tell if she's joking or not. She's never hidden the fact that she wants to be a lead anchor on the national news one day. But I know she still feels terrible for the role she played in my court case—it was her film footage that got me wrongly convicted of Gregory's murder, after all. I think this is her way of making it up to me.

I follow Sigur into the hallway, grateful for the chance to escape.

"So what did you need to talk about?" I say, wiping the Cinderstone powder off my face. "Do you have an update on the break-in?"

"No, we are still questioning people," Sigur says. "I just sensed you needed rescuing."

I grin. "Thanks."

"I do have something I want to show you, though," he says as we head down a flight of metal stairs and enter a large circular hall in the center of the cave.

Sigur's headquarters are located in the nocturnal animals section of the old Black City Zoo. It's perfect, really: dark, secure, with ready-made staff offices to work in and former animal enclosures to sleep in. Of course, my mom made the place really homey when she used to live here, so it doesn't feel like a zoo anymore.

We wander through a network of corridors before reaching Sigur's private suite. The sprawling room is painted red and lavishly furnished with antiques, which Sigur salvaged from Sentry mansions during the war. The majority of the suite is set up like a living room, with elegant sofas and chairs surrounding a fireplace, while a large bed takes up the rest of the space. On the right side of the bed is a small nightstand with a jewelry box, a pottery urn, and a bronze hairbrush. Strands of long, dark hair cling to the bristles. Grief spills over me, knowing they're my mom's.

"I miss her," I say quietly.

"As do I," he replies, walking over to the nightstand and picking up the urn that contains my mom's dual heart. It's tradition for Darklings to harvest their Blood Mate's heart after they die to keep as a memento. "Life feels very empty without her."

I can't imagine what it must be like to lose your Blood Mate. Purian Rose's threat flashes through my mind again. What am I going to do? How can I possibly choose between Natalie and my people? *Would it be* so *bad if we lost the vote?* Sure, the Darklings would be trapped in the ghetto, but at least they'd be alive. Natalie will die for certain if I don't do this. *She's my Blood Mate; Sigur will understand.* If I truly believe that, then why haven't I told him about Rose's ultimatum?

Sigur places the urn back on the nightstand and takes out a photograph from the drawer, and hands it to me.

It's a picture of my mom and her family, taken when she was about ten years old. I smile. For the past few weeks, Sigur has been helping me build up a picture of my Darkling family, finding photos and letters that they sent to friends before the war. I study the picture. The photo seems to have been taken in a forest glen. Peeping through the gaps in the trees is the blurry outline of a mountain with a sharp, talon-shaped peak. I flip the photo over. Scrawled on the back is *The Coombs, Forest of Shadows, Amber Hills.*

"Are these my grandparents?" I ask, pointing to a young couple standing beside Mom.

"Yes, their names were Paolo and Maria Coombs. And that's your aunt Lucinda." He indicates a younger Darkling girl who looks a lot like my mom, except with a round face and shorter hair.

"Who's this?" I say, referring to the stern-looking man with a purple heart-shaped birthmark on his left cheek, standing beside Paolo.

"I don't know. Your mother rarely spoke of her family," he explains, taking out an old leather journal from the nightstand and passing it to me. "But this might help. It's your mother's diary. I found it hidden among her belongings."

"Have you read it?"

"No, it didn't feel right," he says. "However, I am certain she wouldn't mind if you read it."

I flip through the pages, scanning her large, loopy writing, which looks a lot like mine. A photo slips out from between the sheets and falls to the floor. I pick it up. It shows my mom when she was in her late teens. She's with Aunt Lucinda and two other girls inside a run-down tavern. One of the girls is wearing a hooded cape, and is exotically beautiful with full scarlet lips, bronzed skin and topaz eyes. She's perched on the armrest of the second girl's wheelchair. This girl is pretty in an ethereal way, with wide green eyes and wispy blond hair. She's dressed in a barmaid outfit, so I'm guessing her parents own the tavern, since they tend to be staffed by family members. Neatly written on the back of the photo is the caption *T4K. Thrace*.

The sound of yelling rings up through the floorboards. It's Roach and Logan. Concerned, I quickly tuck the photos back into the diary, and we head down to the main entrance. The moment we arrive, I know something is terribly wrong. A group of Darklings have surrounded something on the stone floor, and several rebels are running about, shouting orders at each other. I catch sight of Roach and Logan in the crowd of people.

"That creature should not be here! Who let him in?" Logan demands.

"Someone get a medic!" Roach yells.

Freya is lying on the floor, her dark skin glistening with blood. Air rasps out of her lips as she struggles to breathe, her black eyes wild and panicked. Her chest and stomach have been slashed open, revealing her guts, which are being held in by the man—the *Lupine*—crouched next to her.

He's powerfully built, in his late twenties, with a heavy brow hooding steel-colored eyes and a strip of mottled gray hair down the center of his shaved head. Even though he's crouching, it's clear he's tall—at least seven feet. He's wearing a smoky-gray-colored tailcoat, black leather trousers and steel-capped boots. I understand why Logan is so furious. A Lupine has no right to be here.

I rush to Freya's side, taking her hand. "What happened?" I demand.

"I found her at the Cinderstone plant," the Lupine says. "The guards caught her breaking into the head office."

A weight drops in my stomach. She warned me it was heavily guarded.

"And what were *you* doing at the factory?" Sigur asks the Lupine, clearly suspicious.

"She wasn't the only person there gathering information," he replies gruffly. "I was downloading some files from their computers when this stupid girl barged in and nearly ruined everything."

My fangs throb. "*Don't* call her stupid."

Freya turns her frantic gaze on me and tries to say something, but blood just bubbles out of her lips. Whatever she needed to say evaporates with her last, rasping breath. Her eyes glaze over.

Roach tells the rebels to take Freya's body to the morgue. When she's been carried away, the Lupine stands up, wiping a bloodstained hand on his pants leg before stretching it out to Sigur.

"Rafe Garrick, First Landing pack leader," he says.

Sigur ignores it. "Thank you for bringing Freya back to us, Mr. Garrick. Logan will escort you—"

"I think you'll want to see this," Garrick interrupts, taking out a shimmering blue flash drive from his pocket.

"What's on it?" I ask.

"Schematics for a new super-ghetto in the Mountain Wolf State," Garrick replies.

"Why has Purian Rose built a new ghetto?" I say.

"Because when he wins the vote tomorrow, he plans to ship the Darklings there," Garrick says. "And once you've been rounded up, he intends to kill you all."

4.

ASH

THIRTY MINUTES LATER, all the Darkling ministers and rebels have congregated in the Assembly—the oval chamber where our political discussions take place. Logan shifts uncomfortably in the seat beside me, her cool lilac eyes fixed on Garrick. Sitting next to her are two Darkling ministers. The first is a man named Pullo—a gruff-looking Eloka Darkling, with ebony hair and glimmering black eyes, like mine. Next to him is Angel, a Shu-Zin Darkling, with purple eyes, dark hair and clawed feet, which she's squeezed into a pair of dainty heels. Pullo and Angel occasionally throw cold glances in my direction, barely able to hide their contempt for me. Not all the Darklings appreciate a twin-blood being on their sacred Assembly.

Garrick inserts the flash drive into the com-desk—a large touch-screen computer inset into a table—and everyone falls silent as an image of five Lupines—three men and two women—appears on the digital screen on the back wall. I recognize one of the men. He's the Lupine I saw at the factory with the red leather frock coat and hair ornaments made of teeth.

"I got a tip that a gang of mercenary Lupines, known as the

Moondogs, had been transporting large quantities of Cinderstone out of Black City on behalf of the Sentry government," Garrick says. "I got suspicious. What was the government doing? It couldn't be anything legit if those gangsters were involved."

"We had the same concerns. That's why I sent Freya to investigate," Roach says.

"My pack infiltrated the factory by posing as fellow Moondogs, and I managed to gain access to the head office." He presses a button on the com-desk, and the Cinderstone shipments log appears on the digital screen on the back wall. "You'll notice that the name Mount Alba crops up time and time again."

"The volcano?" Logan says. "But that area has been deserted for decades, ever since Mount Alba erupted."

"Precisely," Garrick says. "So I hacked into the Sentry network to find out why they were sending so many shipments to a volcano. This is what I found."

The image on the digital screen shifts, to zoom in closer to a mountainous terrain within the United Sentry States. I instantly spot the volcano, with its familiar flat peak—it lost its top after the eruption thirty years ago. At its base is a sprawling urban area enclosed by a wall just like the one surrounding the Legion ghetto, but on a *much* larger scale. Written in block letters across the urban area are the words THE TENTH.

"It's the size of a small state!" I say.

"Why do you think they called it the Tenth?" Garrick says.

"Because it's the tenth state," I reply, cottoning on.

He nods. "Really it's more a state-within-a-state, but the name is sort of catchy."

"This isn't evidence the government plans to exterminate us," Pullo says in a brusque voice.

"I agree," Angel chimes in. "It's just a ghetto. It's no different from the Legion, other than it's bigger."

I look at Garrick. "How are you certain Purian Rose plans to kill the Darklings?"

"Not just the Darklings," Garrick says, bringing up some documents stamped CONFIDENTIAL. "From these memos, I was able to determine that Rose plans to send *all* Impurities—"

"Impurities?" Logan says.

"Anyone Rose feels doesn't fit in with his plans for the One Faith, One Race, One Nation campaign," Garrick explains. "This includes Darklings, Bastets, blasphemers, race traitors, Dacians—"

"What about Lupines?" Pullo challenges.

"We weren't mentioned in the documents," Garrick says. "I guess he has other plans for us."

"Then why are you helping us, if you're not at risk?" Pullo says. "What do you have to gain by telling us about the Tenth?"

Anger flares across Garrick's face. "Just because I'm a Lupine doesn't mean I obediently follow everything Purian Rose says and does. I happen to support the rebellion."

"I'm a little confused," Logan says. "Rose's Law only specifies the segregation of Darklings from humans, so how can he justify sending those other people to the concentration camp?"

"The Darklings are just pawns in all this," Garrick explains. "The government is playing on the tension between your two species to garner support for segregation. But once the law passes, they intend to attach addenda to Rose's Law to include *all* the groups—"

"And because they'll be adding to an existing law, he doesn't need another vote to do it," Sigur finishes. "He can send anyone to the Tenth, and it'll be perfectly legal."

There are outraged murmurs among the Assembly.

"You didn't answer my earlier question," I say. "How do you know Rose plans to kill us?"

"From the intel I've gathered, it's clear that the Tenth is divided into three cities." Garrick presses a button, and a trio of urban areas glows on the map.

Each city is surrounded by its own boundary wall and joined together by a complex system of roads and rail networks. Garrick indicates the largest city in the Tenth, which is easily five times bigger than Black City.

"This city is called Primus-One. It's the base camp, where all new arrivals will be sent before they are evaluated and then transported to Primus-Two or Primus-Three." He indicates the two smaller cities, to the south and east of Mount Alba. "Prisoners will be checked for health, age, strength and skills. Those deemed suitable for work will be sent to Primus-Two, to work in the factories."

The screen pans in on Primus-Two. It comprises dozens of large industrial buildings.

"What are they producing in those factories?" Roach asks.

"I didn't have time to access that information before Freya turned up with half the Sentry guard after her," Garrick replies.

"What happens to the people who aren't suitable to work in the factories?" Logan says.

Garrick moves the map to the final city, on the east side of the mountain. "They'll be sent to Primus-III."

He zooms in on a series of white buildings, each with a green cross painted on the roof, just like the ones they paint on medical laboratories. Dread starts to set in.

"He's going to experiment on us?" I exclaim. "Why?"

"I'm not sure," Garrick replies. "But those concrete buildings next to the labs are crematoriums, so whatever they're planning, they don't expect the test subjects to survive."

I think I'm going to be sick.

"It's just like the concentration camp they had in the Barren Lands," Logan says.

"Except on a much bigger scale," Garrick replies. "The Tenth can easily handle twenty, maybe thirty, million prisoners at any one time."

"We must not let Rose's Law pass tomorrow," Sigur says.

There are nods of agreement from around the room.

"But won't Purian Rose still attempt to send us to the ghetto, even if he loses the vote?" Logan says.

"I'd like to see him try!" Roach says. "There would be civil bloody war if he sends the so-called Impurities to the Tenth when over half the country has voted *against* segregation."

I consider the fact that Purian Rose came all the way to Black City to threaten me into supporting his law and suspect she's right. He doesn't want this to break out into a civil war if he can avoid it.

"Then let's not give that bastard any chance to do it!" Roach hollers. "We're gonna win this vote tomorrow, right?"

"Right!" the rebels all chant.

The room erupts into chaos as people discuss this new turn of events, but I'm too numb to hear them. I glance at the map again. This is so much bigger than trying to free my people from the ghettos; the very survival of our species and many others is at risk. So what am I going to do tomorrow? It comes down to this: Whose life is worth more? Natalie's or theirs?

I honestly don't know how to answer that question.

5.
NATALIE

"CLOSE YOUR EYES," Day says as we approach the canal.

The sun has just started to set over Black City, casting a muted peach glow over the buildings. With me are Polly, Day, and her little brother, MJ, plus their parents, Michael and Sumrina. Michael is holding MJ's hand, helping him walk. It's funny seeing them side by side, as MJ's the spitting image of his father; both have the same dark skin, soulful brown eyes and easy smiles, although MJ has a curved back because of his kyphosis. I'm really touched that my sister has come out with us; I know she hates being outside ever since she was tortured and disfigured by Purian Rose.

I wonder if he would've been so cruel had he known that she's his daughter. I search Polly's face for any resemblance. They share the same startling, metallic gray eyes, but otherwise she looks nothing like him. Polly gives me a small smile. She's still breathtakingly beautiful, despite the zigzag of scars across her cheeks. It's wonderful seeing my sister happy. The past two months with Day's family have been good for the both of us.

It's been tough without Mother around, but Sumrina and Michael have made us feel like we're part of the family.

"Where *can* we be going?" I say teasingly as we head along a familiar part of the canal, near to where I first met Ash. My heart stumbles, thinking about that encounter under the bridge. I know they've arranged a surprise party for me on Beetle's boat—Michael accidentally let it slip last week—but I play along, screwing my eyes shut as Day leads me toward the barge.

"Here we are," Day says.

I stretch out a tentative hand so I can be helped on board the barge. A cool, firm hand takes mine in response. An electric shock zings into my heart. *Ash.* He lifts me onto the boat, and I giggle, falling against him.

"No peeking," he says.

He softly kisses me, making butterflies flutter in my stomach.

"Can I look now?" I say when he brings me inside the cabin.

"Go ahead," Ash replies.

I open my eyes and give a little squeal of delight. Beetle has decorated the entire barge with colorful paper chains and ribbons, and a handmade banner hangs over the window announcing HAPPY 17TH BIRTHDAY. Everyone is here: Ash's father, and my former housemaid Martha, as well as Beetle, Roach, Sigur, Amy and Stuart. Amy rushes over and gives me a big hug. We've become quite close since she joined the rebellion. We even got our Cinder Rose tattoos at the same time.

"Juno's running late," Amy says. "She got called to the station because of some breaking news story, yada-yada-yada. You know how it is with reporters."

We all find a place on the long benches. I squeeze in between Ash and Day, wincing slightly as I sit down.

"Is your leg still hurting?" Ash asks.

"A little." I lift up my purple tulle skirt to reveal the nasty bite mark on my leg, where a Darkling boy took a chunk out of me a couple months ago. The wound still hasn't completely healed, and the flesh around it is raised and sore. I scratch at the scab.

"Don't pick at it, or it'll scar," Day chastises.

"Sorry, *Mom*," I say, lowering my skirt.

"Let's get this party started!" Beetle says, clapping his hands together. He's made a bit of an effort to look nice tonight, wearing a clean shirt and black pants with just one tear at the knee. He's even brushed his usually scruffy brown hair. "Who fancies a game of Lady Fortune's Wheel?" Beetle asks.

This is met with cheers from everybody, even Ash's dad, who gives a rueful grin. He may be a minister, but he likes to gamble. Beetle places a twelve-spoke wheel in the middle of the table, and places a container on the end of each spoke. MJ drops a bean in nine of the containers, and coins in the remaining three. Beetle pops the lids on the pots, so no one can see what's inside, and spins the wheel.

"The birthday girl goes first," Ash says, kissing my cheek.

I glance up at him, and my heart squeezes. A thought glimmers in his smoldering eyes. He lowers his long lashes, like he's trying to hide it from me. I don't have much time to analyze it, as my attention is dragged back toward the game.

As the wheel spins, I quickly lift the lid off one of the pots. Inside is a gleaming coin. *Yes!* People ooh and ahhh.

"Lady Fortune's clearly on your side tonight," Ash whispers in my ear, passing me the coin.

It's impossible to concentrate when he's so close by, his cool breath spilling over me, delicious, intoxicating. Yearning unfurls inside me, a flower blooming in winter. Memories of our time together this morning fill my mind, and I touch my glowing cheeks with my hands, willing them to cool down.

We play ten rounds of the game, and Day wins the majority of the coins.

"No fair! Day's cheating," MJ huffs.

"Don't be a sore loser, son," Michael says, ruffling MJ's hair. Day gives her winnings to her brother.

I look at Ash, who is sitting silently beside me. Even though he's right next to me, he doesn't seem to be really here.

"A coin for your thoughts," I say.

Ash smiles, but it seems forced.

"Everything okay?" I ask, suddenly worried.

"Everything's fine."

"You're lying to me."

"Let's not talk about it tonight," he replies. "I'll tell you tomorrow."

"Tell me now," I demand. I hate secrets.

Ash leads me away from the game, and when we're alone, he tells me about the break-in at the Legion, and the Tenth. I lean against him, shaken by the news. I can hear the steady thrum of his heart through his black shirt. It's the only sound that ever calms me in these mad times.

"How did the Sentry manage to build an entire new state right under our noses?" I say.

"No one's lived in that area for years because of the volcano," he explains.

My fingers dig into the material of Ash's black shirt. "We can't let this happen. No matter what, we have to stop Purian Rose."

Ash's body tenses. I look up at him, but he simply kisses my forehead again. We return to the game, but neither of us is in the mood to play anymore. Day senses the shift in the atmosphere.

"Time to open presents!" Sumrina says.

Everyone gathers around the table again, and they jovially hand me their presents. I manage a smile, although all I can think about is the Tenth.

Polly shyly hands me an envelope, and I open it up. Inside is a photo of me and Polly when we were kids, with Mother and Father standing primly in the background. This was back in a time when we were all happy together, before my father died and my mother was imprisoned. Even though we had our differences, I miss them both so much. I give Polly a big hug.

"I love it. And it'll go perfectly in my new picture frame from MJ! Thanks, everyone," I say.

Ash takes my hand. "I want to give you my gift outside."

Out on the deck, the air is cool and crisp, the sky bright with stars. It's a beautiful evening. Perfect. Ash leads me up a small flight of stairs onto the flat roof of the barge. I gasp. The roof has been covered in glass lanterns, which cast a kaleidoscope of colors across the varnished wood. Scattered between them are white orchids, my favorite flower. The sweet scent perfumes the air around us. So this is why I had to shut my eyes earlier?

"It's beautiful," I say.

Ash picks up a flower and passes it to me. "You're beautiful."

I giggle, suddenly self-conscious. I certainly don't consider myself pretty, but I love the fact that he does. He digs around in his pants pocket and retrieves a small parcel, carefully wrapped in brown paper and bound with red ribbon.

"I didn't have much money," he says, passing it to me.

"It's okay. You know I don't care about that stuff."

I untie the ribbon and open the package to reveal a stunning pendant. It has a traditional knotted design intricately etched into the gold, and some Darkling script written around the edge. It's very old and clearly valuable.

"I love it!" I say.

"It was my mom's," Ash explains.

I try to hand it back. "It's too special! I can't accept it."

"She'd want you to have it," he says. "*I* want you to have it."

"Thank you," I whisper, touched by his kind gesture.

His fingers brush my skin as he puts the pendant around my neck, sending little shivers of pleasure down my body. I twist around and kiss him, my hands running through his rippling, silken hair, which coils around my fingers. He lets out a soft moan, his arm looping around my waist, drawing me closer.

"Let's get out of here," I murmur against his lips.

"It's your birthday," he replies.

"So?"

He pulls away, sighing. "I wasn't supposed to tell you, but Day made you a cake, and I think she'll kill you if you don't eat it."

I pout, and Ash laughs.

"I suppose we should get back to the party," I say reluctantly.

"Not just yet," he says quietly, retrieving another parcel from his pocket. This one is smaller than the first and wrapped in beautiful, handcrafted silk paper.

"Another present? You shouldn't have," I say, taking it.

"I hope you like it," he says, rubbing the back of his neck.

He anxiously watches me as I carefully unwrap the parcel. I open the silk paper, and something glimmers.

My heart trips over.

In my hand is a blue diamond ring.

My head snaps up, a question in my eyes.

"I know we're young," he says softly. "But I love you, with every beat of my awakened heart."

I hold my breath, waiting for him to say the words.

"Natalie Buchanan, will you marry me?"

"Yes! Yes, I'll marry you!" I squeal with delight.

He slips the ring on my finger, and I throw my arms around his neck, kissing him over and over. Happiness radiates through me, making my heart swell until I think it's going to burst.

"I love you," I say between kisses.

"I love you too, blondie," he says.

I giggle joyfully as he spins me around, the cool breeze brushing against my skin. Eventually he puts me down and kisses me again, this time softly, slowly, opening a channel between us so I can feel everything he's feeling: his love, his joy, his happiness. We've Soul Shared before, but this time is the most intense of them all, and tears spill down my cheeks. We eventually break the kiss.

"I hope those are tears of happiness?" he teases, wiping them away.

I nod.

We hurry downstairs, eager to break the good news. As we enter the cabin, everyone is silent, an expectant look on their faces. Ash grins sheepishly at me. They must've all been in on it!

"Well? Don't keep us in suspense," Day demands when nobody says anything.

I show them the ring, and everyone cheers.

The women all hurry around me to coo over the ring—even Polly, who manages a few smiles—while the men pat Ash on the back, telling him "well done, mate," and "how did you get a girl like that?" Beetle tops off everyone's drinks and raises his glass.

"To Ash and Natalie—may you have a long and happy life together!" he says.

"To Ash and Natalie!" everyone else responds.

I glance at Ash, and for a second there's worry in his eyes, but he quickly conceals it, giving me the broadest, most beautiful smile I've ever seen. I smile back, but I can't help but wonder why he looked so concerned. Is he already having doubts? No, I'm being paranoid! I push it from my mind and allow myself to enjoy the moment. I can ask him about it later.

The party carries on in full swing. Everyone is in high spirits, dancing and singing—even Sigur, who, as it turns out, has an amazing voice. He teaches Polly and MJ a traditional Darkling song, while Ash's father, Harold, comes over to me and gives me a hug. My cheek scratches against his gray beard, but I don't mind.

"I'm so glad you'll be joining the family," he says. "I've never known Ash to be this happy."

"I promise to take good care of him."

"I know you will."

"You're not worried we're rushing things?" I ask quietly.

He gives me a gentle smile. "I was, but Ash convinced me that he's ready for this commitment, and when my son sets his mind on something, there's no changing it."

I laugh lightly. "That sounds like Ash."

"If you have any doubts . . ."

"I don't," I say, which is true. I have no reservations about marrying Ash. After nearly losing him two months ago, I've learned to grab happiness with both hands and not wait around for a future that may never happen.

Harold hugs me again, and I hold on to him for a bit longer than necessary, but he understands. With a dead father and a mother serving a life sentence in prison, I'm essentially an orphan. When I marry Ash, Harold will become my father too. It's a very comforting thought.

We all gather around the table as Day brings out a lopsided chocolate cake, which is slathered in gloopy icing that's already started to slide off. The large, wonky piping on top reads HAPPY BIRTHDAY NA. She ran out of space for the T. I absolutely love it. It's nice knowing Day isn't perfect at everything.

"It's a masterpiece," I say.

Day rolls her brown eyes. "It's the last time I'm ever baking, so you better enjoy it."

"Make a wish," Harold says.

I blow out my candles, wishing for a positive outcome at tomorrow's vote.

Day serves everyone a slice of cake while I sneak off to the restroom to get a moment to myself. I splash some water over my face and check my reflection in the small mirror above the sink. My cheeks are flushed, and my curly hair is a bit frizzy from being spun around by Ash, but I look *happy*. I smile. I'm about to turn away when something makes me pause. The corner of my left eye looks strange. Is it my imagination, or does it look a little yellow? It must be a trick of the light.

When I join the party again, the mood has shifted, and I soon see why. Juno has arrived, her long red hair a tangled mess, her cheeks pink, as if she ran all the way from work.

"The network got the report an hour ago. The news is about to break on every station across the country—" she says, then cuts herself short when she sees me.

"What is it?" I say.

Sumrina comes over to me and takes my hand.

"It's your mother," she says.

"Is she all right?" I ask, worried.

"Your mom broke out of prison two hours ago," Juno says. "She's on the run."

6.
ASH

JUNO FILLS US in on everything she knows. There was an explosion at the prison, which killed six guards and took down part of the building's west wing. The bombing was just a distraction, to keep the guards busy as Emissary Buchanan was extracted from her cell in the east wing. It took the guards a few hours to notice she had even escaped, and by then, it was too late.

Natalie tightens her shaking fingers around mine, her lips pale.

"Do they know who helped her escape?" she says.

"No, but it was a professional job," Juno replies. "Probably ex-military."

"Where do you think she's gone?" Day says.

"Heavens, you don't think she'd come back *here*?" Sumrina says, worry in her eyes.

"No, she wouldn't do anything so risky," Natalie answers.

"Is Mother going to be okay?" Polly says quietly.

"You know Mother, she's a survivor," Natalie says. "She'll be fine. Just—" Her last word gets caught in her throat. Tears spring to her eyes.

I glance at my dad. He nods, understanding.

"Perhaps it's time to call it a night," Dad says.

Michael and Sumrina take Polly to their house on Cinder Street, while Natalie comes home with me to the Ivy Church. Dad kindly stays at the barge with Roach and Beetle, to give us some time alone.

We climb up the twisting staircase leading to my bedroom in the church's bell tower. The moonlight shimmers off the brass bell hanging down the center of the hexagonal room. Natalie sinks down on the bed while I move the wooden boards over the arched windows to keep out some of the chilled night air. I freeze. Two Sentry guards are sitting on the gravestones outside—they must've been following us. They catch my eye, and one of them waves, a smirk on his lips. I quickly place the board over the window and join Natalie on the bed. I don't tell her about the guards, not wanting to worry her.

"Your mom's going to be all right," I say.

Natalie nods, wiping the tears from her eyes.

"I just wish she'd contacted me."

"It would've been too dangerous," I say gently.

"I know, but it still hurts that Polly and I weren't part of her plan." She sighs, playing with her engagement ring. "I'm sorry. This was supposed to be a special evening, and I'm ruining it."

I tilt her face up. "In good times and in bad, remember?"

She smiles. "I love you so much, Ash. I don't know what I'd do without you."

My heart cramps as I think about tomorrow. What am I going to do? The right choice would be to vote no, but then Natalie will be taken. I simply can't let that happen. So what do I do? With the guards outside, we can't escape, so there's no way I can hide Natalie or get her out of the city tonight without them knowing. Plus, I doubt they're the only guards keeping tabs on us—Purian Rose would've made sure of that. The men outside the church are a warning: he's watching us. All I can do is keep her close.

Natalie gives me a shy smile. "So . . . we're all alone."

I grin. "Yup."

"With no one here to interrupt us."

"Nope."

She looks up at me expectantly, and all thoughts of tomorrow vanish from my mind. It's just her, me, in this moment. I cup a hand around her face and gently kiss her. The echo of her heart tremors inside my chest, nervous and excited, as is mine.

We lie down, and her blond curls spill across the pillow. Anticipation hangs in the air between us. The moment has finally come. My eyes drift over her face, her body, my vision shimmering around the edges. The Sight. It's a force Darklings use to mark their prey, to ward off other Darklings. I envelop her in its enthralling darkness, telling her one thing: *you belong to me.*

My fingers glide over her flushed cheeks and lips, down her neck, stopping at the gold pendant peeking out the top of her purple corset dress. A silk ribbon crisscrosses up the lacy bodice, secured at the top with a simple bow. I playfully tug on the ribbon, and the bodice unravels to reveal the creamy, rose-blushed flesh underneath, marked only by a thin red scar from the heart transplant she had as a child. Fire blazes through my veins, and I let out a ragged breath, barely able to control my thirst.

Natalie's blue eyes simmer as she holds my gaze for a lingering heartbeat, knowing the effect she's having on me. Finally, she entwines her fingers in my hair and draws me toward her. The kiss is like lightning, sending shock waves into my heart. *Baboom, ba-boom!* I hardly notice when she unbuttons my shirt.

There's none of the uncertainty of this morning. Her fingers caress my back, my arms, my chest, sliding over my stomach muscles toward my belt buckle. My poison sacs flood with venom.

She parts her mouth, deepening our kiss, and I let out a low groan. My whole body trembles with pent-up tension; my skin is ablaze. My hands slide up her legs, lifting her tulle skirt at the same time. I roll on top of her and force myself to hold back, just for a moment, and drink her in. I want to savor this perfect moment, because tomorrow everything is going to change. She won't look at me like this ever again, with pure love, trust, desire. One way or another, tomorrow I'll reveal myself for the man I truly am. A traitor.

"I love you," I say, my voice hoarse.

"I love you too," she replies. "With all my heart."

I kiss her, unable to wait a second longer. She gasps, then a sigh, and it's just like I remembered. *Bliss.*

A shaft of sunlight spills between the wooden boards in front of the windows, waking me up. I rub an exhausted hand over my face, struggling to drag myself into the land of the living. My left hand dangles over the edge of the bed, and my fingers brush against the lacy material of Natalie's torn, discarded dress. I grin. I'll have to buy her a new one.

The mattress dips slightly as Natalie rolls over to face me, the white sheet twisting around her body. A tangle of curly blond hair surrounds her flushed face, her blue eyes sparkling the same color as the engagement ring glistening on her finger.

I tuck a curl behind her ear. "Last night was . . . *wow.*"

She shyly bites her lip.

"Are you hungry?" I ask.

"Famished," she replies. "What time is it, anyway?"

I check the clock on my nightstand and then leap out of bed, panicked.

"Grab some clothes—we're late!"

Twenty minutes later, we're pushing our way through the crowds in the town square where one of the polling stations has been set up for the public vote today. I can't believe we're late. Of all the days to sleep in! I snatch a look over my shoulder. Two Sentry guards are walking a short distance behind us, guns slung over their shoulders. They followed us here from the church. Natalie glances at them too, frowning.

"They're not very subtle, are they?" she murmurs. "If they're trying to intimidate us, it's not working."

Yes it is.

I tighten my grip on her hand, my mind racing with ways to protect her, if it comes down to it. I still haven't decided which way I'm going to vote. *My guards will slice bits off her, piece by piece* . . . I look over my shoulder again. I can probably take on those two guards, but not the hundred others patrolling the town square. What am I going to do? I'm running out of time to make my decision.

"Phoenix!"

The three boys I saw playing in the street the other day run over to me, followed by their mom, Sally. She looks anxious and fidgety. Little Phoenix tugs at my jacket sleeve. I'm dressed in my Phoenix outfit today—LLF jacket, black pants and boots—as Roach requested, although I drew the line at putting on the makeup. Natalie's wearing a pair of my pants and a shirt tied at the waist with a leather belt.

"Good luck today," Little Phoenix says.

My stomach knots.

"Leave him alone, boys," Sally says, ushering them away. She doesn't wave good-bye this time.

Everyone's tense, but I'm not surprised; this isn't an ordinary day. On the rooftops of the buildings around us, giant digital screens broadcast live footage of the voting that's happening in the other megastates across the United Sentry States. At the bottom of each screen is a graphic letting us know the results so far.

It's rare to have a vote done in public this way. Usually they're secret ballots, but Purian Rose insisted on it, claiming he didn't want Humans for Unity to "try any tricks" and fix the voting. That probably was *one* of his reasons. I'm guessing the other reason is he wants the whole nation to see me vote in favor of his segregation law.

The polling station has been set up beside the three wooden crosses used to execute traitors. The middle cross still bears the scars of my torture and failed execution, the acacia wood blackened with soot, the cobbled ground forever stained with my blood. I look away.

One of the benefits of the voting being done in public is that the Legion guards are able to watch from the Boundary Wall and report back to the other Darklings. They're not allowed to vote themselves, nor are the Bastets or Lupines, as they're not technically citizens of the United Sentry States. I'm only allowed to vote because I'm half human, and have a citizenship card. I can just picture them: whole families huddled together, waiting to hear their fate, relying on me. *Trusting* me.

Also standing on the wall are Garrick and Sigur. A gold mask obscures Sigur's scarred face, protecting him from the worst of the misty sunlight. It reminds me of the first time I saw him and Evangeline standing there, during his niece's execution.

Evangeline. Desire and grief jumble up inside me as I think about her, the girl who was meant to be my Blood Mate. I haven't heard from her since she left Black City, in search of more twin-bloods. I have no idea if she's still alive, although if anyone could make it on her own, it would be Evangeline.

We finally reach the stage and find a frantic-looking Day waiting for us.

"I was just on my way to get you," she says. "Why are you so late?"

"We slept in," Natalie says.

"You might want to come up with a better excuse than that," Day says. "Roach is out for your blood. You were supposed to be meeting and greeting people hours ago."

"I know," I say. Roach wanted me to help Humans for Unity drum up some last-minute support, before the voting started in Black City.

"Where's Polly?" Natalie asks, looking about her.

"She's babysitting MJ. His back was hurting him too much to come out," Day explains. "Besides, I don't think she could face all these crowds. She's having one of her bad days . . ."

Natalie nods, understanding.

"There you are, bro!" Beetle says, pushing his way toward us, followed by a thunderous-looking Roach.

"You were told to be here hours ago," Roach says to me. "How do you think it looks if Phoenix can't even be bothered to show his fragging face?"

"I'm really sorry," I say.

We're soon met by my dad, Sumrina, Michael and Amy. Juno is on the stage with Stuart, filming the public vote in Black City. She's wearing her signature look—tight black leather pants and corseted white blouse, with heavy Cinderstone eyeliner rimming her pale blue eyes, while Stuart's made less of an effort, wearing a faded patchwork tailcoat and brown suede slacks, his brown hair spiked up in its usual style. TV crews have been placed at all the polling stations across the city, but the one in the town square is getting the most focus, because of me.

On top of the platform is a pair of large glass boxes, each two yards tall and wide, with a metal slot in the front of both boxes for people to post their ballot papers through. All the ballot slips have a microchip built into them, which contains your citizenship identification number, to prevent fraud. A computer, which is hooked up to the voting boxes, records this information as you drop your ballot slip into the box, and your vote instantly appears on the screen behind the stage. A sign above the box on the right says YES, and on the left, the sign reads NO.

"How's it going?" I ask the group.

"Not too bad," Amy says. "We lost the vote in the Plantation State, but it wasn't by much."

The Plantation State was always going to be one of the hardest states to win over, because they rely on government contracts to sell their crops, so the fact that the vote was close is really encouraging.

"The real surprise is the Dominion State," Amy continues, pointing to the digital screen above Black City School.

Currently the people of Centrum, in the Dominion State, are voting, and the screen is showing 8,476,802 YES; 6,098,156 NO. I do a double take, stunned by the numbers. I thought Centrum would vote almost entirely yes, given it's the capital city and Purian Rose's home turf.

"Those numbers are great!" Natalie says.

Beetle grins. "Yeah, and just imagine what they'll be like for the cities that *hate* the Sentry."

No wonder Purian Rose paid me a visit yesterday. He must've known the vote was going to be tight. And it hits me: we could actually *win* this. I'd always hoped we could, but looking at those figures, that hope is becoming a reality. All I have to do is vote no to Rose's Law, and my people could be spared from going to the Tenth.

But then Natalie will die.

My stomach clenches.

Natalie or twenty million people.

Who do I choose?

"Bro, don't make a scene," Beetle suddenly says to me, peering over my shoulder.

I turn, wondering what he means, and my fangs instantly flood with venom as I stare into the callous green eyes of Sebastian Eden. I take a protective step toward Natalie.

"I have to admit, I didn't think you'd show up," Sebastian says, looking pointedly from me to Natalie.

"What, and miss the chance to humiliate Purian Rose on live television?" I say.

"I would tread very carefully, nipper," Sebastian says icily. "Don't forget what's at stake here."

"I haven't," I reply.

A cruel smile breaks out on his lips. "Give my regards to Polly," he says to Natalie, before walking onto the stage.

"God, he's such a jerk," Natalie mutters, then turns to talk to Day.

"What was he talking about?" Beetle whispers to me when she's distracted.

"Nothing. Don't worry about it," I reply.

He presses his lips together, not believing me. Beetle knows me almost as well as Natalie does, so he can tell when I'm lying. To his credit, he doesn't push it.

On the digital screens the cameras cut back to SBN studios. Glamorous news presenter February Fields gives us a wide, glossy-lipped smile.

"The final votes are in for the Dominion State." We all stop talking and look at the screen. "The state votes in favor of Rose's Law."

"Two-zero," I mutter.

"Don't stress about it, mate." Beetle claps a hand on my shoulder, making my scars sting. "We're next. We'll swing the vote back in our favor."

My neck muscles tense up. The time to make my decision is nearly upon me. I look up at Sigur, who is still watching the proceedings from the Boundary Wall. I can't see the expression behind his mask, but his body language is stiff.

Natalie or my people?

The footage cuts to the town square in Black City.

"Next up, Black River State," February Fields announces. "First to vote will be Black City."

My stomach lurches. *Showtime.*

Traditionally, the state capital votes first, mainly so the lesser cities in the state know how they're meant to be voting. It's an unspoken rule among the cities to do this, to show strength and unity in the state, although the lesser cities don't always listen.

The television cameras turn toward Sebastian, who stands primly on the stage next to the glass cubes. Behind him, a row of Sentry guards stand at attention, their guns locked and loaded. The message is clear: vote yes.

Sebastian waves a hand, ushering the first voters up. Normally, the Emissary would vote first, but since Black River State doesn't have an Emissary at the moment—no politician seems willing to take on that poisoned chalice—the citizens go straightaway.

"Here we go," Beetle says as Sally walks up to the stage, her black bustle dress dragging through the ash coating the cobblestones.

The tension in my shoulders unwinds a little, knowing we've got her vote.

Juno commentates live on camera. "The first brave citizen steps up to the podium, a vision in black—the color that has become synonymous with hope in this city," she says, alluding to my Phoenix outfit. "After months of campaigning, it all comes down to these next few moments . . ."

Sally's face is projected on all the digital screens as she walks up to the voting boxes. She glances toward Sebastian, who is standing beside the NO box, his hand resting on the hilt of his sword. She hurries over to the YES box and drops in her vote, then quickly returns to the crowd and drags her boys out of the town square.

"I thought we could count on her vote," Natalie whispers. "I guess we don't know who to trust."

I look behind me. The two Sentry guards who were following us are still nearby, watching me.

The next few dozen votes go like this, with people visibly shaking as they hurry to drop their ballot papers into the YES box. I look up at the screen: 48 YES; 0 NO.

"Fragging hell," Beetle mutters under his breath.

"Hang on," Natalie says.

James and Hilary Madden from Firebird radio walk up the steps to the platform.

I take a deep breath, and Natalie gives my hand a reassuring squeeze.

They fold their ballot papers and walk toward Sebastian. James flashes a look in our direction, and there's a cold gleam in his eyes. In that moment, I know we've lost them. They veer to the right and drop their ballot slips into the YES box.

Beetle swears loudly. "Those *traitors*. I bet they were the ones who stole our weapons! They should be hanged!"

I swallow a hard lump in my throat. *Will he want to hang me as well?* I think Beetle's suspicions are right, though. As prominent members of Humans for Unity, James and Hilary have full access to all areas of the Legion ghetto, including the weapons store. They defiantly walk down the steps, their heads held high.

Beetle spits on James as he passes by, and the man turns, swinging a fist at Beetle, missing him by a hair's breadth. It all happens so quickly: James and Beetle start fighting, throwing wild punches at each other. Day and Hilary try to pull them apart, but they get knocked to the ground as more people join the fray. Two people soon turn into twenty. Fists fly, and people are pushed and shoved. In the melee, James and Hilary manage to flee. Flashbacks to the riot two months ago crash into my mind. I can't let this happen again! I rush onto the stage and grab Juno's microphone.

"STOP!" I yell at the top of my lungs.

My voice reverberates around the town square. Everyone is deathly silent. Thankfully, the fighting stops immediately.

Thousands of faces stare up at me from the crowd, reminding me of the day I was crucified. My mouth suddenly feels dry, and I can almost taste the acacia fumes. *Not now . . .* I lick my dry lips, and start to speak.

"We're here to vote, not to fight," I say. "Don't resort to bloodshed and undermine what we're trying to achieve today.

The government may think it's acceptable to intimidate us with their guns and their soldiers"—I slide a look at Sebastian, who glowers at me—"but that is not our way. We will not be governed by fear."

A lone voice calls out across the crowd. "No fear, no power!"

The chant is picked up by another person, then another, just like on the day of my crucifixion. Soon the whole city is chanting, "NO FEAR, NO POWER!"

I should be happy. This is exactly what the rebels wanted, but I can barely breathe. It's precisely the thing Rose wanted to avoid. I'm meant to be showing my unwavering support of him. *If I don't* . . . I glance from Natalie to the two guards standing a short distance behind her. *They're going to cut her up.* There's still a chance to make this right.

I take out my ballot paper. Never has a slip of paper felt so heavy in my hand.

I shut my eyes.

Vote yes and save Natalie.

Vote no and save twenty million people.

My heart hammers. Everyone in the nation is watching me now, waiting to see what I'll do, including Purian Rose.

Natalie.

Twenty million people.

The girl I love.

Twenty million people.

There was never a choice.

I slip my vote into the ballot box.

"Ash Fisher votes no to Rose's Law," Juno reports to the camera.

I look at Natalie down in the crowd, and my heart splinters into a million pieces. *I'm so sorry.*

The rebels cheer, but I barely hear them as I sprint off the stage and grab her hand.

"We need to leave the city," I say to her in a rush.

She raises a brow at me. "What? *Now?*"

The two Sentry guards are still behind her.

"Yes, now. Let's just go," I say.

I have no idea how I'll get her past all the guards, but somehow I need to get her to safety.

She looks at the line of people forming at the podium steps. "What's gotten into you? We're in the middle of the ballot."

"I don't care," I say urgently. "We need to leave."

"I can't leave Polly, plus I want to vote."

I let out a frustrated sigh. She's right, of course. I haven't thought this through.

A crease forms between her pale brows. "You're frightening me, Ash. What's going on?"

I scan the crowd behind her again. The guards are nowhere to be seen. Where did they go? Maybe Purian Rose ordered them not to take her here, since we're being filmed? I figure as long as we're near the cameras, we're safe.

"Nothing," I say, leading her closer to the stage so we're in the shot. "Everything's fine. I'm just jumpy with all these guards around."

She studies me for a moment, clearly concerned. I kiss her cheek.

"Everything's fine," I say again.

"I should go vote," she says, her hand slipping through mine.

I keep an eye out for the guards as Natalie walks up the steps, ignoring the cold look from Sebastian. She casts her vote in the NO box, then joins me again. The line moves forward, and one by one, the citizens of Black City move up to the stage.

They don't seem as scared as before. Some of them even dare to look Sebastian in the eye as they drop their ballot papers into the NO box. The numbers soon start shifting, the nos overtaking the yeses. Beetle grins at me. I cast a look at Sigur, who is still standing on the Boundary Wall. He gives me a slight nod of approval.

The votes start coming in from the lesser cities around Black River State, and the nos come in thick and fast. Ember Creek, a quaint harbor town on the east coast of the state, is the last city to vote. Their polling station has been set up on a scenic promenade surrounded by market stalls selling fishing supplies. Hundreds of people are crammed onto the promenade, and they've all turned to face the camera, their expressions fierce, defiant. The footage quickly cuts back to February Fields, but not before everyone has heard the citizens of Ember Creek chant "No fear, no power!" at the top of their lungs.

It doesn't take long for the voting to finish, since Black River State is one of the least populated areas in the country, after millions were killed during the war. I stare at the results on the digital screens, not quite believing it. February Fields appears on the monitors, her smile wavering and forced.

"The final votes are in for Black River State," she says. "The state votes no."

There are cheers and whoops of joy in the town square. Everyone is celebrating except me.

"Now the Provinces will vote," February Fields announces.

This sobers everyone up quickly. We may have won over Black River State, but if no other states follow us, then everything we achieved today will be for nothing. Over the next few hours, we watch with apprehension as the votes come in from the final states:

The Provinces—No.

The Barren Lands—Yes.

The Emerald State—No.

Mountain Wolf State—Yes.

Golden Sands—No.

"Well, isn't this exciting? The vote is tied," February Fields says, her girlish voice a little strained. "Four states vote in favor of Rose's Law, and four against. And finally, the Copper State!"

Everything rests on this last vote.

The screens cut to footage of Emissary Vincent, a thin black woman in her midfifties, with a severe haircut that accentuates the hard angles of her face. She's standing in front of a wall similar to our Boundary Wall, except theirs is made from steel and brass, not concrete.

All I can do is watch helplessly as the woman strides up to her polling station, which has been set up similarly to ours. She briefly pauses, allowing the press to take her photo before walking toward the YES box. It's like watching an accident; you know it's going to happen, but you can't stop looking.

Then she does something no one expects.

She turns sharply to the left and slips her ballot paper into the NO box.

There's a pregnant pause as everyone in the town square stares at the screen in disbelief.

Emissary Vincent turns to look at the cameras, addressing the nation.

"Citizens of the Copper State, I urge you to—"

The live feed cuts out, and all the monitors turn black.

7.
NATALIE

THE WHOLE CITY is in pandemonium, everyone wondering what's going on.

"What happened to the feed?" Roach calls up to Juno, who is still filming up on the stage.

"Someone's jamming our signal. We can't broadcast anything," Juno replies.

A graphic suddenly appears on the monitors, with the words *We are experiencing a technical difficulty. Be back soon!*

"Technical difficulty, my ass," Juno mutters.

"I can't believe Emissary Vincent voted against Rose," Day says, bewildered.

"She's always stood up to him," Natalie says. "Emissary Vincent cares about *all* people, not just the Sentry. My mother thought it made her weak."

"If she's flipped sides, this is great for the cause!" Beetle says. "She runs all the munitions factories, and without weapons, he has no power."

Before we can discuss it any further, the monitors spark back to life, and February Fields's face appears on the screens. She breaks out into a smile, but it doesn't reach her sea-green eyes.

"Citizens, our apologies for that short technical glitch. Oh, the perils of live broadcasting," she says, as if it were just some innocent mistake. "Thank you, Emissary Vincent, for that rousing speech. And now back to the Copper State to continue with the voting."

Emissary Vincent is nowhere to be seen, and is it my imagination, or have the television cameras moved position? A young man hurries onto the stage, casting his eyes toward something offscreen. He drops his ballot paper in the YES box. Beetle curses loudly. An elderly woman is called up next. Her eyes also flash toward something hidden just out of view. I squint at the monitor as a dark smudge appears in the bottom right corner of the screen—it wasn't there a moment before. The television camera pans slightly to the left, and the smudge disappears, but not before I've worked out what it was.

Blood.

I gasp. "Ash . . ."

He's seen it too.

"You don't think . . . ?" It's too horrible to say.

He nods. "They shot her."

We lose the Copper State. It's over. We've lost.

"And there we have it, citizens!" February Fields says brightly when it's all done. "The results are in, and the nation votes in favor of Rose's Law, five to four."

The screens cut to footage of each of the state capitals, where people are cheering and clapping wildly. A victory party is happening outside Rose's palace in Centrum, with elaborate decorations and dancers in glimmering outfits performing in the city square. They must've been planning this tableau for weeks. I notice that SBN news skips over the Copper State in their little montage of victory celebrations.

The national anthem plays, and the broadcast ends on a graphic of a stern-looking blond boy and girl, accompanied by the words ONE RACE. ONE FAITH. ONE NATION UNDER HIS MIGHTY.

Sigur and Garrick leave the Boundary Wall, returning to the ghetto on the other side. A moment later, there is a terrible sound as thousands of Darklings wail in grief. Ash shuts his eyes, a pained expression on his face.

"You did everything you could for them," I whisper.

"It wasn't enough," he says quietly.

"What are we going to do now?" I say.

"The only thing we can do—get ready to fight and defend the ghetto," Roach says. "We'll hold the Sentry off for as long as we can, but it's not going to be easy without our stockpile of weapons."

We all look at each other, thinking the same thing: how are we going to protect the Darklings from the full might of Purian Rose's forces? We weren't prepared for this. Until yesterday, we thought Rose's Law was just about keeping the Darklings segregated, not shipping them—and millions of others—off to the Tenth, to be enslaved and exterminated.

"Fight or die trying, right?" Beetle mutters.

Roach goes to talk to Juno, along with the other adults, while I hug Ash, trying to remain calm while the reality of what this means crashes over me. As a twin-blood, Ash will be sent to the Tenth along with the rest of the Darklings. It's only a matter of time before the Sentry guards start shipping everyone out. How long do we have? A month? A week? A day?

"It was all for nothing," Ash whispers.

"No it wasn't," I say. "We stood up for what was right."

Ash brushes his fingertips across my cheek, his eyes dark with grief.

"I'm so sorry," he whispers.

My brow furrows. "You did everything you could."

Sebastian smirks as he walks over to us. I can't believe I ever kissed those toxic lips. He fixes his gaze on Ash.

"So you voted no?" Sebastian shakes his head. "I honestly thought you cared for Natalie more than that. Guess I was wrong."

What does Sebastian mean?

Ash takes a protective step toward me. "If you touch her, I'll—"

"What?" Sebastian quirks a brow.

Ash doesn't say anything.

"I didn't think so," Sebastian says, then turns to me. "Just know it could have been prevented."

I watch Sebastian walk away, my head spinning.

"What was that all about, bro?" Beetle asks.

Ash shoots me a worried look, and my stomach knots as it dawns on me why he's been acting so weird lately.

"They got to you, didn't they?" I say to him.

Ash rubs the back of his neck.

Beetle's mouth hangs open. "Mate?"

"Rose told me if I didn't vote in favor of his law, he'd . . ." Ash looks at me. His black eyes are filled with shame.

My heart cramps. He doesn't need to say it.

"Natalie, I'm so sorry," he says in a rush. "What could I do? So many people were relying on me; I had to do it. I—"

I gently kiss him. "It's okay, I understand."

My life isn't worth more than millions of others. If the roles were reversed, I would've done the same thing. It's a testament to how much he loves me that he even considered voting in favor of Rose's Law to protect me.

"Why didn't you tell me what was going on?" I say gently. "I would've told you to vote no. I'm not afraid of Purian Rose." That last bit is a lie, but I don't want Ash to know how scared I am right now. What does Rose have planned for me?

Ash pulls me toward him, holding me tight. "I won't let him hurt you. I'll die before I allow that to happen."

I look over his shoulder at the three crosses near the Boundary Wall. I don't doubt his words. I know he'd die to save me—he's done it before.

The rest of our families join us.

"We should go home before it gets dark," Sumrina says.

Beetle and Roach head to the Legion to discuss defensive strategies with Sigur, while Amy glumly helps Juno and Stuart pack up the equipment on stage.

Ash glances toward the Boundary Wall.

"You should go with Beetle," I say.

"I don't want to leave you," he says. "Will you come with me? It'll be safer for you there."

"If the Sentry wants me, they'll get me no matter where I am," I say. "Besides, I want to check on Polly and make sure she's all right."

If my sister is having one of her bad days, like Day said she was, then she needs me.

Ash flicks another look at the ghetto.

"It's okay. Go," I say. "I know there's going to be a lot of business to discuss."

"Roach can deal with it," he says. "I'm not leaving your side."

I smile, secretly grateful he's staying with me.

The town square is almost entirely deserted, since the majority of people hurried home when it was clear the vote wasn't going in our favor. All around the city, doors have been locked and shutters closed as people wait for the Sentry government's retaliation for our public defiance of Purian Rose.

The streets are swarming with Sentry guards, and I doubt they'll leave again. They're setting up roadblocks, which is alarming. They obviously don't want people to leave the city. What do they have planned for us? Ash keeps me close to him, while Harold and Michael flank us as we hurry back to the Rise, sticking to the back alleys to avoid the guards. Even so, I keep glancing nervously about me, worried one of Purian Rose's men will appear out of the shadows and snatch me.

My heart races when something to my right catches my eye—a flash of a golden-brown tail disappearing over the rooftop. *A cat.* I really am getting spooked. The sooner I'm home, the better.

The Rise is eerily quiet when we arrive. Curtains are drawn and lights are out in the high-rise tenements and Cinderstone shacks. No children play in the cobbled streets. I feel like a trespasser in my own home. We reach the Ivy Church, where Ash and his father live. Harold says his good-byes, not questioning Ash when he stays behind with me.

We turn down Cinder Street, and I'm almost knocked off my feet by a wave of heat. Men, women and children are running in and out of their homes, all carrying heavy pots and pans, water splashing over the sides. Acrid smoke fills the air. At the bottom of the street, twenty soot-covered men are throwing buckets of water over the source of the fire. It's our house.

"MJ!" Day screams, running down the alley.

My stomach lurches. "Polly!"

I turn to Ash, but he's frozen, transfixed by the flames. I grab his hand, snapping him out of his nightmare. We sprint down the alley, ignoring the blistering heat. This must be torture for Ash, but he doesn't leave my side. We reach the house. Flames spill out of the windows and consume the roof. The whole street could go up if we don't put the fire out soon, but that's not my concern now.

"MJ! MJ!" Michael yells, searching for his son in the crowd.

I grab one of the men carrying buckets of water. "Did you see a teenage girl and a young boy leave the house?"

The man shakes his head. Without pausing to consider the risks, I push past the men and barge into the house, ignoring their pleas for me to stay outside. Ash follows a heartbeat behind, an arm over his mouth and nose. The kitchen is ablaze. The floral wallpaper has been entirely stripped away to reveal the Cinderstone bricks underneath, which glow like embers.

"Polly! MJ!" I yell, and immediately start choking on the scorching fumes.

They're not in the kitchen, so I head farther into the house, raising my arm to protect my face from the heat. Ash grabs the door handle leading into Michael and Sumrina's bedroom and yells out in pain as the flesh on his palm sizzles.

"We can't go in there!" he shouts. "The whole room must be an inferno!"

We hurry to MJ's room. It's billowing with smoke, and I can barely breathe.

"MJ?" I cough.

No answer.

I check Polly's room next. Nothing.

Which leaves one room: the bedroom I share with Day. Paint is peeling off the door, and the wood is warped from heat. *Oh, God, please let them be alive.* I shove the wooden door with my shoulder, the force making my teeth rattle. It doesn't budge. Ash joins me, and we hit it together. This time the door buckles, and I tumble into the room. The air is thick with smoke. Ash and I frantically search for my sister and MJ.

"They're not here! Did they get out?" I call out to Ash.

A sickening thought strikes me. *Are they in Michael and Sumrina's room?* Tears spring to my eyes, and I turn, ready to rush back to their bedroom, when I hear a small moan from the wardrobe near my bed. The sound is barely audible over the crackle of burning wood. A chair has been pushed in front of the wardrobe, and I knock it aside and yank the cupboard door open. MJ topples out. I catch him before he hits the floor.

He's alive, but barely conscious.

"MJ . . . MJ, wake up!" I slap his face to rouse him.

He looks up at me with confused brown eyes.

"Where's Polly? Is she here?"

A shake of his head. "Gone." He slips into unconsciousness.

Polly isn't here. My relief is quickly countered by worry. Where is she? Ash lifts MJ over his shoulder. I snatch my bottle of heart medication off my nightstand, tucking it into my pocket, and we rush out of the room. The hallway is ablaze, and the heat claws at my skin, scorching my eyes and lungs. I hold my breath as we push through the corridor, barely avoiding a pile of burning books as it topples into our path. Flames lick up the walls and over the ceiling, making the wooden beams above us creak and splinter. There's a terrible cracking sound, and Ash shoves me, sending me flying out the front doorway into the street just as the roof caves in behind us.

Cool air smacks me in the face, and I gasp deep lungfuls of it before crashing to the ground. Michael takes his son from Ash, who kneels on the cobblestones beside me, coughing up soot. Someone hands us a pan of water, and I let Ash drink first before guzzling the remainder myself. My throat feels scorched, on fire.

"Are you okay?" I say croakily.

He manages a nod, but his whole body is shaking.

Day rushes over to me after she's tended to MJ.

"Polly?" she says.

"Not here," I reply. "I don't know where she is."

Day gasps. "Natalie!"

She points toward the house. It takes me a moment to realize what I'm looking at through the smoke, and then I see it.

Painted on the side of the house is a bright red rose.

8.
NATALIE

 "POLLY! POLLY!" I yell.

Ash holds me back, and I kick and whale against him like a wild animal. I know the symbol is a message for me. Purian Rose has taken Polly. Sebastian's words ring in my head: *Just know it could've been prevented.* They never intended to kill me. I make these little hiccupping sounds until my chest hurts.

"Why won't Rose leave us alone?" I say.

"Because we're a threat," Ash replies.

"But Polly wasn't a threat. MJ wasn't a threat!" I say. "Why should they suffer because of something *you* did?"

Ash flinches.

I regret the words as soon as they fall out of my mouth.

"I didn't mean that," I say.

"It's true, though."

I pull away from Ash, my whole body shaking with rage at the Sentry. They took my sister, they tried to kill MJ. Who else will they hurt to get back at us? A name suddenly springs into my mind.

"Harold!" I exclaim.

What better way to punish Ash than to kill his father? We push our way through the crowds of people trying to put out the fire, and sprint through the streets until we reach the Ivy Church.

We burst through the front door.

"Dad!" Ash yells.

Harold comes rushing out of the kitchen and goes pale when he sees us.

"Oh, my heavens! What happened?"

We tell him about the house fire, about Polly and MJ and the rose symbol. When we're done, I collapse in a kitchen chair, utterly drained. Ash tentatively rubs my back. I lift my head up to face him, tears in my eyes. It strikes me how gaunt he's looking, with deep shadows under his sharp cheekbones, the stress of the past two months catching up with him. I wonder when he last ate something.

"I really am sorry for what I said earlier, about this being your fault," I say. "It's not."

"It is, in a way." Ash lowers his lashes. "Rose told me he was going to take 'Miss Buchanan.' It didn't even occur to me it could be your sister."

"Did Purian Rose tell you what he had planned for her?" I say quietly.

"No," he says, not looking at me.

He's lying, but maybe it's best I don't know.

Harold fetches Ash a sachet of Synth-O-Blood from the fridge and makes me a cup of herbal tea. I stare at the tea leaves drifting down to the bottom of the cup, thinking about Polly. She must be so scared. Another sob escapes my lips. Ash cradles me in his arms as Harold goes to get Day and her family. The front door closes. We're alone.

"Am I a bad person, Ash?" I say.

"Why would you think that?"

"Because my whole family has been taken away from me," I say. "My father was killed, Polly's been kidnapped, and I have no idea where my mother is. It's too much."

He hooks a finger under my chin, tilting my face up to meet his. "We'll get through this." He kisses me softly, trying to take the pain away. It works for a while, like a dam holding back the tides, but the second he breaks the kiss, it all comes flooding back, worse than before.

"I wish my mother were here," I whisper. "She'd know what to do."

Ash's arms tighten around me, but he says nothing.

Thirty minutes later, Harold returns with the others. He helps Michael bring MJ into the church on a makeshift stretcher while Day carries the few charred possessions they've managed to salvage from the wreckage. Our whole lives fit into one bag. I briefly think about the birthday gifts I was given yesterday. They would have gone up in flames along with the house. I lightly touch the pendant around my neck, grateful that I never took it off. It's covered in soot, but it seems intact.

They bring MJ into Harold's bedroom and make him comfortable, and everyone sorts out where they're going to sleep now that we're homeless. We all get comfortable while Sumrina clatters about the tiny kitchen, the bustle of her cerulean dress knocking into our chairs as she moves about. She manages to find an old apron tucked in the back of one of the cupboards and ties it around her wide hips. Rolling up her sleeves, she sweeps her silken black hair up into a bun and starts making dinner, despite Harold's protests. She seems to need the distraction.

Michael finishes setting up the beds downstairs and reenters the kitchen. The small room doesn't have any of the homeyness that our kitchen did. There's no floral wallpaper, no smell of bread baking in the oven, no woman's touch, but that's hardly surprising, since only Harold and Ash live here, and it's not like Ash has any real need for a kitchen—he can't eat human food.

Day sits beside me. "We'll find her, Nat."

I take in a shaky breath.

"At least she's alive—that's something to hold on to," Day continues.

I don't say anything. There's no guarantee my sister is alive.

Night starts to creep in through the windows, and the air-raid siren wails across the city, letting us know curfew has started. Harold lights some candles while Day phones Beetle to tell him what happened. The instant he arrives, he begins a tirade about how he's going to kill every single Sentry in the country for what they did. Right now, that sounds like a really good idea. I want them to suffer too.

"I've already put the word out around Humans for Unity to look for her," Beetle says. "They're sending out teams as we speak."

"I want to join them," I say.

"Me too," Ash replies.

"No way," Beetle says firmly. "There are Sentry guards swarming all over the place, and it's after curfew. The last thing we need is for you both to get arrested. We're taking care of it."

I sigh, frustrated. But he's right.

Everyone offers suggestions of where we should look for Polly while Sumrina serves dinner. I don't join in the conversation, knowing in my heart we won't find Polly in Black City; I somehow doubt Purian Rose would risk keeping her so close by. She's probably on a Transporter to Centrum by now. A terrible, aching pain balls up in my chest, and I push my plate aside, my appetite lost.

"How are Sigur and the other Darklings doing?" Harold asks Beetle.

"Not so good," Beetle replies. "There was a lot of shouting, a lot of tears. Roach is still with them, trying to work out what to do next. They were hoping to see—"

THUD!

There's a smash of slate tiles as something heavy lands on the church roof, making us all start. It's quickly followed by a scratching, scuffling sound as the animal—or person—slides down the side. There's a moment's silence, then another *thud* as whatever it is hits the gravel pavement outside.

"What the fragg . . . ?" Ash says, kicking back his chair.

I grab a knife and follow him through the church.

Ash yanks open the front door. "Who's there? Show yourself!"

A teenage boy emerges from the shadows, his gold wristbands glinting as he raises his hands. He's dressed in a leather vest and pants, which match the color of his dark russet hair. I gasp, instantly recognizing him. It would be hard to forget a boy with a long tail and markings like a cheetah's down the sides of his face, neck and flanks. It's the Bastet I rescued from the laboratory in Sentry headquarters more than two months ago!

A lazy smile plays over his sensuous lips as he leans against the door frame.

"Hello, Natalie," he says. "I bet you didn't expect to see me again so soon."

I lower my knife.

"And you are . . . ?" Ash says.

"Elijah Theroux," he replies, turning his topaz eyes back on me. "Natalie and I go way back, don't we, pretty girl?"

My cheeks burn with shame, remembering how I found him in Dr. Craven's laboratory, chained up, naked and bruised. The scientist had been draining Elijah's venom to use in the Golden Haze.

"What are you doing here?" I ask.

"I have a proposition for you." He casually studies his nails. "What would you give for a weapon so powerful, it could bring down the Sentry and end the war between our races?"

"Erm, pretty much *anything*," I reply.

"Good." He smirks. "Because I happen to know one exists. I just need your help to get it."

9.

ASH

THIRTY MINUTES LATER, we've all converged in the nave of the church. The pews have been moved to create a square of seats, with the kitchen table in the center. Day is perched on Beetle's lap on the bench to my left, while Natalie is sitting between me and Amy. The Jones sisters arrived a few minutes ago, along with Stuart, who is chatting to Dad about a new camera lens he bought. They're on the pew to my right. All of Day's family has gone to bed, and we're just waiting for the others to arrive before starting the meeting.

Natalie rests her head on my shoulder, lost in thought. I know she's thinking about Polly; she's on my mind as well. I'm at a loss over what to do. We'll search for her at dawn, after curfew is lifted, but where do we even begin to look?

Although everyone is worried about Polly, there's also excitement in the air about the prospect of a weapon that can take down the Sentry government. Elijah strolls around the church, curling his lip as he runs his fingers through the dust coating the pews. Amy giggles slightly when his tail brushes past her legs as he walks by, rubbing his scent on her, marking his territory. I scrunch my nose up, able to smell the offensive musk from here. The humans don't seem to notice it, though. He sighs, and sits on the table in front of us.

"I've never met a Bastet before," Amy says shyly. "Where are you from?"

"Viridis, in the Emerald State," he says. "My dad's the Consul, so I live in the embassy with my family and the rest of the senate." He leans toward Amy, a cocky smile on his lips. "I'm famous among my people, you know?"

Amy blushes.

"Maybe I'll take you there, one day," he continues. "We don't get many humans visiting the city. Certainly not ones as pretty as you."

She turns beetroot red. From across the table, Juno glares at Elijah. She's very protective of her little sister.

There's a knock at the door, and Roach, Sigur, Logan and Garrick enter the church, dressed in hooded robes. My dad quickly introduces them to Elijah. The two Darklings scowl at the Bastet as they cross the room, and I understand what they're feeling. I'm sensing it too—a twisting, seething hatred toward him, like snakes writhing in my belly. It's our basic instinct to distrust Bastets, since they're the Darklings' natural predator.

"So how do you and Natalie know each other, Elijah?" Day asks, pushing her glasses up her nose.

He tenses up.

"Elijah was being held captive in Sentry headquarters," Natalie answers. "I helped him escape."

"She saved my life," he says quietly. "I owe her everything."

Why did she never tell me any of this?

"You're looking much better," Natalie says.

"Thanks. My mom's been taking care of me back in Viridis."

A dark emotion crosses his eyes. "Well, she was, until she went missing."

"Oh my God, what happened?" Natalie takes his hand. Jealousy stirs inside me at the sight.

"My mom went to fetch the Ora—that's the name of the weapon," Elijah says. "She was supposed to call me every day to let me know she was safe, but the last time she got in touch was three days ago. I think she's been captured by the Sentry." He looks directly at me. "That's why I'm here. I don't just need your help to find the weapon; I need your help to find *her*."

Natalie catches my eye. We've both lost our moms recently—mine was murdered, and hers is on the run from the law, so we can understand what he's going through.

"What makes you think I can help you find them?" I reply.

"Have you heard of the Four Kingdoms?" he asks.

"I have," Sigur answers. "They were a rebel group who wanted to overthrow the Sentry government and replace it with a democratic system that represented all four races. They were highly radical in their methods, even by my standards." He looks at me. "Your aunt Lucinda was a member."

"She was?" I say, surprised.

"Yes, and so was my mom," Elijah says.

"I thought the group had disbanded after the incident at the Black City waterworks," Sigur says.

"They did," Elijah replies. "But then a week and a half ago, my mom received this."

He takes out a folded piece of paper from his pocket and lays it on the table in front of us. It's the remains of a letter, which has been torn up, then crudely stuck back together. It's stained in places, obscuring some of the words.

Yolanda,

I'm sure you're angry at me for contacting you, but please understand it's for a very good reason. Purian Rose has built another death camp, bigger than the last, called the Tenth. He intends to send us all there after Rose's Law passes! We <u>must</u> stop him!

I understand we can't have a repeat of what happened at the waterworks—it was reckless and I lost sight of our goal. What we need is a weapon that can bring Rose to his knees, but with limited casualties, and we both know such a weapon exists. The Ora! I know it's very risky, but shouldn't we at least try, when so much is at stake? But I need your expertise to make this work. We'll have to retrieve the container, then find a willing host, but I think we can do it! We can stop him.

I'm at the place we all stayed at in Minar City, with the Twins. Please come. I'll explain everything in more detail when you get here.

T4K

Luci x

"Immediately after receiving the letter, my mom packed a bag and left Viridis," Elijah continues. "She wouldn't tell me where she was going, saying it was too dangerous for me to know."

"What are these stains?" Day asks, picking up the letter.

"Medical waste," Elijah says, and Day drops the letter and hurriedly wipes her hands on her pants. "My mom works in a laboratory—she's a geneticist. She tore up the letter after reading it, and threw the remains into the waste container. I managed to salvage what I could after she left."

"I'm still not sure how you think I can help," I admit.

"Look who it's from," he says.

"Luci. So?"

"As in your *aunt*, Lucinda Coombs." His golden eyes light up with hope. "I thought you might know where she went to meet my mom."

I shake my head, really confused. "It can't be from my aunt. She died in the Barren Lands during the war." I look at Sigur. "Right?"

"It's possible she survived," he admits.

This is news to me! "Why wouldn't she contact us if she were still alive?"

Sigur looks at my dad.

"What is it?" I say.

"Lucinda is angry at us both," Sigur replies.

"Why?"

"Early on in the war, Lucinda came to me and told me about her plan to release a deadly virus into the city's water system. She asked for my help," Sigur explains. "Obviously, I refused. Our war was with the Sentry, not the Workboots."

Logan tenses, and I wonder if she disagreed with that decision.

"I went to Natalie's father, General Buchanan, and told him about her plan," Sigur continues. "He stopped the attack, but Lucinda's Blood Mate, Niall, was killed. After being interrogated, she was sent to the Barren Lands to perish with the other Darklings."

I feel a rush of anger toward Sigur for betraying my aunt like that, but at the same time I know he did the right thing. The Workboots aren't our enemy; they suffered at the hands of Purian Rose almost as much as we did during the war. Just ask Beetle, Juno and Amy, who were all orphaned when their parents were killed in the air raids. Still, it's little wonder Lucinda hates him so much.

"And what about you?" I say to my dad. "What did you do that made her so mad, she hasn't been in contact with us?"

"It's complicated."

"Try me," I say.

He sighs. "I wasn't always a minister, son. When I first met your mom, I was a Sentry guard."

"What?" I sputter. "You're a *Sentry*?"

Why did Dad never tell me this? Come to think of it, he's never really spoken about his parents. I thought they were dead. Is this why? Is he ashamed of them? *Or is it because they're ashamed of me?*

"Lucinda couldn't forgive your mom for marrying me, so they lost touch," Dad says.

I rake my fingers through my hair. This is a lot to take in.

"This is all very enlightening, but I'd like to hear more about the *weapon*," Roach interjects. "What precisely is the Ora?"

We all look at Elijah.

"It's weaponized yellowpox," he replies, and there are a few stunned gasps from around the room. Yellowpox is one of the deadliest viruses in the world. "Well, I'm pretty sure that's what it is. I only got hold of the letter after my mom left, so I couldn't ask her about it."

I frown. "Then how do you know it's yellowpox?"

"I was curious to know more about the Ora, so I hacked into my mom's laboratory computer, looking for answers," he says. "I found some old research documents, dated around the time she was involved in the Four Kingdoms. They weren't specifically about the Ora, but I figured it was probably a code name."

"Or nickname? Like how the C18-Virus is also known as the Wrath?" Day suggests.

Elijah nods. "I discovered my mom had been researching yellowpox, and more specifically how to create a strain of the virus that would only target those with the v-gene—"

"Like the Trackers!" Day says.

The v-gene helps humans sense Darklings and is quite rare; only about 6 percent of the population has it, and most of those are from Sentry heritage, like Natalie and—as it turns out—me as well.

"And you think your mother succeeded in creating this new strain of the virus?" Logan asks.

He nods. "But after the incident at the waterworks, and Lucinda's arrest, my mom fled to Viridis to seek refuge with the Bastets, so I guess they never got to complete the project."

"But now that Lucinda is back, they're hoping to finish what they started?" Sigur says.

"Yeah, that's what I think," Elijah says. "It fits—it's a weapon that can bring down the Sentry, but with limited casualties, since it only targets those with the v-gene. Also, why else would Lucinda need my mom's expertise if it wasn't for this?"

Beetle studies the letter. "It says they need to fetch the container.

How come your mom didn't just keep a sample of the yellow-pox in her lab?"

Day rolls her brown eyes. "Didn't you ever pay attention at school? Yellowpox is highly virulent. You need a specialized facility, somewhere remote and possibly underground, to safely store it."

The tips of Beetle's ears turn pink, and Day kisses his cheek.

"Imagine what we could do with that weapon," Roach says. "We could take out swaths of Rose's forces in one hit, with little risk to ourselves or the Workboots. It would cripple the Sentry."

"Let's not get ahead of ourselves. We need to retrieve it first," Juno says.

"Actually, the first thing we need to do is rescue my mom and Lucinda," Elijah says. "They're the only people who know where the laboratory is. Plus, it's clear from the letter that my mom's skills are needed to finish the project."

"Then that is what we will do," Sigur says.

Everyone starts chatting excitedly, filled with new hope. All we'd have to do is keep the Sentry at bay long enough for us to rescue my aunt and Elijah's mom, and get the Ora. It'll be tough, but we can do it.

"Are we seriously considering infecting people with yellow-pox?" Natalie says. "We'd be no better than the Sentry when they infected all those Darklings with the Wrath."

"This is different," Beetle says.

"How?" she challenges.

"They deserve it, for starters," he says. "Besides, how is this worse than blowing people up, or shooting them? The result is the same—they're going to be dead. The only difference is that fewer of *us* will die if we use the Ora."

Natalie looks at Sigur.

"I must put my people first," he says. "This weapon could be the key to saving us."

She turns her gaze on me. "Ash?"

"I agree with the others," I admit. "And it's not the same as the Wrath. That was designed to kill all Darklings. The Ora will only affect a small percentage of people with the v-gene."

"Like you and me," she says.

"It's a risk I'm willing to take," I say. "We're out of options."

"We'll use it carefully," Roach chimes in. "We'll only hit strategic targets to minimize casualties."

Natalie says nothing more, knowing she's outvoted.

"I'm curious," Juno says to Elijah. "Why aren't the Bastets keeping the weapon for themselves? Why share it with us? It's not like we're allies."

Elijah scratches his neck. "Well, firstly, because we don't know where it is, and need your help to retrieve it."

"And what's the second thing?"

He looks at me. "The senate can't agree on what to do with the Ora. Half of them are too scared to use it, knowing if we do, it'll be starting a war with the Sentry that we can't win. However, the rest of us want to fight, but we need support."

"You want to join the rebellion?" I say.

He nods. "But we have to get the other senators on board with the idea. I was hoping that you and Natalie would come to Viridis with me and convince them it's the right thing to do."

I look at Roach.

"We need all the allies we can get," she says.

Sigur and Beetle both nod in agreement. I glance at Natalie. "What do you think?" I ask.

She gives a faint nod. "All right."

I stretch out a hand to Elijah. "You've got yourself a deal."

We shake hands.

"Well, this is a cause for a celebration," Dad says, going to the kitchen and returning with the bottle of Shine, which I know he stashes behind the boxes of cereal. "To new friends."

"To new friends," we reply, raising our glasses.

The liquid begins to vibrate.

I don't have much time to wonder about this before a low, terrifying rumble above us makes everyone freeze.

"What is it?" Natalie asks.

I stand up. "Only one way to find out."

We all rush outside to see what's going on. The streets are already filled with citizens, their faces fearful as they stare up at the night sky. Unnatural shadows swim across the ocean of stars like a shiver of sharks, blocking out the moonlight.

Destroyer Ships.

A whole fleet of airships, each over eight hundred feet long, floating across the city.

My blood turns to ice.

At that moment, the digital screens across the city spark to life, and Purian Rose appears on all the monitors. We all hold our breaths. I've never heard the city so silent before.

"Citizens of Black City. By now, you will have noticed my airships above your heads," he says.

Natalie shoots me a worried look.

"Your betrayal today did not go unnoticed by me," Rose continues. "And as a response, the government has made an amendment to our segregation laws. Anyone who voted no in the ballot is now considered a race traitor, as are their children, and will be segregated along with the Darklings. You have seventy-two hours to hand all race traitors, and the Darklings, over to my guards. If you fail to do so, you will meet the same fate as Ember Creek."

Ember Creek? Wasn't that the city where people were yelling out "No Fear, No Power!" during the live vote?

My suspicions are confirmed when the footage cuts to an image of the harbor we saw this morning, except everything is ablaze. The pier is gone. The market stalls, boats and houses all destroyed. Bobbing on the bloodred waters are hundreds of dead bodies, their skin like charcoal. Men, women and children; no one was spared from Rose's wrath.

Natalie grips my hand.

I stare at the horrifying image, knowing it'll haunt me for the rest of my life. All those people, burned to death. *Just like I was.*

"I did this," I whisper. "It's my fault they're dead."

A countdown appears at the bottom of the screen, letting us know we have seventy-two hours to comply. The clock starts ticking down—71:59:59, 71:59:58, 71:59:57 . . .

"We'll never do it; we'll never surrender to your demands!" Beetle yells at the screen, as if Rose could hear him.

The camera slowly closes in on Purian Rose's face, so that it fills the entire screen.

"I have one more message, for the boy who calls himself Phoenix—"

My grip tightens around Natalie's hand.

"I've been too lenient on the rebels these past two months, and it's allowed you, like vermin, to multiply and spread," he says. "It's time I rid myself of this infestation. The Sentry government is officially declaring war against your terrorist organization. Anyone found to be involved in your movement will be executed."

I look at Beetle. His expression reflects my own concern.

"Oh, and one more thing . . . ," Purian Rose continues.

The image cuts to grainy footage of a dark-haired girl bound to a metal chair, her head bowed, her body stripped bare. Blood pools around her feet.

"If the rebels attempt to interfere in any way, if you defy me again, I will follow through on my promise," Rose says. *"Piece by piece."*

The girl looks up at the camera, and Natalie screams.

It's Polly.

10.

ASH

DAWN BREAKS over the city, casting misty yellow sunlight over the ghetto. After Rose's announcement last night, the rebels took refuge in the Legion, ironically the only place in the city we're safe now, because of the Boundary Wall. I barely had time to pack a single bag of clothes and belongings before coming here.

I pick up the blue duffel bag and take out an ornate wooden box wrapped in one of my shirts. The box contains all my mom's keepsakes: some old photos, a lock of white hair, a Legion Liberation Front leaflet advertising a rally in Black City, and the diary Sigur gave me.

I flick through the journal, taking some comfort in reading my mom's words. As I turn the page, two photos slip out— one of the family in the forest glen, the other of her as a teenager, with Aunt Lucinda and two girls, taken in a tavern in Thrace. I'd forgotten I'd put them in there. I lift the photos off the floor and study the pictures, my heart pinching at the image of Mom's face beaming back at me.

I put the photos back in the journal and walk over to the

window. All night Sentry troops and packs of Lupines had been transporting down from the airships to secure the city. It seems Garrick was right—Purian Rose does have another plan for the Lupines, and now it's clear to me what it is: he intends to use them like bloodhounds to help hunt down Impurities. From the viewpoint in my bedroom—Evangeline's old room, in fact—I can see at least twenty Sentry and Lupine patrols in the city center alone.

The clock continues to count down on all the digital screens, but alongside it now is a scrolling list of the names of people who have been marked for segregation. These include Darklings and anyone who voted no yesterday, such as Natalie, Dad, Beetle, Roach, Amy, Sumrina, Michael, Juno, Stuart—everyone I know is on that list.

At that moment, an image of Polly appears on the screens. They've been doing this every hour, on the hour, since Purian Rose made his speech to the city. From what we can tell, the message last night and these hourly updates are only being broadcast within Black City, which makes sense. Purian Rose wouldn't want the rest of the country knowing what's happening here. Polly's still strapped to the chair, shaking, afraid. She's in a small, dark room made entirely of steel. I wonder if she's in a cell somewhere—maybe like the one I was in at Sentry HQ? It looks similar. Hope briefly flickers inside me that Polly might still be in the city, although it seems unlikely Rose would risk that. He'd need to keep her somewhere safe and out of my reach.

Angry voices ring up through the floorboards from the council chamber below us, as the rebels and Darkling ministers fight over what we should do. They've been arguing all night. I want to tell them there's nothing we can do. We've lost. Our only hope now is to run.

I glance at Natalie, curled up in the double bed. When she wakes up, I'm going to tell her about my plan to escape to the Northern Territories. Crossing the border will be dangerous, but I think it'll be worth the risk. The people there are said to be more tolerant of Darklings. Of course, I'll have to persuade our families to join us. It'll be hard bringing everyone along, but I'll work that out somehow.

"Polly!" Natalie screams, startling herself awake.

I rush over and pull her into my arms.

"It's okay, I've got you," I say.

She rests her head on my lap, and I caress her golden hair. I wish there was something more I could do to take away her pain.

"I think we should run away," I say quietly, and tell her my plan.

Natalie sits up. "We can't do that."

"I know it'll be hard, but—"

"Not without Polly," she says. "If you want to leave with the others, then I'll understand. But I'm not going anywhere without my sister."

I rub the back of my neck. There's no point pushing it. She won't change her mind, and there's no way I'm leaving the city without her.

We get dressed and head downstairs a few minutes later, to find everyone congregated in the Assembly. All the Darkling ministers are there, arguing with each other while Sigur and Logan look on. The digital screen on the back wall shows the countdown clock, letting us know how much time we have left before the city goes up in flames: 63:42:11, 63:42:10, 63:42:09 . . .

I find a seat at the com-desk between Natalie and Amy, who gives me a small, worried smile. Sitting opposite us are Day, Beetle and Garrick, while Elijah paces up and down the room behind them. I know my dad and the rest of Day's family are still asleep, since I passed their rooms on the way here. Roach is on the phone.

"Where are Juno and Stuart?" I ask Amy, surprised they're not here.

"They've gone into the city. I begged Juno not to go, but . . ." She bites her lips. "Well, you know my sister. She always has to be at the heart of the story."

Roach hangs up the phone. "I've just spoken to Flea. There aren't any airships in the other cities. It's just us."

"Has there been any update on Polly?" Natalie asks.

"Not yet," Roach says.

Natalie frowns, making a small crease form between her eyebrows. Garrick walks over to her and rests a clawed hand on her shoulder. Up close, I see his nails are like shark's teeth, all jagged down the edges. I wouldn't want to be on the wrong end of those.

"I'm sorry about your sister," he says in a gruff voice. "You must be very worried about her—and your mom?" He leans conspiratorially toward her. "I heard a rumor the Emissary had been spotted in the Copper State."

"I wouldn't know anything about that," Natalie says. "It's not like she's contacted me."

"No, of course not. It wouldn't be safe," Garrick replies. "But I'm sure if she could get in touch with you, she'd let you know she was all right."

"I somehow doubt it," Natalie mutters.

Garrick squeezes her shoulder and goes to find an empty seat at the back of the oval room.

"So what's the plan?" I ask, the question posed to everyone in the room.

"We must defend the ghetto!" Pullo, the brutish-looking Eloka Darkling, says.

"No, we should surrender," Angel—the female Shu'zin Darkling—replies. "We will die here, for certain. We have no food, the people of this city want us dead, and even if we succeed in defending the ghetto, Rose will burn it to the ground."

"What about the Ora?" Beetle says. "We're still going to look for that, right?"

"And my mom," Elijah adds, giving me a panicked look. "We have to find her."

I briefly shut my eyes, my head spinning.

"We will send a team to search for the Ora and Elijah's mother as soon as possible," Sigur says, and Roach nods in agreement. "But in the meantime, we must come up with an alternative plan to defend ourselves. We only have three days before the Sentry bombs the city."

"Perhaps Angel is correct," Logan says. "The Tenth may be our best option, until you can retrieve the Ora and rescue us. At least the youngsters will be sent to work in the factories in Primus-Two."

"But what about the rest of us?" Pullo fumes. "I'm not going to be sent to Primus-Three to be used as someone's lab rat!"

"We could try escaping," Natalie suggests. "Ash has a plan to bring everyone over the border into the Northern Territories."

"It was more an idea than an actual plan," I admit. "I don't even know how we'd get everyone out of the city."

A Transporter flies over the ghetto, making the walls rumble. We hold our breaths until it passes by. It makes no attempt to land.

"How come the Sentry guards haven't come to get us yet?" Day asks.

"I can only presume Purian Rose has ordered them not to take us until the deadline has passed," Sigur says. "He wants the people of Black City to fail, to give him an excuse to burn the city to the ground."

"Then why give us three days to hand everyone over?" Day says. "Why not firebomb us now, like he did in Ember Creek, if that's his intention?"

"He needs the prisoners, so they can work in his factories or be experimented on in the Tenth," Garrick says from the back of the room. "He made an example of Ember Creek, so the people of Black City would be scared into doing his bidding."

"It worked," I mutter.

There's a bang as the oak doors to the Darkling Assembly burst open, and Juno and Stuart race into the room. They're both breathless, their hair and clothing a mess, and Juno's cradling her left arm. Stuart's carrying his camera, which he immediately plugs into the digital screen at the back of the room.

"It's madness out there!" Juno says.

Amy hurries over to her sister. "Are you hurt?"

"It's just a sprain," Juno replies. "You guys need to see this."

Stuart presses Play on his camera, and everyone in the room quiets down as we watch the video recording. The first set of footage shows hundreds of people in the town square, demanding that Sigur send out the Darklings, while countless Legion guards line the wall, ready to die to protect their people. *My* people.

"I never thought I'd say this, but I'm actually glad we've got that bloody wall," Roach says.

Stuart fast-forwards the video and stops on some footage of Sentry guards setting up more roadblocks around the city, complete with machine gun turrets and tanks. No one will be able to leave by the roads. The next shot is at the train station, where some families are being ushered onto an armored train.

"Hang on, are those people evacuating?" I ask.

Juno nods. "That's this morning's latest development. Anyone who hands over three or more Impurities to the guards will be given a ticket to leave the city." She tosses a blood-soaked train ticket onto the table, with the words EVACUATION PASS printed on it in bold red letters. "I got that off a dead guy who'd been mauled by some Lupines. I guess he pissed them off."

Garrick's mouth twitches slightly.

"A few of them tried to grab me and Stu, but we fought them off," Juno continues.

I turn the ticket over in my hands. It has a silvery rose-shaped watermark on it to prove its authenticity. It must've taken weeks to get these printed up. Anger rages inside me. Purian Rose has been planning this all along—he guessed I'd vote against him. I've played right into his hands!

"The rest of the country needs to see what's happening here," Roach says. "We have to warn them, before the airships move into their city."

"Can you hack into the SBN news feed and broadcast this?" Sigur asks.

Juno shakes her head. "We already tried."

"The government's somehow jamming any signals going into or out of the city," Stuart explains. "We can't broadcast anything, unless it's within the city limits."

The video footage cuts to an image of a young couple hunched over a tiny figure lying in a pool of blood. Everyone in the room falls silent as the crying mother faces the camera.

"Why aren't you helping us, Phoenix?" the woman sobs into the camera. "We supported you, and this is how you repay us? You've abandoned us!"

Juno mutes the digital screen, but it's no good—I can still hear the woman's words ringing in my head.

Roach strikes her palm against the com-desk. "We need to be out there, fighting!"

"But what about Polly?" Natalie says. "If we interfere, she'll be killed."

"And what about all those people who supported us yesterday?" Roach says. "*They'll* be killed if we don't act now. We have a duty to protect them."

"Can't we just wait until we know where Polly is?" Natalie says.

"Every minute we waste, more people are being taken," Roach replies. "Is your sister's life really worth more than theirs?"

Natalie lowers her blond lashes. "Do what you have to," she says quietly, getting up from her seat. "If you need me, I'll be upstairs."

She leaves the room, and Day and Amy hurry after her.

Elijah stands up. "Excuse me, but I need to make a phone call."

"You can use the telephone in my office," Sigur says.

"Thanks," Elijah replies, walking out of the room.

The others start planning our attack while I wander over to the window and gaze up at the sky.

A Transporter carrying another batch of prisoners cuts through the clouds of ash that hang over the city, making it rain with black snow. The aircraft is an armored tiltwing, nearly one hundred feet long and big enough to carry up to fifty passengers at a time. Painted in large, bright red letters on the side of the ship are its name and number. This one's called *Marianne 705*. Nearby, a second Transporter called *Roselyn 401* flies up to another Destroyer Ship hovering over the Park. I'm guessing the name relates to the Destroyer Ship the aircraft belongs to, and the number distinguishes it from the others in its fleet.

The giant digital screens across the city blink, and Polly's image appears on the monitors again. She looks petrified. I tear my eyes away from her, ridden with guilt, knowing we're about to sentence her to death by defying Purian Rose's orders. *God, are we doing the right thing?*

Beetle catches my eye as I return to the com-desk and gives me a sympathetic look. This isn't easy on him either; he's gotten to know Polly well these past two months, since she moved in with Day's family. I try to listen to the others as they discuss our plan to strike the Transporters, but I can't concentrate. My eyes drift toward the muted video footage that Stuart took this morning, still playing on the digital screen. Families are being torn apart; people are being killed. *You're doing this for the greater good.* There's more at stake here than Polly's life. Still, it's a bitter pill to swallow when I see her terrified image broadcast across the city every hour.

Something Stuart said earlier suddenly flashes into my mind: *The government's somehow jamming any signals going into or out of the city . . .*

I jerk bolt upright in my seat, alarming everyone.

"If the government's blocking all broadcast signals coming into and out of Black City, how are they showing the live footage of Polly?" I say.

Everyone's silent for a moment, then Stuart grins.

"The signal has to be coming from somewhere in the city!" he says.

"Where?" Beetle asks.

"Sentry headquarters?" Juno suggests.

"No, we've broken in there before," I say. "It needs to be somewhere they know we can't get access to."

My mind races. If I had to keep Polly in the city, but somewhere out of reach, where would be the best place to hide her? The answer hits me. I peer toward the window.

"She's in a Destroyer Ship," I say.

11.
NATALIE

I CURL UP on the leather chair beside the stone hearth in Sigur's office and watch the yellow flames as they dance in the fireplace. Amy and Day sit cross-legged on the antique rug in front of me, giving me concerned looks. It's clear neither of them knows what to say, but what *can* they say? I've basically just signed my sister's death warrant. I blink, and the flames blur through my tears.

"Maybe the rescue team will find her," Amy says hopefully.

Pain knots inside my chest, and I try to knead it away with my fist, but it doesn't work. I let out a pitiful groan and crumple in on myself, finally allowing myself to cry. Day rushes over, putting her arms around me.

I cling to her, hating myself for betraying Polly, and hating Purian Rose for tearing my family apart. Again. How can he do this to his own daughter? Would he save her if he knew the truth? Somehow I doubt it.

The door opens.

"Sorry," Elijah says when he sees us. "I was going to make a call. It can wait."

I wipe my eyes. "No, it's fine. Come in."

Elijah hesitates, then crosses the room toward Sigur's desk. I try not to listen in on his hushed conversation with his father.

"Any news about your mother?" I ask when he hangs up.

He shakes his head.

"Your father must be worried about her," I say. "I'm surprised she didn't tell him where she was going."

"They're not together anymore," Elijah explains. "My mom hates him. They rarely speak."

I bite my lip. *Good one, Natalie.*

"Do you have Lucinda's letter with you?" I say.

He takes it out of his pocket.

"Come on, let's try and work out where your mother is," I say, in desperate need of a distraction before my guilt over Polly threatens to devour me.

We gather armfuls of encyclopedias, atlases and old nautical charts from the shelves, then carry them back to the rug beside the hearth and sit down in a circle. Elijah places the letter on the floor between us. Day's glasses keep sliding down her nose as she reads.

"So Lucinda's gone to meet the twins," she says. "Who are they?"

Elijah shrugs. "Mom never mentioned she knew any twins."

"Well, the city they've gone to definitely starts with an *m* and ends with an *r*," Day says. "And given that only a few letters are stained, we're looking for a place-name that's five or six letters long."

"Okay, everyone look through the books and see if you can find anything that matches," I say.

Elijah picks up one of the books. I'm sure he's done this already, but without anything else to go on, it's all we can do. Maybe he missed something.

I pick up an old atlas and flip through the yellowed, musty pages, scanning the tiny print for any reference to a city that could match the name in Lucinda's letter. With every book I get through, desperation rises in me, my desire to save Polly getting muddled with the need to help Elijah. I furiously throw the last book across the room and sink my head in my hands, taking a few deep breaths.

"You all right?" Elijah asks.

I nod, drawing my hair back into a bun. "I didn't find anything that matched. Only Maize, Mercury, Majesty, Monns Peninsula and Molten Lake."

"Same here," Elijah replies, tossing his book on the pile.

"Me too," Day says.

"I found a place called Mountain Shade on one of the older maps," Amy says. "But I don't think the town exists anymore, after Mount Alba erupted."

Elijah's face crumples, the last glimmer of hope gone.

"I'm sorry," I say, taking his hand.

The study door opens, and Ash and Beetle enter. They're both breathless.

"There you are!" Ash says.

His sparkling black eyes flicker toward my hand, which is clasped around Elijah's. I let go.

"What's going on?" I say.

"We've worked out where Polly is," Ash says.

I stand up, my heart leaping. "What? Where?"

"She's in one of the Destroyer Ships over the Park," Beetle replies. "Ash and Stuart worked it out."

"He was able to trace the signal to the airship *Roselyn*," Ash adds.

I run over to Ash and throw my arms around his neck, kissing him passionately. A tremendous weight lifts off my heart; we can save Polly!

He breaks the kiss. "It's not going to be easy getting her back."

"But we'll try, right?" I say.

He nods. "The others have already started planning the rescue mission."

Beetle nudges the pile of books on the floor with his boot. "What are you guys doing?"

"We're trying to work out where Lucinda and Elijah's mom have gone," Day replies.

"But we can't find any cities that match the place referenced in the letter," Amy says. "We've looked through *everything*."

"Maybe it's a code name," Beetle suggests.

"Oh!" Day exclaims, jumping up. "Oh!" she says again.

"What did I say?" Beetle asks.

"Sshh, I'm thinking," Day says, pacing in front of the fireplace. She snaps her fingers. "I've got it! It's the city's *nickname*."

Amy and Elijah exchange confused looks.

"Come on, guys," she says, grinning. "Centrum's nickname is the Gilded City—"

"Viridis is the Vertical City!" Elijah chimes in.

"And Thrace is the *Mirror* City!" She gives us all a smug look as she sits down.

"How do you know all this?" Beetle asks, impressed.

"Some of us actually paid attention in geography."

"Oh, yeah," Beetle mutters.

Ash furrows his brow. "Did you say *Thrace* was the Mirror City?"

"Yeah," Day replies.

He jogs out of the room and returns a few minutes later carrying a leather-bound journal. He takes out a photograph and shows it to us. It's a picture of two Darkling girls—I assume they're Ash's mother and aunt—standing beside a young barmaid in a wheelchair and a stunning girl with honey-colored eyes wearing a hooded green robe.

"That picture was taken in a tavern in Thrace," Ash says.

"That's my mom!" Elijah says, pointing to the girl in the green robe.

"Look on the back," Ash says.

Elijah flips it over. "T4K, Thrace . . . *T4K*? The Four Kingdoms!"

Day looks at the photo. "Huh. I thought the Four Kingdoms were about uniting the four races, but there's no Lupine in the picture."

"Maybe the Lupine was the one holding the camera?" Ash suggests.

I take the picture from him. "Do you think this is where your mother has gone to meet Lucinda?"

"It's very possible," Elijah says, grinning from ear to ear.

"It's not much to go on," Ash admits. "I don't even know the name of the tavern."

"It's more than I had yesterday," Elijah says, looking at the young barmaid in the photograph. "She might know where my mom and Lucinda went to fetch the Ora."

"So we have a plan," Ash says. "We go to Thrace and find the barmaid?"

We all nod in agreement.

I look at Ash, and he returns a smile—we're both having the same thought. If we can find Lucinda, and persuade her to give us the Ora, maybe we'll finally have a way to bring down Purian Rose. I'm coming round to the idea of using the weapon against the Sentry, after they kidnapped my sister, bombed Ember Creek and then threatened everyone in Black City.

But first we have more pressing business to attend to.

I'm going to rescue Polly.

12.

NATALIE

I GLANCE UP at the sky toward the airship that's been my sister's prison for the past two days. *Roselyn.* It's such a pretty name, considering what it is. Roach did a recon mission last night and worked out that our best shot of getting onto the Destroyer Ship is to board one of the Transporters parked on Union Street. Ash gives me a cuddle, kissing the top of my head as I try to calm my nerves. Polly needs me to be brave right now.

We're hidden down a side alley, near Union Street. The city around us is in chaos. People are screaming and running in all directions; there's a pop of gunfire every few minutes; and we catch sight of several Lupine packs stalking the streets, on the hunt for their next victims.

"Okay, let's go over the plan one more time," Ash says.

He goes through the plan again with Elijah and Stuart while Harold helps me with my robe, since my hands are shaking too much to tie the belt.

Elijah lets out a weary sigh.

"I'm sorry. Am I boring you?" Ash says.

Elijah shrugs. "A little."

Ash glowers at him, opening his mouth to say something, but I shoot him a warning look. Elijah's doing us a massive favor by helping us out today, and I don't want to upset him, since he's a key part of the plan. Ash relents, muttering curses under his breath instead.

Harold binds our hands with rope, keeping the knots loose enough for us to break free when we need to. Then comes the bit I'm really not looking forward to: he puts the burlap sacks over our heads. Immediately I feel suffocated and want to tear the hood off, but somehow I manage to restrain myself. Two small holes have been cut in the sack, so I can just about see what's going on directly in front of me, which is better than nothing.

"This sack stinks of fish," Elijah whines, his voice muffled.

"I thought cats liked seafood," Stuart replies.

Nerves start to kick in, and I ball my bound hands into fists.

"Let's do this," I mumble through the sack.

Harold guides us to Union Street and herds us into the steady stream of people being ushered toward the prison Transporter *Roselyn 401*. Through the open hatch at the back of the ship, I can see long rows of metal benches with shackles to lock onto our feet. There's only one window right at the front of the aircraft, so the pilot can see where he's going. There's a mesh grille between him and the prisoners for protection.

Four armed Sentry guards wait by the hatch, loading the prisoners onto the Transport and handing out Evacuation Passes to the traitors bringing them in. One of the guards, a slim man in his fifties with close-cropped silver hair, waves a hand.

"Next," he says.

A man shoves two dark-skinned girls toward the aircraft. They can't be more than seven and ten years old. Fury surges through me, thinking about what that man did to get hold of those little girls. Are their parents dead? The younger of the two girls trips, and he roughly hauls her to her feet. She starts crying. A smack across the cheek silences her, and it takes all my strength not to run over to that man and punch him in the face.

"Name?" the silver-haired guard says.

"Greer, Adrian," the man says. "I brought a nipper here earlier today; it should be against my name."

The guard scans the list and then shakes his head.

"That's fragging ridiculous! I brought it here just three hours ago. Give me my Evacuation Pass!" the man yells, his face turning red.

"If you don't shut it, I'll hand you over to the Lupines," the silver-haired guard says to the man.

The man storms off, escorted by two Sentry guards to ensure he doesn't cause any trouble.

"Next," the silver-haired guard says, bored.

We take another step forward, and that's when I see him.

Sebastian.

I didn't notice him earlier, because my hood blocks my peripheral vision. He's carrying a handheld com-screen and is making a note of the prisoners as they board the Transporter, like we're inventory.

"Harold—" I begin.

"I've seen him," he mutters.

"Will he recognize you?"

"He's only ever seen me without a beard, so I don't think so," Harold says.

I try to steady my growing nerves. There's no reason Sebastian should recognize Harold, not dressed in Workboot clothes and wearing a full, gray beard. The line continues to shuffle toward the aircraft.

"Next," the silver-haired guard says.

"Good luck," Harold whispers as we step forward.

I can't see Sebastian anymore, but I know he's to my left. Every hair on my arms stands on end, sensing him. I can even smell his spicy aftershave; the scent brings back memories of our time in Centrum together, when we spent hours kissing on my bed. I push that revolting thought out of my head.

"Name," the guard says.

"H—James," he quickly corrects, trying to disguise his mistake with a cough. "James Madden."

I daren't turn my head to see Sebastian's reaction to Harold's slipup.

"How many are you transporting?" the guard says.

"Three," he replies, giving our false names.

The guard checks the list and nods approvingly. He passes Harold an Evacuation Pass. "Enjoy your train ride."

Harold mutters his thanks and turns to leave.

"Wait." Sebastian's voice comes from my left.

My heart flips.

"Can I help, sir?" Harold says.

"Have we met before?" Sebastian asks.

Panic rises up inside me, every instinct telling me to run. If Sebastian works out who we are, he'll kill us, I'm certain of it.

"No . . . no, I don't think so," Harold says. "I work at Chantilly Lane Market. Maybe you've visited my stall?"

Silence from Sebastian. Then, "Let me see those prisoners. Take off their hoods."

No, no, no, no, no!

"There's really no need for that," Harold says quickly.

The guard rips off Stuart's hood. He looks fearfully from the guard to Harold. I'm so relieved Amy did some of her makeup magic and added fake bruises and cuts to our faces, to help disguise us. *Good thinking, Amy.*

"Been beating them up, eh?" the silver-haired guard jokingly says to Harold, assuming this is the reason he doesn't want the hoods taken off.

"Yes, well, I had to restrain them somehow," he says.

The silver-haired guard reaches out a hand and starts lifting my hood up. A million escape plans run through my mind as the material inches up my face.

"Don't! She'll bite your hand off, that one," Harold says in a rush.

The hood is getting higher and higher. It's reached my chin, lips, soon Sebastian will recognize me—

"Give me my fragging Evacuation Pass!" the man from earlier yells, running back toward us, the two Sentry guards racing after him.

The hood drops back over my head.

The silver-haired guard and Sebastian subdue the man while one of the other guards leads the three of us onto the Transporter, leaving Harold behind to watch us go. My heart is still racing. It's as hot as an oven in the crowded aircraft, and sweat instantly rolls down my back as I sit on the metal bench. Our ankles are shackled to prevent us from trying to escape. The guard walks away.

"That was close," Elijah's muffled voice says beside me.

"Too close," I mumble through my hood.

The little girls I saw earlier are sitting opposite me, and the younger one is crying again. Her sister attempts to console her, and my heart aches as I think about Polly and how she would comfort me when I was upset. I vow to free those girls if I can.

A moment later, the aircraft's hatch is shut and the engines turn on. People start crying and wailing; some even pray as the Transporter lifts off. This will be the last time they see Black City. Their next destination will be their final resting place.

Two seats away, a skinny woman with strings of blond hair and the black veins of a Hazer is having a full-on hysteria attack, her screams filling the cabin.

"I'm not meant to be here! You've made a mistake!" she wails, even though the pilot isn't listening.

The bumpy journey to the Destroyer Ship takes only a few minutes, but it's enough to cause most of the passengers to throw up. The stench is unreal, and I only just manage to rip my hood off in time to puke all over Elijah's feet. He tears off his hood.

"I'm sorry," I say in a rush. As the Bastet Consul's son, he'd be more used to girls throwing rose petals at his feet, not vomit.

He lightly takes my hands in his, startling me. His hands are so hot, the way mine feel after I've been warming them over a fire. The gold bands around his wrists glimmer, and I focus on them, finding it soothing.

"The air's thinner up here. It makes everyone feel sick." He inspects the mess splashed all over his feet. "Did you have carrots for breakfast?"

I laugh. It's a bit of a hysterical sound, just like the crazy lady two seats down from me, but it's just what I need to calm my growing nerves. I'm starting to think Elijah's exactly the sort of person I need around me during a crisis.

We undo each other's binds, then help Stuart with his, removing his hood in the process. Stuart and I take off our robes to reveal the Sentry guard uniforms hidden underneath, which Roach and Beetle managed to obtain for us last night. The two little girls stare at us with bug-eyed wonder. We wipe the makeup off our faces, and I pull back my hair so I look older and more serious. I shove the robes and spare hoods under the bench, tucking one hood in my pocket to use as a disguise for Polly.

"Elijah, if you'd do the honors," I say, lifting up the chain shackling my feet to the ground.

He bites down on the chain with his saber teeth. It takes a few attempts before the links break and my feet are freed. He does the same with Stuart. Many of the prisoners are staring at us now. A boy around eighteen years old, with shaggy brown hair, alabaster skin and startling green eyes, leans toward me and shows me the Cinder Rose tattoo on his wrist. I show him mine.

"What are you doing here?" he asks.

"Rescue mission," I reply.

"Are you going to save us?" he says.

I nod, unable to say the lie out loud.

The sliver of light from the cockpit disappears as we enter the Destroyer Ship, plunging the cabin into total darkness. Now everyone begins to scream, yanking at their shackles. The Transporter judders as it docks in the Destroyer Ship. There's a blast of cold air, and light floods the cabin as the hatch is opened.

We're inside a cargo bay in the main envelope of the airship. I knew Destroyer Ships were big, but now that we're inside one, I'm overwhelmed by its size. How are we ever going to find Polly in here?

A young male guard with slicked-back hair enters the cabin

and stops when he sees me and Stuart. The name tag on his chest reads VICTOR. Blood pounds in my ears. The prisoners around us watch silently, but no one says anything to give us away.

"What are you doing here? This isn't normal protocol," Victor asks.

"We're escorting this creature," I say, pointing to Elijah. "It attacked one of the guards, so they told us to bring it up with the others."

Elijah dramatically roars and snaps his saber teeth at Stuart.

"Get down," Stuart bellows, slapping Elijah across the face.

Elijah's golden eyes flash with genuine anger, but he sits down, playing along.

"Sebastian didn't radio this up to me," Victor says.

"He's a busy man," I reply. "I guess he forgot."

Victor considers this. "Who did the cat bite? Please tell me it was Holden."

I laugh, like I'm in on the joke. "No, it was some newbie called Wadsworth."

Victor looks disappointed, but he seems to have bought our story. He starts to unshackle the prisoners. When he reaches the hysterical woman, she starts babbling at him.

"You've made a mistake—I love Purian Rose! I voted in favor of segregation," she says. "Please, let me go. I'm not like these other race traitors!"

"That's what they've all been saying," Victor replies, removing the chains.

The hysterical woman springs to her feet, startling Victor long enough to push past him and run out of the hatch. She makes it twenty feet before he shoots her between the shoulder blades. She collapses to the ground midstride, her blood splashing across the floor. Victor strolls over to her and kicks her onto her back. She's still alive, although blood gurgles out of her mouth as she silently pleads for her life. He drags her toward the hatch in the cargo bay. I watch, transfixed, as he opens up the air lock and tosses her out into the sky.

He returns to the prison Transporter.

"Anyone else thinking of running away? If so, you know where the door is." He waits a moment, but no one stirs. "Get up," he orders.

The prisoners all stand, subdued by the horror of what they just saw, and obediently shuffle out of the aircraft. There are scores of armed guards patrolling the cargo bay, monitoring the traffic. Transporters come and go in a steady stream, dropping prisoners off. All the ships are named *Roselyn,* like ours, but have different numbers. I notice *Roselyn 403* seems to be loading prisoners back *on* it. Strangely, all of them are pretty girls and boys. Victor catches me looking.

"They're special orders for Centrum," he says, winking at me.

My stomach churns when I realize what he means. The guards must have a nice little sideline selling those kids to the highest bidder.

We're ushered out of the cargo bay and down a long corridor leading to the prison deck.

"I've not seen you around here before," Victor says as we walk down the passageway. He eyes me up and down. "I would've remembered someone as pretty as you."

I smile, but inside I'm cringing. "I just transferred here."

"Well, if you need anyone to show you around, I'll be happy to do it," Victor says. "Maybe we can get a drink sometime?"

"Maybe," I mutter.

Victor smiles. "Let's chat later."

"Can't wait," I say as he goes to the front of the group.

I hang back with Elijah and Stuart. I notice a steady drop-off in security as we near the prison deck. It seems most of the guards are posted around the cargo bay—this ship's only exit. It's good in one way: it'll be easier to move around as we search for Polly. Not so great when we need to make our escape.

"When we reach the prison deck, we need to head to the bow of the ship," Stuart whispers to me. "That's where we located the signal."

We head down a flight of stairs and enter the prison deck. This part of the aircraft is dank and dark, lit only by a few amber lights hanging overhead.

We wait for our opportunity to escape. It comes a few moments later, when Victor turns down a corridor to our left, momentarily losing sight of us.

"Now," I say.

We peel off down another corridor, leading toward the bow of the ship, and immediately come face-to-face with a group of Sentry guards leaning against the silver walls, on their coffee break. Panic flares inside me. *Act normal.* I nod at them as we pass, praying they don't notice how badly my hands are shaking. They carry on talking, ignoring us. I let out a relieved breath.

"The signal was coming from around here somewhere," Stuart says, pushing open a heavy steel door.

We enter a small control room, crammed with digital screens, a com-desk, a key rack and various filing cabinets. On one of the screens is an image of Polly tied to a chair.

"Which cell is she in?" I ask.

Stuart hurries over to the com-desk. His fingers fly over the keys, pulling up files, searching through the data, while Elijah waits by the doorway, looking out for Sentry guards.

"Do you see anything?" I ask, my nerves building.

He scans through another file.

"Yes! Here!" he says, jabbing a finger at the com-desk. "She's in cell two-ten. It's just down the corridor."

I spin on my heel, ready to run. Elijah grabs my arm.

"Wait! We need to make a recording of the live feed first," Elijah says.

"Yes . . . yes, of course. Sorry," I say.

Stuart needs to record sixty seconds of the live feed, which he'll loop and broadcast so no one knows Polly is missing when they do the next hourly broadcast, which is due in—I check my antique watch—five minutes!

"Hurry up," I say.

I tap my foot, ball my hands into fists, do anything I can to force myself not to run down the corridor to Polly.

Stuart stops pressing the keys on the com-desk and looks up at me, his face ashen.

"What is it?" I say.

"Can't you break into the feed?" Elijah asks.

"It doesn't matter. We'll just grab her and go," I say.

Stuart shakes his head. "It's not that. I broke into the feed . . ."

"Then what is it?" I say, fear rising.

"The footage of Polly . . ." He licks his lips. "It already *is* a recording."

The ground seems to slip from under my feet as it sinks in, what he means. I snatch the cell key from the rack on the wall and rush out of the room, my heart racing, not wanting to believe.

"Natalie, wait!" Elijah says.

I find cell 210 and unlock the door.

Red.

The floor, the ceiling, the walls.

Red as the rose painted on a burning wall.

And curled up in the middle of it all is a small ball of white, frozen in death.

I fall to my knees.

Somewhere in the back of my mind, I realize my sister has been dead for at least a day.

13.
NATALIE

I BARELY REGISTER the others entering the cell. I gently lift Polly's body and cradle her in my arms. Cold leaches from her skin, seeping through my veins, turning them to ice. Her usually glossy black hair is stiff with blood, and I carefully untangle it with my fingers, knowing she'd hate looking such a mess.

Something is clutched in her pale hand, and I carefully pry her fingers open. A small, rose-shaped silver medal falls to the floor. I only know one person in Black City with a medal like that. *Sebastian.* I glance at her bruised thighs, and bile rises up in my throat, realizing what he did. He tried doing it to me once. I wince as if a knife had cut deep within me, making my insides bleed, pour out. The pain is unbearable.

Stuart stands by the doorway, his eyes fixed on his feet, while Elijah sits beside me. His hand finds mine. Its warmth slowly melts the ice in my veins, bringing me back to cruel reality.

"We need to go," he says.

The thought of leaving Polly here makes my throat constrict.

"We have to take her," I whisper.

"We can't carry her. She'll draw too much attention," he replies softly.

He's right of course.

"But she'll be all alone," I say.

"She's not really here, not anymore," he says.

I don't know if I believe in a heaven, but the thought of her surrounded by our lost loved ones makes it easier to let her go somehow. I lay her down and carefully arrange her hair around the remains of her face. I whisper a promise in my sister's ear.

"Are you ready?" Elijah asks.

I try to stand, but the weight of my grief crushes down on my shoulders. Elijah places a strong arm around my waist and takes some of the burden off me, lifting me to my feet. We go into the corridor and shut the cell door, closing the lid on my sister's coffin.

"What do we do now?" Stuart asks.

"We're going to free those kids we saw on the Transporter," I say.

I stride down the corridor, not waiting to hear their protests. I'm a raging inferno, fueled by anger, and nothing is going to stop me now. Purian Rose killed my sister, and now I'm going to make him pay for it, one act of rebellion at a time, until Centrum is nothing but burning rubble around his feet. That's the promise I made to Polly.

We reach the corridor Victor turned down.

"Hang back here, out of sight. I'll return in a minute," I say.

I round the corner. The communal cell is packed with prisoners, their arms stretching out of the bars, begging for water. There's no air-conditioning on the prison deck, so the heat is overwhelming, and many of the prisoners are swaying, ready to collapse. On one side of the cell is a stack of dead bodies, mostly elderly people who died from heat exhaustion.

I purposefully walk up to one of the armed guards by the cell doors. He's a beefy man with a goatee. I don't feel afraid. There's no room inside me for any emotion other than blind fury.

"I have special orders from Centrum," I say to him.

He grins and unlocks the cell door, escorting me inside.

"What are you looking for?" he says. "How about a pretty redhead?"

A teenage girl around fourteen years old stares up at me with luminous blue eyes.

"Yes, she'll be good," I say, scanning the room for the two little girls who were on my Transporter. I find them huddled together, being looked after by the teenage boy with the shaggy brown hair and green eyes. "Those three."

"Really? Fragg, those Centrum types like them young, don't they?" the guard says, looking at the younger of the two girls. "She can't be more than seven years old."

"It's not my concern, as long as they pay us, right?" I say.

He nods, idly scratching his goatee. "You tell Patrick that he still owes us for those Darkling twins. It's not my fault one of them died."

"Sure," I reply. *Patrick?* He must be the man sorting out all the deals in Centrum. I make a mental note to hunt him down and make him pay for this.

I search for more children. There are so many. How can I choose who gets to live and who dies? Impulsively, I decide to pick the children who don't have their parents with them, because they're the most vulnerable. I end up with five more girls and three boys. I want to take more, but that will start raising suspicion.

"That's my quota," I say to the guard, and he escorts us out of the cell.

The green-eyed boy with shaggy brown hair flashes me a thankful look.

I turn to the guard. "Give those people some water, will you? These kids are practically dead—we'll be lucky to get them to Centrum. Patrick's not paying for corpses, you know."

"Yeah, all right," the goateed guard says.

It's not much, but it's something, at least. I escort the children around the corner and meet up with Elijah and Stuart.

"There're so many of them," Stuart says.

"I wasn't going to leave them," I reply. "Come on, we've got to go."

Stuart takes the back of the pack while I take the lead, holding Elijah's upper arm as if I'm escorting a prisoner. The green-eyed boy, who tells me his name is Nick, talks soothingly to the little girls, Bree and Bianca, trying to keep them calm.

"We're playing a game," he says to them.

"What game?" Bree, says.

"It's called Prisoner. We're all pretending to be convicts, and these are our friends, helping us to get out of here," he says. "The aim of the game is to sneak onto an aircraft without getting caught. Can you do that?"

Bree looks at her older sister, then nods. "I'm very good at games."

"That's good," Nick replies.

Bianca keeps petting Elijah's tail, not that he seems to mind.

He's more concerned with looking at me. I wish he'd stop. I don't want his sympathy, because I don't want to be reminded why my insides are being torn apart.

We pass a number of Sentry guards in the corridors, but they don't stop us. It must be common to see children being escorted to the cargo bay, ready to be shipped to Centrum. One guard, though, a woman with a thin face and a blond ponytail, slows down as she passes by us. A flicker of recognition registers in her eyes as she looks at me.

I lower my head and keep on walking, but the blood is swooshing in my ears.

"Natalie Buchanan?" the woman calls out after me.

I almost turn. Rookie mistake. Every part of me is screaming to run, the fight-or-flight instinct taking over, but somehow I manage to keep my composure and carry on walking at a steady pace. I turn my head slightly toward Elijah.

"Is she following us?" I whisper to him.

A faint nod is all the answer I need.

She must not be certain it's me; otherwise, she would've raised an alarm by now. But she keeps a watchful eye on us all the way to the cargo bay. I scan the bay for the prison Transporter heading to Centrum and find it at the far end of the room. A row of children are being ushered onto it by Victor.

The blond female guard goes over to one of her senior colleagues, casting another suspicious look in my direction. I turn my back on her, not wanting to give them a clear view of my face.

"We need to get out of here, right now," I mutter to Elijah.

Victor waves a hand, and the Transporter's hatch begins to close. *No!*

"Wait!" I call out to him.

I shepherd the group of children across the hangar, toward the aircraft.

Bree grips Nick's hand.

"Remember, it's just a game," he whispers. "But we can't get caught, or we'll lose, all right?"

She nods.

We reach the aircraft just before the hatch shuts.

"Phew, that was close. Patrick would've had my neck if I'd missed the transport," I say.

Victor glances at the group of children. "I wasn't expecting any more passengers."

"We got the call when we were down on the prison deck," I say.

Victor lets out an annoyed sound. "They keep doing this. All right, put them on."

Stuart quickly herds the kids onto the Transporter.

I peer over my shoulder. The female guard and her colleague are walking in our direction. My heart races.

"How much do you think we'll get for the cat?" Victor asks me as Elijah climbs on board after Stuart.

"Enough," I reply vaguely. "I'm going to escort it to Centrum. We don't want the creature eating the cargo, right?"

Victor laughs.

The blond guard and her colleague are just twenty-five feet away.

"Stop that girl!" she calls out.

Victor turns at the sound, but I grab his arm, drawing his attention back to me.

"So when should we get that drink? I'm free tomorrow," I say, furtively glancing over his shoulder. The two guards are now running toward us. "Pick me up at nine?"

"Sure." He grins.

"Great. See you then." I quickly step onto the aircraft. The hatch begins to close.

"Hold on," Victor says.

I turn, giving him my most winning smile.

The other two guards are now just fifteen feet away, and getting closer.

"Tell Patrick not to put in any more special orders unless they're through me," Victor says.

"Okay, I'll let him know," I say.

I hurry to find my seat between Elijah and Stuart.

"I've been recognized," I say to them.

"Stop!" I hear the female guard yell.

The engine starts up. The hatch is almost closed. *Come on! Come on!*

Through the gap in the closing door, I see Victor talking to the woman with the ponytail. He flashes a panicked look toward the Transporter. "Wai—"

The hatch shuts, and the aircraft lifts off. It speeds toward the Destroyer Ship's cargo hatch, the clouds and sky beyond it just within our reach—

A voice crackles over the pilot's radio.

"Turn around." Victor's voice sounds over the airwaves. "There's a rebel on board."

The pilot doesn't have time to register the order before Elijah leaps up and tears open the mesh door in front of the cockpit. I'm stunned by his strength. He loops an arm around the pilot's throat.

"Keep flying," Elijah says, baring his saber teeth.

We're just a few feet from the cargo hatch.

"Turn around now! That's an order, pilot!" Victor's voice demands over the radio.

Gray skies fill the windscreen.

Stuart squeezes my hand and says a prayer under his breath.

Daylight floods the aircraft. We're out.

We're getting closer.

I say a prayer.

We're out!

I rush out of my seat and join Elijah. I yank the radio out of the socket, stopping any further communication.

"Land on Union Street," I order.

The pilot steers the aircraft toward the rendezvous point, flying over the smoldering rooftops of Black City. In the distance, I spot a distinctive white marble building. It's Sentry headquarters. We're nearly at Union Street. We'll have only a few minutes' head start on Victor, so we need to be quick. I just hope Roach is waiting for us as promised.

"They'll know you attempted to rescue Polly," Elijah says to me.

I nod, understanding his meaning. The dance that we've been playing with Rose is over. He has no hold over me or Ash anymore, which means there's nothing stopping us from fighting back. He'll have no choice but to kill us, and do it quickly.

The Transporter lands, and the hatch opens, revealing Roach, Garrick and the rebel team, all pointing guns at us. Ash hangs slightly back, his eyes glittering in the shadows of the alleyway.

"Some welcoming party," Elijah says to them.

Roach lowers her shotgun, and Ash pushes past her onto the Transporter. He draws me into his arms, and it takes all my willpower not to just break down there and then. He suddenly pulls away.

"You smell of blood," he says. "Are you hurt?"

"No," I murmur, but that's not entirely true. Inside I'm dying.

Garrick boards the aircraft, his head brushing against the roof. He searches the faces of all the children in the transport.

"Where's Polly?" he says.

My throat tightens. I can't form the words.

"Polly's dead," Elijah says for me.

Ash inhales sharply. "Natalie, I'm so sor—"

"What the fragg?" Roach says, boarding the Transporter. "Who are these kids?"

"They're coming with us," I say.

"I don't think so," she replies.

"We don't have time to argue. There will be guards crawling all over this place any minute now," I say.

We hurriedly take the children off the Transporter. There's a pop of gunfire behind us. Roach has just killed the pilot. I find it hard to care. We split into groups and set off in different directions to make it harder for the guards to find us all, agreeing to meet back at the Legion ghetto.

A few minutes later, there's a low rumble like thunder, announcing the arrival of more Transporters, but Ash and I are already deep within the maze of the city streets. We reach City End, and the Legion guards help us over the wall.

As Sigur greets us in the Assembly, I notice with relief that Stuart and Elijah have already made it back. Day and her parents are also there, anxiously waiting for us, and they run over to me, all three of them crying.

"We heard what happened . . . ," Day sobs.

The others arrive in dribs and drabs over the next thirty minutes, some with a few scrapes and bruises. Juno helps Beetle patch up the wounded while Sumrina finds rooms for all the children we rescued. Nick shoots me a grateful look as he's led upstairs to the living quarters.

When everyone is back, the Darkling ministers arrive for the debriefing. It doesn't take long for the meeting to erupt into chaos as the Darkling ministers and rebels discuss our next steps now that Polly's rescue mission has failed.

"Surrendering is not an option," Sigur says. "Our only solution is to escape."

"How will we get past the roadblocks?" Garrick says. "They're heavily guarded."

Day raises her hand, like she's at school. "What about the humans? We can't just leave them here to die."

"We need a diversion," Elijah says. "Something to keep the Sentry guards distracted while everyone makes a break for it."

"It'll have to be one hell of a diversion, mate!" Beetle says.

I can't listen anymore. Nothing matters. Polly is dead. On the digital screen to my right, the countdown clock ticks away, letting everyone know we've got only thirty-two hours left before Black City is razed to the ground.

An idea suddenly hits me.

"I know how we can evacuate everyone," I say.

"How?" Sigur asks.

"We do what Elijah suggests; we create a diversion." I eye them all steadily. "Tonight we burn down Black City."

PART II

ESCAPE

14.

ASH

NATALIE STARES OUT the window while the rest of us try to catch up with what she's just said. *Burn down the city? Can we really do that?*

A deep, throaty chuckle comes from Sigur.

"I think it is a marvelous idea," he says.

"Where would we go?" Logan says.

"North," I reply. "We'll try and cross the border into the Northern Territories."

"But what about the rebellion, bro?" Beetle says. "Even if we get everyone out of Black City, that still doesn't solve the problem of Purian Rose. We can't just leave the country. People need us. We have to keep fighting."

I glance at Natalie and imagine what our lives could be like in the north. We could get married, move to the country and live a quiet, peaceful existence. But I know these are just dreams. There's only ever been one path for me to follow.

"I won't be going," I say. "I intend to stay to search for the Ora and take down Purian Rose. Anyone who wants to fight with me can do so."

Natalie briefly squeezes my hand, letting me know I have her support, before getting up and leaving the room. I think she wants to be alone to grieve.

"Won't we risk killing innocent people if we set fire to the city?" Day asks.

"Not if we're careful." Roach stands up and presses a few buttons on the com-desk, projecting a map of Black City on the digital screen on the far wall. "We could strategically plant bombs here, here and here." She highlights Chantilly Lane Market, Union Street and the Park. "It will cause a lot of damage, but because those areas aren't residential, the risk to human life will be minimal."

"Won't the fires spread to the inhabited areas?" Garrick asks.

"Yeah, eventually, but it should give people enough time to make a run for it," Roach says.

"We should target the Cinderstone factories first," I say. "That should keep the guards busy."

It's a long shot, but during the air raids last year, Purian Rose didn't bomb the factories because he needed the Cinderstone to fuel his munitions operations, so I'm hoping he gave the same orders this time round and will want to protect them.

There are excited murmurs as people start putting a plan together. I glance at Sigur, and he nods, understanding I need to be with Natalie.

I find her in our bedroom, curled up on our bed, her arms wrapped around herself. I lie down beside her so we're nestled together like spoons. We stay like this for an hour, saying nothing. Only the thrum of her aching heart sounds in my ears. Eventually she turns around and cries against my chest.

"He raped her," Natalie whispers. "Sebastian, he . . ."

I tighten my arms around her as the horror of her words sinks in. They didn't just kill Polly; they made her suffer in every way possible first. My fangs flood with venom. I want to rip Sebastian's head off, tear him to shreds. I'm going to make him pay for what he did.

After Natalie's cried all her tears, she looks up at me. "Ash, will you promise me one thing?"

I nod. "Anything."

"Promise me that when we face Purian Rose, I'll be the one who gets to kill him."

That evening, Natalie and I sit on the roof of the Legion head-quarters, hand in hand, watching the sun set over the city. By the time the sun rises again, the city will be destroyed. Natalie gazes up at one of the Destroyer Ships hovering over the city and says a final good-bye to her sister, the first of many family members and friends we'll be parting ways with tonight.

The Sentry stopped playing the footage of Polly, knowing the jig is up, but so far there's been no other sign they're intending to change their strategy, and they have continued to run the countdown on all the screens across the city. Rose still thinks he's in control.

The inky blue of night slowly seeps into the bloodred sky, until a shroud of darkness descends over Black City.

"It's time," I say to her.

We all meet in the Assembly and go over our plan again. Fifty teams, led by Dad and Logan, Michael and Sumrina, Pullo and Angel, plus all the Legion guards, will escort groups out of the ghetto and head toward the northern border. The rest of us will lead the attack on the city.

"Okay, so does the rebel team know what they're doing?" Roach asks. She's wearing a gray jumpsuit, and her long blue dreadlocks have been tied back. "Garrick?"

"I'll hijack a Sentry truck and travel back to the Mountain Wolf State to gather support from the Lupines," Garrick says. "Then I'll meet you at the rendezvous point in Centrum in the Dominion State, to prepare for the final assault."

"Good," Roach says. "Sigur?"

"I'll head to Fire Rapids and assist with the evacuation of the Darklings there," Sigur says. "Once that's done, I'll send word out to the other ghettos about our plans to head north, then join you in Centrum."

"Excellent," she says. "And while you're doing that, Humans for Unity will begin our strikes against the Sentry government, to keep them distracted. We'll focus on targets like factories, farms, fuel supplies, roads—basically anything that will sabotage their infrastructure and make life hell for them."

Beetle grins at me, making the scar tissue on his cheek pucker. He's looking forward to this.

"Phoenix, you know what you're doing?" Roach asks me.

"Yup. Natalie, Elijah and I will rescue Lucinda and Yolanda," I say. "Once we've located them, we'll retrieve the Ora. Then we'll go to Viridis to speak to the Bastet senate about joining the rebellion, before heading to the rendezvous point."

"You better return with that weapon, Ash," Roach says. "We can only hold off the Sentry for so long. We're all counting on you."

"I won't let you down." I just hope I can keep that promise.

"Right, everyone get ready. We leave in an hour," she says.

Sigur exits the council chamber with Elijah, and I wonder where they're going, but I don't have time to think about it, as Roach walks over to me and Natalie. Garrick's standing nearby, counting out the boxes of ammunition. We were able to gather a few guns and supplies, after our stockpile was stolen, but it's not much.

"You guys got everything you need for tomorrow?" she says in a low voice.

I nod. Getting out of Black City is going to be our first challenge, but we've got a plan. It's risky, but it might just work. Only our families, Roach and Amy know the plan. After what happened with James and Hilary from Firebird, we can't chance telling too many people.

When Roach leaves, Garrick comes over to us.

"I want to come with you and help plant the bombs," he says.

"That's okay, we've got it worked out," I say.

"I want to be useful," Garrick replies. "Besides, if you meet a pack of Lupines on the streets, you won't stand a chance against them."

He has a point. "Thanks."

We can go our separate ways once the bombs have been planted and continue with our original escape plan. Garrick isn't in the loop about our plot to leave the city and head to Thrace, and I want to keep it that way. I trust him, but if he gets captured tonight, I don't want him giving away our escape plan to the Sentry.

Nick laughs as Amy paints his face with Cinderstone powder, decorating his eyes just like she did mine a few days ago so that he resembles Phoenix. He's dressed in my LLF jacket, black trousers and boots, his disheveled hair tinted black with Cinderstone. Except for his green eyes, he looks startlingly like me, which is the whole point. Nick is my decoy.

His counterpart is Amy, who is wearing one of Natalie's

tops, cropped leather pants and knee-high boots; her usually auburn hair has been roughly bleached and curled. Her disguise isn't quite as convincing as Nick's, but we're not looking for perfection—just likenesses close enough to draw the guards away from me and Natalie.

It was Roach's idea, and I was dead set against it, as were Natalie and Juno, but we were overruled by Amy and Nick. They want to help, and they're old enough to make their own decisions. Juno keeps glancing toward her sister, a mixture of worry and pride in her blue eyes. The Jones sisters have never been afraid to stand up to the Sentry, but it still can't be easy for her. At least she'll be going with them, so they'll be looked after.

Nick turns to me, beaming, clearly pleased with his transformation. "Hey, Ash, what do you think?"

"You look hideous," I tease.

"I didn't have much to work with," he zings back.

"Are you sure you want to do this?" I say to him, ignoring the frosty look from Roach.

"Yeah, sure! Look, we're all in this together, plus I owe you after Natalie rescued me from that Destroyer Ship." A shadow passes over his eyes, but he blinks it away. "Besides, I'm digging the makeup."

"Okay, five-minute countdown, everyone," Roach says. "Say your good-byes now."

Sigur stays outside in the ghetto with the Legion guards, splitting the Darklings into their groups. We said our farewells earlier today, knowing he'd be busy. We kept the conversation light, although we both knew it could be the last time we'd ever see each other.

Elijah enters the room at that moment, and I can smell blood on him, sick, *diseased* blood. It quickly becomes apparent what

Sigur asked him to do. I bet the hospital ward where the Wraths were being cared for is now empty. It was the kindest thing. We couldn't take them with us, and since normal poisons don't work on Darklings, a dose of Bastet venom would've done the trick. At least it would've been fast—I doubt they felt much pain, and Elijah's not at any risk of getting infected; he has a natural immunity to the Wrath since the C18-Virus is present in his venom.

"Sigur wanted you to know that Martha's arrived," Elijah says. "She's outside with him now. She'll be going with Harold's team."

Natalie lets out a relieved sigh. I know she loves her old Darkling housemaid very much. Martha's been staying with some members of Humans for Unity the past two months.

We check our provisions, and then it's time to say our good-byes. Beetle's group is the first to leave, as they'll be planting the bombs in the Cinderstone factories.

"See you in Centrum, bro," Beetle says.

"Try not to get blown up again," I tease, referring to the time he bombed the Boundary Wall.

He laughs. "I can't promise anything."

Roach just nods a curt good-bye at me, her mind already on the mission ahead. Day hugs her family members, trying hard not to cry. MJ clings to her. His burns from the house fire are healing nicely, and we gave him plenty of pain medication to take along with him for his back, so he should be all right.

"Be a brave boy, okay?" Day says.

MJ nods, sniffing.

Sumrina gives a little squeak as she holds back her tears. "Take care, my precious girl. I love you so much."

"I love you too, Mama, Papa," Day replies, hugging them again.

Day wipes her eyes, then comes over to us. We awkwardly shake hands—Day and I have never really managed to form a friendship—then she briefly hugs Natalie before picking up her satchel and rushing out of the room.

Natalie takes a shaky breath. I lightly kiss her forehead.

"She'll be okay," I say. "Beetle will take care of her."

Next out the door is Juno's group; they are going to plant the bomb in the Park—the neighborhood in the city where the rich used to live, like Natalie's family, before it was destroyed in last year's air raids. Nick, Juno and Stuart say quick good-byes, while Amy flings her arms around Natalie. It's strange seeing the two of them side by side, looking so alike.

"Good luck! Oh, heavens, is that bad luck? Do I mean 'break a leg'?" Amy says in a rush.

"I think that only applies in the theater," Natalie says.

"Phew! Well . . . good luck! I'll see you in Centrum." She leans conspiratorially toward us, keeping her voice low. "Do you remember how to apply your makeup?"

"I've got it," Natalie says kindly. The makeup is part of our escape plan.

Amy hugs Elijah, then turns shyly to me. "Bye, Ash."

I give her a quick peck on the cheek, and her face flushes bright red. She hurries over to Juno, and they leave.

I check the gray satchel beside my blue duffel bag, by my feet. The satchel holds the explosives we'll set around Chantilly Lane Market. Roach gave us a crash course in how to detonate the bombs. It sounds simple enough: in Roach's words, "just flip the switch and run like hell."

Garrick strides over and picks up the satchel. "I'll carry these."

"No, it's fine, I'll—"

"No one's going to care if my head gets blown off," he interrupts, his metallic eyes glinting.

I don't argue. "Thanks."

Natalie and Elijah deal with our final preparations while I find Dad. He's standing by the window at the far end of the room, away from everyone else.

"I didn't think I'd be saying good-bye to you again so soon," he says, referring to the time we said farewell in my prison cell, just before my execution.

"Hey, on the plus side, at least I'm not about to be crucified," I say. "That's better than last time."

He chuckles, but the sound gets caught in his throat. He pulls me into an embrace, and I wrap my arms around him, holding on for as long as I can.

"I'll be okay," I whisper.

"I know you will," he says, releasing me. "I'm so proud of you, son."

I smile. "Love you, Dad."

He ruffles my hair. "Get on out of here."

I join Natalie, Elijah and Garrick by the door and sling my blue duffel bag over my shoulder; it contains our disguises and my mom's keepsake box. Natalie and Elijah each carry their own duffel bags filled with provisions.

I take one last look at my friends and family, and say a silent good-bye to them all. Despite all our promises, I suspect we're never going to meet again. As we walk past the window, I peer up at the Destroyer Ships blocking out the starlight. I don't think I'm going to survive this war. I may have risen from the ashes like a phoenix, but like the mythical bird, I know my fate is to die in flames.

15.

ASH

CHANTILLY LANE MARKET is deathly silent as we navigate the dark, narrow alleyways between the market stalls. Even the colorful flags outside each stall are still, like the very city itself is holding its breath. Every few hundred yards, Garrick carefully plants a bomb under one of the stalls, targeting the shops with the most flammable merchandise.

"How long do we have?" Natalie asks.

I check the digital monitors on the buildings surrounding the market. The bright yellow numbers of the countdown display read 24:10:00.

"Ten minutes before the factories blow up," I say. "Let's get a move on."

We reach Mollie McGee's Tavern—a popular drinking establishment with the Sentry guards—and Garrick breaks down the door. We grab bottles of Shine from behind the bar and pour it all over the floor before going outside and dousing the flags and market stalls with the flammable liquid. It'll help carry the flames to the other stalls, maximizing the damage to the area. I plant the last bomb outside the tavern, and look at the countdown again.

"Five seconds before first strike," I say.

We watch the seconds tick away:

24:00:05

24:00:04

24:00:03

24:00:02

24:00:01

24:00:00

BOOM!

The explosion roars through the city, sending vibrations up and down our bodies. In the distance, a plume of fire and smoke over a hundred feet tall soars into the air, lighting the sky. It can mean only one thing: the Cinderstone factories are ablaze. Beetle has succeeded.

We've barely had time to recover from the shock waves before the digital screens around the city flicker and start broadcasting a live feed of Amy and Nick running through the Park, their backs to the camera so you can't get a good look at their faces. Everyone will assume that they're me and Natalie. We're able to do this because we're broadcasting within the city limits, like they were doing with the "live feed" of Polly, so the Sentry's jamming signal doesn't work, as that only prevents signals coming in or out of the city bounds.

Nick and Amy deposit some explosives outside Natalie's old family home, a derelict white mansion covered in brambles, then hurry toward the manhole cover in the middle of the street, dropping down into the sewers just as the bomb explodes and another shock wave hits the city. A series of explosions take place in rapid succession as the other bombs in the Park detonate. The old, dry wood from the abandoned houses provides the perfect kindling, and that area of the city is soon an inferno.

Almost immediately, there's another explosion to the west—this time a power plant—and all the digital screens and streetlights start to pop out one by one, sending a rolling tide of darkness across the city.

There's a moment of stillness before all hell breaks loose. Air-raid sirens wail, people scream, footsteps echo in the streets as citizens run for cover. Everything is going according to schedule. Right now, I know Dad and Logan are leading the first teams out of the ghetto under the cover of darkness. I say a silent prayer for them all. We've done everything we can; now it's up to fate to determine whether they get out of Black City alive.

"Our turn," I say. "You ready?"

Garrick, Natalie and Elijah all nod. Our bombs are on a time delay, so once I flip the first switch, we'll have just three minutes to get out of the market before the first bomb detonates and sets the others off in a chain reaction.

I peer up at the sky. The first Transporters start to drop from the Destroyer Ships. Some head toward the Cinderstone factories, others to the Park, where the bombs have gone off. There's no time to wait. I flip the switch.

The three-minute countdown begins.

We sprint through the market, tearing through the warren of alleyways, me leading the way, as my eyesight is best in the dark.

Two minutes.

I turn a corner and immediately realize I've gone the wrong way when we're confronted with a brick wall. Fragg!

"Ash, this way," Natalie says, guiding us down another passageway.

The colorful bunting around the market stalls flutters as we rush by. We pass the fishmongers, the jewelry stores, finally reaching the clothing stores on the outer rim of the market.

One minute.

We reach a crossroads.

"Which way?" Elijah asks.

"I don't know," Natalie says. "I always get lost around here."

We don't have time to waste. I just follow my gut and pick the passageway on the right.

Thirty seconds.

As we run down a narrow alleyway, Natalie's foot slips on a loose cobblestone, and she stumbles. Garrick roughly drags her to her feet.

Ten seconds.

"There! Look!" Elijah says.

A crack of light between two stalls.

We run toward it.

Five seconds.

We're not going to make it.

Three. Two. One.

We burst out of the market just as the first bomb detonates.

The blast knocks us off our feet, and we crash to the ground ten feet from where we started. My ears are ringing, and every bone and muscle in my body aches. Everything sounds muffled, like I'm swimming underwater. I lie on my back and watch as confetti rains down on me. Another explosion sends more colorful bunting and bits of flaming debris up into the air. I try to move, but my body refuses.

Through the fog in my head, I make out the sound of marching boots against cobblestones. It's getting louder and louder. The Sentry guards are coming. A voice screams in the back of my mind to get up, but my legs aren't responding. Everything's still in a haze, and I can't concentrate. *Get up, Ash. Get up, Ash. Get up—*

"Ash!"

Natalie's voice makes my world whoosh back into focus. I struggle upright in time to see her being slung over Garrick's shoulder, about fifteen feet away. For a second, I think he's trying to carry her away from the approaching Sentry guards, but then I notice her fists pounding against his back, the fear in her eyes. My heart leaps into my mouth. He's trying to kidnap her!

"Let me go!" she screams.

I lunge for Garrick. He yells as I sink my fangs into his leg, injecting him with a heavy dose of Haze. Startled, he drops Natalie. Elijah helps her to her feet while Garrick staggers back, one step, two steps, before crashing to the cobbled ground, grinning like an insane man as the Haze courses through his veins.

"Down here!" Sebastian calls out to his men. They're in the street next to us.

"We have to get to the safe house," I say.

We grab our bags and stagger out of Chantilly Lane just as the first guards approach the market square. We hurry down the passageway, getting as far away as possible.

The streets start to fill with people as they evacuate their homes, carrying clothes, food, pets; some even attempt to carry heavy paintings and other heirlooms with them in their panicked state.

"Put up your hoods," I tell the others.

We join the throng of people, using them for cover as more Sentry troops rush by. Everyone is running in all directions, uncertain where to go. With the factories, the Park and Chantilly Lane in flames, most head toward the Rise to take refuge there.

We walk for twenty minutes until we reach City End, where the safe house is. I'm just grateful I never told Garrick our plan, that fragging traitor! I think back to the first time I met him, after he'd brought Freya to the ghetto, and recall the slash marks down her stomach. I'd thought they were made by a guard's sword, but now I suspect the Lupine was responsible. Was that what Freya was trying to tell me before she died? We pass dozens of houses, searching for the right one, but they all look the same, with black Cinderstone-brick walls and red doors.

"Which one is it?" Elijah asks.

I quickly check the top right-hand corner of each door until I find what I'm looking for: a small burning rose carved into the wood.

"This one," I say.

We enter the safe house, slamming the door behind us. It is small and cramped, with dust on every surface and bedsheets covering the old furniture. The owner died a year ago, and Humans for Unity has been using it as a refuge ever since. We head up to the attic, as Roach instructed us to, and find a couple of sleeping bags, an oil lamp and some tins of food. There's no Synth-O-Blood for me, but I didn't expect there to be; everything in the attic has been here a while. My stomach growls, and I try to remember the last time I ate anything. It's been ages.

There's a small round window in the attic, giving us a great view over the city. Infernos rage in the three districts where we planted the bombs. Thankfully, the fires are still contained within those sections, but it'll only be a matter of time before they reach us. We'll stay here for as long as we can, then head to the station on the outskirts of the city.

Elijah sits down on one of the sleeping bags and begins to

groom himself, licking the dust and blood off his arms, while I stalk about the room.

"I can't fragging believe Garrick's been playing us all this time," I spit.

"Who do you think he's working for?" Natalie asks.

"My money's on Purian Rose," I reply.

Elijah stops cleaning himself. "Then why tell us about the Tenth?"

"To gain our trust, so he could infiltrate the rebel headquarters." I punch my fist against the wall, making my knuckles ache. "Fragg! He knows *everything*! He knows where the Darklings are going and that we're looking for the Ora."

"At least he doesn't know we're going to Thrace," Natalie says. "That's something."

I rake my fingers through my hair, trying to think of ways to warn the others, but come up empty.

"Why did he try and kidnap Natalie, though?" Elijah asks me. "Wouldn't it have made more sense for him to kill you both?"

We all look at each other, trying to work this out, but none of it makes sense. It would have been the perfect opportunity for Garrick to kill me, so why didn't he?

"So what do we do now?" Natalie says.

"I guess we carry on with our plan," I say. "Garrick doesn't know how we intend to escape the city; he'll assume we're already on our way out."

"I hope he's having a really bad Haze trip," Natalie says, wincing as she sits down.

"Are you hurt?" I ask.

"It's just that old bite mark on my leg," she says. "Nothing to worry about."

She opens one of the tins of soup, cooking it over the oil

lamp, and we settle down for the evening. I keep a close eye on the window, to see if the fires are spreading in our direction. Elijah curls his lip at the soup when Natalie passes it to him.

"Fine, go hungry. I don't care," she snaps.

He quickly takes the soup and drinks it down. Honestly, where does he think we are? The Golden Citadel? As the Bastet Consul's son, he's probably used to getting the finest foods. I enviously watch them as they eat their dinner, my own stomach roaring with hunger.

Another eruption rumbles across the city. Something else has just gone up in flames.

"Do you think the others made it out okay?" Natalie asks.

I nod, although I just don't know. Pain balls up in my chest, thinking about Dad and Sigur, not to mention Nick and Amy.

Natalie and Elijah finish their meager dinner while I triple-check the contents of my duffel bag, making sure we have everything for our escape plan tomorrow: wigs, contact lenses, veneers, makeup, clothes, Evacuation Passes. It's amazing what Amy managed to cobble together for us in terms of disguises in such a short space of time. A lot of it was stolen from Black City School's props cupboard and the makeup department at Juno's work. I'm concerned that we have only two Evacuation Passes—the bloodied one Juno got hold of from a dead guy and the one Dad collected during the attempt to rescue Polly. We still need a third pass, which is another item on the long list of things that can go horribly wrong tomorrow.

Right now, our plan relies on the Sentry believing Natalie and I have already left the city. With Garrick still out there, our chances of escaping have just gone from bad to worse. I just pray Nick and Amy get out okay, for their sakes as well as our own.

"Do you think the Sentry will still honor the Evacuation Passes?" Elijah asks.

"I think so," Natalie says. "If Purian Rose evacuates those who have been loyal to him, it'll give other people around the country incentive to support him, rather than join forces with us."

"I hope you're right," he mutters. "I *have* to get to Thrace. My mom needs me."

"We'll get there." Natalie touches his arm reassuringly, and I feel a twinge of jealousy.

When Natalie's done with her meal, she climbs into her sleeping bag and drops off almost instantly. Her skin is covered in a fine sheen of sweat, like she's feverish, and I wonder if she's coming down with something.

"You were with Natalie when she found Polly, weren't you?" I ask Elijah quietly.

He nods.

"Did she die quickly?" I've been clinging to that small hope all day.

"I don't think so, given the number of defensive wounds on her arms and hands. They took their time," Elijah responds. "The Sentry likes to make their prisoners suffer."

Elijah rolls over, turning his back on me. I remember what Natalie said about Elijah being held captive in Sentry head-quarters, and realize this mission isn't just about finding his mom or retrieving the Ora. It's about vengeance.

16.
NATALIE

THICK BLACK CLOUDS of soot and steam billow out of the train, covering the platform in a viscous fog that hides everyone's feet. It gives the impression the station is haunted with hundreds of disembodied ghosts trying to board the ten fifteen to Centrum, our ride out of this city.

All around us sirens wail as the city continues to burn. Choking ash drifts down on us in a blizzard of dark snow, obscuring our visibility. It's been a blessing in disguise, though, as it allowed us to get to the station this morning unnoticed.

Parents say tearful good-byes as their children are ushered onto the train. One little girl in a red dress refuses to let go of her mother, and her father literally has to pry her off and carry her onto the train. His expression is grief stricken as he returns to his wife.

"She'll be all right," he says to her. "She'll be safer in Centrum."

That's if she even makes it there. The steam train is armored by heavy sheets of silvered steel, while the windows have been barred in a bid to protect passengers from bandits and Wrath attacks as the train travels through the wild and deadly Barren Lands.

The only possible points of weakness on the train are the emergency escape hatches in the roof, but they're protected with layers of acacia wood, which Darklings are severely allergic to, so I *think* we'll be okay. I've done this ride before, when I moved from Centrum to Black City a few months ago, but that train was for government officials, so it had much better security. Right now, I'm more worried about the Sentry guards patrolling the platform, checking passengers' Evacuation Passes and making sure they're not on Purian Rose's Most Wanted list. *Like us.*

There's a blast of steam from the train, stirring the ash-snow, revealing a figure in a striking black uniform and flat cap striding down the platform, followed by a troop of Sentry guards. *Sebastian!* His head has been cleanly shaved to reveal the rose tattoo above his left ear—the mark of a Pilgrim, a devoted follower of the Purity faith. There's a small tear on his black jacket, where his silver rose medal used to be, before Polly ripped it off. I quickly turn my back on him just as he walks by, although I know it's unlikely he saw me lurking in the shadows under the iron stairwell. We really have to get out of here before he sees us, but we can't go anywhere until we've got the last Evacuation Pass.

"What's he doing here?" Ash whispers.

"Maybe they've found Nick and Amy?" Elijah replies.

I bite my lip, worried for them and us. I couldn't stand it if Amy got hurt because of me. Images of Polly's dead body instantly flood my mind, but I force them aside, along with my grief. I can't think about my sister, not right now, because if I do, I'll just crawl into a hole somewhere and never get out again. So instead of heartache, I fill the void with another, more productive emotion: anger. This is what will fuel me until the day I look Purian Rose in the eye and drive a knife into his chest.

I snatch a look in Sebastian's direction. He's standing farther down the platform, overseeing a pack of Lupines who are load-ing crates, antique furniture and paintings onto the train. It's all from the Sentry HQ. My mother's belongings! But I guess now that she's a fugitive and Sebastian pretty much runs the city, it's his stuff. It makes me sick that Sebastian is more concerned about saving his property than people's lives, but I'm not sur-prised. He talks quietly to one of the male Lupines, who's wear-ing a dark red leather frock coat and has teeth braided into his hair. Clearly visible on his neck is a crescent moon tattoo. He must be the leader of the Moondogs, which Ash told me about.

At that moment, five tall figures appear on the other end of the platform, smoke swirling around them. I stifle a cry. It's Garrick and four of his Lupine pack: two men, two women. They all look similar, with gray clothing, silver eyes, and fur-like hair styled to look like a shark's fin down the center of their heads, except the others are shorter than Garrick and one of the females has dyed her hair to match her shocking-pink lipstick.

The people on the platform hurriedly get out of their way as they stalk toward Sebastian and the Moondogs.

"There you are—I've been waiting for you," Sebastian snaps at Garrick. "Did you find them?"

"No," Garrick says. "They've left the city."

The Moondog in the red coat scoffs.

"You got something you want to say to me, Jared?" Garrick growls.

The man glowers at Garrick, but says nothing more. I'm get-ting the impression Garrick holds a high position in their so-ciety, if he's able to talk to the Moondog pack leader that way. Tension bubbles between the two packs, with Garrick's gray-clothed First Landing pack on one side, and the red-clothed Moondogs on the other.

"We'll find them," the female with pink hair says to Sebastian.

"You better, or you'll find yourself in the Tenth with all those other animals," Sebastian replies.

Garrick growls.

"Make yourself useful, *dog,* and get this stuff on the train," Sebastian says, unperturbed. "I haven't got all day."

Garrick's hands ball into fists, but he gives a faint nod. His pack helps the Moondogs load the furniture onto the train while Sebastian leaves. My heart is racing. How are we going to get out of here with Garrick still around?

I check my watch. The time is 10:05. The Humans for Unity guys we're waiting for are five minutes late. What's holding them up? In addition to securing another Evacuation Pass for us, they were also meant to pose as our parents to help get us on the train along with all the other children being evacuated from the city. It would raise too much suspicion if three kids tried to board the train on their own. The ruse was Ash's idea. *Hide in plain sight,* he'd suggested. *They'll never expect us to be so brazen as to board the train with the other evacuees.*

I tug on the hem of my jacket, which is a little too short for me. We've all got on disguises. I'm dressed like a boy in gray slacks, a workman's shirt and patchwork woolen jacket. My hair has been pulled back into a cap, and my breasts have been bandaged. I look surprisingly convincing as a young boy, which doesn't do much for my ego. My diamond engagement ring is attached to the necklace Ash gave me for my birthday, hidden under the collar of my shirt.

Elijah is wearing leather pants under a long black tailcoat, fake glasses and a cap. His tail is curled up under his coat, his saber teeth are fully retracted, and his distinctive brown spots are covered by makeup, so he's passable as human.

The most startling transformation out of the three of us is Ash. His skin has been painted with stage makeup so it looks sun-kissed and healthy; he's wearing veneers to help hide his fangs, and they've given him bright blue contact lenses to hide his sparkling eyes. To complete the disguise, Amy and Roach managed to find a blond wig in the props cupboard at school for him. He looks . . . *human*.

I check my watch: 10:09.

"Is Garrick still there?" Ash asks.

I peer down the platform. Garrick loads the last chair onto the train, then orders his pack to leave.

"He's going," I say, relieved.

Garrick takes a few paces down the platform before pausing. He tilts his nose up and sniffs the air; catching a scent, he turns. His silvery eyes slide in our direction. I slam my back against the iron stairwell.

Ash flashes me a panicked look. "Did he see you?"

"I don't think so," I reply. "Besides, I'm wearing a disguise." *But that won't help if he can smell us.* I'm just grateful there are so many people around us, to help hide our scent.

Blood pounds in my ears as we all wait.

A whole minute passes, and nothing happens.

I risk another quick peek down the platform.

Garrick has gone.

I let out a shaky breath.

A whistle blows, letting passengers know the train is about to depart. I check my watch again—10:13. We've got exactly two minutes to board the train; otherwise, our best chance of escaping Black City will have gone. There's still no sign of the Humans for Unity members. *Where are they?*

"Fragg it, let's just try and sneak on," Ash says. "The smog from the train is pretty thick in places; it could provide some cover—"

"They're here!" Elijah says, nodding toward three people who have just appeared on the platform, looking flustered and nervous.

I let out a relieved sigh.

"Right, do you remember the plan?" Ash says to me. "You go first. Your name is—"

"Matthew Dungate. I'm fourteen years old, and I live in the Rise with my father, Robert Dungate. I remember. We've been over this a hundred times," I say.

"I'm sorry," he says quietly. "Just . . . stay safe. I'll see you on the train."

I glance around to make sure no one is looking, then quickly kiss Ash, trying to pour as much love and emotion as I can into that brief touch. He wraps his arms around me.

"Guys, can you hurry this up? The train's about to leave," Elijah says.

We hold on to each other for a second longer before letting go. Adrenaline courses through my body as I sling my duffel bag over my shoulder and step out of the shadows onto the platform. This is it. We went over the plan countless times yesterday, and it seemed simple, but now I'm not so sure. What if the guards see through my disguise? Why did we think this was a good plan? It's insanity! There are guards *everywhere*.

A Sentry guard with a neatly trimmed black beard fixes me with a hard look as I stroll over to my "father," a tall, blond-haired man called Weevil, one of the highest-ranking Humans for Unity members in Black City. My hands are clammy with sweat.

"Matthew, there you are. I told you not to run off," Weevil says as the bearded Sentry guard studies us.

"Sorry, Dad," I say in a gruff voice.

The Sentry guard looks at us for another few seconds, then turns his attention away. *Phew.*

"Where have you been?" I say under my breath.

"We hit a bit of trouble getting the Evacuation Pass, but I've got it," he replies, ushering me toward the train. There's no time to waste.

"How are you going to get out of the city?" I ask him.

"Don't worry about me," he says, leaving it at that.

The two other Humans for Unity members meet up with Ash and Elijah by the stairwell, and they head toward a different carriage farther down the platform. Ash peers over his shoulder at me. He seems calm, except for the tension around his beautiful—now blue—eyes. I know he's nervous for me. The four of them are soon shrouded by the smoke and steam spewing out of the train's smokestack.

Weevil leads me to a line of children waiting with their parents to board the train. In front of me is a chubby red-haired woman dressed in a knee-length patchwork frock coat, fussing over her two equally chubby red-haired daughters. The younger of the two girls clings to the hem of her mother's jacket, tears welling up in her eyes.

To my frustration, the carriage I've been booked on is being guarded by the bearded Sentry who was watching me a minute ago. Just my luck! He peers over at me, his hand resting on the stock of his rifle, and I swallow a hard lump in my throat. *My disguise is good; there's no way he'll recognize me.*

The line moves quickly as kids are loaded onto the train like cattle, but even so, butterflies fill my stomach, nervous I won't make it. The woman in front of me hands over her two Evacuation Passes to the Sentry guard, then helps her children onto the train. There's certainly no time for tearful good-byes, but she doesn't seem to realize this as she blocks the doorway.

"I love you, my darlings. Call me the instant you get to Centrum," she sniffs.

I tap my foot impatiently, and Weevil anxiously checks his pocket watch. *Come on! Come on!*

The last whistle blows, and the train's engines roar.

I throw a panicked look at Weevil.

"Move it, lady!" he yells, thrusting my Evacuation Pass into the Sentry guard's hands while simultaneously shoving me onto the train.

I tumble into the carriage, knocking over the two chubby red-haired girls. Behind me, their mother and Weevil shout at each other.

The doors hiss shut, and I clamber to my feet, grabbing my bag and helping the girls up with my free hand. The train lurches forward, nearly knocking me off my feet again, then chugs away from the platform. I catch sight of Weevil through the barred windows. He's still fighting with the Sentry guard and woman. Things are getting heated, and there's lots of pushing and shoving. He catches my eye, and a small, triumphant smile forms across his lips just as the guard raises his rifle and shoots him in the head.

Weevil's blood splashes against the window, and all the children scream. I slam my back against the wall, screwing my eyes shut. Panic rushes through me. What if they've caught Ash or Elijah? I force myself to open my eyes and calm down. I have to find them.

The dark carriage is hot and muggy and crammed with children. Every seat is already taken, and many kids sit on the metal floor. The place is already unbearably hot. Sweat drips down my face and back, and I wish I could take off the suffocating bandaging around my chest, but people might be a bit alarmed if Matthew Dungate suddenly sprang a set of C cups.

I help the two red-haired girls find a place to sit and give them both a quick cuddle. The younger girl with the gap tooth grabs my hand.

"Don't leave us," she whispers.

"You'll be all right. Centrum is a great place to live. All the kids are really nice, and there are loads of parks to play in." This seems to cheer the girl up a little bit. "I have to go and find my . . . er . . . my brother. We got separated, and he'll be worried. Will you be okay?"

The little girl sniffs and nods.

I stand up and scan the carriage, searching for Ash and Elijah—they were supposed to meet me here. Nothing. I check again, remembering they're disguised. Worry bubbles up inside me as I check every face for a third time, but don't see them. They're not on the train.

17.

NATALIE

MAYBE THEY'RE WAITING *for me in the wrong carriage?* I reassure myself as I hurry through the train as fast as I can, accidentally bumping people's shoulders with my bag in my haste. "Sorry, sorry," I mutter all the way down, my heart in my mouth, hoping more than anything Ash and Elijah made it on board. What if they got caught? Ash could be on his way to a prison cell right now while I'm stuck on this train, unable to help him.

Black City whizzes by the barred windows as the train picks up speed. In two days we'll be in Georgiana, where everyone, except us, will disembark to get their connecting ride to Centrum. We'll be taking another train to Thrace. I scan the faces of everyone in the next carriage, then the next, desperation rising inside me when I don't see them anywhere. I pass through a cargo carriage, which is packed to the ceiling with red-and-white enameled bowls, then yank open the steel door to the next car on the brink of tears.

I stop dead.

The whole carriage is full of Sentry guards. There must be at least fifty of them, all laughing as they play cards and drink

Shine. On their tables are portable digital screens, streaming the latest news from SBN. Leaning against their legs are their rifles and swords. They peer up at me, and I quickly lower my cap, hiding my face.

"Sorry, looking for my brother," I mumble and hurry down the aisle.

I pass a skinny guard with a shaved head and a red rose tattooed just above his left ear. He watches me intently, his eyes narrowed, and my stomach flips when I realize I know him. His name's Neil . . . something. He used to work at the Sentry HQ when my mother was the Emissary there. I must've passed him in the hallways a hundred times.

He kicks out a foot, blocking my path.

"Don't I know you?" he says.

I shake my head. "No, sir."

He runs a thumb over his lip, trying to place me. There's no way I'm hanging around while he works it out. I step over his leg and rush into the next carriage. A tall, beautiful boy with startling blue eyes and sun-kissed skin walks down the aisle toward me, anxiously scanning everyone's faces and receiving a number of appreciative glances in return. It takes a second for me to realize this tanned Adonis is Ash. Elijah is behind him. Relief washes through me. I clamber over people's outstretched legs and bags and meet them in the middle of the carriage. Ash pulls me into a tight embrace.

"I was so worried about you," he whispers.

"Me too," I reply, stroking the side of his face.

We get a few funny looks from a group of kids nearby, and I remember I'm dressed as a fourteen-year-old boy.

I reluctantly pull away from him. "We can't go that way—I just bumped into a guard I knew."

"Did he recognize you?"

"He knew I looked familiar, but he couldn't place me."

"We should go back that way," Elijah says, indicating the carriage they've just come from.

We head to the next carriage, and Ash finds us an empty section of floor to sit down on, wedged between a row of seats and a filthy toilet, which has a screen in front of it instead of a proper door. It *stinks*. I try not to look too disheartened that we're going to be stuck here for a few days.

"I will not sit there," Elijah says through gritted teeth. "I'm the Consul's son. I won't be treated like some dog."

"There's nowhere else for us to go. Unless you want to sit on the fragging roof?" Ash says, pointing to the escape hatch above us.

Elijah scrunches up his nose.

Beside us, a teenage girl with curly black hair flashes us a curious look. I start to feel tight around my chest, my anxiety mounting as it hits home that we're trapped on this train, with over fifty Sentry guards just a few carriages away. This was a crazy plan! I tug at the bandages under my shirt.

"You okay?" Ash says.

"I have to loosen these bandages." I go to the restroom and pull the screen over the entranceway.

The cramped cubicle is lit by a single oil lamp overhead, casting an orange glow over everything, which does little to improve the look of the rusting metal toilet and sink. The smell is overpowering, but I try not to let it bother me as I frantically open my shirt and loosen the bandages underneath. I turn on the faucets and take a few sips of tepid water, starting to feel better.

"Look at her again, and I'll rip your fragging throat out," Ash snarls on the other side of the screen.

I peer through the thin gap in the divider to see Ash's hand gripped around Elijah's neck. It doesn't take a genius to work out Elijah's been watching me undress. The creep!

"Ash, let him go before someone calls the guards," I say through the screen.

He releases his hand, and Elijah rubs his bruised throat.

I button up my shirt, then rummage around in my pants pocket for my heart medication. I pop one of the white pills, washing it down with water, and then check my reflection in the cracked mirror above the sink. I curl my lip up at the sight. I look awful with no makeup on. How do guys look so good without it? Even my eyes look all dull and yellow . . . *yellow?*

I lean closer to the mirror. The white of my left eye does seem a little yellow, especially at the corner, like it did on the night of my birthday. There's definitely something wrong with it. Have I caught an infection or something? *That's all I need.* I sigh and leave the toilet, deliberately kicking Elijah's leg as I sit down. This gets a wry smile from Ash.

"You feeling better?" he asks.

"Much," I say.

"Well, we'd better get comfortable. We're going to be here for a few days," Ash sighs.

Over the next six hours Elijah and I entertain ourselves with stories and games, trying to stave off our boredom and anxiety, while Ash reads his mother's diary, hoping to find some clues about the tavern in the photograph, since it's our only clue to finding the Ora and Elijah's mother. Time seems to drag, and every hour feels like three, so I'm disappointed when I check my watch and discover it's only four o'clock in the afternoon. I sigh, and lean against Ash, who is still reading the journal.

"Find anything interesting?" I ask.

He shakes his head. "I've scanned the journal for any mention of the Ora, Thrace, Mirror City or Yolanda, and they're not mentioned anywhere." He puts the diary down. "Most of the entries are about my mom's life in her late teens and early twenties. It's interesting, but not very useful, I'm afraid."

I study the photograph he's using as a bookmark. It's a picture of five Darklings, taken in a forest glen with a mountain in the background.

"Is that your mother's family?" I ask.

He nods, passing the photograph to me.

"That's my mom, grandparents and Lucinda," he says, pointing everyone out.

"Who's this man in the background?" I say.

"I don't know," he replies.

I flip the image over and notice the writing scrawled on the back. "*Forest of Shadows, Amber Hills*? Where's that?"

He shrugs. "I haven't had a chance to look it up on a map yet."

"Can I see the other photo, of the tavern?" I say.

Ash passes it to me, and I study the picture of the four girls in the tavern in Thrace. Elijah leans over so he can look too, enveloping me in his warm, spicy scent. I trace my finger over the picture, trying to reveal its secrets, but there's not much to go on. It's just a normal tavern, with a wooden bar, shelves packed with bottles of Shine, and a long mirror on the back wall.

Something catches my eye in the mirror. I bring the photo closer to my face, inspecting it closely. *Could it be . . . yes!* I let out a squeak of delight, drawing the attention of the black-haired girl nearby. She studies me for a moment before facing the other way again.

"What is it?" Ash asks in a low voice.

I point to the mirror.

Ash arches a brow. "Yeah . . . it's a mirror. So?"

"Look at the reflection, silly," I say, gesturing toward a rectangular object reflected in its glassy surface. "It's a tariff board, advertising room rates. And I'm betting that writing at the top of the board is the name of the place."

Elijah beams at me. We take it in turns studying the picture, trying to work out what the reflected writing on the tariff board says.

"I don't recognize the language," I whisper, so the other passengers can't hear us.

"It's Thracian, the local language they use in the Provinces," Elijah explains in equally hushed tones. "This might be *luma* or *luna*?" He points to the second word.

"I think the first word is *la* and the last one *estrella* . . . ?" I say. "It's hard to read when it's all backward."

"La Luna Estrella? What does it mean?" Ash asks.

"My Thracian is a little rusty, but I think it translates as 'the Moon Star,'" Elijah replies.

Ash grabs his mother's diary and flips through the pages until he finds what he's looking for.

"I saw this earlier," he says, passing it to me.

I read the passage out loud, but keep my voice low. *"Dear diary . . .*

"What a week! The rally was a huge success, even though the Sentry guards arrested several of the speakers. There were thousands of people outside the city hall at one point, many of whom had traveled hundreds of miles to get there, just like us! It was wonderful being around so many like-minded people. We made some great friends at the boardinghouse where we were staying. Luci was particularly taken with this really obnoxious girl named Landie—"

"Landie?" Elijah interjects, snatching the diary from Natalie.

"Hey!" I say.

"Sorry, it's just Landie was my mom's nickname," he says, studying the diary entry.

"That would've been useful to know earlier," Ash grumbles. "You know, preferably before I'd scanned the entire diary for any reference to *Yolanda.*"

He glares at Ash. "It didn't occur to me. No one called her Landie except my dad."

"What else does it say?" I prompt.

Elijah picks up where I left off: *"We talked for hours about politics and how we dreamed of having a fair, democratic government that represented all four races. I have real faith that we'll learn to peacefully coexist one day, but Kieran thinks I'm being naive. He believes a war between the Sentry and the Darklings is inevitable after everything that happened in Amber Hills."*

"Who's Kieran?" I ask.

"He's a Lupine my mom knew growing up," Ash explains.

Elijah carries on reading from the diary. *"Luci and I are heading to Black City, as she heard the civil rights movement is gaining a lot of traction there. We tried to persuade Kieran to join us, but he's got his heart set on staying at the Moon Star with the landlord's daughter, Esme, who can't leave because her father is ill."*

His eyes catch mine at the mention of the Moon Star. "This has *got* to be where my mom's gone!"

I pick up the photo. "Do you think the barmaid could be Esme?"

"Yeah, it's very possible," Ash replies, taking the diary back from Elijah. "And listen to this . . . *I think it's sweet how in love*

Kieran and Esme are. They go everywhere together, like they're joined at the hip. Luci doesn't get it, but she's never believed in love at first sight." He closes the journal. "I think Kieran and Esme are the twins Lucinda was talking about in her letter. It adds up."

Elijah leans back against the wall, letting out a relieved sigh. "So that's where my mom went to meet Lucinda. *The Moon Star.*"

"Hopefully Esme can give us some clues to where they went," I say.

Ash smiles at me, his eyes glimmering with hope. I'm feeling it too, although I know there's still a long way to go before we find the Ora. First, we have to get to Thrace without being discovered. I stretch my legs, feeling stiff from sitting on the hard floor for so long. The black-haired girl on the seat nearby gets up and turns to her friend.

"I'm getting some food. You want anything?" she says.

Her friend nods. The girl heads down the aisle.

"You hungry?" Ash says.

I nod and he gets up.

"I'll have some fish and a glass of milk," Elijah says. "Oh, and maybe some Kalooma berries, if they have any, but only if they're ripe. I hate them when they're green."

"You'll get whatever they have," Ash growls.

"Be careful," I say.

He squeezes my hand, then heads down the carriage on the hunt for something to eat.

The train rhythmically sways as the world outside the window flashes by. During the course of our train ride, the sky has turned from azure blue to a startling crimson, which can only mean one thing: we're approaching the Barren Lands. The red skies are a result of the desert sand being whipped up into the air by tornadoes so vast, they can swallow whole towns. A deep canyon cuts through the desert like a bloody slash, stretching on for as far as the eye can see.

Elijah sighs, tugging at his shirt collar. "They could do with opening a few windows. I'm sweating like a pig in these clothes."

"Delightful," I say. "The windows are shut to keep the Wraths out."

Elijah undoes the top few buttons of his shirt, revealing the smooth, tanned skin underneath. Glistening beads of sweat slowly roll down his throat, making the tiny hairs on his flesh shimmer. Inexplicably, my cheeks warm up. I cast my eyes away, but not before he's caught me looking.

"Like what you see, pretty girl?" he says.

I snort. "Oh, please. I'm trying not to vomit."

"Well, I liked what I saw earlier very much." His eyes drift down to my breasts.

I kick his leg. "Don't *ever* spy on me again."

He smirks.

The door at the end of the carriage opens, and my heart leaps; it could be a Sentry guard. I relax when the black-haired girl appears, carrying a tray with some stale bread, two rotting apples and a bottle of milk on it. The other kids look at the food hungrily. She catches my eye as she sits down. I'm looking forward to getting off this train and away from that carriage of Sentry guards. There's a hiss of steam as the train rapidly decelerates, the sudden shift in speed knocking me into Elijah. I push myself away from him, flustered.

"Your hat," Elijah says through his teeth.

I touch my head and realize my hat has fallen off, revealing my hair. I hurriedly replace it, stuffing my curls back under the rim, but not before the black-haired girl has spotted me. I give her a quick smile. She stares at me for a moment, then smiles back. I relax.

I go over to the window, curious to know why we've stopped. We're at a train station—well, it's more of a wooden platform with a single ticket office. There's a bunch of crates on the platform; each has CENTRUM and something that looks like a red butterfly stamped on the side.

Several of the guards, including Neil, get off the train, and while they're loading up the boxes, one of the men loses his grip and drops a crate. The lid bursts open, and a dozen bottles of a resin-colored liquid crash to the ground, sending glass everywhere. I recognize that liquid—it's acacia solution. They doused Ash's cross with it before his execution. This must be where they make it, since acacia wood is prevalent in the Barren Lands.

Once they're done loading the crates, the train slowly begins to chug away from the platform, passing a tall, hand-painted sign that reads DUSTY HOLLOW. Hanging from it are several decaying Wrath corpses to ward off any others of their kind. I shudder.

During the war, thousands of Darklings were held captive in the nearby concentration camp, where my father used to work. They were experimented on, and deliberately infected with the deadly C18-Virus to test its effects. When the war ended, having become Wraths, they were set loose to fend for themselves. It's a miracle they've survived so long—the disease is very aggressive. But maybe they were given a different strain of the virus than the one used to infect the Darklings in Black City? It's the only reason I can think of for why they've lived this long.

The carriage door opens again, and this time Ash appears,

carrying a tray. There's something bumpy under his jacket. Children ravenously look at the tray of food as Ash walks down the aisle. He hands one particularly skinny boy some bread, and it strikes me how much the boy looks like the twin-blood Sebastian murdered in front of us a few months ago. I guess that hadn't gone unnoticed by Ash either.

Ash sits down and passes me a piece of stale bread and an apple. Elijah holds out his hand and gets handed a bottle of milk.

"Where's the food?" he says.

"That's all they had left. I saw some mice in the other carriage. You could always eat those," Ash replies.

Elijah glances over at the boy, who is greedily eating the bread Ash gave him. His saber teeth extend, and I quickly tear my bread in two and pass the larger half to Elijah. His saber teeth retract.

"No need to say thank you," I mutter.

"Thanks," he replies through a mouthful of bread.

"Aren't you hungry?" I ask Ash.

He shuts his eyes. "They don't serve what I need."

It's going to be days before we get to Thrace. Ash will be starving by then without any blood.

"You can drink from me," I whisper.

"No. I don't want to drug you with Haze," he replies.

"I could try siphoning some off—"

"With what?" he says.

He has a point; it's not like we have any equipment to safely drain my blood.

"Don't worry. If I get hungry, I can always eat Elijah," Ash teases.

Elijah hisses at him.

I lean against Ash, and my head bumps against something solid under his jacket.

"Oww," I say, rubbing my head. "What's that?"

He pulls out a portable digital screen from under his coat. "I swiped it from the guards' carriage. No one will miss it. They've got loads of them in there," he says. "I want to know what's going on with the rebellion."

The three of us huddle around the screen as he turns it on, keeping the volume low. The picture is a little pixelated, but I can still make out February Fields's glossy blond hair and bright pink lips.

"—twenty guards confirmed dead, and many others wounded in the worst terrorist attack this country has seen since the war. Many more would have perished if it hadn't been for the Sentry government's quick action."

The image cuts to a montage of families being loaded onto the trains with the help of smiling Sentry guards. The vehicles are sparkling and new, and all have the Sentry crest painted on their sides. Ash lets out an annoyed grunt. The footage is totally fake! Purian Rose has re-created the evacuation to show his guards in a more favorable light. I guess he doesn't want people to know what really happened—that families were being torn apart and people were getting shot. I wince, thinking about Weevil.

"Purian Rose has put out arrest warrants for those responsible for this atrocity, which was masterminded by the traitor known as Phoenix," February continues. "Rewards will be given to anyone who has information on their whereabouts."

Photos flash up on the screen: Ash, me, Sigur, Roach, Beetle, Juno—

The broadcast is suddenly interrupted, and cuts to the footage Stuart shot in Black City, when the Destroyer Ships invaded. People are crying and screaming as they're gunned down by the

Sentry guards or mauled by packs of Lupines. The camera whips up to get a shot of the sky, where the Destroyer Ships hang over the city, then pans down toward one of the giant digital screens, zooming in on the image of Polly tied to the chair. Seeing my sister again, so unexpectedly, knocks all the wind out of my lungs.

"Your government is lying to you," Juno's voice says over the footage.

The promo ends with a shot of Ash, dressed as Phoenix, with the words NO FEAR, NO POWER.

I turn off the digital screen, not wanting to see my sister's image anymore, every part of me aching with grief.

"Sorry," Ash says, tucking the portable digital screen inside his duffel bag.

I eat my bread, then rest my head against Ash's shoulder. My eyelids droop as the train gently rocks, and I'm soon asleep, my dreams filled with red rooms, roses, and cities burning down.

When I wake up, I'm drenched in sweat from my feverish nightmares. I blink the sleep out of my eyes, and check my watch. Nine o'clock! I've slept through most of the evening. I notice the black-haired girl isn't in her seat. She must've gone to forage for more food, although didn't Ash say they'd run out? Maybe she just wanted to exercise her muscles; I know mine are aching.

"Hey, sleepy," Ash says, kissing my burning cheek. He frowns. "You feeling all right?"

I nod.

A shadow flies past the window, catching my eye. "What was that?"

"Probably a condor," Ash answers.

"What?" Elijah says, alarmed.

"Are you okay?" I ask him.

"Uh-huh," Elijah says, his eyes fixed on the window. "I just don't like birds. It won't get inside here, will it?"

Both Ash and I laugh.

"It's not funny!" he says. "Some people hate spiders, I hate birds. Get over it."

"Sorry," I say, still laughing. "It's just . . . you're a *cat* . . ."

He glowers at us.

I force myself to stop giggling. "No, it won't get in here, unless the bird somehow learns to open up the escape hatch."

Elijah looks up at the hatch in the roof.

The carriage door opens and the black-haired girl walks down the aisle, empty handed, and takes her seat. I snuggle against Ash's chest, not worrying so much about keeping up the pretense I'm a boy, since the black-haired girl beside us already knows the truth.

I keep an eye on the window, not entirely convinced that what I saw was a condor —it seemed much too big—but I don't see anything except a blur of stars. At first they're just white smudges against the night sky, but they slowly begin to take form, their shimmering outlines becoming crisper. It could only mean one thing.

"The train's slowing down again," I say, confused.

"Are we in Georgiana already?" Elijah asks.

I shake my head. "We're over a day away."

"Maybe we're stopping for more supplies?" Ash suggests.

Another shadow passes the window, but I barely have time to register it before the carriage door bursts open and five Sentry guards enter, led by Neil—the shaved-headed guard I recognized earlier. The girl with the curly black hair stands up.

"They're over here," she says, pointing at us.

So that's what she was doing earlier? Ratting us out to the Sentry guards!

Neil draws his sword. "Halt! You are under arrest!"

There's a faint *thud* on the roof of the train.

Ash pulls off his false veneers, revealing his fangs. Elijah bares his saber teeth.

Neil takes a step toward us. "There's nowhere to run. You're completely—"

The escape hatch above us is torn off its hinges.

We all begin to scream.

18.

NATALIE

THE WRATH GLARES DOWN at me with menacing yellow eyes, its fangs dripping with venom. Ash pulls me behind him just as the creature folds its wings and drops into the carriage, followed by two females. The male's hands are covered in welts from the acacia wood, but he doesn't seem to notice. The Wraths let out a terrifying howl.

All the children around us stampede into the aisle, tripping over each other in their haste to escape, but the only door out of here is blocked by the Sentry guards who came to arrest us.

The first Wrath—a gigantic creature over seven feet tall with strings of sticky white hair—grabs the black-haired girl and rips her head off in one gruesome movement, spraying hot blood over the carriage. Screams fill the air. The Sentry guards draw their swords and push past the children, knocking them out of the way as they approach the two female Wraths. The animals screech, baring their jagged fangs, and leap at the Sentry guards. Four of the men are felled within seconds, their bodies torn apart like tissue paper, so only Neil is left.

"We have to get the kids out of here!" I say to Ash as the

larger male Wrath drops the body of the headless girl and turns his focus on the group of children huddled by the door.

Ash lunges for him while Elijah attacks one of the female Wraths, plunging his saber teeth into her jugular vein. She howls in pain before crumpling to the floor, dead. The other female whips her head around and fixes her yellow eyes on Elijah. She knocks over the skinny Sentry guard, Neil, with one sweep of her hand, making him drop his sword, and jumps at Elijah.

There's no time to think. I grab Neil's discarded sword and thrust it into the female Wrath's heart. Sticky, hot blood spills over my hands, covering them in red.

"Thanks, I owe you one," Elijah says breathlessly, but I barely register him as I stare down at my bloodstained hands. A memory of Gregory Thompson flashes into my mind. *I killed him just like this, with a sword through his chest—*

"Natalie!"

Ash's gargled voice rouses me out of my stupor. The male Wrath has Ash by the throat. Reflexively, I swing the sword, slashing the Wrath's arm. It lets Ash go, and he falls to the floor. I drop the blade and rush over to him while Elijah finishes the beast with a bite to the neck.

The carriage falls silent.

Neil shakily gets to his feet and surveys the carnage. His gaunt face and shaved head are splattered with blood. All his men are dead, but thankfully, only one of the children—the black-haired girl—was killed. He picks up one of his men's swords just as running footsteps approach the door.

Neil turns to me and holds up his sword. "Sebastian's here to get you."

So that's why the train stopped? I didn't hear the telltale hum of the Destroyer Ship through the train's armored walls.

"Please let us go," I say.

His eyes flicker to the dead Wraths on the floor.

"You know me, Neil. I'm not a bad person," I continue. "We could've let them kill you all while we escaped, but we didn't."

Doubt crosses Neil's face.

"Please," I say.

He lowers his sword.

"Thank you."

Ash gives Elijah a boost through the escape hatch, then lifts himself through before stretching out a hand toward me.

"Wait, your bag!" I say, knowing his mom's keepsake box is in there.

When I turn to grab his duffel bag, my eyes snag on the lifeless Wrath near my feet. My heart slams against my chest as I stare down at its dead, yellow eyes.

Yellow, just like mine.

Suddenly I can't breathe, can't think, can't do anything but listen to the blood pounding in my ears. I can't have the Wrath. *Can I?*

"Natalie!"

Ash's voice penetrates through my terror, dragging me back to reality. I pick up the duffel bag, then take his hand. There's a moment of weightlessness as he lifts me through the hatch, and not a moment too soon: below, the carriage door bursts open and the guards spill into the cabin.

Icy cold air instantly hits my skin as I step onto the train roof, chilling the sweat soaking my body and clothes. My father once told me how deathly cold it gets in the Barren Lands at night, but I didn't truly understand what he meant until now. High above us in the moonlit sky is the Destroyer Ship, its engines omitting that low, ominous hum. I hope it's too dark for them to see us without its searchlights on. Parked across the railway tracks is a Transporter, blocking the train's path.

"Where are they?" Sebastian says, inside the train carriage.

"Escaped during the Wrath attack," Neil replies.

There's a disgruntled growl. *Garrick*.

I hand Ash his bag, which he slings over his shoulder, while Elijah gracefully leaps off the train, landing silently on arid earth. Ash carefully passes me down to Elijah, whose warm hands accidentally slip underneath my jacket as he takes hold of me. His calloused fingers slide over my stomach, making every part of me suddenly hot. The instant my feet touch the ground, he lets me go, and I hastily readjust my jacket, embarrassed. He looks away. There's a soft *thud* as Ash's boots hit the sand. His fingers entwine with mine, then we're running, running, running, as fast as our feet can carry us, trying to get as much space between us and the train as possible before they come after us.

It's so dark, I've never known blackness like it, and I'm running blind, trusting Ash to keep me safe as he steers us past jagged boulders and thorny desert plants that threaten to trip us up.

"Over there!" Ash says, pointing toward something I can't see—it's just black on black—but I know what he means: the canyon I saw out of the train window.

"We can't jump off a cliff!" I exclaim.

"I wasn't suggesting that," Ash replies. "There's a horse trail over there. We can follow it down the ravine to the riverbed."

"Are you mad? It's too dangerous," Elijah says.

Behind us, the Lupines cry out. They've caught our scent.

"We don't have any choice," I reply.

Adrenaline's the only thing keeping me going as my shinbones splinter with every footfall, pushing my body to its limit as we approach the cliff edge.

"They went this way," Garrick calls out.

The canyon is getting closer, closer. We're running too fast to stop.

"Ash, are you sure there's a path?" I say, panicked.

"Trust me." Ash turns sharply to the left, bringing us with him.

I see it! The trail entrance is just visible between the prickly brush and rocks—there's no way you'd notice it unless you knew it was there or had great night vision like Ash. The track is steep and narrow—probably only a yard or so wide, with the jagged cliff face on our left side and a sheer drop on our right. We take it fast, too fast, and the gravel shifts under my feet. I fall. My heels frantically dig into the loose dirt as I slide down the trail, rushing toward a sharp bend in the path. I cry out in fear, knowing there will be nothing but air to greet me, followed by certain, horrible death.

A hand grabs my collar and drags me back just before I fall over. Elijah smirks at me, his dark hair falling around his boyish face.

"We're making it a habit tonight of saving each other's lives," he says, helping me to my feet.

"Thanks," I reply.

Ash pulls me into his arms, holding me tight. "Fragg, fragg, fragg, I thought I'd lost you."

A bloodcurdling scream suddenly pierces the air, and we all look up to see the shadow of a Lupine tumbling over the edge of the cliff and into the abyss below. A moment later, there's a bone-shattering crunch as his body hits the rocks. The other Lupines manage to skid to a halt before they follow him over the edge, kicking sand and grit into the ravine. I spot Garrick at the top of the cliff, silhouetted against the iridescent moonlight. He sniffs the air, then walks in our direction. He's spotted the path, but thankfully not us yet. We shrink into the shadows.

The female Lupine with pink hair joins him.

"They've gone this way," Garrick says.

"Well, let's go after them," she replies.

Garrick flashes a look over his shoulder at the Lupine in a red leather frock coat—I recall Garrick referring to him as Jared at the train station. There's a pause, and I hold my breath. Then:

"No, it's too dangerous. We'll track them at first light," Garrick says.

"But—"

"That's an order, Sasha," he says.

"The boss won't be pleased," Sasha says as they trudge away from the cliff edge.

I exhale. Thank heavens it's dark; otherwise, they certainly would've come after us.

Ash leads the way as we cautiously head down the path, which thankfully gets wider after the first mile. Large rocks and boulders from an old landslide litter the trail. This slows down our progress but, on the plus side, offers us some much-needed cover. The air gets colder the deeper into the ravine we go, and my teeth soon begin to chatter. I'm just glad I'm wearing these woolen clothes, although I'm sure I won't be so thankful for them tomorrow when we're out in the blistering heat. I rub my arms, trying to get some warmth into them. A moment later, something slides over my shoulders. Elijah's coat. I peer over my shoulder at him.

"You'll freeze," I say.

He shrugs. "Don't worry about me, pretty girl."

"Thank you," I say.

"No problem. If it gets too cold, I'll just ask for it back," he adds.

I roll my eyes.

Above us, the Destroyer Ship circles the canyon, its searchlights scanning the deep ravine for us. We duck every time the light swoops near us and try to blend in with the surrounding rocks and desert shrubs. I'm hopeful they won't be able to spot us since they're so high up and we're all dressed in dark clothing, although Ash's blond wig might draw some attention to us.

"Ash, your wig," I say. He yanks off the hairpiece and tosses it over the edge of the trail, raking his fingers through his rippling black hair before quickly removing his blue contacts. The transformation from Human-Ash to Darkling-Ash is instant, and I much prefer this version: dark, deadly and breathtakingly beautiful. Elijah takes this opportunity to remove his own disguise—a cap and glasses—and tucks them into his pocket.

We hike all night. Progress is slow going for the first few hours, as we have to time our movements between the sweeps of the searchlight, but as the night draws on, the Destroyer Ship moves away, looking for us farther up the canyon. Halfway down the trail, we stumble across the Lupine's body. My stomach churns at the sight of his broken, contorted limbs. I catch Ash holding his breath, struggling with his hunger.

"Maybe you should take some of his blood," I say quietly.

Elijah curls his lip, and I shoot him a warning look.

Ash hesitates, but his hunger wins out. He kneels down and dips his fingers in the pool of blood, bringing it to his pale lips. He tentatively tastes it, then gags, wiping his hand on his pant leg.

"Sour," he says.

We leave the dead man and carry on down the path. By the time we reach the river at the base of the canyon, the pink hues of dawn have begun to rise over the valley. I yawn. I've never felt so exhausted, both physically and mentally, as my thoughts keep wandering back to the same topic: the Wrath.

Have I really got the virus? I think about the Darkling bite on my leg. *It can't cross species.* I don't know that for a fact, though, and I have been feeling sick lately. But if I *am* infected, why has it taken so long for the first symptoms to appear? The Darklings in Black City who contracted the Wrath began showing symptoms within a week of infection, so why is it different for me? Is it because I'm human? Will I get any sicker?

Am I going to die?

The thought hits me so hard, I stop walking, and Elijah bumps into my back.

"Oww," he says, rubbing his nose.

"Sorry," I mutter.

Ash turns around to see what the commotion is about. Worry must be etched all over my face, because a crease forms between his brows.

"You okay?" he says.

"Yes, I'm fine," I say, not wanting to worry him. I don't even know if I *am* infected. It's just a hunch. Now more than ever, I wish my mother were here. She may be a little blunt and clinical when it comes to emotional matters, but that's what I need right now—someone with a clear head who can tell me everything is going to be okay. *Where are you, Mom?*

"So what's the plan?" Elijah says.

"Keep walking until it gets too hot, and then find somewhere shaded to hide," Ash says. "As soon as night falls, we'll climb out of the ravine and hike into the nearest town."

"Maybe we should go back to Dusty Hollow," I say. "At least we know where that is."

"No!" Elijah says. "We have to keep moving forward. If we go back, it'll add days to our journey."

Ash looks behind us, and I follow his gaze. The Destroyer Ship is heading upstream, in the direction of Dusty Hollow.

"I think they're expecting us to go there," Ash says.

Elijah starts walking. "Then that's settled. Onward it is."

Ash catches my eye, giving me a worried look. I know what he's thinking. Once we head out of the ravine tonight, there won't be anywhere to hide. If we don't find a town before dawn, then we'll be in serious trouble.

We trudge through the canyon, our spirits low. Thrace feels like a million miles away, the Ora so far out of our grasp. We follow the path of the rushing river, which carves through the ravine, occasionally wading into the shallows or briefly splitting off in different directions to throw the Lupines off our scent when they eventually come after us.

The sun continues to rise over the canyon, lifting away the last tendrils of night and turning the cliffs a burnt shade of orange, the river a brilliant turquoise. Beneath the clear waters, hundreds of small shadows dart about. There's a surprising amount of life around here. Lizards bask in the sun, rattlesnakes slither between the rocks, condors glide across the sky. Elijah flinches every time one flies overhead. Nearby, a herd of wild horses drink by the river edge, their chestnut tails swishing as they swat at mosquitoes. The sound of our footsteps makes them look up, and they immediately gallop away, kicking clouds of dust into the air behind them.

As the heat intensifies, I shrug off Elijah's coat, handing it back to him, while Ash pulls out a black cotton scarf from his bag—the type the Legion guards wear in Black City—and wraps it around his head and neck, so only his sparkling eyes are visible. He must be uncomfortably hot, but he can't risk exposing his skin.

The gorge is remarkably peaceful, the sound of rushing water and the call of wild animals our only companions, and for a while, I forget why we're here as I take in the dramatic scenery, thinking about Polly and how much she would have loved it. I feel her presence everywhere, like she's with me. Perhaps it's just wishful thinking. I hope not. I like to think of her in a better place, not curled up in a ball in a bloodred room.

My reverie is quickly shattered when far in the distance a man howls, his cry echoing throughout the ravine and turning my blood to ice. It can only mean one thing.

The Lupines are coming.

19.

NATALIE

WE CUT ACROSS the river, wading across the cool water until we reach the other bank to try and throw them off our scent. My clothes are heavy with water, weighing me down, and it's a struggle to keep up the pace with Ash. Only the knowledge that the Lupines are after us keeps me going, but every step feels like I'm dragging my body through mud.

"Ash, I need to stop," I say after an hour, unable to take another step.

The Lupines howl again. The sound seems to be coming from both sides of the gorge this time.

"They've split up," Ash says distractedly.

"That's a good thing, right?" I say. "It means they're having trouble tracking us?"

Ash doesn't say anything. Instead he surveys our surroundings, then leads us into the shallow waters of a stream, I presume to cover our scent. We follow it through a crevice in the cliffs to our right, the water splashing around our boots. The light immediately dims as we enter the passageway.

The sandstone walls close in around us the farther we walk,

making me feel claustrophobic. At one point, the passageway gets so narrow, we have to turn sideways to squeeze through the gap. Ash grunts as the stone scrapes at his chest, tearing a button from his jacket.

"Fragg," Ash mutters, getting jammed.

I shove him with my shoulder, wincing as my arm collides with his hard body, and we burst through the other side of the passage. My eyes widen with surprise as we're greeted by a natural pool inside a giant cavern. A large section of the cave's roof has fallen in, so sunlight streams down on its glittering surface. Boulders and green thorny shrubs line the embankment, while silvery fish dart about underneath the jade waters.

We find a place to rest on the stony banks. I lay our coats on the ground while Ash removes his black headscarf, tucking it into his duffel bag.

"I'll take the first watch," Elijah says, walking to the water's edge. He finds a boulder to sit on, and turns his back on us.

Ash and I lie down on the coat-bed, facing each other. Tingly sparks of electricity shoot through me, the way they always do when I'm close to him, because of our Blood Mate connection. He smiles softly at me as his fingers brush over my cheek, making my blood temperature turn up a notch. He closes the gap between us, and we gently kiss. This is all I need: him, me, like this. His hand slips under my top and lightly traces up my spine. I melt against him, my moan muffled against his lips.

"Ahem."

The sound of Elijah's exaggerated cough makes us both start. We stop kissing, and grin sheepishly at Elijah. He shakes his head, then turns around again. Ash holds me against him as we fall asleep.

In my dream I'm walking through the canyon, but it looks

different: the skies are storm gray, the earth as black as cinder, the river rose-red with blood. The sight should repulse me, but instead I feel *thirsty*. Up ahead, Ash kneels by the water's edge, drinking from the blood-river like the wild horses we saw earlier.

"*Ash?*" I call out.

He raises his head, and I gasp. His eyes are sickly yellow, his flesh rotting from his bones. He lifts his hand and points an accusing finger at me.

"You . . . did . . . *this,*" he says.

I shake my head.

"*No, it wasn't me,*" I cry out.

"You . . . did . . . *this,*" he says again, then points to the river.

Confused, I glance down at my reflection in the glassy red water, wondering what he means. My scream echoes around the canyon as a monstrous Wrath stares back up at me—

I start awake, my chest heaving. I blink, trying to erase that image from my mind. The air is warmer than before, suggesting it's close to noon. Have I really been asleep for a few hours? It felt like seconds. Ash's arm is wrapped around my waist. His breathing is ragged, his eyes moving rapidly under his pale lids, clearly trapped in his own terrible nightmare.

"Stop, oh God . . . the flames . . . oh God, oh God . . . Natalie," he says in his sleep, panic rising in his voice. "Natalie!"

"Sshh, it's okay," I whisper soothingly. "You're safe. I'm here. It's not real."

Ash's breathing immediately starts to slow. It breaks my heart that he has to relive his execution every night. I wait a few minutes until his breathing is back to normal, and then carefully move his arm, getting up. I walk over to the water's edge, shading my eyes from the bright shafts of sunlight coming through the hole in the cavern roof. Elijah's standing in the middle of the pool, deep in concentration. He's taken off his shirt to reveal his lean, tanned torso, which glistens with water. I feel embarrassed seeing him half dressed like this, which is ridiculous, considering I've seen him completely naked before, when he was being held captive in Sentry headquarters back in Black City.

He's bulked out a lot since then—which is hardly surprising now that he's not being starved and tortured. His chest and arm muscles are firm and defined, his neck muscles thicker. The beautiful brown markings on his flanks continue down his narrow hips, darting below the waistband of his pants. If memory serves, those markings go all the way to his feet. I flush. Why did I put *that* image in my head?

He's staring at the water with great intensity, his dark russet mane hanging around his face. His tail stirs the water around him in circular motions, coaxing the silvery fish to form a tight ball in front of him. All of a sudden, he thrusts his hand into the water and plucks out a fish. It flaps wildly in his hand, its mouth gaping. He bites its head, killing it, then tosses it onto the embankment by my feet, where another two fish are lying. Elijah wades out of the pool, his black pants slick against his thighs.

"What's this?" I say, pointing toward the dead fish with the toe of my boot.

He grins. "Lunch."

We sit on some flat rocks while he starts to gut the fish with a piece of flint, the sun beating off his back. Up close, his skin has a reddish hue, like the sandstone around us. It's a stark contrast to Ash's alabaster skin. They're like winter and summer. While Ash is tall, Elijah is short. Ash's face is long and angular; Elijah's is square and strong. Even their lips are different—Ash's pale and straight, Elijah's scarlet and curved. I tear my eyes away, realizing I'm staring.

"I think the Lupines have lost our scent," he says. "I haven't heard them in over an hour."

My shoulders relax. I hadn't realized I'd been hunching them.

"I've never seen anyone catch fish with their bare hands before," I say, nodding toward our lunch.

"My brother Acelot showed me how to do it. It's usually the dad's job, but . . ." He sighs, hurt flickering across his features. "He doesn't have much time for me."

I slide off the rock and sit beside him to help prepare lunch. I'm not keen to eat raw fish, but I'm too hungry to argue. My knee accidentally brushes up against his as I lean across him to pick up one of the fish, but he doesn't make any attempt to move away. I squeamishly dig my fingers into the slit Elijah cut into the fish's belly, pulling out its insides.

"You mentioned your mother was a geneticist?" I say, trying to keep my mind off the fish guts.

He nods. "Her work is mostly focused on xenotransplantation—"

"Xeno-what-now?"

"She transplants cells or organs from one species into another," he explains. "Because there are so few Bastets left, organ donation among my people is almost unheard of these days, so she's finding alternatives that we can use if we get sick."

I think about the scar on my chest, from my own heart transplant when I was a kid. I would've died if Dr. Craven hadn't ripped out Evangeline's heart and given it to me.

"I like to help my mom around the laboratory. Well, I did before she . . ." He stares at his hands, which are covered in fish blood. "Do you think they're torturing her, like they did with Polly?"

My heart stings, thinking about my sister. In all honesty, if the Sentry has Elijah's mom, then I'm certain she's being interrogated and tortured. It's what they do. He doesn't need to hear this, though.

"We'll get her back," I say, lightly touching his tanned arm.

He glances down at his arm where my fingers touch him, and a deep flush rises up his neck. He lifts his honeyed eyes and holds my gaze for a lingering moment, and suddenly I'm the one who feels too hot.

"You're getting fish blood on your leg."

I start at the sound of Ash's voice. Flustered, I quickly drop my hand from Elijah's arm. Ash is leaning against the cave wall, his thumb hooked in one of his belt loops. There's a hard edge to his expression I've never seen before. I place the gutted fish on the rock.

"I thought you were asleep," I say.

"Sorry to disappoint you," Ash replies as Elijah puts on his shirt.

My cheeks burn. I'm not sure whether I'm furious at Ash for insinuating that something was going on between me and Elijah or embarrassed that maybe he was right, at least a little bit. Ash stalks over to the water's edge. I go over to him.

"Nothing was going on," I reassure him.

I try to take his hand, but he puts it in his pocket, preventing me.

"Why are you being like this?" I say.

"Sorry," he mutters, finally taking my hand. "I guess it pisses me off when a half-naked guy flirts with my fiancée."

"He wasn't—"

Ash raises a brow.

"Even if he was, it doesn't mean anything," I say. "You know what he's like."

"Yeah," Ash replies. "It's you I'm confused about."

I snatch my hand away from his, definitely angry now.

"You're being ridiculous," I snap. "*Nothing happened.* He was upset, and I was consoling him, that's all. I—"

My words are cut off as we're suddenly plunged into twilight. Confused, I peer up at the gap in the cavern roof just as the air around us starts to hum. My heart freezes as the Destroyer Ship slowly stalks across the sky.

They've found us.

We sprint away from the large hole in the cavern roof and slam our backs against the stone wall, trying to make ourselves invisible. The shadow of the Destroyer Ship blocks out most of the light, the aircraft's engines making the surface of the water vibrate.

"Did they see us?" Elijah whispers.

"We'll know soon enough," I murmur, keeping my eyes fixed on the airship's hatch. If they know we're here, any moment now it'll open up and a Transporter will come down to get us. We wait for second after agonizing second as the Destroyer Ship cruises by overhead. After what seems like an eternity, light floods back into the cavern, and the blue sky returns. It's gone.

I exhale, my nerves shot.

"How many hours until nightfall?" Ash asks.

I check my watch. "Six."

"We'll leave as soon as it gets dark," he says.

We sit down on the coats while Elijah finishes cleaning the fish. Tension bubbles between me and Ash, still upset from our fight. Elijah returns and offers some pieces of fish to me, but I've lost my appetite. Instead, I retrieve the portable digital screen from Ash's bag and watch the news with the sound down low, not wanting to draw attention to our position on the off chance the Lupines are still in the area.

"I'm sorry," Ash whispers to me.

"Me too," I reply.

He loops his arm around me, all forgiven.

The three of us huddle around the digital screen. There's been some fighting in Fire Rapids in the Black River State, plus three rebel strikes against munitions factories in Gallium. Roach, Beetle and Day are certainly sticking to their end of the deal by keeping the Sentry busy while we search for the Ora, but how much longer can they hold them off?

Eventually night falls and it's time to leave. We gather our belongings, exit the cavern the same way we entered and wander along the river for a few hours, passing a herd of resting horses. I keep an eye out for any sign of the Destroyer Ship, but don't see it anywhere.

Ash stops and points toward the cliff. "There's a trail up ahead. We should follow it up to the top of the ravine."

In the moonlight I can just make out the path snaking up the rock face.

"It looks very steep," I say, concerned. "It could take all night to climb."

"Why don't we ride the horses?" Elijah gestures toward the herd of animals.

"You can't be serious," Ash says.

Elijah smirks. "You scared?"

"No," Ash replies, then adds under his breath: "Good luck catching one."

I watch, intrigued, as Elijah cautiously approaches one of

the chestnut mares. The horse clambers to its feet, neighing loudly. He raises his hands.

"Whoa, girl," he says in a strangely hypnotic voice. "I'm not going to hurt you."

The horse scuffs its hoof against the ground, agitated.

"Maybe you should back off," I say.

Elijah ignores me and holds the animal's gaze. He gently places his hand on its nose, and the horse immediately calms down.

"How are you doing that?" I whisper as we approach him.

"It's just a gift my people have," he says.

I let out a panicked yelp when he lifts me onto the horse without warning. Elijah chuckles.

"That wasn't funny," I say.

"Your turn," Elijah says to Ash, his eyes bright with amusement.

Ash clumsily slings his leg over the horse, somehow managing to clamber onto it behind me. The horse lets out a disgruntled snort, but thankfully doesn't buck us. Ash slips an arm around my waist, taking the horse's mane in his other hand. Elijah confidently mounts one of the other horses and rides off without another word. Ash nudges our horse with his heels. It jerks forward.

Riding a horse isn't as scary as I thought it would be. In fact, it feels freeing, exciting, as the wind whips past my face. I squeeze my thighs around its flanks, getting a better grip. We carefully trek up the horse trail. This one is wider and better tended than the one we took to get down into the ravine, which is an encouraging sign. We must be near a settlement of some sort. All the way up, I keep glancing over my shoulder, expecting to see the Destroyer Ship coming for us, but it's nowhere to be seen. *Where are they?*

The journey is much faster on horseback, and we reach the top within a few hours. By now the sky has turned from the deep blue of twilight to the empty black of night. Only the moon and stars offer any sort of light across the wild desert plains. The rocky landscape seems to roll on to infinity, and I start to worry we've made a mistake coming up here. Perhaps we should've stayed in the ravine.

"Which way should we go?" Elijah says.

"That way." Ash indicates a spot on the horizon directly in front of us. "There's something in the distance. It could be a town."

I just pray to heaven that he's right, because if we're not out of the desert before the sun rises, we won't survive long.

20.

NATALIE

I CLING TO the horse's mane as we gallop toward the buildings that Ash saw on the horizon. Elijah rides beside us, expertly steering around the rocks and brush jutting out of the arid earth, despite the poor light. He wasn't exaggerating when he said he had a gift with horses. After several miles, Ash yanks on the mane, and the horse stops so suddenly, I have to fling my arms around its neck to prevent myself from sliding off.

"Are those what I think they are?" Elijah says.

"Yeah," Ash replies flatly.

I look up to see what they're talking about. Up ahead is the familiar ragged shape of Crimson Mountain, silhouetted against the bright, full moon. It's a famous landmark of the Barren Lands, known commonly as the Devil's Fork because of its three peaks, but I'm pretty sure Ash didn't stop to admire it. Then I see what caught his eye. At the base of the mountain is a small town, and beside it is a forest of strange-looking trees. I blink, not understanding. A woodland in the desert? The shapes of the trees start to properly form as I continue to gaze at them: tall, narrow trunks, unnaturally straight branches. A gasp catches in my throat—they're crosses. Hundreds upon hundreds of crosses.

We've inadvertently stumbled across the Barren Lands concentration camp, the place where thousands of Darklings were executed during the first war. My father described it to me only once, but there's no mistaking what it is. He was responsible for sending the Darklings to the camp as part of the government's "Voluntary Migration Scheme" at the start of the war, and the horrors he witnessed here eventually caused him to flip sides and work for the Darklings.

It's one thing hearing about it, and altogether a different matter seeing it for myself. It makes me fully realize the true horror of the Tenth. That camp is large enough to imprison tens of millions of Darklings, humans and Bastets.

Ash nudges the horse forward. We're all deathly silent as we ride through the forest of crosses. Goose bumps prickle my skin, but they aren't just caused by the cold desert night. This place has the haunting feel of a graveyard, and I guess that's what it is: a mass grave for thousands of Darklings. The wooden crosses are charred and covered in soot where the Darklings caught fire in the intense desert heat, just as Ash did during his crucifixion. They must have suffered terribly.

I fix my gaze on my horse's neck, not wanting to look any more. I can't believe my father was responsible for this. After a few minutes, the horses' hooves hit stone, and I know we've reached the main camp. The iron gates are open, which strikes me as odd, but I suppose there was no need for the guards to close them when they abandoned the compound. We ride through. The camp is nestled in the shadow of Crimson Mountain, surrounded by a tall chain-link fence topped with barbed wire. Gun turrets are spaced at even intervals around it, and at every corner of the fence are tall metal pylons with these silver orbs on them.

"What's that sound?" Elijah says, his ears twitching.

"What sound?" I ask.

"That high-pitched noise, like a mosquito buzzing in your ear," he replies, wincing.

"I can't hear anything," I reply.

"Me neither." Ash gestures to one of the pylons. "Maybe those are sonar towers?"

A sonic alarm? That would make sense if Elijah can hear it but we can't.

"Why would they keep them on? No one's here," Elijah grumbles.

"They probably heard you were coming," Ash says, and Elijah glares at him.

We ride deeper into the camp, following a wide road that resembles a main street, with sidewalks and buildings on either side. Most of the buildings are houses, but there is a hairdresser, a tailor, and something that looks like a small convenience store, where the guards probably went to stock up on luxuries like Shine and cigarettes.

"It's not what I expected," Ash mutters as we pass a number of elegant three-story houses done in the same colonial style as the houses found in the Plantation State. Some even have front yards, although the lawns and flowers are long dead. It looks like any pretty suburban street, except that there are iron security grilles in front of all the buildings' windows and doors, and machine gun turrets on their roofs.

"I think this is where the guards slept. They certainly wouldn't live with the Darklings," I say.

I briefly wonder which house was my father's. Did he ever

enjoy a leisurely drink on his front lawn with his friends while a hundred feet away, Darklings were being starved and slaughtered? I can't imagine him doing that, but maybe he did. My father wasn't always a good man.

From my vantage point on the horse, I get a good view of the camp's layout. At the entrance of the compound, where we are now, are the Sentry living quarters, where the guards slept and socialized. About fifty feet away, a set of railway tracks cuts across the road, creating a natural break between the guards' living quarters and the heart of the concentration camp, where the Darklings were imprisoned. Then at the far end of the compound is a large, blocky gray building. I'm guessing that's the main administration building and hospital, where the Sentry employees worked and did their experiments on the Darklings.

"Let's hide out in one of these houses," Ash says, pointing to a colonial house painted a pale pink color. He dismounts and approaches the house. He's about to slide open the iron grille blocking the front door when—

"Stop!" Elijah shouts. "The grilles are electrified."

Ash snatches his hand back.

I strain my ears, listening for the telltale hum of electricity. It's faint, but it's there.

"We'll need to turn the power off before we can go inside," I say.

"Maybe we can turn off that annoying sonic alarm while we're at it," Elijah suggests.

Ash gets back on the horse, muttering thanks under his breath to Elijah. We ride down the street and cross the rusting train tracks, which lead into a railway tunnel carved into the mountain, about thirty feet away. The tunnel entrance has been hurriedly boarded up. I vaguely recall my father mentioning that they used the passageway to bring supplies into the camp from the depot on the other side of Crimson Mountain.

The instant we cross the tracks, the conditions in the camp deteriorate. This is where the Darklings lived. In place of three-story houses are a hundred run-down prison barracks, with no windows, and armored doors. Instead of gardens are open sewers and wooden stocks stained with dark blood.

Elijah covers his nose with his hand, trying not to breathe in the stench. Despite the fact that the camp's been out of use for over a year, the smell of death and decay permeates the air. I try not to think about all the suffering that went on here as we ride toward the administration buildings at the end of the camp, but it's impossible not to imagine the Darklings crammed like sardines in those metal huts, baking in the heat with no air, no food, no hope. I swear I can still hear them crying, but it's just the wind whispering in my ear.

"How did my aunt survive this?" Ash murmurs.

We dismount the horses, and Elijah softly pets their noses, talking to them in that strange, soothing voice, until they lie down and go to sleep.

We enter the main administration building. Inside is cool and still and painted clinical white, with the occasional portrait of Purian Rose hanging on the walls. The offices are still packed with furniture, books, computers, overflowing In trays—it's like the bureaucrats just got up and left halfway through their working day. Maybe they did. I know once the cease-fire was announced, they had to immediately shut down the camp, but I'm surprised they didn't clear out their offices. The only evidence of a cleanup is the remnants of burnt paper in the fireplaces, where I presume the most incriminating documents were hastily destroyed. I guess Rose intended to keep the camp in working order, in case he ever needed to use it again. It was always his plan to continue his persecution of the Darklings.

"Let's find the generator room," Ash says.

We head down a flight of stairs and find ourselves in a hospital wing. There's a strong smell of antiseptic mixed with the metallic tang of blood. Ash swallows, flicking me a hungry look, and I can tell he's struggling to deal with his thirst. It pains me that I can't help him, but I can't risk it. Not until I know for certain if I'm infected with the Wrath. Elijah turns on a few lights, and we hurry onward, locating the generator room at the end of the hallway.

The room is boiling hot, and the sound of the generator's whirring fan is deafening. The silver machine reminds me of a heart, with a complex series of valves and tubes. I circle the generator, trying to work out how to turn it off.

"Which one?" I shout at Ash, indicating three levers: one red, one green, one blue.

"Turn them all off, just to be safe," he says, yanking on the red lever. Elijah picks the green one, I take blue. All the lights in the building go out, plunging us into darkness. The fan slows down, and I can finally hear again.

"It's odd they kept the electricity on when there are no prisoners here," Elijah says in the gloom.

"They probably forgot to turn it off. They seem to have left in a hurry," I reply.

We head outside again and search for the horses, but they're nowhere to be seen.

"Fragg! Where are they?" Ash says.

"Something must've spooked them," Elijah replies.

"Let's not stick around to find out what it was," Ash says.

We sprint back to the stately houses and hurry to enter the

first one we reach. The house is cold and smells of rot, but it's better than being outside in the unforgiving desert. Elijah takes the master bedroom without even asking, leaving me and Ash to sleep in a smaller room. Ash washes his face while I nudge the twin beds together. We climb into bed, fully clothed, and snuggle under the blankets. Somewhere in the distance, a wild dog howls at the moon, and I squeeze closer to Ash.

He draws little circles on the back of my hand with his fingertip. It's such a faint touch, but it makes my body ache for him. Ash props himself up on his elbows so his face is just inches from mine.

"You know, you look surprisingly good in boys' clothes," he says, unbuttoning my jacket. "But I prefer you out of them."

"Nice try, lover boy," I say, stopping him.

"Can't blame a guy for trying," he replies.

He smiles, melting the last of my resistance. I draw him toward me. His kiss is soft, slow, tender. Perfect. I don't stop him this time when he unbuttons my jacket, or the shirt underneath, or even when his fingers tug at the bandages around my chest. The fabric unravels, and I'm a girl again. Ash dips his head, his rippling hair tickling my bare skin as he plants feather-light kisses down my body. I sigh, my fingers digging into the mattress, and for a moment, I forget where I am, forget that I could be sick. Then it hits me.

You might be infected . . . You could kill him . . . Don't risk it . . . Stop . . . Stop—

"Stop," I say, roughly pushing him away.

I know we made love recently, but that was before I suspected I might have the Wrath. I'm not sure if it can be sexually transmitted, but I won't chance it again. I scan his flushed face, looking for any of the telltale signs of the Wrath, but there's no gangrene or yellowing of the eyes. If he had the virus, he would've started showing symptoms by now, like the other Darklings did in Black City. I think it's affecting me differently because I'm human—assuming that I *am* infected. Ash sits on the edge of the bed, rubbing the back of his neck the way he does when he's agitated.

"Sorry, I misread the signals," he mutters.

I stretch a hand out to comfort him, to tell him that I love him, but I snatch it back. What excuse can I give for pushing him away? I don't want to tell him my fears about being ill until I have all the facts. There's no point worrying him unnecessarily. *There's a way I can find out, though.* I can test my blood in the science laboratory I saw earlier. Then I'll know for sure.

"I'm just tired. It's been a long day," I say, buttoning up my shirt.

He nods and kicks off his shoes, getting into bed without saying another word.

"I'll keep first watch," I say.

"Thanks."

"I love you, Ash," I say quietly.

"I love you too," he murmurs, turning his back to me.

I wait until he's asleep before creeping out of bed. I sneak down the corridor and pass Elijah's room. The door is ajar. He's sitting on the window ledge, reading Lucinda's letter. He must be so worried about his mother. Elijah looks up, sensing me.

"Natalie?" he says.

I hurry away before he comes after me, and head outside, glancing toward the wrought-iron gates leading out to the crucifixion fields. Shadows creep through the forest of not-trees, almost like they're slinking toward me, but I know it's just a trick of the eye. Even so, it gives me chills. I imagine millions of tormented Darkling souls haunting their final resting place.

I go straight to the hospital wing in the administration building, using the moonlight to search the laboratory for a microscope, a scalpel and some glass slides. I feel at home in the laboratory. Science was the one subject at school I excelled at. I even got on the Sentry's science Fast Track program and spent some time as Dr. Craven's intern back in Black City. He showed me samples of the Wrath virus, so I know what to look for.

I cut my finger and put a drop of blood on a microscope slide. I prepare the blood smear the way Dr. Craven taught me, and place the slide under the lens of the microscope, flipping on its battery-powered light. The C18-Virus's particles are large enough to see under an optical microscope, so I should be able to spot them if I'm infected. I take a deep breath, then peer through the lens.

Please don't let me find anything, please, please . . .

I twist the focus knob and the cells come into view.

All the typical things you'd expect to see are there: red blood cells, leukocytes, platelets. But there's something else there too. Amid the blood cells are the unmistakable spiky-rimmed virions characteristic of the C18-Virus.

I stagger back, clamping my hand over my mouth to muffle the scream. My legs buckle, and I drop to the cold floor. I draw my knees up to my chest and sit there for about ten minutes as the truth slowly sinks in.

I have the Wrath.

I bury my head in my hands and let out a pained wail. I'm sick, and there's a good chance I'm going to die. *Oh God.* My stomach turns over, and I'm sick into a nearby trash can.

There's not much to bring up—I've hardly eaten in the past few days—and I slump back against the desk, shaking all over. How am I going to break the news to Ash? It's going to kill him.

Think, Natalie. You're in a science lab. This is where the Sentry created the Wrath; perhaps there's a cure. I drag myself to my feet and start scouring the laboratory. I open up filing cabinets, poring through documents, trying to find anything related to the C18-Virus. The Sentry scientists must have left some files on their research, and maybe, if I'm lucky, I'll find some clues about a possible cure. I can't believe they would develop something as deadly as the Wrath virus without also developing a vaccination against it, in case it ever spread to humans. They must've foreseen that as a possibility, surely.

I have no idea how the virus is going to progress; clearly it's not affecting me in the same way as the Darklings, considering it took two months for my first symptoms to surface. I think about all those kids who took the Golden Haze—the ones who didn't immediately die from it, that is—and wonder if they've contracted it too. There haven't been any reports of humans getting sick from the Wrath, but maybe they haven't started showing any symptoms yet.

I sit cross-legged on the floor and start reading through all the documents I've found. I toss file after file onto the ground, my hope fading with each dead end. One of the files catches my eye. It has a bright red butterfly on it, similar to the crates at Dusty Hollow. I scan through the document. It appears to be a lab report about something called Chrysalis. There's no mention of the C18-Virus, but I'm curious about what it could be—knowing the Sentry, it can't be good. I rip off the top sheet and tuck it into my pants pocket to read later.

The rest of the documents are notes from the other sadistic

experiments they did on the Darklings. Actually, I wouldn't call them experiments; they were vile acts of torture, performed by the very men and women who had taken a vow to help the sick. Frustrated, I fling the documents across the laboratory, accidentally hitting Elijah on the leg as he enters the room.

"I wondered where you'd gotten to," he says. "I checked in on you and Ash, and you weren't there. I was worried."

I wipe my eyes, hoping he can't tell I've been crying. "Sorry."

"What are you doing here?" he asks.

I stand up. "Just doing a spot of bedtime reading."

He picks up the documents. "You call this bedtime reading?"

I shrug, tucking a curl behind my ear.

"What were you really doing here?" he presses.

I look into his concerned golden eyes. It's the same look he gave me after we found Polly. We shared that experience, that horror. He was such a support to me then, and I really need some comfort now. I could go to Ash, but I haven't got the strength to deal with the fallout of that devastating conversation. What I want now is someone who can just listen to me, who will let me be selfish and cry and feel what I'm feeling without worrying about how the news is hurting him.

"I've got the Wrath," I blurt out. I show him the bite mark on my leg and explain about how I was bitten. "I've been feeling sick ever since, but I didn't put two and two together until I saw my eyes."

I start to cry again, and Elijah pulls me into his arms, holding me against him. He smells like sandalwood and the earth. His hair is coarse against my cheek, his full lips soft as they whisper assurances into my ear. I allow myself to fall deeper into his embrace, needing the comfort. Elijah tenses slightly, but he doesn't let me go.

"What are you going to tell Ash?" he asks.

"Nothing. At least not yet. He'd be devastated," I whisper.

"You can't keep this from him. He needs to know," Elijah says.

I shake my head. "It'll break his heart."

"Natalie—"

"I just need some time," I say. "You can't say a word to him. Promise me."

Elijah places a finger under my chin, tilting my face up to look into his. Pale moonlight glows off his bronzed skin, accentuating the brown markings down the sides of his chiseled face. His tousled hair has an almost purple tinge to it in this light, and it falls in unkempt waves to his shoulders.

"I promise," he says.

Movement to my right catches my attention. I pull away from Elijah and glance toward the door, but there's nothing there.

"What is it?" he asks.

"I thought I saw something," I say. "It may be nothing, but we should probably go and look."

"Okay." He takes my hand. "Will you be all right?"

"No," I admit.

"Don't worry, pretty girl. We'll find a cure."

"I hope so," I say. If we don't, within a short time, I'll be dead.

21.
ASH

THE COLD AIR hits me like a sucker punch as I sprint outside the administration building. I drag in a deep lungful of it, trying to catch my breath, but my chest is too tight, my throat constricted. There's nothing I can do but fall to my knees as the world shatters around me. The two duffel bags I'd been carrying, belonging to me and Natalie, slide off my shoulder and hit the ground. I brought them with me in case we had to make a quick getaway.

Natalie and Elijah . . .

I can't get the image of the two of them out of my head—his hand cupping her face, her arms wrapped around him.

What are you going to tell Ash?

Nothing. At least not yet. He'd be devastated.

You can't keep this from him. He needs to know.

It'll break his heart . . . You can't say a word to him. Promise me.

I promise.

I don't want it to be true, but the evidence is there.

Natalie's cheating on me.

What other explanation is there? Is that why she pushed me away earlier? Couldn't she stand being touched by me when Elijah was in the next room? I just don't understand. How is it possible they're together? They've only known each other a few days! But that's not true, is it? They met months ago, when he was being held captive in the laboratory in her house. A lot can happen in that time, and wasn't my attraction to Natalie just as fast, just as powerful? *You're Blood Mates—that's different.* Is it? People fall for each other all the time; it's not unique to Blood Mates. I think about how the girls all look at him, and the way he was flirting with Natalie at the pool, and realize it's not so surprising she's attracted to him.

I'm so wrapped up in my thoughts, I don't immediately notice the sweet tang of blood. My hair stirs, sensing it. I pick up the two bags and follow the scent down the side of the administration building. One of the horses is lying on the dirt, its guts ripped out. I suddenly realize why they needed sonic fields. It wasn't to keep people in the camp. It was to keep something *out*.

Around the corner, a door swings open and there's a sound of footsteps. Natalie and Elijah are heading back to the house. They don't realize they're being hunted. We all are. I run back to warn them. No matter how betrayed I feel right now, I can't let anything happen to Natalie.

"Ash, I thought you were asleep," Natalie says, casting a worried look at Elijah.

My blood boils as I glare at Elijah. I would love nothing more than to tear his throat out. "We need to get back inside, right—"

A low growl comes from behind me, and I slowly turn. A shadow stalks out of the gloom, taking form in the moonlight. A jackal. Although it's unlike any wild dog I've ever seen before. It's twice the normal size, with dripping fangs, rotting flesh and terrifying yellow eyes. The jackal snarls, taking a step toward us.

"Natalie, run," I say calmly. "Now."

"I can't," she whispers.

I risk a look over my shoulder. Another five dogs have us surrounded.

"Head back into the building," I say, not taking my eyes off the dogs.

We cautiously edge toward the administration building. The dogs take another step toward us. We reach the door. Elijah fumbles for the handle in the dark.

"Hurry up," I say under my breath.

"I'm trying," he says.

The pack leader studies me with hungry eyes.

They move closer.

"Now would be good, Elijah," I say.

The pack leader howls, and the jackals bound toward us.

"Elijah!" Natalie exclaims.

The handle clicks, and we tumble through the open door. I kick it shut just as the dogs reach us. They slam into the door, splintering the wood. I scramble to my feet and twist the lock. The animals howl and snarl on the other side, their claws scratching at the wood, trying to get in.

"Did you see their eyes?" Elijah says.

"They're infected—they've turned into some kind of Wrath Hounds," I confirm. "They must've eaten contaminated Darkling meat."

It's the only explanation I can think of, although I didn't realize the virus could jump species. But the how or the why is the least of my concerns right now. There's a loud thud as one of the Wrath Hounds leaps at the door.

"Did they bite you? Are you hurt?" Natalie stretches a hand out toward me, but I flinch away as if her touch were fire. How can she act like she cares about me, after what I saw?

She furrows her brow. "Ash?"

"I'm fine," I say. "We need to get to the roof before they find out how to get in."

"I'm going to turn on the electricity. I'll meet you upstairs," Elijah says, darting off before we can stop him.

Natalie and I run in the opposite direction, in search of the stairwell. We find it just as there's the sound of shattering glass. The Wrath Hounds have found another way in. Natalie tugs on my arm, stopping me.

"We can't leave Elijah," she says.

"Forget him," I snap, dragging her farther up the stairs.

"Ash, what's gotten into you?"

She looks up at me with beautiful blue eyes, which are so full of concern for *him*. Pain rips at my heart.

"Will that make you happy?" I ask quietly.

She looks at me, bewildered. "Yes. I don't want him to get hurt."

Her words tear through me, but as upset as I am, I'll do anything for her—even save the boy she's cheating on me with.

I release her hand and thrust our duffel bags into her hands.

"Fine, I'll go get him," I say. "You head to the roof."

I don't wait for her to answer, just race down the stairs in search of Elijah. I run past the office with the broken window. One of the dogs must've scratched itself on the glass, because there are drops of foul-smelling blood on the floor. The scent leads me all the way to the generator room.

The place is boiling hot and pitch-black, and I'm grateful for my night vision. I catch glimpses of five shadowy creatures lurking down the walkways, prowling toward Elijah, who is standing at the end of the room, searching for the levers to turn the power back on.

For a moment, I consider leaving Elijah with the jackals, but quickly cast that thought aside and look around for a weapon. Normally I'd use my fangs, but I can't risk infecting myself. I yank some steel piping off the wall and quietly stalk the jackals as they in turn hunt Elijah.

He finds one of the levers and pulls it, turning the generator fan back on. The sound startles the Wrath Hounds, and they howl, the noise echoing around the room, making it hard to pinpoint the source. Elijah looks about him, fear etched on his face. Bastets have great hearing, but their eyesight isn't as good as a Darkling's.

A Wrath Hound scurries across the walkway behind him, ready to pounce.

"Behind you!" I call out in the dark.

He turns just as the dog leaps toward him. Elijah takes it down in one swift movement, snapping its neck.

"Three o'clock!" I shout as another dog springs for him.

The animal lands on him and they fall to the floor. Elijah grips the dog's throat, holding its gnashing teeth at bay as I dash toward him. I swing the steel pipe, cracking the animal's skull. It rolls off Elijah, and I help him to his feet.

"There's three more," I say to him, scanning the room. "I'll hold them off—you turn on the electricity."

Elijah races back to the generator while two of the Wrath Hounds bound toward us, their fangs dripping. I strike one of them, the pipe easily tearing through its gangrenous flesh. Warm blood sprays out of its wound. The second jackal turns on its fallen comrade and starts tearing at its flesh, overtaken by a feverish bloodlust.

Elijah finds the second lever, and all the lights blink on.

"Ash!" he calls as the last Wrath Hound lunges for me.

There's no time to block the attack, and I'm knocked off my feet. The pipe rolls under the generator. The Wrath Hound is inches from my face. I struggle to hold the creature back as it snaps at me with its deadly fangs, my fingers slipping through its rotting flesh.

"Help me!" I yell.

My arm muscles start to shake from the strain. I can't keep this up much longer.

"Elijah!" I say, panicked.

There's a *clunk* as another lever is pulled, and the Wrath Hound immediately rolls off me, whimpering as it writhes around the floor in agony. I can't hear it, but the sonic shield must be on again. A shadow falls over me. *Elijah.*

"You alive?" he asks.

I get to my feet.

"That was close," he says, grinning. "I thought we were—"

I punch Elijah in the face.

He lets out a pained yell as blood squirts out of his nose. The bones in my hand rattle, and I know my knuckles are going to be bruised for the next few days, but it was worth it.

"What did you do that for?" he says through his bloodied hands.

"You know what that was for," I snarl, shoving him against the generator. "Leave her alone. She's *mine.*"

"What?" he says.

I don't answer. I'm not interested in hearing his excuses. I pick up the pipe and kill the last two Wrath Hounds, pretending their heads are Elijah's.

"I think they're dead," he says, dabbing his nose with his sleeve.

I take a deep breath, trying to calm myself. We study our handiwork.

"Weren't there six dogs outside?" Elijah asks.

He's right; there are only five hounds here, which can mean only one thing.

"Natalie!" we say in unison.

We run out of the generator room, through the corridors and up the stairs. My heart is racing. *Please let her be okay, please, please.* We burst onto the roof. It's unnaturally dark out here, as something blocks out the moonlight. At first I don't see Natalie, but then I make out a shape slumped on the flat roof. Blood stings my nostrils.

The night becomes still. I can't move.

Elijah rushes over to the figure.

"It's the dog! Just the dog!" he says.

I let out a sigh of relief.

"Natalie?" I call.

"Sshh," she whispers, walking out from behind a chimney stack. She points upward.

We all turn our heads up to the sky. At first I don't know what she's referring to, then I realize what's blocking out the moonlight. My blood turns to ice.

The Destroyer Ship.

22.
NATALIE

"**IT ARRIVED** a few minutes ago," I whisper. "I don't think we've been spotted yet."

Down below, in the center of the compound, there are two Lupines writhing on the ground.

"Garrick and Sasha?" Ash whispers to me.

I nod. "They collapsed about a minute ago. I don't know why."

"That's when we turned on the sonic shield," Ash replies. "It seems to affect canines."

"How do we get out of here?" Elijah asks. I notice his nose looks slightly swollen. He must've been injured while fighting the jackals.

I point toward Crimson Mountain, which is a few hundred feet away, to our left. At the base of the mountain is the boarded-up railway tunnel I noticed earlier, when we entered the compound.

"I think the Sentry used the tunnel to transport supplies into the camp," I say. "It should lead to a depot."

"Let's go before they realize Garrick and Sasha are in trouble," Ash says.

He takes his duffel bag from me, while I carry mine. He refuses to meet my eye as he rises to his feet. We sneak back inside the administration building. I reach out my hand toward Ash, but he ignores it. I lower it. Is he mad at me for some reason? He can't be upset that I rejected his advances earlier, surely. Ash isn't like that. I get a terrible sinking feeling. Did he overhear my conversation with Elijah? But even if he had, that wouldn't explain why he'd be angry at me. Unless . . . *unless he's not mad at all.* Maybe he's repulsed by me? I never considered that as a possibility; I thought he'd be devastated by the news, not sickened by it. Humiliation burns at my cheeks.

Ash edges the front door open and peers outside, just as a searchlight comes on from the Destroyer Ship. He swiftly shuts the door. The blue light shines through the dusty windows, filling the corridors with its eerie glow. We crouch down as the light scans the building once, twice, before moving on.

"Now," Ash says, opening the door.

We run outside and hurry for cover between the barracks. They don't offer much protection; if the searchlight turns on this area, we'll be spotted immediately. Ash takes the lead as we dart from building to building. The light sweeps toward us, and we slam our backs against the wall. I shut my eyes, whispering a prayer. It passes by, just missing us. Adrenaline courses through my veins, making my pulse race. Ash takes my hand, sensing my panic, and immediately my heartbeat slows. His touch means more to me than he realizes. Perhaps he simply didn't notice my outstretched hand earlier, and that's why he didn't take it?

We run to the tunnel, hand in hand, Elijah following. The searchlight fixes on something in the center of the compound: it's found Garrick and Sasha. We have a few minutes at most before a Transporter comes down for them and the area is crawling with Sentry guards. I don't understand why they didn't bring the guards down with them in the first place, though. It doesn't make much sense, but I'm not going to complain about a bit of good fortune.

We reach the tunnel, and Ash and Elijah start pulling at the wooden boards nailed in front of the entrance. Above us, a hatch opens in the Destroyer Ship and something metallic streaks across the night sky. A Transporter.

I help Ash and Elijah with the boards, yanking at them with all my might, ignoring the splinters digging into my hands.

Dust stirs in the air as the Transporter lands nearby.

"Hurry!" Elijah says, pulling at the wood.

He tears off another plank, creating a hole just big enough for us to squeeze through. Ash and I toss our bags through the gap, and then the three of us clamber through the hole, dropping to the other side just as bright lights flood the camp. We don't hang around to find out if we've been spotted. We sprint into the depths of the pitch-black tunnel. I've never known darkness like it—I'm totally blind. My feet keep getting caught in the wooden ties of the railway track, making me stumble more than once. I run my hand along the stone wall until my fingers find a cold, hard metal railing about four feet from the ground, and I cling to it, trying to rein in my terror.

There's a loud grumble, and at first I'm worried we're having a cave-in. Then Elijah gives a small laugh.

"Was that your stomach, Darkling?" he whispers in the dark.

"I haven't eaten in days," Ash replies through gritted fangs. He leans against the wall for a moment, letting out a low groan as his stomach rumbles again. Yet again, I wish I could do something to help.

"Are you all right?" I ask him.

"I'll be fine." He staggers onward into the blackness.

Somewhere deep in the passageway, I hear the chatter of bats and just pray they're not infected with the Wrath as well. I can't deal with flesh-eating bats and man-eating dogs all in one night. My eyes start to adjust to the dark, not so much that I can see things clearly, but enough to differentiate between the shades of black: lighter black is air; darker black is the curved tunnel walls. Even so, I keep my hand firmly grasped around the cool railing as I follow Ash.

I'm starting to get the vibe that he doesn't know I'm ill. It's just the way he's acting around me—he seems concerned, but only the normal amount you'd expect given our predicament, not "my fiancée is going to die of a horrific virus" kind of worried. I don't think he overheard my conversation with Elijah earlier. If he had, I'm certain he would've mentioned it by now.

In one way it's a relief—I can spare us both the heartache for a while longer, until I find the strength to tell him. But eventually, I will have to break the news to him, and that's not a conversation I want to have. I know that as soon as the words fall out of my lips, it'll mean the end of our relationship. I'll *have* to leave him, not just for his own safety, but because it'll be the kindest thing to do. I can't let him watch me rot and die the way his mother did. My heart cramps at the thought of losing him, and Ash sucks in a breath, feeling my pain. That's the only problem with being Blood Mates; every time my heart bleeds, he feels it too. He looks over his shoulder again at me, his eyes glimmering with concern.

We walk through the dark tunnel for hours, until I think I'll go mad if we don't get out of here soon. Thankfully, I don't think we're being followed. I'm sure we would've heard them by now.

"What do you think the others are doing right now?" Elijah asks.

Ash stops and rummages around his bag, pulling something out. "I forgot I had this, sorry," he says. There's a flick of a switch and immediately the portable digital screen's bright light fills the tunnel. The sudden change in light hurts my eyes, but it's a relief to be able to see again. We listen to the latest news reports, while Ash uses the digital screen like a flashlight.

For over an hour we hear story after story about members of Humans for Unity being rounded up and executed. The Sentry's hit rebel factions in Fire Rapids, Red Winter, Lithium, the list goes on. I quickly do the sums. That's over two hundred people, dead. The numbers are really shocking when you consider Purian Rose only declared war on us a few days ago. If things continue on at this rate, the rebellion won't last long. I glance at Ash. His face is illuminated by the bluish glow of the digital screen. His mouth is set in a grim line. He's obviously thinking the same thing as me: we have to find the Ora, and fast.

"Can we take a break?" Elijah says. "My feet are killing me."

I don't want to stay in the tunnel forever, but I'm sweating from exhaustion, and I know Ash can't carry on much longer, given the way he's clutching his stomach. We find a recess in the tunnel wall and sit down, using our coats as pillows. Ash puts the digital screen on the ground between us so we can share the light.

"I'm going to use the little girls' room," I say, hurrying down the tunnel until I find another recess in the wall. It's much darker down here without the light of the digital screen, and I try to be quick, spooked out by the idea of rats, cockroaches and heaven knows what else scurrying about in the gloom.

When I'm done, I rush back toward Ash and Elijah, tripping

on a railway strut in my haste. I crash to the ground, cutting my hand and arm on a broken wooden tie. Wincing, I sit up and check my wound. A large splinter is sticking out of my arm. I bite my lip as I pull out the splinter of wood. Blood oozes out of the wound, and I gingerly get to my feet, keeping my arm elevated.

"Ash? Elijah?" I call out, unable to see them. "I've hurt myself. I—"

There's a terrifying growl, which echoes down the tunnel, chilling me down to my marrow. Something lunges toward me in the dark, hitting me with such force that all the wind is knocked out of my lungs. I can't even scream as the creature yanks my head to one side, exposing my throat. All I think is *Wrath Hound*. But then I notice the cotton of a shirt, the scent of bonfires and musk, the warmth of Ash's breath spilling over my skin. My heart clenches with fear, for me, for him.

"Don't!" I scream as his fangs prick my skin.

Suddenly his weight lifts off me. There's a loud crunch of bones hitting stone as Elijah flings Ash against the tunnel wall. Blood pumps out of the wound in my arm. Ash snarls and pounces at me again, but Elijah swiftly hooks an arm around Ash's throat, holding him back. Ash's boots kick at the dirt as he struggles against Elijah, but the Bastet is too strong. Eventually, Ash's thrashing slows down, until finally he stops, subdued, his bloodlust gone. Even so, Elijah doesn't let go.

I check my neck, relieved to find Ash didn't puncture my skin.

"Are you okay?" Elijah asks me.

"Yes," I say, although the crack in my voice gives me away. *Ash attacked me.* How can I possibly be okay? I know Darklings drink human blood, but it's the first time he's ever tried to feed on me like I was prey.

"He's hungry, and the smell of your blood made him crazy," Elijah says quietly as I edge toward him. "He didn't know what he was doing. You might want to bandage that arm, though."

I go back to our recess and find Ash's black headscarf in his bag. I rip a length of material from the headscarf and wrap it around my arm in an attempt to bandage it. It's not perfect, but it stems the flow of blood and seems to calm Ash down a little. I sit on the pile of coats, still shaken.

"I'm sorry," Ash manages to say.

"I know. It's okay," I reply, and then look at Elijah. "We need to get him some food. I heard some bats earlier. Maybe we can catch one of those . . . ?"

Elijah shakes his head. "Even if we could catch one, it wouldn't be enough to feed him."

Tears sting my eyes, and I wipe them away, hating the fact that I can't help the boy I love. The Wrath isn't just killing me; it's killing him. Without saying another word, Elijah bites his wrist, causing blood to spill out of the puncture wounds, and holds his bleeding arm up to Ash.

"I'd rather die," Ash spits out.

"You will die if you don't eat," Elijah replies.

"Won't your blood kill him?" I say.

"No. Only Bastet venom is toxic to Darklings. Our blood can sustain them," he says.

I turn to Ash, keeping my voice soft, pleading. "Please drink, Ash. For me?"

Ash briefly shuts his eyes and then reluctantly takes Elijah's arm. He places his lips over the puncture wounds and begins to feed, tentatively at first, then with more fervor. A groan forms in his throat, and he draws Elijah's arm closer, drinking greedily. Elijah sways slightly, but he doesn't pull away. Blood spills over Ash's lips, dripping onto the earth. He twists his fingers through Elijah's hair and yanks his head to one side, sinking his fangs into Elijah's neck. A sigh escapes Elijah's lips as the Haze floods his bloodstream. He droops against Ash, his breathing labored.

"That's enough," I say after a minute, when I know Elijah can't take any more.

"No," Ash snarls, his lips berry red. "More."

"Let him go," I say firmly.

He releases Elijah, who falls back against the wall, drugged and drained. Ash's thirst is still evident, his eyes wild and predatory. Just like the eyes of the Wrath that murdered my father. He sees the fear on my face, and it's like a switch is flicked off inside him, the animal tamed. Ash wipes his mouth and somehow manages to get to his feet. He mutters something about needing to go to the restroom and heads farther up the tunnel, although I know he's just trying to get away from me.

When Ash is gone, I tend to Elijah, checking his pulse. It's slow but steady.

"Are you all right?" I ask him, ripping another strip off the black headscarf and wrapping it around his bloodied arm.

"Everything's sparkling," he says dreamily.

"That's the Haze. It makes you feel funny," I reply. That's an understatement. I remember the time Ash accidentally gave me a hit of Haze—the euphoria and visions were intense. I'm actually a bit jealous of Elijah right now. I could do with a little happiness, even if it is chemically induced. The pain of my sister's death and the grief over my own illness aches through me, weighing me down.

I unbutton his shirt so I can wipe the congealing blood off his neck and chest. Elijah softly purrs, enjoying my touch as I dab the rag over his toned muscles. I try to ignore him, knowing he's under the influence right now and can't help himself. Still, it feels illicit, wiping his bare chest when my fiancé is nearby.

"Thanks for helping Ash," I say quietly when I'm done patching him up.

"Anything for you, pretty girl." Elijah raises a hand and strokes my cheek. "I love you."

I flinch away from him, struck by his words. *It's the Haze,* I remind myself. *It makes people think they're in love with you when they're not.* Elijah falls asleep, a smile on his sensuous lips, and I know he'll have good dreams. I doubt I'll sleep a wink.

There's movement behind me, and I turn. Ash silently walks out of the shadows, his eyes glittering. Grief is written all over his face. He doesn't look at me, just sits down on the ground and leans back against the wall, shutting his eyes.

"Will he be all right?" Ash says after a moment.

"He'll have a killer headache when he wakes up, but he'll be fine."

Ash gives a faint nod, then turns his face from me, but not before I see the tear slide down his cheek.

23.

ASH

THE LIGHT of the digital screen dims slightly as the battery starts to run out of juice. I've been watching the news all night, trying to keep my mind busy, but it hasn't worked. All I can think about is how Elijah declared his love to Natalie, confirming my fears that she's cheating on me with him. I turn off the digital screen to conserve the last of its energy.

Natalie's head is on my lap. I gently brush her blond hair away from her face, grief aching through me. Despite my pain, anger and humiliation, I still love her. I can't blame Elijah for being so infatuated with her—she's incredible. *Does she feel the same about him?* Natalie seemed startled when he said he loved her, so maybe she doesn't feel as strongly for him as he does for her. That gives me hope that maybe I haven't lost her yet.

Elijah stirs, waking up. He sits up and groans, cradling his head. Haze Headaches are a common side effect when you've been injected with Darkling venom. The puncture wounds on his arm and neck are still raw, making my thirst return with a vengeance. I try not to think about how good he tasted. Bastet blood isn't like anything I've ever had before. It's such a rush. *I want more.*

"Don't get any ideas, Darkling," he says, reading my mind.

"I can say the same thing about you." I must look pretty appetizing to a hungry Bastet right about now.

He rolls his eyes. "Don't flatter yourself. You're not my taste at all."

"No, blondes are more your thing, aren't they?" I reply.

He looks at Natalie, then back up at me, a furrow between his brows.

"I'm not interested in Natalie," he says.

"Don't lie to me. I saw you with her in the laboratory. She made you promise not to tell me something that would hurt me. So if you're not trying to sleep with her, what is it?" I demand.

Elijah glances at Natalie again, clearly torn about something.

"Well?" I say, my anger rising. *Why won't he just admit it?* "Last night, you said you loved her."

He seems genuinely surprised by this. "I did? That was just the Haze talking."

"Bullcrap." A horrible thought strikes me. "How long has it been going on between you two?"

Natalie released Elijah from the laboratory months ago. Have they been secretly keeping in touch ever since, while I've been busy working with Roach and Sigur? The thought, the betrayal, is too much to comprehend.

Natalie's roused by my raised voice, and her eyes sleepily blink open.

"Everything okay?" she says.

I stand up, my body shaking with rage. "Everything's fine. We need to go."

I'm halfway down the tunnel by the time they catch up with

me. Natalie tries to take my hand, but I just can't hold it, not yet. The pain is too raw. We walk down the railway tunnel in complete silence. Anger and humiliation surge through me, poisoning my mind. It's one thing to think Natalie and Elijah hooked up over the past few days because they shared an intense physical attraction—that I can just about handle. But it's altogether a different matter if they've been sleeping together for months. That would mean they have genuine feelings for each other, that they're in a *relationship*. That, I could never forgive.

What I don't understand is why she agreed to marry me if her heart doesn't belong to me anymore. Was it out of a sense of duty? Fragg, does she feel *sorry* for me? I picture the burns on my arms and shoulders, the night terrors that plague my dreams, and realize she must pity me. Elijah does seem like an attractive prospect by comparison.

The tunnel exit can't come soon enough, and I'm relieved when we reach it within the hour. We pull back one of the wooden planks boarding up the exit, allowing us to slip outside. Despite the blistering heat prickling my skin, the daylight is a blessing. *Anything* is better than being trapped underground with Natalie, Elijah and my thoughts.

I spoke too soon.

We surface on the rim of a bustling rail and truck depot. There must be fifteen train tracks feeding in from all directions, plus scores of cargo trucks hauling long metal containers. On the roofs of the depot buildings, digital screens show the latest news from SBN. Sentry guards busily unload the cargo from the trains onto the trucks, ready to be transported to their final destination. A lot of the cargo seems to be weapons, medical supplies and food.

Hovering above the depot is a familiar-looking Destroyer

Ship. My stomach plummets. We've walked straight into the lions' den.

We slink back into the tunnel, out of sight. When Natalie said the Sentry guards used the tunnel as a rail link to the camp, I hadn't realized that the depot on the other end of it would still be in use. But of course it would be—it was stupid of me not to figure this out earlier. Still, we weren't faced with many options at the time.

"Should we head back to the camp?" Natalie whispers. "If the Destroyer Ship's here, they're probably waiting for us to show up."

I shake my head. "If they were waiting for us, there would be a hundred guards patrolling the tunnel at this end. They don't know we're here—they must think we escaped back into the desert."

"So why are they here?" Elijah asks.

"Refueling?" I suggest.

"We should go back to the camp," Elijah says.

"And go where after that?" I reply. "We still have no means of transport, we're miles from anywhere, and I can't survive in this heat for long. No, we stay here. We just have to find a way to get on one of those trucks undetected."

"How do you propose we do that?" Elijah says.

"Throw you out as bait?" I suggest.

Elijah scowls and Natalie gives me a stern look.

I scan the depot from our vantage point within the railway tunnel, although my view is partially blocked by crates and up-turned carts abandoned in front of the exit. I watch as groups of Sentry guards load crates onto rows of trucks, parked side by side, with just a few feet between them. The wooden boxes all have different locations printed on them: Centrum, Athena, Gallium, Leopolis, Thrace—*yes! Some luck at last.*

"There," I say, pointing to the green truck where the crates marked for Thrace are heading. "We'll escape on that."

"We don't have any disguises," Natalie says. "They'll recognize us."

"Then we just have to do this the old-fashioned way and stay out of sight," I say.

We cover ourselves in sandy dirt from the cave floor, darkening our skin and clothes, in hopes that this will serve as some sort of camouflage. I flinch slightly at the sight of the black cloth around Natalie's forearm, remembering what I did. She rolls down her shirt sleeve, covering it.

"We ready?" I say.

"No," Elijah mutters.

Natalie nods.

I cautiously approach the tunnel exit. About twenty feet away, three Sentry guards are loading cargo onto a red truck destined for Gallium. That's our best shot at cover. The trucks are parked close together, so we can easily run from one to another, hiding under them until the coast is clear. I'll need to distract the guards, though. Scanning the area, I spot a pile of smaller crates to the right of the truck, each with a green cross and the word FRAGILE printed on it. Medical supplies. *Perfect.* I grab a stone from the ground, weighing it in my hand. I've got only one shot at this. Taking a deep breath, I lob the rock at the pile of crates. It smashes into the middle box, and the medical supplies crash to the earth.

The guards all run to assess to the damage, shouting at each other. We've got mere seconds to get across the dusty path.

"Go," I say.

We sprint out of the tunnel, bursting into the blazing sunlight. Adrenaline pumps through my veins, and my mind is thinking just one thing: *RUN!* We keep our heads low, darting between the crates and upturned mine carts for cover. The Sentry guards are still fighting over who stacked the medical supplies, blaming each other.

Just as one of the guards finds the stone, we reach the truck. The guard inspects the stone in his hand, his brow creased. I usher Natalie under the vehicle. Elijah's next.

The guard starts to turn.

Fragg!

I dive, rolling under the truck just as the guard looks in our direction. My heart crashes against my chest as the guard walks over to the vehicle. *Did he see me?* A pair of brown leather boots stops directly in front of us. I hold my breath. There's a long pause. Eventually: "Come on, you lot, we haven't got all day," he calls over to his two colleagues.

I exhale.

There are loud clangs above our heads as they continue to load the heavy crates into the truck.

"I can't believe we've been lumbered with shipping this fragging crap to Gallium, given all the trouble there," Brown Boots moans to one of his colleagues.

"What's going on in Gallium?" his colleague asks.

Elijah impatiently taps my shoulder and motions for us to leave, but I shake my head. I want to hear what the guard says.

"Fragg, Spinner, don't you ever watch the news? The Darklings broke out of the ghetto. It was a bloodbath," he says. "Why do you think they need all these weapons and medical supplies?"

When did this happen?

"I didn't really think about it," Spinner says.

"You don't think, period," Brown Boots says.

"I heard rumors that Phoenix was there," the third guard chimes in. "Apparently he single-handedly killed fifty guards."

"I heard it was a hundred," Brown Boots says. "Ripped their throats out and drained all their blood."

"No kidding?" Spinner says nervously.

My mind reels with this news. The Darklings have staged a rebellion in Gallium, the capital of the Copper State? This is *huge*. The Copper State is where all the munitions factories are located. With the rebels causing havoc in the state and Emissary Vincent executed, the place will be in chaos. This is . . . this is brilliant!

I wonder who spread the rumor that I was involved in the uprising. Probably Roach. It's a good plan. Not only does it keep the Sentry off my tail as I search for the Ora, but it's made the guards scared of me. Sometimes the myth of a person is more powerful than the real thing. Little do they know that the real Phoenix is hiding under their truck, covered in dirt and frightened as hell.

"Did you hear what Pearson's got in his cargo hold?" Spinner says.

"I'll believe it when I see it," Brown Boots replies. "He's always making up crap. One time he said he shot a Lupine, and it turned out to just be some guy's dog."

The third guard laughs. "Yeah, and what about that time he claimed he took on a whole nest of Wraths?"

"No, this is real this time. He said he caught it two days ago in Fire Rapids," Spinner says a little defensively.

Fire Rapids? Why does that name ring a bell?

"If it's true, why hasn't he shown it to anyone?" Brown Boots challenges.

"He was worried someone would try and steal it."

"He's lying," the third guard says.

"If he's lying, why would he have called Sebastian Eden down here?" Spinner says.

"Because Pearson's as stupid as you are," Brown Boots replies.

Brown Boots and the third guard chuckle heartily while Spinner mutters curses under his breath. Natalie gives me a questioning look. That explains why the Destroyer Ship is overhead. It's a relief knowing for certain they're not here waiting for us, but whatever is in that cargo hold must be pretty important if Sebastian's paused his search for us to check it out.

As they continue to load the cargo, the guards' leather boots kick up plumes of red dust, which tickles our noses. Natalie covers her nose just as a sneeze escapes. She gives me a panicked look.

"Did you hear something?" Brown Boots says. I wave at Natalie and Elijah to move. We crawl across the sand to the truck parked a couple of feet away, just in time to avoid being spotted as Brown Boots peers under the red vehicle, where we were hiding.

"Huh," he mutters, shaking his head.

We scamper under the next vehicle, keeping out of sight, and after a few heart-stopping minutes, we make it to the green truck heading to Thrace. It's parked next to an armored cargo train, but the cargo isn't medical supplies: it's prisoners. People scream and groan inside the carriages, their hands stretching out of the barred windows, begging passing guards to free them or give them water.

"We have to help them," Natalie says.

"We'll be spotted," Elijah replies.

A Sentry guard opens the truck door and climbs in. We don't have much time.

"Ash, look!" Natalie whispers, pointing to three figures walking alongside the cargo train, heading right toward us. It's Sebastian and Garrick, plus a third man—a Sentry guard, who I'm assuming is Pearson.

The guards scurry out of Sebastian's way as he's led toward one of the carriages. The silver buttons on his Tracker uniform glisten in the sunlight as he walks. His head and face are both clean shaven, highlighting the rose tattoo above his left ear. The ink has darkened from a vivid scarlet to a deep mahogany where his olive skin has caught the sun.

By comparison, Garrick looks bedraggled and tired, and there's blood around his ears where the sonic shields must have burst his eardrums. His expensive clothes are torn on one side, and I'm guessing he came face-to-face with a pack of hungry Wrath Hounds. They must've turned off the sonic shields like we did, not realizing what they were for. Only the guards who worked at the Barren Lands camp would've known about the jackals. It would explain why they didn't find us in the tunnel; they probably didn't stick around long enough to thoroughly search the area.

He sniffs the air and peers in our direction, his eyes squinting against the desert sun. We slink deeper into the shadows.

"Do you think he saw us?" Elijah whispers.

My muscles tense. It's dark under the truck, and we're covered in dirt, so it's unlikely he can see us. I'm more worried that he can smell us, although the stench of the prisoners in the cargo train should help camouflage our scent. Garrick continues to look in our direction for what seems like an eternity before turning his attention back to Sebastian and the Sentry guard. The tension in my muscles uncoils.

"This had better be worth it," Sebastian snaps at Pearson.

"Oh, it's worth it," the guard says.

He slides open the door of one of the carriages, revealing the cargo inside.

Natalie clamps a hand over her mouth, stifling her gasp.

Inside the carriage, chained and hanging from the ceiling, is Sigur.

That's why Fire Rapids sounded familiar. It's where Sigur said he was going when we discussed our escape plans. His wings are shredded, and he's been badly beaten, his white hair soaked through with red, his face almost unrecognizable. For a fleeting moment, I hope Sebastian won't be able to identify him.

Sebastian steps into the carriage and grips Sigur's face, turning it from side to side, inspecting it closely. A cold, frightening smile breaks out on Sebastian's lips.

"My day just got a lot better," he says.

Sigur spits in Sebastian's face. The Tracker punches him in return. Sigur grunts, bending double.

"Bring the nipper up to the Destroyer Ship," Sebastian says, wiping the spittle off his cheek.

Pearson stops the Lupine. "Hey, not yet. What about my reward?"

Garrick growls, and the guard recoils.

Sebastian draws his sword, and with two swift movements, cleaves off the remains of Sigur's wings. His pained howl echoes throughout the depot as dark blood pours down his back.

Sebastian tosses the wings at Pearson. "There's your reward. Now, untie that creature and bring him to the ship." He steps off the train.

Pearson and Garrick untie the chains holding Sigur up. He crashes to the ground, exhausted and broken. His head lolls in our direction, and alarm registers on his face when he spots us hiding under the truck.

The truck's engine begins to rumble. They're about to leave.

"We need to go," Elijah whispers.

"We have to save Sigur," Natalie replies.

If I'm going to rescue him, now is the time to do it.

The engine revs.

This is our best chance to get to Thrace.

My eyes lock with Sigur's.

He's your Blood Father.

Sigur shakes his head slightly, understanding.

"Come on," I say to the others, and run to the end of the truck, climbing on board.

They hurry onto the vehicle after me. We duck for cover behind the towers of crates as a third guard approaches the truck. He slams the doors, blocking out the world, but not before I've heard Sigur's scream.

PART III

MOON STAR

24.
NATALIE

THE TRAILER SWAYS as we travel along the bumpy desert road, the crates of food and military supplies threatening to topple on us at any moment. We find a recess in the crates and make ourselves comfortable, since we're going to be here for at least a day, if not two. I retrieve a few lanterns from one of the supply crates and light them with Ash's cigarette lighter. The firelight casts a soft, orange glow around us, reminding me a little bit of the burning Cinderstone houses of Black City. *Home.* I'll never see it again. There's no home to go back to.

The atmosphere in the truck is subdued. We're all still reeling about what we saw in the depot with Sigur. I can only imagine the horrors he's enduring right now. Did they take him into a cell, like Polly's? Grief rips through me. How many more friends and family members are we going to lose before this conflict is over?

Ash sits opposite me, his legs outstretched and his eyes shut, deep in thought. I know he's worried about Sigur, but he hasn't said a word to me since we boarded the truck. It hurts that he doesn't want to confide in me, but maybe he just needs some time. I can understand that.

Sighing, I search the food crates for a bottle of water, but then a wave of nausea hits me. I place a hand over my stomach, waiting for it to pass. I've been feeling sick on and off all day, and I suspect it's the Wrath.

Elijah raises a quizzical brow at me. "You feeling okay?"

Ash's eyes snap open.

I could kill Elijah. "I'm *fine,* thank you. Just a little queasy from all the rocking."

Elijah gives me an apologetic look, realizing he's put his foot in it.

"You look very pale," Ash says, walking over to me. He presses a hand against my forehead. "You're burning up. You need to lie down."

"I'm okay, really," I say. This would be more believable if I weren't sweating.

Ash searches the crates for some clothes and pulls out a bunch of Sentry jackets and some black winter robes, laying them on the ground. I lie down on the makeshift bed, and he places my head on his lap, stroking my hair.

"I'm sorry about Sigur," I say.

His hand pauses for a second, and then he continues to caress my hair.

"Ash—"

"I don't want to talk about it right now," he says.

I gaze up at him, but don't push it.

Elijah brings over a bottle of water, and Ash snatches it from him.

"I'll do that," he says.

What's going on between those two? Ash unscrews the

bottle top and cradles my head while he pours the water into my mouth. I only manage a few gulps before I throw it back up.

"Sorry," I mumble.

Ash holds back my hair as I'm sick again. Elijah curls his lip, but says nothing, even though he has every right to complain. Instead, he rummages around the crates until he finds some crackers.

"These should settle Natalie's stomach," he says, tossing them to Ash.

Over the next hour, Ash feeds me water and crackers while Elijah does his best to clean up the mess I've made. Ash creates a pillow out of the jackets and mops my brow with a damp rag, making sure I'm comfortable. He looks so worried, like he thinks I might shatter into a thousand pieces. How's he going to react when I tell him I've got the Wrath? It'll crush him, I know it.

The nausea finally passes, and I curl up against him. "I love you," I say to him.

He sucks in a shaky breath, as if those words pain him.

"I love you too," he replies quietly. "With all my heart."

We hold on to each other in silence. Occasionally, Ash rubs his thumb over my palm, subconsciously drawing two hearts on it. One for him, one for me. *How much longer do we have? How many more moments in each other's arms?* It doesn't seem fair that we've barely had any time together. But these have all been stolen moments, with a stolen heart. Is this nature's way of trying to redress the balance? Sorrow weighs down on my shoulders until I think it's going to crush me. I turn my head from him, worried that he'll see the yellowing of my eyes.

Over the next few hours, the trailer's rocking gets less noticeable, until it's just a gentle sway. The temperature inside the vehicle drops by a few degrees, confirming that we've left the Barren Lands and are now in the Provinces. Elijah yawns, tired and bored. I get up, feeling slightly better, and I find some fresh clothes—a Sentry guard's uniform that's a size too big for me—and put them on. I suddenly remember my heart medication and the document I took from the science lab at the Barren Lands camp, and retrieve them from my discarded pants and slip them into my bag.

"So how are we going to rescue Sigur?" I say. It's time we addressed this.

"We're not," Ash says simply.

"But he's your Blood Father."

"He wouldn't want us to abandon the mission," Ash replies.

"But—"

"I don't want to talk about this anymore, Natalie," he says firmly. "We're not going to save him. It's what Purian Rose would expect us to do."

Ash pulls a robe over himself, like he's going to sleep. Conversation over.

I take one of the lanterns and walk to the other end of the long trailer, giving us both some breathing space before I say something I'll regret. It's Ash's choice what we do about Sigur, but that doesn't mean I agree with him. I hide in a nook between two towers of crates. A moment later, Elijah slips in beside me. It's really cramped in the nook, and his tail tickles my toes, but I don't mind so much. His golden eyes glimmer in the orange light.

"I can't believe Ash doesn't want to rescue Sigur," I say. "He's probably being tortured as we speak."

"Probably," Elijah admits. "But Ash is right; Rose will expect us to attempt a rescue mission, and that would be suicide. We can't break into Centrum unarmed and unprepared."

"We should at least try," I mutter. "If you were being held captive, wouldn't you want us to save you?"

"Of course, but I'm a little self-centered," Elijah says.

I manage a laugh. "You, self-centered? Never."

Elijah grins. It looks good on him. I bet he isn't short of female attention back home. It's not just his good looks, but underneath his pompous outer shell is a sweet guy.

"Do you have anyone special waiting for you? Like, a girlfriend?" I ask him, curious to know more about his life.

He smirks. "Why? Are you jealous, pretty girl?"

"Urgh, never mind," I say. "Sorry I said anything."

"No," he says eventually. "There's no one."

I have to admit, I'm surprised.

"I'd have thought the Consul's son would have girls falling at his feet," I say.

"Yes, well, obviously. But I'm not interested in those sorts of girls." He distractedly plays with the gold bands around his wrists, and I sense he doesn't want to talk about home anymore. "Are you feeling any better?" he asks, keeping his voice low so Ash can't hear us.

I nod. Although I'm feeling rotten, it's not from the illness.

"Ash is in a mood with me, and I don't know why," I whisper. "Has he said anything to you?"

"He thinks we're sleeping together," Elijah says.

"What? Why?" I say, my mind racing.

Elijah relates what Ash told him. "He obviously didn't hear our whole conversation in the lab."

"You didn't tell him?" I say.

"I promised you I wouldn't," he says. "But you have to tell him the truth at some point."

"I will."

"When?"

"When the time's right," I say. "I can't tell him now, not with everything that's happened with Sigur. Plus we're in the middle of a mission . . ."

"You're making excuses."

"No I'm not," I say.

"Yes you are."

I sigh. "Maybe I am. But I just need some time. I'm not ready for our relationship to be over."

"He won't break up with you just because you're sick."

"No, he loves me too much to do that," I reply. "And that's exactly why I'll have to break up with him. I don't want him to see me die. He's suffered enough."

I glance through the gaps in the crates and watch Ash sleeping. His black hair gently ripples around his pale face, and his lips are slightly parted, revealing the tips of his fangs. He seems at peace, for now, although I know it's not going to last long. I lightly touch the engagement ring still hanging from my gold necklace. We were going to spend the rest of our lives together, and now . . .

"I don't want to say good-bye to him just yet," I whisper. "Given the speed at which the symptoms are coming on, I think I've got a couple of months before I get really sick. We should finish the mission first, then I'll tell him when we get to Centrum."

"The longer you leave it, the harder it'll be on him."

"Not if I gently ease myself out of his life," I say, a plan formulating in my mind. "If I slowly distance myself from him over the next few weeks, then it won't be so hard on him when I go. Plus, if I wait until we're in Centrum to break up with him, he'll have Beetle there to pick up the pieces."

"I don't know . . ."

"Elijah, please," I say. "Let me do it my way, in my own time."

"What if your symptoms come on faster than you think?"

"Then I'll have to tell him, obviously," I say.

Elijah leans back against the wooden crate. "All right," he finally says. "But how do I explain what he overheard in the laboratory?"

"I . . ." This has me stumped. "I don't know."

I don't like the idea of Ash thinking I'm cheating on him with Elijah, but it will be easier for him to let me go if he thinks my feelings toward him have changed.

Elijah lets out another sigh, clearly guessing my thoughts. "If he asks me about it again, I won't deny his accusations, but I won't exactly confirm them either, okay?"

"Thank you," I say quietly. "I'm really sorry to put you in the middle of all this, Elijah."

He gives me a tight smile. "Yeah, well, if he punches me again, then the deal's off."

"When did he punch you?" I say, surprised.

"Back at the concentration camp," he says.

"Oh," I reply. "Sorry."

He shrugs. "I probably deserved it. I have been flirting with you."

My cheeks flood with color.

"I probably shouldn't have told you that," he says, his own face flushing.

"No, it's fine," I reply, but I'm suddenly painfully aware of his leg pressed up against mine. "I thought Amy was more your type," I add, remembering how he flirted with her back at the Ivy Church.

"She's cute," he replies. "But I have a thing for girls who save my life."

I blush harder. I saved his life twice, in fact. The first time when I helped him escape the Sentry laboratory, and the second time back on the train, when I killed that Wrath.

"I suppose guys hit on you all the time," he says.

I laugh. "Hardly. I'm not one of those leggy models from *Sentry Youth Monthly*."

A crease furrows between his russet brows. "You have no idea how people see you, do you?"

I shake my head. "How do they see me?"

"You're the girl who shouted 'No Fear, No Power' in front of the whole nation," he replies. "You're beautiful, and you're brave. Don't you see how guys might develop a crush on you?"

I laugh, embarrassed.

"Sorry," he mumbles. "I don't seem to have a filter between my brain and mouth sometimes."

"It's all right." I take his hand. "Really. I'm flattered."

He gazes down at our clasped hands. "Yeah, well, you should be. I'm quite the catch." I know he means it as a joke, but his voice is flat.

I laugh, trying to keep the mood light, but I don't know what to say. Elijah is a sweet guy underneath the arrogant veneer, and clearly very attractive, but my heart belongs to one boy.

"I'm sorry, Elijah," I say. "You know nothing can ever happen between us, right?"

"I know," he says, releasing my hand. "Ash is a lucky guy. You clearly love him a lot."

"Until my dying breath," I reply.

I just wonder when that will be.

25.

NATALIE

AT SOME POINT during the journey, I slip into a troubled sleep, my dreams filled with images of Polly. She starts off as my sister, then her gray eyes turn yellow and she becomes a Wrath Hound, her fangs dripping with venom. I call out to my mother for help, but she's not there. Then I remember she's run away. I'm alone. Slashes appear in the Polly-Hound's stomach, spilling her innards across the ground, and suddenly she's my sister again, curled up on the cell floor, surrounded by a pool of blood in the shape of a rose—

The truck hits a pothole, jarring me awake. My legs are aching from being curled up in a ball all night next to Elijah. His strong arms are wrapped around my waist, his face nuzzled against the back of my neck. My cheeks are wet. I must have been crying.

"Sleep well?" Ash's cold voice says close by.

I sit up, alert. Ash is perched on the edge of a nearby crate, dressed in one of the hooded black winter robes we found with the rest of the supplies. I wonder how long he's been watching us.

Elijah stirs and wakes up, yawning loudly. "What time is—"

He stops talking when he sees the thunderous expression on Ash's face.

Ash tosses two robes at us. "Put these on. We've arrived."

We pull on the long robes just as the truck slows down. Around us I can hear the sounds of the city: merchants calling out to each other, carts rolling down the street, music spilling out of taverns. It must be early afternoon—my body clock is all out of sync after being trapped inside the trailer with no natural light.

Ash lifts the truck door, letting in a welcome blast of cool air, which smells of spices and herbs. We're in Thrace's bustling central market, which puts the one in Chantilly Lane to shame. There are hundreds, if not thousands, of round buildings made from red sandstone bricks. Many of the buildings have murals painted on the walls, so the city is a vision of color. But this isn't what's most striking. All the buildings have elaborately tiered roofs, covered in tiles made from a strange, shimmering metal I've never seen before. It's highly polished and reflects the light, so the whole city seems to be glittering, like sunlight on the sea. It's beautiful.

"I see how Thrace earned the nickname the Mirror City," I whisper to Elijah.

"They're solar tiles," he explains. "It's how they get their energy. We use them in Viridis too, but not to this extent."

Without saying a word, Ash lifts his hood over his head and leaps off the moving truck, his cloak billowing behind him like phoenix wings. Elijah takes my hand, and we jump together, landing heavily on the dust tracks.

We hurry away from the truck, getting as much distance from it as possible, and slip into the crowds of people dressed in corset bustle gowns, jewel-toned frock coats or vibrantly colored robes. I pull my hood up, disguising myself, as we follow Ash deeper into the market.

Flags flutter in the cool spring breeze like butterfly wings, bright against the cobalt-blue sky. Swarthy-skinned traders sing ancient merchant songs as we pass by, which weave and layer over each other in a beautiful melody, reminding me of birdsong. The whole place is so joyous and alive. It's a welcome change from the Barren Lands.

Even so, the farther we go in the maze of alleyways, the more disheartened I feel. Everywhere I turn, there's another tavern or inn. Frustratingly, none of the establishments have a sign hanging over the doorway.

"None of these places are named," I say. "How are we ever going to find the Moon Star?"

Elijah frowns. "I guess we'll just have to ask around."

Occasionally we pass large digital screens on top of wooden platforms scattered throughout the market. On every single one, the same eight photos are displayed under the words WANTED DEAD OR ALIVE:

Ash

Me

Sigur

Roach

Mother

Beetle

Juno

Day

Thankfully Elijah's not mentioned, and neither are Harold, Nick or Amy, but none of them are high-ranking members of the rebellion, or escaped convicts, so that's probably why. Sigur's photo has been crossed out on all of them. News of his capture must have already spread across the country. Rose didn't waste any time making that victory public. *What are they doing to him? Is he even alive?* I pull my hood lower over my face.

"Ash, slow down," I say a few minutes later, breathless.

Ash stops and waits for me, his eyes glittering like the mirrored roofs around us. His expression softens when he sees how tired I look. I'm feeling nauseated again, probably from the overpowering scents of perfumes and spices in the market. He gently takes my hand. I catch Elijah looking at us, a stung expression on his face. I wish he hadn't told me he has a crush on me; it's made things awkward.

"Are you feeling all right?" Ash asks me.

"I think I have a stomach bug," I lie. I don't know how many more excuses I can come up with before he starts getting suspicious.

He kisses my forehead. It's a small gesture, but it shatters my heart. I can't believe I'm intending to break up with him. I love him so much. But I remind myself that's why I have to do it.

"Let's find somewhere to stay," Ash says. "There must be a Humans for Unity stronghold around here somewhere. Keep an eye out for the Cinder Rose emblem on the doors."

We stroll past the round buildings, casually checking the door frames for any sign of a burning rose. Each time we pass a tavern, Elijah darts inside and checks to see if it's the Moon Star. Each time he returns, shaking his head. We pass stalls selling spices, sweatshops creating Sentry banners and swordsmiths forging silver-plated weapons, which are useful against Lupines and Darklings, both of whom have an allergy to the metal.

Outside one of the market stalls, a Pilgrim of the Purity faith stands on a crate as he preaches from the Book of Creation. His flock of faithful followers listens, enraptured, occasionally chiming in with "so sayeth His Mighty." The Pilgrim has a shaved head and rose tattoo, just like Sebastian, which is startling enough to look at, but there's something else about him that makes me pause. It takes a fraction of a second for me to realize he's got these silver halos around his irises. I've never seen anything like that before. It must be some sort of genetic eye condition.

We skirt around the Pilgrims, keeping our heads bowed, and continue to search for a safe house.

"Let's look for the Darkling ghetto," Ash suggests. "Where there are Darklings, Humans for Unity won't be far behind."

I notice a sign for Spice Square. Assuming the Darkling ghetto will be next to the plaza, like it is in Black City, we head in that direction. Occasionally Ash's fingers brush against mine, like he wants to hold hands, but neither of us takes that next step. It's like we're back to when we first met, uncertain about how the other person feels. As soon as we approach Spice Square, I can tell something's wrong. A second later, I hear it: the crack of a whip and the scream of a girl, followed by the laughter of men.

Ash takes my hand as we enter the plaza. "Stay close."

The town square is three times bigger than the one in Black City, and at the north end is a long stone wall, where the Darkling ghetto begins. At the other end is a stunning, centuries-old building made from red sandstone. It has an ornate façade and a massive decorative door almost half the height of the building, painted burnt orange, with a much smaller access door built into it. I recognize the building from my history books as Thrace City Hall.

In the center of the town square are three Sentry guards, who are beating up a couple of Dacian kids. Passersby ignore them, not wanting to get involved. The Dacians are a traveling community who live on the fringes of our society, and they get treated with even less respect than the Workboots. The first Dacian is a boy who can't be more than ten years old, with dark tanned skin, black curly hair and eyes as blue as the cobalt sky. There's blood over his face where he's been punched, while the second—a teenage girl, around seventeen years old—has had her dress ripped at the shoulder. Her flowing auburn hair tumbles in waves down her tanned back, the ends touching the dusty earth. Colorful feathers have been woven into its strands, so she looks like an exotic bird.

One of the attackers, a shaved-headed man with a broken nose, pins her arms behind her back while another man thrashes her with a short horsewhip.

"Thieving Dacian scum!" the guard with the horsewhip says. "I'll teach you to pick my pocket!"

She spits at the man, cursing at him in some of the most colorful language I've ever heard. Despite her injuries, she struggles against her captors like a wild animal.

A third guard grabs the girl's face, inspecting it.

"You're a pretty thing for a peasant," he says, kissing her.

The sight of the guard roughly kissing the girl makes me think of Sebastian and how he forced himself on Polly.

"We have to help them," I say.

"They'll recognize us," Ash replies, glancing at our photos on the nearby digital screen.

The Dacian girl bites the man's lip, and he staggers back, grunting in pain. She's rewarded with a hard slap across the face, which knocks her to the ground.

I wince. "Ash, we have to do something."

Ash scoops up some dirt from the ground and rubs it around

his eyes and down his nose. Without another word, he strides over to the Sentry guards, his cloak billowing behind him. Elijah and I race after him.

The people around us continue to go about their business, deliberately keeping their eyes downcast as they hurry past the Sentry guards. The man with the horsewhip raises his hand to strike the girl again. Ash grabs his wrist, stopping the swing in midair. The man flinches.

"Do you know who I am?" Ash growls, his voice low, menacing.

All the color drains out of the man's face. He shoots a terrified look at his colleagues.

"Phoenix," the man whispers.

"That's right," Ash snarls. "And do you know what I do to people like you?"

The man nods again. He's obviously heard the rumors from Gallium, where Ash supposedly killed one hundred guards with his bare fangs.

"Then I suggest you leave this boy and girl alone, or else I may have to"—Ash flashes his fangs—"make an example of you too."

Ash releases the guard's wrist, and the men sprint off.

"You know they're going to tell everyone we're here?" Elijah says.

"I'm sure they will," Ash replies. "So we'd better go find somewhere to hide out."

Ash helps the boy to his feet, checking his injuries, while I help the girl up. She's tall, with an hourglass figure and a striking face: sharp cheekbones, catlike eyes ringed with black Cinderstone powder and pouting lips painted the color of bronze coins. Elijah looks her up and down, clearly liking what he sees. I roll my eyes, feeling a pang of resentment.

"There was no need to get involved; I could've handled those guys myself," the girl says, wiping the dust off her purple dress.

Well, that's gratitude for you.

"Are you hurt?" Ash asks.

"I'll live." She sticks her hand down her ample cleavage, pulling out a leather pouch of coins. "But this certainly helps."

So she did steal that man's money? Still, it's no excuse for beating her.

"Are you really Phoenix?" the boy says.

Ash nods. "And you are?"

"Lucas."

"And I'm Giselle," the girl says, openly admiring Ash. "I have to say, those Wanted photos don't do you any justice at all."

Ash rubs the back of his neck, embarrassed.

Lucas laughs. "Giselle always gets these goo-goo eyes when you're on the news."

Giselle slaps his arm. "Sshh."

I possessively take Ash's hand, already distrusting this girl.

Elijah tilts his head toward the ghetto wall. "I can't hear any Darklings on the other side."

"That's because they're all dead," Giselle explains. "They caught some virus last year."

The Wrath has spread to the Provinces already?

Ash frowns.

"How will we repay you?" Giselle asks.

"We need somewhere to rest for the night," Ash replies.

"I know just the place." She beams. "I'll take you to Madame Clara's."

26.
NATALIE

GISELLE BECKONS US to follow her. I hesitate, not trusting her, but the boys don't seem to share my concerns, given how willingly they go with her. It reminds me of how the Sentry boys at school used to chase after Polly. They would do anything she wanted, not that she ever took advantage of this fact. My sister had the purest heart of anyone I ever knew.

Giselle leads us down a labyrinth of back alleys, which get narrower and darker the farther into the city we go. The round market buildings are soon behind us, replaced by narrow brick buildings, their crumbling walls painted vivid reds, purples, blues and golds. I peer into one of the shop windows, and my skin crawls at the sight of the sinister objects: monkey heads, jars of frogs, chickens' feet, snakeskins. Elijah curls his lip up at them, as grossed out as I am. An uneasy feeling comes over me. *Where's she taking us?* I tug on Ash's sleeve.

"I don't like this," I whisper to him. "Let's go back to the market."

He gives me a kind but slightly patronizing look. "Just because Giselle's a Dacian doesn't mean she's untrustworthy."

No, stealing that man's money is what makes her untrust-worthy. I can't help but feel he's being blinded by her beauty. Or maybe . . . maybe it's just me, I admit. I don't like the way she keeps looking over her shoulder at Ash, flashing him a dazzling smile.

Lucas walks beside us. He's intrigued by Elijah's tail, which is just visible beneath the hem of his robe. The boy keeps grabbing it and laughing when Elijah swats him away like a pesky fly. It becomes a bit of a game between the two of them, and although Elijah seems annoyed at the boy, I know from the glint in his eye that it's just an act. I think this happens a lot with him when kids are around, remembering how the little girl we rescued from the Destroyer Ship, Bianca, also played with his tail.

We turn down a side alley, and Giselle stops in front of a violet-colored house with a tiered roof covered in glimmering solar panels and topped with a weather vane in the shape of a sun.

"Welcome to Madame Clara's," Giselle says, pushing open the black door.

A bell tinkles as we step inside the gloomy shop. The walls are painted the color of night, with silver stars stenciled on them. There's a heady smell of incense in the round room, making my stomach churn. The wooden shelves are packed with leather-bound books, potions, candles and colorful crystals.

Sitting at a round table in the center of the room is an elderly woman wearing a traditional folk dress like Giselle's and heavy silver bands around her wrists. Intricate tattoos of the ancient zodiac decorate her arms and face.

Her long hair is coarse and gray; her dark olive skin is weathered with wrinkles and the strange tattoos. She's wearing a pair of brass-rimmed sun goggles, and she lowers them. I stifle a gasp as I stare at her eyelids, which have been sewn shut.

She turns her head toward me, and her lips spread into a gold-toothed smile. "Do you want your palms read? It's only two coins."

"They're not customers," Giselle says, dropping the pouch of coins on the table. "Clara, this is Ash Fisher, Natalie Buchanan and—"

"Elijah Theroux," he says.

"They need a place to stay. They're hiding from the Sentry," Giselle explains.

Madame Clara spits at the mention of the Sentry, muttering curses under her breath. She gets up, struggling slightly with arthritic hips, and waves at us to follow her into the back room. I soon realize the shop is just a tiny portion of the ramshackle building, which sprawls over five floors. Every room is painted a different rainbow color, and there's a mural running up the stairwell, which was clearly painted by the ten children who are running about the building, laughing and playing.

Lucas tugs Elijah's tail and sprints on ahead, wanting to continue their game of cat-and-mouse. Elijah laughs and races after the boy. The sight makes me smile. I catch Ash looking at me. He turns away, his expression pained.

"Why are there so many children here?" I ask as we walk up the creaking steps to the third floor. I can't imagine they're Clara's kids, since she's too old to be their mother.

"Madame Clara runs a refuge," Giselle explains. "All the kids here ran away from home for one reason or another. She keeps us off the streets."

That explains why she was pickpocketing earlier. She needs the money to help support all these children, the same way Ash had to sell Haze to support his father. Madame Clara shows us to a double room with bare wooden floors and colorful silken fabrics draped down the blue walls. Directly opposite us are wide bay windows, which lead out onto a balcony with loads of potted plants. To our right is the bed, which is covered in a handmade quilt, and to our left is a simple tin bath and sink. It's not much, but after many hard nights spent on trains and trucks and in caves, it looks like heaven.

"For you and Ash," Madame Clara says to me. "There are dresses in the wardrobe, if you want to change. Elijah can sleep next door with Lucas and the boys."

Giselle smiles at Ash. "My room is at the end of the hall, in case you need me."

She sashays down the corridor after Madame Clara, putting a little extra sway in her hips. Ash gives a lopsided smirk, enjoying the view. Fury spikes in me, and I mutter a few rude words as I stomp into the bedroom.

I open up the balcony windows to let in some air, then sit on the bed and take off my shoes while Ash runs the bath. It's the first time we've been alone since the Barren Lands, and it feels weird. There's a wall of tension between us that's getting higher by the day. Ash keeps glancing over at me, like he wants to talk to me about something, but then changes his mind. Nerves fill my stomach, worrying that he's going to ask me about the conversation he overheard with me and Elijah, and I don't know what to say if he does.

"Natalie?" he finally says.

My tummy flips. "Yes?"

He looks at me with such deep intensity that I feel burnt by his gaze. He must notice my body tensing, because he looks away.

"Nothing," he mumbles. "Do you want to wash first?"

"No, you go," I say.

He pulls the modesty screen across the bath and gets undressed. I catch glimpses of him through the gaps between the panels—the curve of a biceps, the knot of muscles on his flat stomach, a naked hip. Yearning aches through me. There's a splash of water as he slides into the bath.

A stab of pain shoots through my thighs. I look down and realize I'm digging my nails into my legs. I quickly get up, feeling flustered. I twist my hair up into a bun, then pull off my black robe, top and pants, so I'm just in my vest and underpants. I walk over to the wardrobe and find three gowns inside. I select a folk-style teal dress, with off-the-shoulder sleeves and little gold coins sewn into the hem of the pleated skirt. I lay it out on the bed quilt and begin unfastening the mother-of-pearl buttons.

There's another splash of water, followed by the sound of footsteps padding across the wooden floor. I turn around, my heart racing. Ash stands a few inches away from me. Beads of water snake down his bare torso, sliding past his belly button toward . . . I swallow, flushing. He stretches out a hand and rests it on my hip. I can't focus on anything but those five fingertips pressed against my skin.

He doesn't do anything for a long moment, just gazes at me, silent and uncertain. A warm breeze flows through the open balcony windows, stirring his wet hair. Finally, he pulls me toward him, and dips his head. The kiss is slow, beautiful, intense, and I'm instantly lost in him. I lace my fingers through his inky hair and draw him closer, deepening our kiss. The beads of water on his body soak through my cotton vest, making goose bumps break out across my skin, but I don't care; all I can focus on is his hand sliding down my back. It rests above the waistband of my underwear.

"I've missed you," he murmurs, his fingers slipping under the elastic waistband of my underwear.

I have the Wrath.

The thought slaps me so hard, I stagger back from him, gasping for air. *Oh God, oh God, oh God.* How could I be so reckless? I gaze up at him, tears brimming in my eyes.

"What did I do?" he says, his face stricken.

I cover my mouth, trying to stifle the sob that's going to break out at any second. How could I be so stupid? I could infect him!

He stands there for a moment, stunned and confused.

"Is it the scars?" he asks quietly.

"No! God, I told you I don't care about those." I blink, trying to compose myself.

"Then what is it?"

"I—" I don't know how to end that sentence. *I have the Wrath, and I'm going to die, and I love you, and I'm going to leave you, and I'm sorry, I'm sorry, I'm sorry.*

He grabs his clothes off the floor and tugs them on.

I chase after him. "Ash—"

He pushes past me and storms out of the room, slamming the door behind him.

"I'm sorry," I whisper.

I sink down on the floor and cry.

27.

NATALIE

ABOUT AN HOUR LATER, I head downstairs, freshly bathed and wearing the teal dress. The coins sewn into the hem jangle as I walk, making me sound more cheerful than I feel. Around my neck is the gold pendant that Ash gave me for my birthday. My engagement ring hangs from the chain, and I tuck it under the top of my dress, hiding it from view.

I find everyone in the kitchen, watching an SBN news report about Sigur's capture on Madame Clara's old portable digital screen. I take a seat at the large oak table. The kitchen is warm and inviting, with terra-cotta tiles on the floor and wooden cabinets painted with colorful images similar to the mural in the hallway. Bunches of herbs hang from hooks on the cabinets, while jars of tea leaves line the shelves.

Even though she can't see, Madame Clara moves deftly about the kitchen as she prepares a simple rice dish for supper, skirting around Lucas, who is sitting cross-legged on the floor, tying a red ribbon to Elijah's tail, which is already covered in gaudy bows. Giselle laughs, shooing him away.

"Go play in the garden, you pest," she says.

Lucas sticks his tongue out at her and runs to join the other children.

Giselle's arms are laden with jars, and she places them on the table. She's changed into a tulip yellow dress that clings to her curves, and has tied some bright orange feathers in her auburn hair. A purple bruise has started to form on her cheek where the guard slapped her.

Ash sits stoically in the corner of the room, watching the news report. He raises his eyes briefly as I sit down.

"They're holding Sigur for questioning in Centrum," Ash says flatly. "He's going on trial next week for his role in burning down Black City."

"Well, he's still alive. That's good news," I say, trying to see the positive side. "Maybe Roach will send in a team to rescue him?"

"Don't be stupid. They're not going to rescue him. It's too dangerous," Ash says. "He's as good as dead."

I bite back my reply, stung by his harsh words. Elijah quirks a concerned eyebrow at me.

Giselle perches on the edge of the kitchen table beside Ash and begins writing some labels for the jars filled with something that looks like ground peppercorns. The gold rings on her toes glimmer as her foot keeps brushing up against his leg. Whether it's accidental or not, I don't know, but thankfully Ash moves his leg away before I lunge across the table and rip the feathers out of her hair.

Elijah unscrews the lid of one of the jars and sniffs its contents. His face scrunches up.

"What *is* that?" he says, thrusting the jar into her hand.

"Ground-up night whisper," Giselle explains, putting the lid back on the container. "We mix it into our tea to help us relax. It's quite potent, but my people have a natural tolerance to it, so we don't feel its effects as much as others. It just gives us a nice, sleepy buzz."

The digital screen beeps, and the Sentry crest appears on the monitor, with the words NEWS FLASH. Everyone falls silent as Ash turns up the volume.

"Citizens, we interrupt your program with an urgent newscast," February Fields says. "Reports have just come in that the traitor known as Phoenix has been killed during a firefight in Iridium. Once again, the traitor known as Phoenix is dead."

We're all so stunned, it takes a second for the news to sink in.

"How can Phoenix be dead?" Giselle asks, confused. "You're here."

Ash groans slightly. "Oh no," he mutters.

"Purian Rose will now make a statement to the nation," February says on the digital screen.

A moment later, Rose appears on the monitor. He approaches a podium on the Golden Citadel balcony, which overlooks the city square in Centrum. The Sentry flag flutters behind him. He's dressed in his ceremonial robes, and although his eyes are stern and fixed on the camera, there's a barely disguised smirk on his lips.

There are cheers from the thousands of Sentry citizens congregated in the city square below him. Many are wearing white Pilgrim robes, their heads cleanly shaved, but others are dressed in the latest fashions—bright corset dresses and feathered hats for the women, long tailcoats and silken waistcoats for the men.

Rose addresses the crowd, talking briefly about the dark times they have faced recently, and saying that the time of hardship is over. The rebellion is defeated. The false prophet Phoenix is dead. Ash was not immortal, he was not a messiah. He was just a boy.

The image cuts to footage of the firefight in Iridium, which took place inside the Darkling ghetto. It's hard to see clearly through the smoke and rain, but even in the poor conditions, you can make out the shape of thousands of bodies—Sentry, Darkling—piled on top of one another where they were shot down. They weren't lying when they said it was a massacre. Suddenly a tall boy with black hair, an LLF jacket and Cinderstone powder painted on his face runs into the frame. It's Ash! Except I know it's not him at all. It's Nick.

He charges toward a Sentry guard, who has his gun pointed at a woman's head. I can't see her face, but the long ginger ponytail is unmistakable.

I gasp. "Juno!"

Before Nick can reach her, a bomb detonates. Dirt and gore explode into the air, showering the battlefield in a rain of blood. When the dust settles, there's a shallow crater in the ground where Nick once stood. There's nothing left of him to identify. Nearby, Juno lies facedown in a pool of blood, unmoving, the Sentry guard clearly dead beside her.

The footage cuts back to the city square in Centrum. The people seem stunned. Then they realize they're on camera and all begin to cheer again, as if on cue. Rose finishes his speech, warning that his forces will not rest until all the remaining rebels have been hunted down and captured. No one will threaten this great nation. The broadcast ends with the Sentry crest and the words ONE FAITH, ONE RACE, ONE NATION UNDER HIS MIGHTY.

We're all too shocked to speak at first, saddened by Nick's death and the certainty that Juno is either dead or seriously wounded. It makes me worry about Amy and Stuart as well. Did they make it out of Iridium alive?

Ash leans forward in his chair, hooking his hands behind his head. I want to comfort him, but I don't think my affections would be welcomed after what happened upstairs.

Elijah gets up. "Madame Clara, may I make a phone call? I want to check in with my family."

"The phone's in the parlor," she replies.

Elijah leaves the room and closes the door behind him.

"What's my dad going to think?" Ash says quietly. "He'll be so worried."

"He'll know it wasn't you," I reassure him. "He knew Nick and Juno were traveling together."

Ash scrapes his chair back. "I'm going upstairs."

I stand up, expecting to go with him.

He looks at me coldly. "I don't want any company."

I flinch, but what did I expect? I really hurt his feelings earlier. He leaves the room, shutting the door behind him. Giselle bounces to her feet and turns off the digital screen.

"At least they think Ash is dead. That's good news," Giselle says. "They won't come looking for him in Thrace now."

"Giselle!" Madame Clara chides. "That boy was their friend."

Giselle bites her lip slightly. "Sorry. I don't always think before I speak."

"It's fine," I say, a little tersely. "Excuse me. I'm going to find Elijah."

I stroll down the hallway, thinking about what Giselle said. I hate to admit it, but in a small way, Nick's death is good news. If those guards from earlier tell anyone they saw him here, people will assume they were mistaken, since Purian Rose just proclaimed that Phoenix is dead. I poke my nose into all the rooms until I find the parlor. It's a small but cozy room, with sumptuous pink walls and glimmering fabrics thrown over the chairs and chaise longue.

Elijah is sitting on the window ledge, talking quietly on the phone. He seems agitated.

"I know what's at stake . . . I'm being as quick as I . . ." Elijah runs his fingers through his dark brown hair. He spots me by the doorway. "I have to go."

He hangs up the phone.

"Is everything okay?" I ask.

"Just my dad being a jerk, as usual."

"I'm sure he's just eager to get his hands on the Ora. We all are," I say. "Has there been any sighting of the Destroyer Ships near Viridis?"

"Not yet, thankfully," he says. "I guess Purian Rose is waiting until they've collected all the humans who voted no in the ballot first, and then he'll add a new addendum to Rose's Law and come for us."

I nod. *One thing at a time,* my father always used to say, and Purian Rose is a patient man. It's not like a few thousand Bastets pose much threat to him, so there's no need to waste his resources on them when he's got his hands full with the rebel attacks.

We head back to the kitchen, where dinner is being served. I sit down as Madame Clara scoops some rice into a bowl and places it on the table between us. I don't have any appetite.

Elijah starts serving us dinner, putting a few dollops of rice on everyone's plates. He catches me looking and immediately sits down, a deep flush spreading up his neck, although I don't know why. What's he got to be embarrassed about? He was being nice!

"Elijah was telling us earlier on about the Tenth and your search to find his mother," Madame Clara says. "You think she was staying at a place called the Moon Star?"

"Yes. Have you heard of it?" I say.

"No, I'm sorry, my dear," Madame Clara replies. "There are hundreds of taverns in the city."

"Their names tend to describe some distinctive feature of the building, though," Giselle chimes in. "For instance, the Scarlet Sun has a bright red sun painted on its door; the Witch's Hat has a roof in the shape of a pointy hat, that sort of thing."

"Wouldn't it be more convenient just to put a sign outside the building?" I say.

Madame Clara laughs. "Part of the joy is working out the name of the place. You get one chance to guess the name. If you're right, the barmaid gives you a free shot of spiced Shine."

"Isn't the tavern's name written on their tariff boards, though?" Elijah asks.

"Yes, but most merchants are either illiterate or too dimwitted by the pretty barmaids to notice it," Giselle says.

"The locals must get a lot of free drinks," Elijah murmurs.

Giselle laughs. "We do. But in return, we bring merchants into the taverns and keep them entertained, so they stay and buy loads of drinks. They nearly always end up having to rent out one of the tavern's rooms to sleep it off. So everybody wins."

Elijah catches my eye and frowns. This is really going to slow down our progress.

I sigh, pushing my plate aside. "I'm going to look for the Moon Star."

"Should we get Ash?" Elijah says.

"I'd rather he didn't come," I say.

Elijah doesn't push it as we put on our hooded robes and head out into the city.

28.

NATALIE

THE SUN HAS STARTED to set over the Mirror City, making the solar panels on all the rooftops shine with amber light. Everything about the city is warm and inviting, with laughter and music spilling out of the taverns, and children rushing through the streets, jovially chasing each other. It's so at odds with my mood. I keep replaying the image of Nick getting blown up in my mind, and my stomach knots.

"Are you okay?" Elijah asks me as we turn down Saffron Street.

"No," I admit.

"Giselle's a nice girl, isn't she?" Elijah says, clearly wanting to divert my mind from thoughts of Nick and the others.

"Not really," I say.

Elijah grins at me. "Jealous?"

"No!" I say, then look down. "Maybe. I don't like how she looks at Ash."

"Yeah, well, get used to it, pretty girl," he says. "He's famous now."

A couple of merchants sing loudly as they pass us, their faces red from a mixture of sunburn and drinking too much spiced Shine. I tug my hood lower around my face.

"So what's going on with you lovebirds?" Elijah asks as we wander down the street. "Things seemed tense earlier."

"It's nothing," I say, then add in a rush, "We were kissing, and he wanted to take things further, and I couldn't because I'm sick, so now he's upset." I blush. It's really embarrassing talking to Elijah about my sex life, or lack thereof.

"Oh," he says. "Maybe it's time to tell him you're—"

"Don't even say it, Elijah," I say.

"Natalie . . ."

"In the past year, I've lost everyone I love," I say. "I'm not ready to lose Ash yet."

"You're being selfish," he says. "And you're hurting Ash by *not* telling him."

"I know," I whisper. "But I can't let him go, not yet. I'm not strong enough."

"Well, if you're going to continue with this charade, then at least stop sending him mixed signals," Elijah replies. "It's cruel to lead him on if you plan to leave him."

I chew on my nail, saying nothing. He's right, though. It's unfair to give Ash hope when there is none.

Elijah nods toward a nearby tavern with a green door made out of tree branches.

"Should we go in?" he says.

"We might as well start somewhere," I say.

He holds the door open for me as we go inside.

The tavern is crammed with merchants from all walks of life—some wear fine silk shirts, pocket watches and elaborate tailcoats, others are dressed in tattered rags, their gnarled hands cupped around glasses of spiced Shine. But everyone is chatting and mingling happily, like there are no differences between them. People barely notice us as we walk up to the bar, keeping an eye out for the tariff board, but even so, we keep our hoods low and heads bowed.

A curvaceous barmaid with wild curls of brown hair walks over to us. Her lips are painted the color of copper, and her luminous hazel eyes are heavily circled with Cinderstone powder. She's wearing a typical folk dress, like mine, although she fills hers out a lot better than I do—something that doesn't go unnoticed by Elijah, given the way his eyes keep drifting down.

"What's my name, merchant?" she says in a thick Thracian accent.

Elijah spots the wooden tariff board by the stairwell. "The Olive Branch," he says, translating the Thracian name.

The barmaid beams and pours two shots of spiced Shine, then places them in front of us. He picks up the glass of amber liquid. "To Nick and Juno."

I hesitate, then raise mine. "Nick and Juno."

We knock back our drinks in one go. I gasp as the choking heat scorches down my throat. The taste is unpleasant, but the effect is immediate. Already I feel more relaxed. It's nice. It's been such a horrible couple of days; I want to forget everything for a few hours.

Elijah turns to the barmaid. "Do you know where we can find La Luna Estrella?"

"No, sweetie," she replies. "But why don't you stay here and have another drink?"

"Another time." Elijah winks at her, then takes my hand and leads me out of the tavern.

She swears at us as we leave—this is not how the game is meant to be played.

We head into the next tavern a few doors down. This one's the Yellow Duck. Another dead end. We hurry to the tavern on the next street, then on to another, and another. We visit over twenty bars in the space of three hours, only allowing ourselves to have a drink at every fifth stop, but even so, I'm feeling a little lightheaded. It's nice.

I hook my arm through Elijah's as we wander down the bustling street. No one pays us much attention; Thrace is a city of strangers. I'm surprised there are so many people out after dark, but I guess without any Darklings in the city, there's no reason for a curfew like we had in Black City.

We enter Thyme Plaza, which is smaller than Spice Square. In the middle of the plaza is an ornate marble fountain, topped with a statue of two lovers entwined in an embrace. A flock of pigeons nest at its base. They scatter into the sky as we pass by.

"Argh! Get them away from me," Elijah says, swatting at the birds.

I don't mean to laugh, but I can't keep the sound from escaping my lips.

"It's not funny," he says huffily.

"I'm sorry," I reply, plucking a gray feather out of his hair. "But honestly, what's so frightening about a *bird*? They're cute."

"No they're not! They have these horrible, beady little eyes and disgusting clawed feet." He shudders, and I burst out into a fit of giggles again. "That does it," he says, grabbing me.

He tickles me until I can barely breathe.

"I'm sorry, I'm sorry," I gasp.

He grins, releasing me. "There must be something you're frightened of."

"Yeah, Wraths," I say, my voice cracking.

Elijah pulls me toward him, and I lay my head against his

broad chest. "I'll take care of you, Natalie. You don't have to go through this alone," he murmurs.

His arms briefly tighten around me, and then he lets me go. I'm surprised at how quickly my heart is beating.

"Let's check out this tavern," I say, indicating a building with a blue door.

We go inside. This time the barmaid is a blonde, with pale green eyes. Excitement briefly bubbles up in me, thinking it could be Esme, but then I remember she's in a wheelchair and would be in her late forties or fifties by now, and this woman is in her thirties. The barmaid walks over to us, and her smile falters. For a second I'm worried she's recognized us, despite our hooded capes. But then her smile returns.

"What's my name, merchant?" she asks.

Elijah glances at the tariff board. "The Pink Apple."

We're rewarded with two more free shots of spiced Shine.

"We're looking for a tavern called La Luna Estrella. Have you heard of it?" Elijah asks her.

She shakes her head. Even if she did know the place, I doubt she'd tell us.

"Enjoy your drink," she says, giving Elijah a flirtatious wink, which he returns. For some idiotic reason, I feel jealous.

Elijah sits down and knocks back his drink.

"Shouldn't we go to the next place?" I say.

"You look tired," Elijah says.

"Oh, thanks," I mumble.

"You know what I meant. We can pick up our search at first light."

"Are you sure? I can carry on for a few more hours . . . ," I say unconvincingly. I'm exhausted.

He gives me a crooked smile, pulling back a stool for me.

I sit down. "Okay, just one drink, then we'll go back to Madame Clara's."

One soon turns into two, then three, then four, and I've soon lost track of the time, but it's hard to care as the drinks keep flowing. I don't even recall us ordering them, let alone paying for them, but the barmaid seems happy to keep topping off our glasses. Elijah keeps me entertained, telling me funny stories about his fishing trips in Viridis and about his three brothers.

"So let me get this straight," I say. "Acelot is your oldest brother?"

He nods. "He's a decent guy. I've always liked him. Then there's Donatien, who's a *real* mommy's boy, and finally there's Marcel, my youngest brother. He is a total ass."

"How come none of them are here, helping you find your mother?" I ask. "Aren't they worried about her too?"

"No, but she's not their mom. Acelot, Donatien and Marcel are my half brothers," Elijah explains, knocking back his drink. He slams his glass on the counter. "Our relationship is complicated."

"I get it," I say. "My mother cheated on my father, and Polly is . . . *was* . . . my half sister."

He gives me a sad smile.

The barmaid tops off our glasses again. She nervously glances over our shoulders toward the door, so I turn around a little too fast, wondering what she's looking at, and nearly fall off my stool. I laugh as Elijah catches me.

"Okay, pretty girl. Time to take you home," he says.

"Just one more drink?" I say.

"No, we've both had enough."

I pout, and he grins.

"You're going to regret this in the morning," he says.

"I don't care," I say. "You only live once, right?"

I reach out for my drink. My hand pauses by the glass. The honey-colored liquid is vibrating. My head snaps up, suddenly very sober. I've seen this happen once before and know what it means. I strain my ears. Beneath the din of music and chatter of merchants is the unmistakable hum of Destroyer Ships.

"We need to get out of here," I say, pushing back my stool.

We race outside and instantly stop dead. Overhead, the stars are blocked out by the outline of five Destroyer Ships hovering over the city. But that's not what's caused the blood in my veins to freeze. Parked in Thyme Square is a Transporter. The hatch door opens, and Garrick and the pink-haired Lupine, Sasha, step out, their steel-capped boots clunking against the stone. How did they know we were here? *The barmaid!* She must've tipped the Sentry off. That's why she kept plying us with drinks—she was keeping us there until they turned up.

Garrick pulls up the collar of his gray coat and sniffs the air. His head turns in our direction, his silver eyes glinting in the dark.

"Run!" I say to Elijah.

We race down a busy side alley and push through the crowd of people, bumping against their shoulders as we weave between them at top speed. The world is a blaze of color and glimmering lights, and my ears ring with the hum of music and Destroyer Ships. Everything feels hazy, like I'm in a dream, but I know it's just a side effect of alcohol and adrenaline.

A man bumps into me and my hood falls down, but I don't have time to put it back up as Elijah drags me onward. More people spill out of the taverns into the street as word gets around that the Destroyer Ships are in the city. Thankfully, they're all looking up at the sky rather than at the two of us rushing past them.

I risk a look over my shoulder. Garrick and Sasha are at the end of the street, scanning the sea of faces for us. They both stand almost two feet taller than everyone else, so they can easily see over the crowd. Sasha spots me.

"There!" she says.

They roughly shove some men out of their way as they race toward us.

People drag their eyes from the sky and, seeing the Lupines bounding toward them, hastily get out of their way. Garrick and Sasha pick up speed, closing the gap. They're going to catch us!

A tavern door swings open, and a group of drunken merchants stumble out into the street, blocking their path. The Lupines slam into the men. They all fall over into a tangled heap on the ground, all shouting and swearing at each other. Garrick yells something, but I don't hear it as Elijah yanks my arm and leads me down a back alley. The passageway is dark and quiet. Crates are stacked up against the buildings, and trash cans overflow with garbage. He releases my hand and nimbly leaps up the crates onto the tavern's circular roof. I scramble onto the crates, and he hauls me up to the roof. My foot skids on the slippery solar tiles, and Elijah grabs me just as Garrick and Sasha enter the alleyway.

I clamp my hands over my mouth, trying to disguise my ragged breathing. The Lupines wander down the alley, their noses in the air. They're trying to smell us, but they seem to be having trouble picking up our scent over the reek of garbage.

The solar panel under my foot starts to crack.

Panic pulses through me. If it breaks, I'll fall.

The Lupines walk to the end of the alley, then turn back in our direction. The solar tile fractures a little more, and my foot slips an inch. My heart leaps into my throat. Garrick and Sasha are below us. Garrick peers through the window of the tavern, checking to see if we're inside.

"They're not here," he growls.

"Fragg," Sasha mutters. "Let's check the other alley."

They leave the passageway and are soon swallowed up by the crowds on the main street.

I release my hands from my mouth and exhale. My whole body is shaking.

Elijah helps me up, and we quickly climb over the rooftop just as the digital screens across the city blink on. Purian Rose's face appears on the monitors.

The city falls silent.

"Citizens of Thrace, by now you will have noticed my Destroyer Ships above your city," he says. This is all starting to sound scarily familiar. "It has come to our attention that the Dacian residents of your city recently voted against Rose's Law. In accordance with the new addendum to the law, this now classifies them as race traitors, and they have been marked for segregation."

Elijah gives me a worried look.

"You have precisely seventy-two hours to hand over all your Dacians to my men, or you will be severely punished," Purian Rose says. "If you have any doubt about my sincerity, I have left a message for you in Spice Square. Good evening."

The image cuts to a live feed from Spice Square. Kneeling in the center of the plaza are six Pilgrims, all wearing the white robes of the Purity faith. They recite from the Book of Creation as several Sentry guards—Sebastian included—walk around them, splashing gasoline over the Pilgrims' clothes. "What's going on?" I say, dread slowly creeping through me.

"They're Pilgrims, not Dacians. What could they have possibly done wrong?"

"Nothing," Elijah says darkly. "That's the point. If Purian Rose can do this to his most devoted followers, imagine what he'll do to the people of Thrace if they disobey him and don't turn over the Dacians?"

The guards move away, and Sebastian picks up a flaming torch and tosses it at the Pilgrims. They're instantly engulfed in flames, but not one of them screams—only words of praise for Purian Rose fly from their lips.

Rose is sending us a message, all right: if this is what he'll do to his most devout followers, imagine what he'll do to the people of Thrace if they disobey him.

29.

ASH

THE HOUSE is in an uproar around me as Lucas and the children run about, gathering their clothes and toys in readiness to escape. I help Giselle drag a bookshelf in front of the door while Madame Clara bolts the window shutters. We saw Purian Rose's message thirty minutes ago, and already a few men have gathered outside the house, trying to break in. I don't think they know I'm here; otherwise there would be a full-on lynch mob.

I snatch a look at the grandfather clock. It's past eleven o'clock. "Did Natalie give you any indication when she'd be back?" I ask Giselle.

She shakes her head as she drags a few chairs in front of the bookcase to create a blockade.

I touch a hand to my chest and feel the steady thrum of my heart under my fingertips. Natalie is alive. That much I know. If she weren't, my heart would've stopped beating. As soon as Madame Clara's kids are safe, I'm going to find Natalie. Then . . . I don't know what. One thing at a time.

There's another loud thud against the front door.

"Go to hell!" Giselle screams at the men on the other side. "They're just kids!"

"Where will we go?" I say to Madame Clara as I pile more chairs in front of the door.

"The Rainbow Forest on the outskirts of the city," she replies. "We can take refuge with Neptune."

"Who's Neptune?" I ask.

"The leader of our people," Giselle replies. "He's got a commune up in the forest. They keep moving around, so it's hard for people to track them down unless you know what to look for."

It sounds like our best shot at getting the kids to safety. I check the clock again. *Where are you, Natalie?* I rush over to the window and pull the curtain aside. On the digital screen on the street opposite us, the countdown clock has already started ticking down: 71:28:14, 71:28:13, 71:28:12 . . .

I drop the curtain as a platoon of Sentry guards marches down the street. They've been arriving in their Transporters for the past thirty minutes, setting up roadblocks to stop people from escaping. I don't know how we're going to get out of here.

There's a sudden thud on the roof, quickly followed by a second thump.

I bound up the stairs, Giselle following, and race into my bedroom. Standing on the balcony are Natalie and Elijah. Relief crashes over me as I yank open the doors and pull Natalie into my arms. She's clearly exhausted, barely able to catch her breath. She smells of Shine, and so does Elijah—I can smell him from here. So that's what they've been doing? If it were any other time, I'd be furious at Natalie for being so thoughtless, but I'm so glad she's safe, it's hard to be mad. I hold her tight.

Elijah flops down on the mattress and runs a hand over his face. "That was close."

"What happened?" Giselle says.

"Garrick and Sasha," Natalie replies. "But we managed to lose them. I'm sorry, Ash. Sebastian will know we're here now."

"Well, you and me," Elijah corrects her. "They think Ash is dead, remember?"

There's more banging on the front door, downstairs.

"It's okay. We need to go," I say. "We're heading into the forest."

Natalie struggles to her feet. "Okay. Let's go."

I collect my duffel bag while Natalie stuffs a few dresses into her bag. When we get downstairs, Madame Clara is already waiting for us in the hallway with Lucas and the other kids. They all look terrified.

There's a series of loud thumps as the men outside hammer against the door. The wooden frame starts to splinter.

"Come out here, you Dacian scum!" one of the men shouts from the other side.

The door begins to buckle. They'll be inside at any minute.

"How are we going to get away?" Natalie asks.

"Through the service tunnels," Madame Clara says.

She ushers us all into the kitchen and shoves the heavy oak table to one side. Underneath is an oval rug. Giselle kicks it to one side, exposing a wooden trapdoor. She lifts the lid to reveal a flight of rickety steps, which leads into a dark basement.

Giselle picks up the lantern from the countertop and then helps the blind old lady down the stairs. The children go next, followed by Natalie and Elijah. I drag the kitchen table back into its original position, then duck under the table and climb through the trapdoor, shutting it behind me. The basement is musty and is stacked with crates and forgotten furniture. Elijah helps Giselle lift a few crates of spiced Shine to one side, revealing an old metal door. It creaks as she pulls it open, causing flakes of rust to fall to the floor. On the other side of the door is a redbrick tunnel, about seven feet high and four feet wide. It leads into a black abyss.

She enters the tunnel, followed by Lucas and the other children.

Madame Clara grips the strap of my bag for guidance as the rest of us head into the tunnel after them. Just before Elijah slams the metal door behind us, I hear the front door burst open upstairs.

The passageway is pitch-black, except for the light coming from Giselle's lantern. The air around us is damp and cool, and the ground is covered in dirty rainwater, which has seeped through the crumbling mortar. The children all link hands as they follow Giselle. Madame Clara walks behind me, while Natalie and Elijah bring up the rear.

For over a mile, we walk in complete silence, other than the sound of our feet splashing through the puddles in a rhythmic beat. I listen out for other footsteps, but no one appears to be following us. That doesn't mean we're safe, though. Who knows what else is down here? I think about the Wrath Hounds and shudder.

A truck rumbles by on the road overhead, and brick dust falls into my hair. I shake my head to get it out.

"Where do all these tunnels go?" I ask Madame Clara.

"Most lead to the ports," she says. "The merchants originally used the passages to bring black market goods into the city. But they've been abandoned for a long time because they're not safe."

Another truck rolls by overhead, shaking loose a chunk of mortar, which splashes into the water in front of me. *No kidding.*

Giselle takes a number of turns, and I soon lose track of where we're going as we head deeper into the tunnel network. A person could easily get lost in here. It's eerily quiet, a stark contrast to the world above us. The city is in pandemonium. People are running; there's screaming and the occasional pop of gunfire. It's like the siege on Black City all over again.

I glance over my shoulder at Natalie to make sure she's okay. She looks utterly exhausted, her feet dragging through the puddles, her skin glistening with sweat despite the cool air. I worry she's coming down with something, but then remember she's been drinking all night, not to mention running from Garrick. No wonder she's tired. She's leaning heavily against Elijah, who's got his arm looped around her waist. My fangs throb. He notices me looking and drops his arm.

Giselle turns down a tunnel to our right. This one is much smaller and is on a slight incline; I have to stoop to prevent my head from hitting the arched ceiling. We follow this passageway for a few hundred yards. The farther we go, the quieter the city above us becomes, until eventually, there's complete silence. We reach a flight of stairs and exit through an abandoned service hut, which leads into the Rainbow Forest.

Even in the moonlight, it's immediately apparent how the woodland earned its name. The forest is densely populated with eucalyptus trees, whose bark is a patchwork of bright colors: lime green, sunset orange, purple amethyst, sea blue, maroon. Scattered between them are a few sap-green conifers and Carrow trees, with their famous star-shaped amber leaves.

I turn around to get a better look at the city below us. We're on a hill, so from this vantage point, I can see across most of Thrace. Thousands of people run through the streets as a steady stream of Transporters brings more troops down to secure the city. Every few seconds there's the rat-a-tat-tat of machine gun fire. It's utter bedlam, and somewhere in the middle of it all is the Moon Star. A crushing weight presses down on my shoulders, knowing the mission's over. There's nothing for us to do now but get the hell out of Thrace.

30.

ASH

WE WALK DEEPER into the forest, putting Thrace as far behind us as possible. Natalie glances at me, her expression reflecting my own disappointment. How can we possibly bring down Purian Rose, when we're so outnumbered and outgunned? Elijah walks next to her, his head bowed, no doubt thinking about his mom. Natalie places a consoling hand on his arm. It's such an innocent touch, and yet it rips my heart in two.

"Why is Rose doing this to us?" Giselle says beside me.

"I don't know," I say, tearing my eyes away from Natalie and Elijah. "I think he's afraid of anything that's not like him."

"So his solution is to kill us all?" Giselle says. "What could have frightened him so much that he has to resort to *this*?" She gestures toward the Destroyer Ships in the night sky.

"I have no idea," I reply. "It's impossible to understand what goes on in his mind."

"I won't let them take Lucas or any of the children to the Tenth," Giselle says. "I'd rather slit their throats than allow them to be sold as slaves or gassed like vermin."

The violence of her thoughts knocks me back. Giselle stops and turns to me, her gray eyes blazing.

"I want to start my own rebellion here in Thrace," she says. "Will you help me?"

I consider her proposal. I may have failed to locate the Ora, but I can still help the rebellion. I have to do *something*. What's the point of being Phoenix if I don't stand up to the Sentry and fight?

"All right," I say. "I'm in."

We continue our hike through the forest for the next hour. Giselle and I chat quietly about our plans to start an uprising, while Natalie and Elijah hang toward the back of the group, deep in their own private conversation.

I start to understand what Madame Clara meant about no one finding us in the forest. It seems to go on for eternity, and all the pathways look the same. You could easily lose your way. Giselle stops at one of the trees and traces her fingers down the colorful bark, finding a small circle carved into the wood.

"They're at the Circle Glade," she says.

Giselle leads us up a steep incline, and my muscles groan with the effort. I don't know how Madame Clara's managing it. I peer over my shoulder at the old lady, who is holding hands with Lucas and chuckling at one of his jokes. The other children race around her, their fear gone now that we're in the woods.

"What happened to her eyes?" I ask Giselle.

"Neptune cut them out."

I stop dead in my tracks. "*What?* Why?"

"Madame Clara fell in love with a woman, and Neptune didn't take it well," Giselle says.

"Fragging hell," I mutter, wondering if it's the best idea to seek refuge with this violent man.

"I don't want you to think badly of our people because of what he did," she adds quickly. "We're not all like Neptune, and this *was* thirty years ago. Attitudes have changed."

We mercifully reach the top of the hill. Up here the forest flattens out, but the vegetation is denser, making progress slow-going. Wild animals call out to each other in the dark as we trudge through the bracken.

"How many Dacians live with Neptune?" I ask.

"Only a few hundred," Giselle says. "Everyone else lives in the city, because that's where the work is. But representatives from each of the five clans have stayed with him."

"Which clan do you belong to?" I ask.

"Lambert, technically," Giselle says. "But I just think of myself as Clara's kid." We carry on trekking through the woodland.

"So, are your parents . . . um . . ." I don't know how to put this delicately.

"Dead?" she asks. "Yeah."

"How come your other family didn't take you in after they died?"

"They didn't want me," she says. "My dad was a Dacian, but my mom wasn't, and neither family approved of the match, so I was shunned. There wasn't anywhere for me to go, so I was on the streets for a while, until I met Clara."

"It sounds tough."

"I can handle myself," she says, subconsciously touching the bruise on her cheek, where the guard hit her. "Ah! Here we are."

We step into a large, circular clearing in the heart of the forest. Parked around the outer edges of the glade are dozens of traditional Dacian caravans, painted in reds, golds and greens, while directly to our right are five large tents. In the center of the glade is a fire pit filled with glowing red embers. A metal sheet is suspended a few feet over it, to prevent the fire from being visible from above at night.

Congregated around the fire pit are over a hundred Dacian men and women. A few of the people have bags by their feet, and I'm assuming they came from the city looking for refuge. They're in the middle of a heated discussion.

Sitting at the far end of the fire pit, listening to everyone argue, are five men and two women. One of the women looks similar to Giselle, with flowing auburn hair and gray eyes, except she's considerably older.

Giselle notices me looking. "That's Pandora Lambert. She's one of the five clan elders. The blond woman next to her is Miranda Hicks."

Miranda is in her midforties and painfully gaunt, with heavy Cinderstone powder drawn around her eyes.

"Who are the men?" I say.

"The guy in the glasses is Sol Becket, and beside him is Gilderoy Draper." The latter has wavy black hair and bright blue eyes, like Lucas. "The man in the middle is Neptune Jack."

Neptune's in his midsixties, stocky, with swarthy skin and a thick gray beard that matches his curly hair. Like Giselle, he has feathers and beads woven into his hair. The way he holds himself, with a quiet, confident power, makes it clear he's in charge.

Everyone stops talking as we approach him. Several of the men draw their daggers, but Neptune signals for them to hold back as Giselle, Lucas and the other children kneel before him, bowing so low, their noses touch the moist earth. Only Madame Clara stays standing out of their group, her chin lifted defiantly.

"You have some nerve bringing your litter of runts here, Clara," Neptune says.

"We seek refuge," she says. "Will you accept us, brother?"

Brother? I look at Neptune and realize there are similarities in their faces—they have the same wide nose, broad cheekbones and dark complexion, although Madame Clara's face is covered in tattoos and slightly disfigured from the scars over her eye sockets.

Neptune scratches his beard as he ponders her request. His gaze lingers on Elijah and Natalie before fixing on me. He sits up straighter.

"We'd heard you were dead," he says.

"Yeah, I heard that too," I reply. "But here I am, and I want to help."

Giselle lifts her head slightly, her auburn hair fanning around her shoulders. "We intend to stage an uprising in Thrace."

Natalie gives me a questioning look.

"When were you going to tell me about this?" she says under her breath.

"I'm telling you now," I reply.

Neptune stands up and waves his hand. "Follow me."

Giselle gets up and joins me, Natalie and Elijah as we follow him and the clan elders into a large tent while Madame Clara stays outside with the children. Inside, the tent has been draped with deep red and purple fabrics. In the middle of the tent is a fire pit with a circular bench covered in silken cushions surrounding it. Neptune gestures for everyone to take a seat on the bench while he sparks up a pipe.

"So you want to take on Rose, eh?" Neptune says.

"They've already started rounding us up," Giselle says. "It's only a matter of time before we're all captured and taken to the Tenth."

I explain what the Tenth is, and Neptune's eyes darken with

fury. The other clan elders pass angry looks between each other, equally outraged as their leader.

"How can we help?" he says.

I tell him the plan Giselle and I formulated while we were walking through the forest.

"What about the Destroyer Ships?" the red-haired woman, Pandora, says.

"We'll have to infiltrate them," I say.

"Once our people are inside, they can rescue the prisoners, then set bombs throughout the ships and take the Transporters out of there," Giselle adds.

"I've been on a Destroyer Ship," Natalie says. "There's not much security on them, beyond the hangar. It can work."

I give her a grateful smile, thankful she's on board.

"The Sentry could just send in more reinforcements via the roads," the gaunt woman, Miranda, says.

"Then we'll blow them up too," Gilderoy Draper replies.

"I don't think Purian Rose will send any reinforcements. He can't spare the men after the massacre at Iridium," I say, referring to the battle that killed Nick and possibly Juno. "The fact that he's sent only five Destroyer Ships here confirms that—in Black City there were a dozen."

"Plus Thrace isn't of military importance," Natalie chimes in. "He can't risk exposing his strategically important targets."

"We'll have to take control of the news station," the man in the glasses, Sol Becket, says.

"My cousin works there," Pandora says. "He'll get me in."

Neptune sucks on his pipe, considering. He gazes at the other clan elders, and they each nod in turn.

"It's madness, but it might just work," he finally says. "We'll begin preparations at dawn."

31.
ASH

I ROLL OVER in the bed and wipe a hand over my face, trying to rub the sleep away. The light coming through the window shutters suggests it's just after sunrise. I gaze around the room, confused for a moment where I am, then remember I'm in one of the Dacian caravans. It's a long, thin wagon with a curved wooden roof painted scarlet and emerald green, and tie-dyed fabrics draped over all the surfaces.

The other side of the bed is empty, the pillow cool. I pull on my clothes and go outside in search of Natalie. The glade is already brimming with life as the clan elders prepare for tomorrow's attack on the Sentry. Sol is by the fire pit with several of his men, cleaning a pile of rifles and swords by their feet and loading the guns with ammo, while Gilderoy and Miranda laugh and chat with each other as they shoot glass bottles off a fallen log, their aim deadly accurate. I can't see Pandora, so I assume she's already gone into Thrace to infiltrate the news station. I hope she succeeds, as it's an important part of the plan.

Natalie, Elijah and Madame Clara are sitting on the steps of a nearby caravan, drinking cups of tea. Natalie looks tired and pale, and I don't think it's just from a hangover. It's more like a weariness that's enveloped her whole body. I'm stunned by how skinny she's looking. I didn't notice it yesterday, when we were in the bedroom at Madame Clara's, but my mind was on other things at the time.

Giselle steps out of the green caravan next to me, wearing the same bright yellow dress as yesterday, although today she's got some peacock feathers woven into her auburn hair. They shimmer turquoise in the sunlight, matching the makeup lining her startling eyes. Her smiling lips are painted gold, and her cheeks flush slightly when she sees me. She hasn't made any attempt to hide her attraction toward me, and you know what? I like it. It's nice to feel wanted by somebody, even if it isn't the girl I love.

"They seem cozy," Giselle says, nodding toward Elijah and Natalie.

I follow her gaze. Elijah's hand is now resting on Natalie's back, his thumb moving in small circles against her spine. She edges away and he lowers his hand, but it's too late, the damage is done. My insides are completely shredded. I need to get out of here.

"I'm going into the city to do some recon," I say.

"I'll join you." Giselle quickly fetches some robes from the caravan, and we head into the city.

A few hours later, we're in the heart of Thrace. The city is in chaos. Doors are smashed, shutters are up on windows, and some of the buildings are on fire. I keep an eye out for any taverns that might be the Moon Star, but see none that could fit the bill. We do pass one tavern with an enormous crescent moon–shaped, solar panel on the top of its intricately tiered roof, but

I can't see the star anywhere, so I discount it. Sentry trucks roll through the near-empty streets while Lupine packs barge into homes and emerge with whole families, who kick and scream as they're dragged to Spice Square, where the Transporters are waiting to take them up to the Destroyer Ships.

Giselle and I climb onto the roof of a building overlooking Spice Square, to get a better view of the plaza. The place is buzzing with activity. I count six Transporters, plus eight trucks. Sentry guards load supplies off the vehicles and carry them into the city hall, where they've set up their base camp.

Across the square, a giant digital screen broadcasts the latest news from SBN. My image is on all the monitors as the news channel runs a report on my supposed death. It's all the same information as yesterday, which is comforting—they don't mention Amy or Stuart, so I can only assume they're still alive somewhere. SBN replays Nick's death on a constant loop in the bottom right-hand corner of the screen. Every time I see the bomb explode, I wince, feeling it.

The broadcast flicks off, and the countdown clock returns, letting us know how much time we have left. Sixty-three hours, twenty-eight minutes. It's not much time to prepare a full-scale assault on the Sentry, especially without Roach and the rest of Humans for Unity to help me.

Giselle edges a little closer to me as we lie on the rooftop and watch the Sentry guards loading the prisoners onto the Transporters in the town square below us. As in Black City, Evacuation Passes are being issued to citizens when they hand over their captives to the guards. It makes me sick that people are so willing to turn over their neighbors, but it does mean the city will be relatively deserted by the time we start our attack, so casualties will be kept to a minimum.

"This is where we'll stage the attack tomorrow," I say. "We'll strike at noon, when the guards are changing shifts, so there are few people on the ground."

We stay on the rooftop for as long as we dare, watching the guards and trying to work out their shift patterns. There appear to be only around a hundred guards on the ground at any one time. The rest stay up in the Destroyer Ships. Anger boils up inside me when Sebastian, Garrick, Sasha and the Moondog in the red leather frock coat, Jared, walk down the steps of Thrace City Hall. Sebastian's dressed in his black Tracker uniform, while Garrick and Sasha are in their usual gray jackets, pants and steel-capped boots. Garrick scowls as he surveys the scene, his silvery eyes glinting beneath his heavy brow. He tilts his head up, sniffing the air. His head turns in our direction.

We scramble off the roof before he spots us. Not wanting to push our luck any more, we hurry back to the forest to meet up with the others. Madame Clara sits with Lucas and the other children around the bonfire, sewing hoods onto black robes, while Natalie and Elijah prepare lunch. There's a big pile of apples beside them, which they're in the process of peeling. Relief crosses Natalie's features when she sees us. She races over to me and flings her arms around my neck. For a moment, it's how things used to be, and I draw her close, my heart aching.

"I was so worried," she says. "You didn't tell me you were going."

"Sorry," I murmur against her cheek. "It won't happen again."

She looks up, and I think she's going to kiss me. But then she catches sight of Elijah watching us and pulls away. The brief moment of joy I felt evaporates, and the hollowness returns.

We join the others. While I tell them what we saw in the city,

Giselle plucks a shiny green apple from the pile beside Elijah and polishes it with the cuff of her yellow dress.

Natalie throws her an annoyed look. "Those are for lunch."

"So? If you want something, you should just take it." Giselle slides a look at me, her gray eyes gleaming mischievously as she takes a bite out of the apple.

Natalie gets to her feet, wiping her hands on her dress. "I'm going for a walk."

She pushes past me and heads to the other side of the glade. Elijah gets up and follows her.

"Was it something I said?" Giselle says innocently.

I frown, a little annoyed at Giselle for upsetting Natalie, but secretly a little pleased that Natalie's jealous. It proves she still has some feelings for me.

We spend the rest of the day getting everything organized for tomorrow's assault on Thrace. Just as the sun starts to set, a group of women return from the city holding piles of folded blue cloth. I run my hand over the cerulean material, which reminds me so much of Natalie's eyes. That's why I picked the color, not that anyone knows this.

Neptune comes over to me.

"I have news from Pandora. She's gotten inside the station, and everything's been set up. She'll stay there to oversee things tomorrow."

I nod, relieved. That was the final piece of the puzzle we had to put into place. There's nothing more to do now except wait. Tomorrow we take back Thrace.

By the time we're finished, night has fallen. Everyone congregates around the bonfire for dinner. The children play around the fire as if they have no worries in the world, while the adults solemnly drink glasses of spiced Shine, knowing that many of us could be dead within the next twenty-four hours. I glance at Natalie, who is sitting on the log bench with Elijah. They both just gaze at the fire, quiet and contemplative. Sensing me looking, Natalie turns her head toward me. My heart clenches.

An old man with a tattoo of a mermaid on his arm has an accordion with him, and he starts to play a folk tune, his fingers nimbly running across the keys. The children spin and dance in time with the music. Madame Clara and Giselle clap along, while a few of the men go and fetch instruments from their caravans and join the old man. One by one, people get up and dance, clearly grateful for the distraction.

Natalie smiles as she watches everyone, her blue eyes glimmering in the firelight. She looks a little better than earlier, now that she's had time to rest. Elijah stands up and stretches a hand out to her. She hesitates, then takes it.

A familiar ache spreads through my chest at the sight of them dancing. He's very good at it, but I guess as the Consul's son, he has time to learn these things. They get a lot of admiring glances from the others, not just because of the ease with which they move, but because they look good together. Great, in fact. He twirls Natalie around, and she throws her head back and laughs, a sound I haven't heard since her birthday. *The night I proposed.*

A new tune begins, led by the drums. The music fills the night sky with its animalistic beat. Nearby, Giselle spins and swirls in time to the rhythm, her yellow dress and red hair fanning around her until she looks like the flames of the bonfire. She catches my eye, and a smirk plays across her lips. She provocatively beckons me toward her. I look jealously at Natalie and Elijah.

Two can play this game.

I walk over to Giselle and take her in my arms, dancing with her to the exotic music, our bodies swaying in unison. I cup a hand around her waist, pulling her hard against me. She lets out a small gasp, her silvery eyes sparkling mischievously.

I look at Natalie. She frowns, her eyes fixed on me as Elijah twirls her around in circles.

The music deepens into something slower, more sensual. Giselle's fingers lace through my hair, causing a sensory overload as she grinds against me. Her lips are so close to mine. All it will take is one misstep, and we'll kiss. Giselle's cheeks flush; her eyes dilate. I've seen the same reaction from Hazers after a hit. *Lust.* Fragg, it feels good to be *wanted*.

My hand runs down Giselle's back, toward the curve at the end of her spine, but all the time my focus is on Natalie. Anger flits across her face, and she wraps her arms around Elijah's neck. He moans, pulling her closer to him. In retaliation, I dip Giselle, lightly running my hand down her voluptuous body. She shivers with delight, her lips parting. I pick her up and whirl her around in time to the music. She lets out a joyful laugh of delight, her eyes glimmering. Her intent is clear, and I'm tempted, even if it is just to make Natalie suffer for the way she's hurt me.

Elijah holds Natalie close, his hands caressing her body, his face pressed against hers, his eyes closed. He looks lost, enraptured. In love. Pain rips through me. It's too much. I release Giselle, defeated, and storm away from the dance floor, away from Natalie.

I head straight for my caravan, my whole body shaking with anger. I sink down on the bed, my chest heaving. I think I'm dying, unable to breathe.

"Are you okay?" Giselle says quietly from the doorway.

"She's leaving me for *him*," I admit, my voice splintering. "I don't know what to do."

"You can't control her heart, Ash."

"I know," I say. "But I can't control mine either, and I love her so much, it's killing me."

Giselle pads over to the bed and hugs me. Her body is soft, warm, inviting. She smells of rose water.

"I want her back," I whisper.

"There's still a chance," Giselle replies. "You just need to remind her why she fell in love with you. In the meantime—" She presses her lips against mine. Her kiss is fire, burning hot, exciting, teasing. She pulls away. "You're a catch, Ash. If she doesn't see that, then she's a fool."

She winks at me, leaving the caravan. The door swings shut behind her, but not before I catch a glimpse of Natalie running into the forest.

32.

NATALIE

 "NATALIE, WAIT!"

I slow down so Elijah can catch up with me. He's carrying a small oil lantern, the light bouncing as he runs. My pulse is racing, my head pounding. Everything is spinning; sky, trees and earth all blend into each other. My knees buckle, and Elijah grabs me before I fall.

"He kissed her," I manage to say as the tears start to fall.

"I know," Elijah replies quietly. "I saw it too."

"Why did he do it?"

"Because he's in pain. He thinks you have feelings for me." He tilts my face up, and his eyes search mine. "Do you?"

I flush. "Elijah, I—"

Before I can finish my sentence, Elijah leans down and touches his lips to mine. His kiss is confident but tender, his lips soft, sumptuous. He tastes like honey—sweet, delicious. His tongue slips between my lips and lightly caresses my mouth, his touch gentle and inquisitive. A breathy moan forms in my throat, and I part my lips further, allowing him to fully explore me. My fingers twist through his fur-like hair, and I press my body against his, needing the comfort.

The echo of a second heartbeat flutters inside my chest. *Ash,* it's saying. *Ash, Ash, Ash.* What am I doing? I break off the kiss and bury my face in my hands, feeling so confused. Eventually, I glance up. Elijah looks at me expectantly, waiting for my answer.

"I can't . . . I don't feel . . . Elijah, I'm so sorry," I say.

The dappled moonlight shimmers across his skin, the gentle breeze ruffling his chocolate-brown mane. In another time, another world, I could possibly fall for him. But that's not the reality I live in. There's only room for one boy in my heart and soul, and that's Ash.

A muscle flexes in his square jaw. "It's okay, Natalie. I knew it was a long shot, but I had to try."

There's a snap of twigs, and a moment later, Ash and Giselle emerge from the darkness, stopping a few feet away from us. There's a challenging look in Ash's sparkling eyes as he waits for me to confront him. He knows I saw the kiss with Giselle. Did he see mine with Elijah? We're in an emotional standoff, everyone hurting, everyone betrayed, all of us wanting someone we can't have. And it's my fault.

This needs to end now.

I unhook the gold chain from my neck and slide off the engagement ring. It glitters in the starlight. It represents everything I want and everything I can never have. Not anymore. I walk over to Ash and drop it into his hand. He studies the diamond ring resting on his open palm, and a mixture of emotions flits across his face: bewilderment, anger, grief.

Finally his fingers close around the ring.

It's over.

"I'm going for walk," I say flatly.

Elijah joins me. We've barely gone a hundred feet before I hear Ash howl.

The walk through the forest is one of the loneliest of my life, even though Elijah is by my side. He holds the oil lantern, lighting our way. My whole body is numb, and I welcome it. I don't want to feel, because I know that as soon as I get over the shock of what I've done, I'm going to break into a million pieces.

It's no good, though. The cracks inside me splinter with every footstep, until I finally shatter. I crumple to the earth. Strong arms hold me as I rock back and forth, letting out a low-pitched wail. *What have I done?* "It was the right thing to do," Elijah whispers to me. "At least now he can let you go."

He holds me for a long time, maybe an hour, maybe two, until we both begin to shiver from the chilled night air. I rub my puffy, tearstained eyes and suck in a shaky breath.

"So what will you do now?" he asks gently.

"I'm going to head to Centrum to meet with the others, then find my mother," I tell Elijah.

I've been thinking about her a lot recently. I've had this aching need to see her, to be comforted by her, to die in her arms. But I don't even know where she is. She could be dead, for all I know, although I suspect if she were, Purian Rose would've splashed that all over SBN news.

"You can't go now. What about the rebellion?" Elijah asks.

"The rebellion doesn't need me."

"I need you," he replies.

My heart constricts. "Please don't say that."

I get up and Elijah springs to his feet. The Rainbow Forest is at the top of a steep hill, so we get a wonderful view of the city as we come down the grassy slopes. Thousands of solar panels glint in the moonlight, so the rooftops look like the stars above us. Even at night, the Mirror City lives up to its reputation.

The effect is slightly ruined by the Destroyer Ships hovering overhead, their searchlights scanning the dark streets. A light scans past the buildings on the rim of the city, illuminating their glassy roofs, and something catches my eye. I stop and blink, uncertain whether what I'm seeing is real or a figment of my imagination.

"Elijah, do you see it?"

"See what?" he asks.

I wait until the light passes the buildings again.

"There!" I say, pointing to a building with a star-shaped roof that tapers up into a steeple. At the top of the spire is a glimmering solar panel cut into the shape of a crescent moon.

"The Moon Star?" Elijah says, grinning.

I grab his hand. "Only one way to find out."

33.

NATALIE

IT TAKES ABOUT AN HOUR to reach the point in the city where I think the Moon Star should be. We cling to the shadows, ducking between buildings as Sentry guards march by on their evening patrols. Thankfully most of the lights are off in the buildings, so apart from the occasional sweep of the search-lights, we're covered by darkness. The streets are also empty, since many of the citizens have already left, having earned an Evacuation Pass. Those who remain stay indoors, hiding.

Overhead, the Destroyer Ships continue to hum, making the air vibrate. Once in a while, a Transporter streaks past, flying so low, it makes my hair whip around my face. It was risky coming down here, and I'm starting to regret it, but there's no turning back now.

I glance at Elijah and see a light in his topaz eyes that hasn't been there before. *Hope.* We wait for a platoon of guards to walk past before running across the street to the next alleyway. We dart between the buildings, using the narrow side alleys as much as possible to keep away from the Sentry guards. The coins on my dress jangle as I run, drawing more attention than I'd like.

"Wait," I say, stopping to rip the coins off the skirt. They roll into the gutter.

Elijah glances over his shoulder suddenly and looks across the street.

"What is it?" I whisper.

He narrows his eyes, then shakes his head. "Nothing. I thought I saw someone, but there's no one there." We don't hang around, in case someone is following us. We weave through the warren of side streets, heading deeper into the city.

"I think the tavern's around here somewhere," I say, scanning the skyline, in search of the crescent moon–shaped solar panel. I spot it peeping between the rooftops at the end of the road. "There!"

Like all the other taverns in the area, the Moon Star's shutters are drawn, the lights off. It's impossible to tell if anyone is inside. I try the handle on the ebony door. It's locked. We circle the building, looking for another way in. Elijah pushes a trash can aside to reveal a trapdoor leading into the storage cellar. He yanks on the handle. To my relief, the trapdoor opens.

We hurry down a flight of creaky wooden steps into the basement, closing the trapdoor behind us. The storage room is damp and musty, filled with crates and wine racks. To our left is a steel service door, similar to the one at Madame Clara's, while up ahead is the stairwell leading into the main bar. We pick our way through the clutter, trying our best not to hit anything, but Elijah's tail accidentally sweeps past a wine rack, knocking a bottle onto the floor. It smashes.

"Sorry," Elijah says.

"Do you think anyone's home?" I ask.

"I don't know. It is very quiet," he says, frowning.

I follow him up the stairs into the bar. We're immediately greeted by two rifle blasts, which miss us by an inch. Elijah and I both hit the floor, covering our heads.

"Who are you?" a woman's voice says.

I risk a look up at our assailant, catching snapshots of her along the way: a pair of scuffed brown boots, patchwork leather pants, a blue corset blouse, a rifle. She's sitting in a wheelchair. My eyes finally rest on her face. There's no doubting the middle-aged woman looking coldly back at me is Esme.

"I'm Natalie Buchanan, and this is Elijah Theroux," I say. "I believe you know his mother, Yolanda?"

Esme lowers her gun. "What are you doing here?"

We get to our feet, and Elijah briefly explains about Lucinda's letter, and our search for Yolanda and Lucinda.

Esme rests the shotgun on her lap, grabs a bottle of spiced Shine and some glasses and wheels over to one of the round tables. We join her at the table, putting the oil lantern between us.

"Were Lucinda and Yolanda here?" I ask.

"Yeah, they were here." Esme pours us all a drink. "Lucinda was on one of her mad rants, claiming she'd worked out a way to bring down Purian Rose, and needed Yolanda and Kieran's help."

"Kieran's your partner, right?" I say.

She nods. "I begged him not to get involved. Lucinda's a bit—" Esme taps her head. "You know? Especially after Niall died."

I remember Sigur telling us about Lucinda and her Blood Mate, Niall, and how he died during their attack on the Black City water plant. I wonder if my father pulled the trigger.

"Kieran didn't listen to me, but when it comes to Lucinda he never does. They go way back. The three of them went off on their mission, and left me here to tend the bar," Esme says bitterly, taking a gulp of her drink. "I would've slowed them down anyway."

She frowns, and I'm guessing it wasn't her choice to stay.

A sound of footsteps outside the tavern draws our attention. Esme reaches for her gun, while we silently wait for the guards to move on. The footsteps fade as they turn down another street.

"Where are Lucinda and the others now?" I ask, once they've gone.

"I don't know," Esme says. "They were heading to the Claw—"

"The what?"

"It's a mountain," Esme explains.

I glance at Elijah, and his expression mirrors my own surprise. The Ora's located on a mountain? But then thinking about it some more, it's a good location for a rebel laboratory that's storing weaponized yellowpox. It's remote and unpopulated.

Esme looks down at her glass of spiced Shine. "The last time Kieran called, he said they'd reached Gray Wolf—"

"That's in the Mountain Wolf State, isn't it?" Elijah asks.

Esme nods. "But I haven't heard from him since. That was nearly a week ago."

"That's around the last time my mom called me," Elijah says.

He sinks his head into his hands, letting out a pained groan. Esme's just confirmed our fears—that his mother and Lucinda have been captured, and by the sounds of it, Kieran too. Esme knocks back her drink, and pours herself another. I notice her hand is trembling. She must've reached the same conclusion as us.

Elijah raises his head.

"I'm going to rescue them," he says fiercely.

"Good luck with that, darling," Esme says. "They're either

dead or will be soon, once the Sentry's got the information they need."

"My mom won't tell the Sentry anything about the Ora," Elijah says assuredly.

Esme furrows her brow. "The Ora?"

"The weapon . . . ?" Elijah says.

Esme's eyes widen. "Oh, do you mean—"

There's a smattering of gunfire, and we duck for cover as the front door and windows are shredded with bullets. Glass rains down on me, ripping my dress and slashing my skin. I cry out in pain as a shard of glass digs into my left thigh. My head swims as I pull the glass out of my flesh. My teal dress instantly turns purple with blood.

"Stop shooting! I want her alive!" a voice shouts on the other side of the door.

Sebastian.

There's a bang against the heavy oak door as the guards try to get in.

Esme picks up her rifle. "Get out of here. Take the service tunnel."

Elijah helps me to my feet. His face is covered in blood, and there's a gruesome gash in his cheek.

"What about you?" I say.

"I'll hold them back for as long as I can," Esme says. "Go!"

Elijah grabs the lantern on the table, then helps me as we climb down the stairs into the basement. I drag my left leg, which feels leaden and white-hot with pain, but adrenaline keeps me moving. We reach the cellar just as the front door bursts open.

"Where are they?" Sebastian's voice booms through the basement ceiling.

"I don't know who you're talking about," Esme replies.

"Don't give us that. One of my girls followed them here," another voice says. *Garrick.*

So Elijah was right, someone *was* following us earlier.

I find the metal door leading into the service tunnel and twist the rusted handle. It doesn't budge. Elijah has a go, putting all his strength behind it, and this time it turns. The door opens, and we're immediately hit with a blast of cold, stagnant air.

"Get the hell out of my bar!" Esme says.

There's a pop of gunfire, and Garrick howls in pain. All hell breaks loose upstairs. Bullets fly, glass breaks, bodies hit the floor.

Elijah shoves me into the tunnel, just as I hear Esme scream. He slams the door behind us.

"We have to help her!" I say.

"It's too late," Elijah replies. "Come on, we need to go back to Ash and tell him about the Claw."

He's right, this is too important. Ash needs to know about the location of the Ora. So many lives depend on us retrieving it.

I sling my arm over Elijah's shoulder for support, grit my teeth, and run.

34.

ASH

EVERYONE IN THE CAMP has gone to bed, although I doubt anyone will sleep tonight. I sit alone on the fallen tree trunk beside the dying embers of the fire and stare at the engagement ring resting on my palm. It weighs barely anything, and yet it's crushing me. After everything we've been through and all the sacrifices we've made, all it took was one kiss to break us. I close my fingers around the ring and throw it across the glade. It lands in some bushes. I regret it immediately and rush over to the bush to retrieve it.

"Couldn't sleep either?"

I whip around at the sound of Giselle's voice and nearly drop the ring again in surprise. I slip it into my pocket. Giselle stands a few feet away, nervously playing with one of the feathers in her auburn hair. She's taken off her heavy makeup, and she looks much nicer without the thick eyeliner and metallic lips. Natural, beautiful. She seems self-conscious, though, unable to meet my eye.

"I thought you were in bed," I say.

"I couldn't drift off," she says. "Guilty conscience, I think.

I'm sorry, Ash. I shouldn't have kissed you. Madame Clara says I have no impulse control, and I'm starting to think she might be right."

"It wasn't your fault. I shouldn't have let it happen," I say.

Giselle sighs. "I don't know what's wrong with me sometimes. I always want the one thing that's out of my reach, like if I get it, somehow it'll mean I'm worth something. Does that make sense?"

I study her for a long moment, and for the first time, I see the real Giselle—an orphan girl shunned by her family, who has to steal to survive. I think about those men beating her in Spice Square, and how people just walked by, and I wonder how many times that's happened before. She wears her confidence like makeup, to disguise the broken girl underneath.

"I get it," I say.

My hair suddenly stirs, sensing blood. I whip around, just as Natalie and Elijah stumble out of the forest. They're both drenched in blood, their clothes ripped and torn. The right side of Elijah's face is swollen, while Natalie drags her left leg. I race over to them, my hurt and betrayal instantly pushed to one side.

"What's happened?" I demand as Elijah helps her to the log. Natalie winces as she sits down, clutching her left thigh. Blood seeps between her fingers, igniting my thirst. I swallow it down.

Elijah gives me the highlights while Giselle goes to fetch Madame Clara. They soon return, carrying bandages and jars of herbal remedies. Giselle tends to the wound on Elijah's face while I help Madame Clara with Natalie's leg.

I roll up her skirt to reveal the gash in her thigh. Blood pumps out of the wound with every heartbeat, turning her white skin a gleaming red. I reach out a hand, intending to inspect the wound, but Natalie violently flinches away.

"Don't touch me!" she says.

"Christ, Nat. I'm only trying to help," I reply, stung by her reaction. "I need to check it."

I reach out again.

"No, wait! Ash, STOP!" she cries out as my fingers touch her blood-soaked skin. "I have the Wrath!"

I snatch my hand back. "What did you say?"

Natalie peers up at me, her blue eyes shining with tears.

"I have the Wrath," she whispers. "I must have caught it from the Darkling boy who bit me."

"Are you certain?" I say hoarsely.

"I ran a test in the laboratory back in the Barren Lands."

A low groan escapes my lips as I bend double, my body crumpling under the weight of her words. *I have the Wrath.*

Suddenly everything makes sense—the way she's been pushing me away, the fact that she hasn't been able to hold any food down, the conversation with Elijah in the laboratory. Somehow I find the strength to lift my head.

"Why didn't you tell me?" I say.

"I wasn't ready to lose you," she says. "I'm sorry, Ash. I never stopped loving you, I—"

I kiss her.

I put as much meaning in it as possible—I'm going to be there for her, she's not alone. She returns my kiss, wrapping her arms around me. My heart aches, with love, with grief. I've got her back, but for how long? A week? A month? A year? We have no idea how this disease affects humans.

"I love you," I murmur against her lips.

"I'm so sorry I hurt you," she replies.

"Me too," I say, referring to Giselle. "But all that matters is that we're together."

I hold her hand while Giselle and Madame Clara patch up her leg. The wound isn't as bad as we first feared—it's deep, but it didn't hit the bone or any major arteries. Once she's bandaged up, I walk over to Elijah. He gazes at me, his swollen cheek covered in a sticky-looking ointment.

"You're taking the news well," he says, glancing toward Natalie.

Grief aches through me. "I think I owe you an apology."

"No, you don't," he says quietly. "I've overstepped the mark a few times myself. Sorry about that."

I sit down beside him. "So, you found Esme?" I say.

He nods, and tells me everything they learned.

"So the laboratory's on a mountain near Gray Wolf?" I say.

Elijah nods. "I've never heard of the Claw before, though. Have you?"

"No," I admit.

"It's probably another nickname," Natalie says, overhearing our conversation. "Like the way Crimson Mountain is also known as the Devil's Fork."

"We should head to Gray Wolf after the attack tomorrow," I say. "Someone might've seen where the Sentry took your mom and my aunt."

"Can we stop off at Viridis on the way?" Elijah says. "It's only a few days away by boat, and it'll be safer than trying to take the roads. You can talk to the senate about joining the rebellion while I gather supplies, and then we'll continue on to Gray Wolf."

"Sounds like a plan," I say, reinvigorated.

Elijah lowers his eyes. "Good; I'm certain my dad will be excited to meet you."

I return to Natalie and scoop her up in my arms. I carry her to our caravan and gently lay her down on the bed and help her undress. There's a nasty purple bruise on her shoulder, and her skin is covered in scratches. *Soon her skin will be rotting and covered in welts.* The thought hits me like a sucker punch, and I have to place a hand on the dresser to steady myself.

"You okay?" Natalie asks quietly.

I nod, finding a shirt and passing it to her. Once she's dressed, I take off my own clothes and climb into the narrow bed. There's not much space, so we're pressed close together. I wrap my arms around her, and she rests her head against my chest, her fingers lightly tracing over my scars.

"I'll understand if you want to leave me," she says quietly.

I tighten my arms around her. "That's never going to happen."

"I'm really sorry I got bitten, Ash," she says.

"It wasn't your fault," I reply, grief clawing its way up my throat. "Let's not talk about it anymore, okay?"

Natalie doesn't protest. She nestles closer to me.

"Are you worried about tomorrow?" she asks sleepily.

"A little," I admit, kissing her head again. "Try to rest."

She shuts her eyes. It doesn't take long for her breathing to slow down and deepen.

"Natalie, you still awake?" I whisper.

She doesn't respond.

Only now that she's asleep do I let the tears fall.

35.

ASH

THE SUN IS HIGH over Thrace, making the whole market sparkle as thousands of mirrors catch the light. We're inside a tavern at the end of Spice Square, about fifty feet away from the Thrace City Hall. The two white-and-red Sentry banners still hang down the front of the city hall, fluttering slightly on the breeze. For the past few hours, I've been watching the guards come and go from the building, trying to gauge their movements. There's nothing out of the ordinary.

To our right, directly opposite Thrace City Hall, are the giant digital screens, showing the countdown: 36:04:01, 36:04:00, 36:03:59, 36:03:58 . . . Situated on top of one of the digital screens, carefully camouflaged, is a camera.

So far, I've spotted around a hundred Sentry guards, several squads of Trackers and two Lupine packs coming and going from that building, including Sebastian and Garrick. They're heavily armed, but because they're not expecting trouble, we've got the element of surprise on our side. Plus, unless they open up the large decorative doors that dominate the façade— which doesn't look possible, considering how rusted the hinges are—all the guards will have to exit the building via the small access door one at a time, making them easy pickings for us.

Across the square is the ghetto wall, punctuated at even intervals by guard towers. These appear deserted, but I know better. Gilderoy Draper and his team have been up there, hidden from view, since dawn. The fact that the Darkling ghetto is empty has worked in our favor, as it means the guard towers have been unmanned for over a year.

Above us, a Transporter travels to one of the Destroyer Ships, carrying a platoon of guards who have just finished their shift. There's only one Transporter left, parked down Cinnamon Street, next to the city hall. Everything is going as planned. First thing this morning, two dozen of the Dacian rebels, including one of the clan elders, Miranda, allowed themselves to be captured and taken up to the Destroyer Ships. Hidden under their clothing were homemade bombs.

My stomach knots as I anxiously watch the airships. If everything is going to plan, the rebels have already freed the prisoners from the cells and are making their way to the hangar deck to capture the Transporters so they can get the Dacians off the airships before they blow up. So much can go wrong, and we're relying on Miranda and her teams to take out the airships; there's no other way we can seize Thrace.

Natalie, Elijah, Giselle, Neptune and Sol Becket are with me. I check my watch. It's almost noon. In two minutes, we'll be unleashing hell on this city. I flick a look at Natalie, who is adjusting her sword. I know she's had experience using a sword, so that brings me some comfort. She's wearing a black hooded robe, and has Cinderstone powder painted over her eyes and nose like the rest of us. She glances up at me, her face almost entirely hidden in the shadow of her hood. I smile at her, and she smiles back. Madame Clara gave her some medicine to manage the pain in her leg, so she'll be able to fight.

I check my rifle for the umpteenth time, and then adjust the canvas bag hidden under my robe. It's loaded with ammunition and smoke grenades, cobbled together from ingredients Neptune's men were able to gather for us yesterday. Everyone else has a canvas bag similar to mine, as well as a sword, dagger or rifle. It's not much, but it's all we have. I hope it's enough.

Neptune pats me on my shoulder. "You ready, boy?"

"Yeah, I'm ready," I reply.

"Ash, look!" Natalie says, pointing up at the sky.

On cue, the azure sky fills with Transporters. They zoom away from the Destroyer Ships and fly toward the agreed-upon rendezvous point a few miles outside the city. A second later, there's a tremendous explosion to the north of Thrace—it's the Destroyer Ship hovering above the docks. Burning ash and debris rains down on the city as the scorched skeleton of the airship crashes into the ocean.

The access door to Thrace City Hall bursts open, and Sentry guards spill out of the building to find out what's happening. Now it's our turn. We each light our smoke grenades, causing white vapor to swirl around us as we run into Spice Square, just as scores of Dacian wagons speed up the side streets, blocking the Sentry's only escape routes. The Dacians leap off their vehicles, guns and swords in hand. They're all dressed in black robes with Cinderstone powder painted on their faces, like me. The guards skid to a halt, stunned, as a hundred Phoenixes glare back at them through the smoke, our hooded capes billowing like wings. *Rose thinks he's killed the Phoenix? He can think again.*

The Sentry guards barely have time to register what's going

on before Gilderoy's men appear in the watch towers and begin shooting. A dozen guards are killed before the others snap out of their stupor and start firing back. Their aim is wild, disoriented by the smoke. There are screams all around me as Dacians and Sentry guards are gunned down in the cross fire. Blood stings my nostrils, making my fangs throb, but I control my thirst as I lob a smoke grenade through one of the shot-out windows of Thrace City Hall, hoping to flush out the remaining people inside. Natalie and Giselle do the same, while Elijah pounces on a Sentry guard, sinking his saber teeth into the man's throat.

A thunderous sound suddenly rips through the city as a second Destroyer Ship erupts into a ball of flames, then a third goes down toward the west, crashing into the Rainbow Forest. The ground vibrates with the weight of metal smashing against the earth. One by one, the bombs detonate, tearing through the remaining two Destroyer Ships. They lose altitude fast, but the pilots manage to steer the aircraft toward the fields outside the city, perhaps trying to keep civilian casualties to a minimum or maybe just hoping to escape. Either way, as soon as they hit the ground, the airships explode.

The skies are empty.

Now all we need to deal with is the enemy on the ground.

I toss another smoke bomb through a broken window, and Natalie and Elijah follow suit, causing a string of explosions. It does the trick, as the Moondogs bound out of the access doors, led by Jared. They snarl and snap their jaws as they charge toward us, their red coats flaring behind them. I don't see Garrick's pack anywhere. The smell of blood in the air is intoxicating, and the Lupines trample the dead Sentry guards with their steel-capped boots, crushing their bones in their thirst to feed. They don't care who they kill, consumed with bloodlust: Sentry,

Dacian, it makes no difference to them—it's all just flesh. They tear apart ten rebels before we manage to draw our rifles and swords.

We rush at the Moondogs, slashing and shooting at them as we run. Neptune, Giselle and Sol take the creatures on the left, while Natalie, Elijah and I tackle the ones on our right. Natalie spars with a smaller, female Moondog who has a mane of dark black hair and is wearing a scarlet top and pants. The woman swipes at Natalie with her razor-sharp claws, but Natalie ducks out of the way and plunges the tip of her blade through the Moondog's heart, killing her.

"Good one!" Sol calls out to Natalie. His glasses are splattered with Lupine blood.

"Sol! Watch out!" Giselle cries as another Moondog lunges for the man.

It seizes Sol and mauls his throat. A blade to its stomach from Neptune finishes the creature, but Sol's already dead. Movement to my left draws my eye. Through the smoke, I spot five figures climbing out a first-floor window in Thrace City Hall and dropping onto Cinnamon Street below: Sebastian, Garrick, Sasha and two more of their Lupine pack. Garrick appears to be limping slightly. They shoot the Dacian rebels who block their path and manage to reach the Transporter parked on the street. A moment later, the engines whir, and they fly off, leaving the rest of their men to fend for themselves.

Fragg!

I don't have time to dwell on it, as there are still the Moondogs to contend with. There are three left—two females and Jared. I shoot one of the females in the chest, then whip my gun around on Jared. I'm about to pull the trigger when he grabs Giselle. I can't shoot him without hitting her.

Her gray eyes snag on mine.

"Do it, Ash!" she cries out.

I hesitate.

"Shoot!" Giselle yells as Jared plunges his canines into her neck.

I pull the trigger, once, twice.

Giselle and Jared collapse on the ground, unmoving.

Natalie and Elijah take down the remaining Moondog, bringing an end to the fight.

The square falls silent. All the Lupines are dead, and the Sentry guards that are still alive are cowering behind the pile of bodies near the city hall steps. The only people left are the Trackers, who have yet to leave the sanctuary of the city hall.

I walk forward, smoke swirling around my feet, and stop in front of the steps. I fix my eyes on the Sentry guards. At that moment, the digital screen on the west wall flickers, and a live feed of Spice Square appears on the monitor. Pandora and her band of rebels have successfully taken control of the news station. Right now, my image is being broadcast on every screen, in every city across the United Sentry States.

"You have one chance to surrender," I call out to the guards, my voice loud enough for the Trackers inside the building to hear. "Lay down your arms and come peacefully with us. If you refuse, we will have no choice but to respond with force."

There's a long pause, and I think the Trackers aren't going to come out. Just as I'm about to give the order to storm the building, the access door opens. The Trackers file out of the city hall, flashing furious looks at me as they pass. The Dacians bind their hands and line the prisoners up in front of the ghetto wall. They'll stay there until we decide what to do with them. I'll leave that up to Neptune. This is his city now.

Taking their cue, Natalie and Elijah head to the roof of the city hall. I walk up the stone steps, disturbing the smoke spewing out of the broken windows. It whips around me until it's impossible to tell where my robe ends and the smoke begins. I turn and gaze up at the camera, perched on top of the digital screen directly opposite me. My face fills the screen. There's a splash of blood on my cheek, and the Cinderstone powder around my eyes is streaked and messy, not at all like the perfect makeup job that Amy always did. This is the real me. This is the true face of Phoenix: bloodied, battle-worn and wearing a torn black robe coated in ash.

Behind me, the two white-and-red Sentry banners flutter on the breeze, creating a stark and vivid image. I let it linger on the screens for a moment, so the whole country can see me. The square is so quiet as everyone waits for me to speak that I can actually hear my heart beating.

"This is a message for Purian Rose," I finally say to the camera. "You thought we were defeated. You thought I was dead. But you were wrong. I am alive. I have been *resurrected*. I am Phoenix, the boy who rose from the ashes."

That's the signal. Natalie and Elijah, now on the roof of Thrace City Hall, cut down the Sentry banners and replace them with ours—a burning black Cinder Rose on a cerulean background. The flags tumble down the building's façade. The message is clear: Mirror City is ours.

The broadcast ends, and the digital screens turn to SBN news, which is already showing commentary from a very flustered February Fields. Purian Rose must be in a murderous mood right now. I suspect a few Sentry generals will be executed for mistaking my identity at Iridium and causing him this political nightmare. Rose made such a show of me being "just a mortal boy" that his army killed, and yet here I am, alive and kicking. The rest of the country will believe I've miraculously been resurrected *again*. It'll give them courage to fight alongside the rebels, knowing Phoenix, and the rebellion, will not be stopped.

The Dacians start moving the dead and wounded into the surrounding buildings, emptying Spice Square, and only then do I see the real carnage. Blood seeps down the steps, and everywhere I turn, there are bodies: Sentry, Lupine, rebel. It's not quite the massacre at Iridium, but it is more death than I ever want to see again. Elijah and Natalie search the pile of bodies for any signs of life. Neptune wanders over to me. There's soot over his craggy face and blood in his curly gray hair—some of it is his blood, some of it belongs to the guards he killed.

"Did we lose many people?" I say.

"At least thirty so far, and we don't know how many made it off the Destroyer Ships yet. It could have been worse," Neptune adds when he sees the anguish on my face.

He pats my shoulder and tells me he'll take over from here. I let him. These are his people, after all. I silently walk across the plaza, looking for Giselle's body. I spy her flame-colored hair underneath Jared's corpse. I roll his body off her, then gently scoop Giselle up in my arms. There's a bright red stain on her dress where the bullet's torn through her chest. I'm surprised how numb I feel looking at her, but once the shock's worn off, I'm certain the magnitude of what I've done will sink in. *I killed her.*

I carry her into a nearby tavern, which has been converted into a makeshift mortuary. Madame Clara and a few other Dacian women are cleaning up the bodies, preparing them to be buried. The old lady tilts her head up at me as I lay Giselle's body on the table in front of her. A waft of Giselle's rose water perfume fills the air, and Madame Clara clamps a hand to her mouth, recognizing it.

"No," she whispers.

"I'm so sorry," I reply. The words sound hollow coming from my mouth.

Madame Clara's lips tremble slightly. She reaches out a hand, and I take it. It's a small gesture, but it means a lot.

I kiss her on the cheek, give Giselle one last look, then go and find Natalie and Elijah.

It's time to get the Ora.

36.
NATALIE

THE NORTH DOCKS are in chaos, with fires blazing and debris everywhere. The shell of the Destroyer Ship sticks out of the harbor waters like a strange sculpture. The water is strewn with dead bodies. I tear my eyes away from the scene. It's one thing knowing there were people aboard the airships; it's another thing seeing their charred remains bobbing up and down on the waves.

"We're looking for a boat called the *Merry Weather*," Elijah says to us as we hurry down the promenade.

We inspect the ships' names until we find a lone steamboat anchored near a rocky outcrop. It's a fishing vessel, with nets and hooks dangling from the sides. The words *The Merry Weather* are painted in perfect yellow calligraphy over the emerald-green paint. Ash tosses our bags onto the deck and leaps on board, before helping me and Elijah on.

Ash pulls up the anchor, while Elijah takes the wheel, since he knows where we're going. He steers us out of the port, being careful to avoid the hull of the Destroyer Ship. I pretend the thumps I hear against the side of the boat are just debris and not bodies.

I'm relieved when Elijah puts the engines on full throttle and we reach the open water.

Ash wraps his arms around me as we sail away from Mirror City. Despite the devastation, it's still beautiful. The cracked solar panels on the surviving buildings glint in the sunlight.

When the city is nothing more than a glimmering speck in the distance, I head down to the cabin. It's small but functional, with a tiny kitchen area complete with table, a restroom that's seen better days and one bedroom filled with a bed just big enough for me and Ash, if we squish together. I guess Elijah will sleep on the deck.

I drop my bag on the creaking bed and check my reflection in the small silvered mirror, curling my lip at the stranger who stares back at me. How can Ash want to be with me, when he knows I'm just going to get worse? My skin will rot, my hair will fall out, and I'm going to become a monster. Worry grips me again, but there's no point getting upset—the cat is out of the bag, and we're just going to have to deal with it.

The boat rocks as we hit a rough patch of water, and my stomach churns. Urgh. I don't know how I'm going to stay on this boat for the next few days, but I don't have a choice. It's the fastest way to Viridis.

I rub my stomach, trying to ease the nausea. It seems to be worse in the evening. I rummage around my bag for one of Madame Clara's herbal remedies and swallow a few drops of her gingerroot tonic. It helps a little. The door swings open, and Ash silently enters the bedroom, fire in his eyes. He knocks my bag onto the floor, scoops me up and lays me down on the bed, then slowly, teasingly, undresses me. He kisses me from head to toe, until I'm tingling all over. My heart is racing, and I want him more than anything, but we shouldn't risk it. The night of our engagement was a one-off. We got lucky. I couldn't bear it if he got sick because of me.

"I don't think we should . . ." I bite my lip.

His fingers trail down my stomach. He's not making this easy for me.

"All right," he says, pulling the covers over me.

"I'm sorry," I say.

He strokes my cheek. "Don't be. It's not important. All I care about is being with you."

I shift across the bed, giving him more space. He wraps his arms around me, and we nestle together, our hands locked. I'm never going to let him go again. The light slowly changes in the bedroom as we sail across the sea, turning from turquoise blue to salmon pink as the sun dips below the horizon. Dark gray clouds start to form across the sky. When I was a kid, I used to watch the sunset with Polly and my father while my mother worked in her office. I feel a twinge of sorrow, thinking about my mother.

"Ash, I've been thinking," I eventually say. "I'd like to find my mother."

"All right," he says without protest.

Wow, that was easier than I expected. Searching for my mother isn't the best use of our time, considering we're in the middle of a war, plus my mother isn't exactly Ash's favorite person in the world after everything she did to him and the Darklings, but he understands why I need her around me now.

"She's going to be devastated when she finds out I'm sick," I say. "Especially after losing Polly."

"It's not going to be an issue, because I'm going to find a cure," he says determinedly.

I don't say anything. It's a futile quest, and he must know that. There is no cure for what I have. My best chance at finding one was at the Barren Lands, where the Wrath was created, and there was nothing there.

"Maybe Elijah will let the rebel scientists do some experiments on him, work out how he's resistant to the virus," Ash continues.

I turn around to face him. His inky black hair gently stirs around his pale face, and there's a smudge of Cinderstone powder down the bridge of his narrow nose.

"I won't let anyone do experiments on Elijah, not after what my mother did to him," I say, wiping the powder away. "He's been through enough."

"But—"

"No," I say firmly, ending that conversation.

Ash doesn't push it, although I can tell his mind is whirring, thinking of ways to save me. I let him. If he needs that glimmer of hope in order to get through these next few months, then who am I to deny him that? Hope isn't a luxury I have anymore, but I want him to have it.

I shut my eyes, exhausted after such an eventful day, and let the boat rock me to sleep. I dream of Polly again, only this time we're kids running around the mansion back in Black City. We're playing hide-and-seek. I go searching for her, skipping down the corridors, but something is wrong. I can't find her. She's not under her bed, or in Mother's closet, or in the pantry, where she usually hides. I start to run around the house in search of her, until I reach my father's study. There's a red rose painted on the door. Something warns me not to go inside, but I need to find Polly and win the game. My hand turns the brass knob, and I open the door and—

I start awake, shivering all over. The bed is empty—Ash isn't here.

I don't have time to really register this as I grab my robe and rush to the toilet and throw up, tears streaming down my face as grief grips me again. The loss of my sister keeps hitting me in waves. Some days I manage not to think about her much at all, but then I have moments like this, when the horror of her death—her *murder*—bubbles up to the surface again. I rock back and forth, crying, until the pain starts to subside. The one and only bonus of having the Wrath is that at least I'll be united with my sister again soon.

When I'm able to stand, I splash some water over my face and then quietly pad toward the kitchen, hoping to find some food to settle my stomach. I hear voices coming from the deck above me and head upstairs.

Ash and Elijah are leaning against the railing, both looking out at the inky sea. They talk in hushed tones.

Ash sighs heavily. "I just love her so much, it's . . ."

"Killing you, knowing she's sick?" Elijah finishes for him. "I know how you feel."

"You really care for her, don't you?" Ash says.

"Do you blame me?" Elijah gazes down at the ocean. "Ever since she rescued me from those labs, she's been on my mind night and day." He sighs. "She's never thought of me as anything but a friend, though."

"I'm sorry," Ash says.

"No you're not," Elijah replies, smiling slightly.

Ash tilts his head up to the moon. "I don't know what I'm going to do without her. I already lost her once; I can't stand the thought of losing her again."

Elijah surprises me by gripping Ash's shoulder.

"We'll find a cure," he says.

"And what if we don't?" Ash asks.

"Then you know what I have to do," Elijah replies. "It's the most humane solution."

Ash looks Elijah in the eye. He gives a faint nod of his head.

They don't say it explicitly, but I know what's just been promised. When I fully turn into a Wrath, Elijah's going to kill me.

37.

NATALIE

FOR THE NEXT few days, we sail across the ocean. We hit a rough patch of weather on the first night, causing the boat to tilt wildly, until I'm positive we're going to sink. Ash comforts me as I cling to the toilet bowl. This nausea is just getting worse, hitting me at all times of the day, making it impossible to hold anything down except dry crackers.

The next morning, the storm passes and the waters become calm and still once more. I even manage to make it out onto the deck to enjoy the fresh, salty air. Ash wraps a blanket around my shoulders to keep me warm, and kisses my forehead. Elijah pretends not to notice, although a flash of jealousy flickers over his face.

Ash spends the day reading his mom's diary to me. He uses the photograph of his mom's family as a bookmark. The picture is faded and curling at the edges, but since it's around thirty years old, that's hardly surprising.

When we're not reading the diary, the three of us are huddled around the portable digital screen that Ash stole from the guards on the train back in the Barren Lands. The reception is poor, but we see enough to work out that there's been more fighting in Thrace, but so far the Dacians have held the city. As we suspected, Purian Rose has kept his armies positioned at the most strategically important locations.

The bounty on our heads has also gone up to a hundred thousand coins each. Ash grins, finding that amusing, although it concerns me that everyone in this country will be desperate to turn us over—even a few of the rebels. It's a *lot* of money.

Elsewhere around the United Sentry States, there have been more uprisings—this time in Niobium, Old Bay Town, and Ashfall. It seems our victory in Thrace has encouraged more people to join the fight, but all of these later uprisings have failed. We watch the government's footage from each of the cities. All the captured rebels are hung from the ghetto walls, as a reminder to everyone of what happens to race traitors. At this pace the rebellion will be over in a matter of weeks. It doesn't give us much time to complete our mission. I turn off the digital screen, not wanting to see any more.

That night, Elijah finds a bottle of spiced Shine hidden away in one of the cupboards. The boys drink—I haven't the stomach for it—while we listen to music on the crackling radio, the stars glittering above us. Elijah shows us a traditional Bastet dance, which makes us giggle.

"All right, your turn," he says, disgruntled.

Ash gets up and does a funny jig, which he claims is a Darkling folk dance, but I know he's just making it up. I burst out laughing, as does Elijah.

"You mocking my moves, blondie?" Ash teases.

I nod.

He sits down beside me, and we kiss. It's so wonderful to be kissing him again, to have his fingers laced through mine. I don't think this moment could be any more perfect. I hope I can hold on to the memory of this night. As the temperature drops, Ash picks me up and takes me back to our bed and kisses me until dawn.

It must be around noon when Elijah's voice wakes us up.

"Land ahoy!" he calls down to us.

We quickly dress and hurry up to the deck. It's a beautiful day: sunny but not too hot, with clear blue skies and a fresh floral perfume in the air. The boat sails past a sheer cliff face hundreds of feet high and covered in twisting vines and lush green foliage. Colorful birds fly overhead, calling out to each other in beautiful song. The foliage starts to thin out as we approach Viridis—the "Vertical City."

"Oh!" I say, amazed, as Elijah slows the steamboat so we can get a better look.

Built into the cliff face is a sprawling city, which reminds me of the famous favelas in the Southern States. The hundreds of blocky, rose-hued buildings with flat roofs are packed so closely together, it's impossible to tell where one house ends and another begins—they all appear to be part of the same organic structure. Crumbling stone steps zigzag through the favela, toward the main city at the top of the cliff. What really takes my breath away is the waterfall that cascades down the middle of the city, spraying clouds of mist into the air.

"Pretty impressive, huh?" he says, smiling.

Once we're safely docked, Elijah turns off the engine and lowers the anchor. We put on our hooded robes, collect our bags and follow him up the steep pathway through the favela, climbing an endless number of steps. My injured leg throbs with the effort, and we have to stop every few minutes so I can rest. Ash takes my bag from me and slings it over his shoulder, along with his own bag. The street is so narrow in places, you can touch the crumbling walls of the buildings on either side of you if you stretch out your arms.

Ash and I keep our hoods low over our faces, so the passing Bastets don't recognize us, although they're not paying any attention to us—they're more interested in Elijah, who is strutting around like he owns the place. I suppose he sort of does— he *is* the Consul's son.

The farther we go through the city, the more I notice how impoverished it is. Many years' worth of graffiti is scrawled over the houses, quite a few of which are on the verge of collapsing and are being held up by the buildings around them. Paint peels off the doors and windows, and the sinking roofs have been crudely repaired with whatever material is at hand— cloth, sheet metal, wood.

Elijah leads us through a network of side streets and up more steps, until we reach an enormous plaza. The ground is made of thousands of tiny, colorful mosaic tiles, which form a dizzying geometric pattern.

Up ahead is a sprawling villa, made of the same rose-hued stone as the rest of the buildings in the city. It looks centuries old, its walls cracking and flaking; part of the west wing is falling down. It's not exactly the embassy I was expecting.

"Home, sweet home," Elijah mutters.

We enter the villa through the arched doorway into the atrium. The long hallway is cool and airy, thanks to the vaulted glass ceiling. On either side of the atrium are four closed doors, while directly in front of us is a set of large rosewood doors. I can hear voices on the other side.

The foyer is devoid of sculptures or paintings, but there are several large, freestanding cages around the room, filled with small red birds with thin, forked tails. They're incredibly pretty, but they could be venomous snakes, given the way Elijah looks at them. The birds let out a terrible screeching cry as we walk past them, and Elijah quickly whistles a four-note tune. The birds immediately stop squawking.

"What sort of birds are they?" I say, my ears still ringing.

"Siren birds," he replies. "We use them to alert the guards to intruders." On cue, two Bastet guards rush out of one of the side rooms, their rifles raised. Both men are packed with muscle and are wearing matching outfits—dark pants, leather vests, black boots, and gold bands around their wrists—the exact outfit Elijah wore the night he turned up at the Ivy Church, which I find odd. They lower their guns when they see Elijah.

"Is my dad in the senate chamber?" Elijah asks.

One of the guards nods, and they beckon us to follow them. They open up the large rosewood doors at the end of the corridor, and we enter a spacious, airy room with arched windows and jade pillars holding up the vaulted ceiling, which has been painted to look like the sky outside. Hanging from the back wall is an enormous tapestry of the United Sentry States, which is old and out of date.

Around the chamber are a dozen armed guards, who have their guns trained on us. They're here to protect the people sitting at the circular table in the center of the room. At the head of the table is a middle-aged Bastet man, with thick russet hair, full lips and dark spots down the sides of his face. There's no doubting he's Elijah's father, Consul Bezier Theroux. He's smartly dressed in a hunter-green tailored frock coat, with a copper and gold embroidered vest, white shirt and silken cravat.

Beside him is a beautiful but stern-looking Bastet woman, her long brunette mane carefully teased into ringlets. She's wearing an amber-colored bustle dress, with delicate beading down the bodice. The markings on her face are much lighter than Elijah's dad's markings, and I'm guessing this is Rowanne, the Consul's wife. To her left are three teenage boys, who must be Elijah's brothers, based on his descriptions of them.

Acelot, the eldest and tallest of the brothers, is the spitting image of his father, with the same russet mane and fierce eyes. He's dressed more casually than everyone else, in a simple white shirt with the sleeves rolled up, a cobalt green vest and black pants. His younger sibling, Donatien, is so skinny, he shrinks inside his expensive clothes. Finally, Elijah's youngest brother, Marcel, slouches in the seat farthest from his father. He's immaculately dressed, like the Consul, and is startlingly attractive, with lips as sensuous as Elijah's, razor-sharp cheekbones and beautiful dark-brown markings down the sides of his face and neck. The whole effect is ruined, though, by the arrogant sneer on his lips.

The other nine senators—five men, four women—wear either frock coats and frilled shirts like the Consul, or bustle dresses similar to Rowanne's, but in varying jewel colors.

Elijah bows. "Father, I've brought you Natalie Buchanan and Ash Fisher."

Bezier gives Elijah an approving look. "I wasn't sure you'd be able to persuade them to come. I underestimated you, son."

Elijah beams, as if he's been paid the greatest compliment. "Thank you, Father."

Marcel rolls his eyes.

"It's an honor to meet you, Consul," Ash says, bowing slightly.

"The pleasure is all mine, I assure you." Bezier smiles, but there's something unsettling about the gesture.

"I don't see your mother," Rowanne says to Elijah. "Does this mean you've failed to retrieve the Ora?"

"Yes, but I know where it is," Elijah says in a rush.

She sighs heavily, and turns her honey-colored eyes toward me and Ash. They have none of the warmth of Elijah's. Hers are cold, calculating, just like my mother's.

I nervously clear my throat. "Elijah asked us here to speak with the senate."

"We'd like you to consider joining the rebellion," Ash continues. "With your support, we can—"

Bezier raises his hand, cutting Ash off midsentence.

"We know why you're here, but I'm afraid we're not interested." Bezier smirks at the senate. "As if we would ever side with the *Darklings.*"

All the Bastets laugh, except for Elijah and his eldest brother, Acelot.

I turn to Elijah. "What's going on?"

He flicks a remorseful look at us just as the Bastet guards rush at me and Ash.

I realize now we weren't here to persuade the senate to join the rebellion.

Elijah's led us straight into a trap.

38.

ASH

THE GUARDS GRAB US, pushing us roughly to our knees. The bags fall off my shoulders, spilling their contents across the stone tiles, including my mom's keepsake box.

"Get off me!" I growl.

"Call the Sentry guard," Bezier orders.

"Elijah, stop this!" Natalie pleads.

He doesn't look at us as he leaves the chamber, shutting the doors behind him.

I struggle against my captors, but they're too strong. They roughly pin me against the stone floor.

"Take them down to the vault and tie them up until our guests arrive," Bezier says.

"Father, must we really do this?" Acelot interjects. "They'll be killed."

"That's not our concern," Bezier replies. "It'll prove to Purian Rose that we are loyal to him."

"Until we get hold of the Ora, at least," Rowanne adds.

Bezier smirks. "These two will buy us some time."

The Bastet guards drag us out of the room. The siren birds

squawk at us as we're hauled across the atrium and down a flight of stone steps leading into the basement. I twist around to make sure Natalie is okay. She kicks, spits and scratches at the guards, even managing to bite the hand of one of them. In retaliation, he punches her, knocking her unconscious. Venom floods my fangs, and I thrash some more, but it's hopeless.

The vault is cold, damp and dark, with stone pillars holding up the domed ceiling. A few torches light the chamber, casting long shadows over the walls and sodden earth. They bind my hands and ankles, then chain me to one of the pillars before doing the same to Natalie. She's still unconscious, her head drooped. There's a lump on her head where the guard hit her.

The instant the Bastets leave, I try and free myself, but the binds are too tight.

Natalie's eyes blink open, and she groans.

"Where are we?"

"In the basement," I say.

"You take me to all the best places," she replies.

"I'm going to fragging kill Elijah when we get out of here."

Natalie sighs. "I can't believe I fell for his lies. I feel like such a fool. He's been manipulating me this whole time, making me feel sorry for him, making me *trust* him."

"He conned us both," I say.

"What do you think is going to happen to us?" Natalie says quietly.

"I think Rose will have us tortured, then publicly executed," I admit. There's no point in sugarcoating this.

"That's what I thought," she says.

Time seems to pass slowly down in the vault. Every minute stretches into an hour; every hour feels like ten as we wait for the Sentry to arrive. I spend most of my time trying to free myself from the chains until I'm exhausted with the effort. It's no good; the binds are just too tight. I let out a frustrated howl. We're never going to get out of here. Natalie just stares off into the distance, subdued and tired.

"How are you feeling?" I ask.

"Not too good," she admits.

The door to the vault opens and Acelot appears, carrying a tray of food. There's some soup for Natalie and a glass of blood for me.

"What's this? Our last meal?" I say to him.

He gives me an apologetic look. "I thought you might be hungry."

"I'd rather starve," I spit.

He puts the tray down on a nearby wooden crate and scratches the back of his head. He seems nervous. Acelot's much taller than Elijah, but less broad in the shoulders. At a guess, I'd say he's about nineteen years old. His sleeves are rolled up to his elbows, and his nails are bitten down to the quick.

"I'm sorry about this," he says, gesturing toward our binds. "For the record, I don't agree with what they're doing."

"Then why are you going along with it?" Natalie says tiredly.

"Because we don't have much choice. When we found out about the Tenth from Lucinda's letter, we knew it was only a matter of time before the Sentry came for us." Acelot perches on the edge of the crate, his tail brushing against the dirt floor. "Elijah told us what he'd discovered about the Ora. The senate saw the opportunity to get their hands on a powerful weapon to defend ourselves with, but we needed a backup plan."

"Let me guess; you're intending to hand us over to the Sentry in return for your lives?" I say.

"Pretty much," Acelot admits.

I shake my head disbelievingly. "You're fragging crazy if you think the Sentry's going to agree to those terms."

"I'm not convinced they will, but we don't have many options," Acelot replies.

"You could've joined the rebellion," I say.

"That's what I wanted." Acelot sighs. "I just couldn't persuade the others to work with the Darklings." He leaves the tray and heads upstairs, briefly pausing on the steps. "I truly am sorry."

The door closes behind him. As soon as he's gone, I slump my head back against the pillar, my temples throbbing. I shut my eyes, trying to block out the headache.

The sound of siren birds wailing wakes me up. I blink a few times, trying to adjust to the dark, and glance over at Natalie. I don't even remember drifting off. How long have we been asleep? She turns her head toward me.

Overhead, we hear footsteps marching through the atrium toward the senate room.

They're here.

Fear spikes in me.

"Ash!" Natalie says, hearing the footsteps too.

"I won't let them hurt you," I say.

There's a clamor in the senate room above us. Chairs scrape back. Footsteps march across the room. I recognize Garrick's distinctive gait.

"Where are they?" he says gruffly, his voice muffled through the ceiling.

"Downstairs," Bezier replies.

"Go get them, then," Sebastian orders.

More footsteps cross the floor. Shortly after, the door to the vault opens, casting a shaft of sunlight into the room. I expect the Bastet guards, but instead Elijah appears. A set of keys jangle around his shackled wrists. He hangs his head slightly as he stands in front of us.

"How could you betray us?" Natalie says.

He raises his eyes. "What would you have done in my place? I was just following orders."

"You make it sound like you didn't have a choice in this," she says.

"I didn't!"

She fixes him with a hard, unforgiving look.

"I *didn't*," he insists, subconsciously playing with the gold bands on his wrists. Bands just like the ones the guards upstairs wore.

"You're a servant," I say, understanding.

Elijah nods slightly.

"So Bezier *isn't* your father?" Natalie says.

"He is," Elijah says. "But when Rowanne found out about his affair with my mom, and that they'd had a kid, she demanded that I work as their servant, to punish my mother."

"Is this the bit where we're supposed to feel sorry for you?" I say.

"No," Elijah replies. "But maybe you can understand that I didn't have a choice. He's the Consul; I have to follow his orders."

Natalie rolls her eyes. "Whatever. You were just trying to impress him."

Elijah flushes.

"We could have *helped* you," I say. "With the Ora, the rebellion might have succeeded. Now there's no chance. You've condemned us all."

Elijah sits down on the damp earth, his shoulders slumping. "I'm so sorry."

"Pardon us if we don't believe you," Natalie replies.

"I mean it," he says. "I care for you. I never wanted to hurt you."

"Give me a break," she says. "It was all make-believe."

"It wasn't! It *isn't*," he says. "I wanted to confess to you a million times—"

"Then why didn't you?" she challenges.

"I thought I was doing the right thing for my people," he says. Natalie glares at him.

"And I wanted to impress my dad," he admits.

"I'm glad that worked out well for you," I retort, looking at his gold shackles.

He rubs his wrists, a frown on his lips. "I did hope—"

"What? That your dad would suddenly accept you into the family if you delivered me and Natalie to him? You're an idiot," I reply. "You're not even a person to him. You're just a tool to be used and tossed away when he's done with you."

Elijah rakes his hands through his mane. "I don't want it to end like this."

"It doesn't have to. You can release us," Natalie says.

"I can't—"

"You owe me," Natalie says. "I released you from the Sentry HQ, remember?"

"Sebastian will kill my dad and brothers if I don't hand you over," he says. "You know he will."

I glance at Natalie. I have to get her out of here; it's her only chance to live.

"Leave me behind. I'm the one Sebastian wants anyway," I say to Elijah.

"Ash, no!" Natalie says.

"Please, Elijah," I say. "If you truly care about Natalie, then set her free."

Uncertainty crosses his features.

"*Please,*" I say.

In the room above us, I can hear Sebastian and Garrick pacing around the senate room, getting impatient. Elijah looks up at the ceiling, then at Natalie. He briefly shuts his eyes, clearly conflicted. Finally, he gets up and unties her. Relief crashes over me; there's a chance she'll escape, a chance she'll live. That's all I need to keep me going.

"Thank you," I say to Elijah.

"Don't thank me yet," he says, surprising me by removing my binds. "I still have to get you both out of here."

I scramble to my feet, confused about why he's letting me go.

"Why are you doing this?" I say to him.

"Because someone has to save my people," he says. "And I don't think my father's the man to do it. Promise me you'll protect them."

"Aren't you coming with us?" Natalie says.

He shakes his head. "I need to stay and defend my family."

"You'll be killed," she says.

A sad smile crosses his lips. "Don't worry about me, pretty girl." He looks at me. "Do you promise?"

I clamp a hand on his shoulder. "I promise."

We race up the stairs into the atrium, but skid to a halt as we spot the two Bastet guards from earlier, patrolling the corridor. They've got their backs to us, so they haven't seen us yet. We quickly slink back into the shadows just as one of them peers over his shoulder. My muscles tense, waiting to see if he's spotted us. My body relaxes when he turns away.

The Bastet guards pace down the hallway, then enter one of the rooms on the left. As soon as the door shuts behind them, Elijah emerges from our hiding place and whistles the four-note tune to silence the siren birds. He beckons us forward, and we follow him. We hurry past the large rosewood doors leading into the senate room.

"I haven't got all day, Bezier," Sebastian snaps from the other side of the closed doors. "Bring them to me *now.*"

"My servant has gone to get them," Bezier replies. "Now, about our terms—"

There's a gunshot, followed by the sound of a body hitting the stone floor.

Elijah spins around, his face ashen. "Dad!"

Pandemonium instantly breaks out in the senate: people scream, more gunshots are fired, bodies hit the floor. The doors burst open, and the Bastet senators run out of the room, tripping over one another in their haste. There's a smattering of gunfire, and they fall into a heap on the mosaic floor. My nostrils flare with the scent of their blood.

Through the open doorway, I see Acelot and the other Bastets fighting the Sentry guards, while Marcel takes cover under the table. Donatien lies lifeless on the floor beside his mother and Bezier. In the center of the melee are Sebastian, Garrick, Sasha and two other Lupines.

The loud noises startle the siren birds, and they begin squawking. Sebastian turns, drawn by the sound, and catches my eye. Surprise briefly registers on his face, and then it hardens into a snarl. He barks an order at the Lupines.

Garrick and his pack bound toward us, followed by Sebastian and a pair of blood-soaked Sentry guards. The Lupines leap over the pile of dead senators, barely breaking their stride as they chase us down the corridor, although Garrick has a definite limp as he runs. The agitated siren birds wail as we dash by, their cries echoing around the atrium.

We burst out the front door, into the main plaza. Parked on the far side of the plaza is the Transporter that Sebastian and his men took to get here. The hatch is open. We race toward it, knowing it's our best chance of escape. I risk a look over my shoulder. Garrick has reached the front door. He charges toward us, closely followed by Sasha and the other two Lupines.

"Hurry!" I cry out.

Natalie gasps as her injured leg buckles beneath her and she slams to the ground. I turn on my heel and run back for her, but I know I'm sealing my own fate by doing so. I reach her at the same time as Garrick. He knocks me out of the way, grabbing Natalie. I hit the ground, hard. The two guards grab Elijah, while Sebastian draws his sword on me, a triumphant look on his face.

He's so focused on me, he doesn't notice Acelot by the doorway, gun raised. The Bastet shoots the Sentry guards holding Elijah before aiming his gun at Sebastian. He pulls the trigger. *Click.* Nothing happens. The chamber's empty.

"What are you waiting for, dog?" Sebastian says to Garrick. "Kill the cat."

Garrick moves, as if he's going to get Acelot. Then something happens I wasn't expecting. Garrick slings Natalie over his shoulder and runs onto the Transporter, along with Sasha and the other two Lupines.

Distracted, Sebastian briefly lets his guard down, and I take my chance to strike. I lunge at him, putting my full weight behind the tackle. We crash to the ground, rolling across the plaza, each trying to get the upper hand. We've been in this situation before—two months ago, in fact, during the riot in Black City. But this time I'm not going to let him go.

On the other side of the plaza, the Transporter's engine starts up. *No!*

"Get Natalie!" I call to Elijah.

I don't know if he's heard me; I'm too busy fighting with Sebastian. I manage to pin him under me and punch him in the face, over and over, until my knuckles bleed. He slumps against the ground, alive but unconscious, blood spilling out of his nose and mouth.

The Transporter's rotors begin to spin, drawing my attention.

Elijah sprints toward the aircraft just as the hatch door starts to close.

He's not going to make it!

Through the crack in the closing door, I see Natalie being shackled to the metal bench.

"Natalie!" I yell.

She turns, catching my eye through the slit in the closing door.

"Ash!" she cries out.

Elijah leaps at the hatch, nimbly rolling through the gap just as the door shuts and the vehicle takes off.

"No!" I scream as the Transporter flies overhead. "Natalie! NATALIE!"

I yell until I have no voice left, but it's no use.

She's gone.

39.

NATALIE

I PULL AGAINST the chains around my wrists and ankles, immediately regretting it as they dig into my sore flesh. We've been on the prison Transporter for hours, and Garrick hasn't said a word to us this whole time. He just sits silently at the pilot seat while Sasha and the other two Lupines watch over us. She occasionally lets me use the tiny restroom near the cockpit, but that's the only interaction we've had.

When I'm not worrying about Ash, which isn't often, I plot ways to attack Garrick and take over the ship, although I know it's futile. The Lupines would kill us before we even got close to him. Besides, it's not like either Elijah or I know how to fly the airship.

Elijah stares ahead, his face etched with worry. He must guess that Garrick probably intends to kill him as soon as we get to our destination. I'm briefly reminded of the last time we were on a prison Transporter together, during our failed mission to save Polly. He was such a comfort to me then. I gently take his hand, and he looks gratefully at me. His fingers tighten around mine.

Clouds drift by the cockpit window. It's impossible to tell where we are, although my best guess is that we're on our way to Centrum. Garrick no doubt wants the reward money for himself and didn't want to share it with Sebastian. What I don't understand is why Garrick took me and not Ash. I'm of little value to Rose, other than . . . *oh God*. There's *one* use for me. Purian Rose can use me to distract Ash, the same way they used Polly. They're going to keep me alive, torture me, knowing it'll drive Ash insane. He won't be able to function; he'll be useless to the rebellion.

I think Rose understands now that killing Ash isn't the best move. Ash has already been "resurrected" twice; people won't believe he's dead, and if they do, he'll be turned into a martyr, which is the last thing Rose wants. There's no point arresting him either. That would make him a political prisoner, which will just rally more support for the rebels. No, all Purian Rose can hope for now is to keep Ash distracted, and to do that, he needs me.

"So how much are you going to get for me?" I ask Sasha. "I hope it was worth all the effort."

She doesn't say anything, just curls her bright pink lips.

The Transporter suddenly banks to the left, and I snatch a look out of the windscreen. The clouds disappear, making way for plumes of choking black smoke.

The aircraft descends rapidly, and the peaks of industrial buildings come into view, copper chimneys glinting as we pass by. We're flying dangerously close to them, weaving through the buildings at breakneck speed, and I cling to my seat, terrified we're going to crash.

"You all right?" Elijah whispers.

"Feeling a bit nauseated," I admit.

"If you're going to be sick, could you do it over your own feet this time?"

I laugh weakly.

We fly over a distinctive steel and brass wall, which I immediately recognize as the ghetto wall in Gallium. We're in the Copper State!

"This is Alpha One, requesting permission to land," Garrick says into his headpiece.

The radio crackles, and a moment later, a man's voice replies. Something about it sounds so familiar, but I can't place it over the static.

"You're clear to land. Good to have you back, Alpha One," he says.

The Transporter turns sharply to the right, missing a factory roof by inches, and lands in a massive courtyard outside a smelting works. Two of the Lupine pack remove the shackles around our feet, but leave the ones on our hands. The hatch opens, and we're blasted with hot, stinking air.

We march through the courtyard into the smelting works and down a maze of metal walkways before we reach two enormous steel doors. They slide open, and I realize it's an elevator.

"Where are you taking us?" I ask Garrick.

"You'll see," he says as the doors shut behind us and the elevator descends into the earth.

My heart is pounding a mile a minute, and my hands shake with nerves. I ball them into fists as Elijah slides a reassuring look at me.

The elevator slows to a halt, and the doors ping open. I blink against the bright fluorescent lights. We've arrived in a bustling subterranean railway network, with a vaulted copper ceiling about twenty feet above us, creating a surprisingly airy feel.

Subway cars rattle by, transporting people around the enormous compound. Wide concrete platforms the size of a regular sidewalk run alongside the rails. They connect the metal-walled buildings and adjoining tunnels, giving the impression we're in the center of a busy town. In fact, as we're ushered down the sidewalk, I see a sign on the wall saying MAIN STREET.

Hundreds of people dash around us, wearing simple orange factory overalls with guns slung over their shoulders. *Where are we?* A petite black woman in her midtwenties, with waist-length cornrows and intense brown eyes, greets Garrick at the crossing of Main Street and Second Avenue. She gives me a quick smile. I vaguely recognize her, but I don't know from where. *What's going on?*

"They're waiting for you in command central," she says.

"Okay, Destiny, tell them I'll be there in five. I've got to take these two to their rooms first," he says.

He tries to grab my arm, but I yank it away from him.

"Don't touch me!" I spit.

"She's a feisty one." Destiny winks at Garrick and heads off.

"This way," Garrick says.

We're taken down Second Avenue, past rows of green doors built into the corrugated copper walls. He stops in front of a door marked BUCHANAN. I glance at Elijah, who raises his brow at me. *I have my own room?* How long have they been expecting me? I'm more confused than ever.

He opens the door, and I go inside, knowing I have no other option right now than to play along. The room is about fifteen feet long, with a pair of bunk beds, a storage space built into the metal wall, a small desk, mirror and sink. There's a vase of flowers on the desk.

Garrick removes the shackles from our wrists.

"Make yourselves comfortable. We need to debrief you in ten minutes," he says, leaving the room.

The door shuts behind him.

Elijah sits down on one of the bunk beds and rubs his sore wrists. "What's going on?" he asks.

"I have no idea," I say, "but I'm starting to get a vibe they're not intending to kill us." *At least, not yet.*

I walk around our room, checking it for clues. There's nothing to give any indication of who these people are. All I find is four orange jumpsuits inside the storage space. The whole setup seems very organized and professional, the kind of thing I'd expect the Sentry government to be involved with, although if this were a Sentry stronghold, surely they would have put me in a cell, not decked me out with my very own room. No, this all seems too . . . *cozy.*

"Is she here? Is she all right?" I hear a woman say outside the door. My heart leaps into my mouth, recognizing her voice but not quite believing.

The door bursts open, and a tall, thin woman wearing an orange jumpsuit stands in the doorway, her jet-black hair flowing in waves around her bony shoulders. She's wearing a slick of bright red lipstick, which makes her alabaster skin look ghostly pale. Even so, she's as beautiful as ever.

She stretches out her arms toward me. "My darling girl."

I run into them. "Mother!"

I cling to her, and she folds her arms around me. The last time I saw her, she was being dragged kicking and screaming out of my prison cell back in Black City, after I was arrested for Gregory Thompson's murder. She's even thinner than normal, her bones jutting out through her jumpsuit. She pulls back and gently tucks an unruly curl behind my ear.

"I'm sure you have a lot of questions," she says. "But right now, there's someone who wants to talk to you."

I furrow my brow. "Who?"

"Hello, sweetheart," a male voice says by the doorway.

I turn around.

A blond man stands in the doorway, dressed in a jumpsuit similar to my mother's. His face is badly scarred, the flesh puckered with numerous bite marks and slashes, making it hard to determine his features. Even so, I'd recognize those bright blue eyes anywhere.

I rush over to him, tears spilling down my cheeks, and he pulls me into an embrace. That's why the voice on the radio sounded so familiar.

It's my father.

40.

ASH

◗ **I SIT ON THE EDGE** of the harbor, overlooking the ocean, the rambling favela rising up the cliff behind us. Abandoned fishing boats bob up and down on the waves, the sound of their bells ringing hauntingly across the bay. I rub a hand over my face. I'm so goddamn tired. I haven't slept in over thirty hours, since Garrick took Natalie.

Where has he taken her? Sebastian's refusing to speak to me, which is hardly surprising, but even if he did talk, I doubt he'd be able to offer any clues to her whereabouts. He seemed as surprised as I was by Garrick's actions. Sebastian is currently being held captive in the villa's vault, until we decide what to do with him.

I shut my eyes and place a hand over my chest, feeling the thrum of Natalie's heart beating in time with mine. She's alive. I know that much. But that's only a small comfort. They might be torturing, beating and abusing her this very moment. Pain grips my stomach, and I bend double, groaning. *I couldn't save her.*

Acelot walks down the wooden walkway and sits beside me. He looks as exhausted as I do. He's spent this whole time tending to the wounded Bastet guards and surviving senators, and assisting with the cleanup of the villa. We sit in silence, watching the clouds drift across the cobalt-blue sky. The color reminds me so much of Natalie's eyes. I let out a shaky breath.

"Elijah will protect her," Acelot says, reading my mind.

"What if he can't?" I say. "I need to find her. I can't just sit around here doing nothing when she could be . . ."

Acelot grips my shoulder as grief washes over me.

"Where do you think they are?" he says.

"Centrum would be my best guess. I think Garrick took them to the Golden Citadel to be interrogated." It's the most likely scenario I can think of. "I need to get there. Do you have any vehicles I can use?"

"We have the boats," he says. "And there's my father's Transporter, but it's pretty beaten up. Marcel took it out for a joyride a few months ago and crashed it, so it'll need fixing."

I nod. "Okay. As soon as it's ready, I'll head to Centrum."

"It's a suicide mission," Acelot says.

"I know, but I'm going anyway," I say. "Besides, I won't be going in unarmed. I intend to find the Ora first; it's my best hope of saving them."

"Then I will come with you." Acelot stands up. "I owe you, and Elijah, that much."

We walk back up the cliff, to the villa.

The scent of death still lingers in the air as we head through the plaza. There are pools of dried blood on the mosaic tiles. The majority of the bodies have been taken to the local morgue, ready to be cremated, while those of the Consul, his wife, and their son Donatien have been taken to the family mausoleum. All across the city, black flags have been hung out of windows, in mourning for their lost leader.

Signs of the battle are visible all the way through the atrium into the senate chamber. The room is in disarray. There's broken furniture, paintings are punctured with bullet holes, and the tapestry of the United Sentry States has been torn off some of its hooks, so it hangs at an angle. Marcel is slouched in his dad's seat, the contents of my bag spilled out on the table. My mom's diary is open in front of him, and in his hand is one of the photographs.

"That's private!" I say, snatching it from him.

It's the picture of my mom's family in the forest.

"I'm bored," he says, crossing his arms over his chest.

My fangs pulse with venom. I don't know how he can act this way, when half of his family has been killed. He doesn't seem affected by *any* of it. There's something not right with that kid.

Acelot grabs Marcel by the ear and lifts him off the seat. "Make yourself useful, and fix the tapestry."

He lets Marcel go, and the younger boy bares his saber teeth at his brother.

We sit down while Marcel fixes the tapestry. I put my mom's photograph on the table in front of me, studying the faces in the portrait. My eyes are drawn to Lucinda.

"So where will we find this weapon?" Acelot asks.

I look up. "It's at a place called the Claw. It's a mountain. Have you heard of it?"

Acelot shakes his head.

I sigh, glancing at the tapestry, wondering where it is. I know the mountain is close to Gray Wolf, so I locate the city on the old map and scan the surrounding mountains, hoping for some clues. My eyes snag on a familiar name: MOUNT ALBA.

I get up, confused. That can't be right. The mountain in the tapestry has a sharp peak, but Mount Alba has a flat top, and it certainly doesn't have any towns around it, like this map suggests. No one's lived there since the eruption around thirty years ago. But then again, the map *is* old—it must've been woven a hundred years ago, long before Mount Alba last erupted and blew its top. I study the towns around the volcano, having never heard of any of them before—all the maps at school were modern ones, given to us by the Sentry government. There's a place called Mountain Shade, and another called Carrow Falls, and—

My heart stops.

At the base of the volcano is a small town labeled AMBER HILLS.

I rush back to the table and snatch my mom's photo. I turn it over, and check the scrawled writing on the back: *The Coombes, Forest of Shadows, Amber Hills.*

I flip it over again and study the picture carefully. My mom's family is standing in a forest glen, and peeping through the trees behind them is Mount Alba, the way it looked *before* it erupted, with a sharp, talon-shaped peak.

The Claw.

It has to be! It's the most significant mountain near Gray Wolf, where Lucinda and the others have gone, and it's where my mom, aunt and Kieran first met. It can't just be a coincidence. I feel certain this is where they were going to retrieve the Ora, before they went missing. It would've been the perfect place to build their laboratory too, as they're familiar with the area and would've known it would be uninhabited for miles. This should be good news, but my stomach sinks. I stare back at the tapestry.

The last time I looked at a map of Mount Alba, I was at the Legion ghetto; Garrick was telling us about a deadly new concentration camp that the Sentry government had built at its base. I suddenly understand why Lucinda and the others haven't been in touch. I know where they are.

I turn to Acelot.

"Get the Transporter fixed," I say. "We're going to the Tenth."